DANCING WOMAN

ALSO BY ELAINE NEIL ORR

DANCING WOMAN

••••••••••••••••••

Elaine Neil Orr

—BLAIR—

Printed in the United States of America
Cover design by Laura Williams
Interior design by April Leidig

Blair is an imprint of Carolina Wren Press.

*The mission of Blair/Carolina Wren Press is to seek out, nurture, and promote
literary work by new and underrepresented writers.*

We gratefully acknowledge the ongoing support of general operations by the
Durham Arts Council's United Arts Fund and the North Carolina Arts Council.

This novel is a work of fiction. As in all fiction, the literary perceptions
and insights are based on experience; however, all names, characters, places,
and incidents are either products of the author's imagination or are used
fictitiously. No reference to any real person is intended or should be inferred.

Library of Congress Cataloging-in-Publication Data
Names: Orr, Elaine Neil, author.
Title: Dancing woman / Elaine Neil Orr.
Description: [Durham] : Blair, 2025.
Identifiers: LCCN 2024017745 (print) | LCCN 2024017746 (ebook) |
ISBN 9781958888339 (hardcover) | ISBN 9781958888445 (ebook)
Subjects: LCGFT: Novels.
Classification: LCC PS3615.R58843 D36 2025 (print) |
LCC PS3615.R58843 (ebook) | DDC 813/.6—dc23/eng/20240510
LC record available at https://lccn.loc.gov/2024017745
LC ebook record available at https://lccn.loc.gov/2024017746

All my favorite people are broken
Believe me, my heart should know.
— LINFORD DETWEILER

What you have to experience before you die
is a driving rain transformed into light.
—MURIEL BARBERY

For Robert Doty,
who gave me the world of literature,
and for Sena Jeter Naslund,
who inspired me to write.

Together they gave me a life.

Kufana, Nigeria

• • • • •

February 1963

The message from her husband was perfectly logical, as was always the case. Nick would stay through the weekend near Kafanchan where he was planting an acre in Neem trees. There was no sense driving home for two nights only to return Monday.

It was too early to be planting. In the heat of the dry season, birds ceased their movement midmorning. The trees would have to be watered. But Nick was eager. He had left a week ago. Eventually her young husband meant to plant several acres. Isabel let her gaze run along the bougainvillea hedge that bordered her yard.

Inside, she picked up pen and paper. *Message received. I do understand how important the project is. And yet,* she wrote and marked through those last two words. What would she say? *And yet, I long for a journey, a night of love, a discovery.* None of that was quite right or sufficient, and all of it made her sound trite. She signed, *Yours, Isabel* before folding the paper and slipping it into the same dust-stained envelope the courier had delivered to her. A pearl of anger pulsed at the back of her skull. How could he be so forgetful of their plans? Back in the yard, she handed the young motorcyclist the envelope. He wore a pale blue shirt embroidered around the neck in yellow thread, and her eyes followed the sinuous motion of the design.

She pulled her gaze from the man's chest. "Safe travels."

"Allah ya sa'," he said, *May God make it so.* He revved the engine. The machine chugged and coughed, and then the courier was gone in a swirl of dust and fumes.

Isabel glanced over her parched front yard. For weeks, she had been anticipating the Valentine's party sponsored by the International Women's Club in the lovely city of Kaduna. The invitation had arrived early in the New Year, bearing a photograph of the pop star, Bobby Tunde. He sat at a piano, in a garden of potted plants and brass instruments, a slightly squashed, gold cap on his head, his sideways glance and neatly trimmed beard disastrously alluring. He reminded her a little of Harry Belafonte, whom her parents, to her great surprise, adored. She imagined Tunde's music as an array of color, heavy in blue and orange.

In Kaduna, there would be a feast, dancing, and beer. Nick had forgotten all about it, though Isabel had made a new dress, green as a lime, with a V-neck and a gathered skirt. She had finished the hem and sleeves yesterday, sitting by the window to catch the breeze. The dress fell perfectly to her knees and brushed lightly against her thighs. In her impatience, she had worn it down the lane to purchase a can of Spam for her dinner. She'd even found small potatoes to add to her solitary meal. Now she would not attend the party because her husband had the car.

Suddenly a boy in a faded tunic stood before her. His eyes were large, his forehead brightened to silver in the sun. He held a bird captured by a bit of twine fastened tight around its tiny, black feet. In his other hand, he held a woven basket. "Please, buy," he said.

The bird seemed all tuckered out, its feathers wilted, eyes dim. Isabel would not keep a bound bird nor a bird in a cage.

"No," she said, still annoyed with Nick, with the heat, with the lonely weekend to come.

Now the boy looked as listless as the bird, his eyes blank. He shook his head but with little passion. An image of a chained bird floated into Isabel's mind. A goldfinch. She had studied it in art history at Hollins, back in Virginia. She had loved and hated the painting. The gold highlights on the bird's feathers stopped her breath, but she despised the chain. How could an artist paint a bound bird? She was sure she would have let it go.

At times, Isabel felt she could see beneath the surface of things. She had always felt so. "How much?" she said.

The boy revived and stood upright. "Six pence," he said.

For the second time that morning, Isabel mounted the steps to the front porch and moved into the house. She returned with several coins and placed a sixpence in the boy's hand.

He set the basket at her feet as if it was now Isabel's, and then he reached for her hand to transfer the twine and the poor attached bird into her ownership. "Wait," she said. She wetted her thumb, ran it over the poor bird's head and down its feathered back several times until a skim of dust was lifted, revealing bright green feathers and a band of gold on its wing. "It's a beauty," she said, and the boy smiled. "Untie it, please. Set it here." She placed a hand on the concrete pillar at the base of the porch.

The boy did as she asked.

The bird teetered. It took a few halting steps and shook itself out, catching the sun in its feathers. It bobbed its head as if trying to remember something. And then it took wing, across the road and into a tall hardwood.

Isabel felt golden.

"Now," she said. "Don't catch any more birds. I will give you two shillings. Go to the market and purchase a bucket. You can make more money fetching water from the stream." She handed him the coins.

He looked at the money in his upturned palm. "Thank you," he said and dipped his head. At the first bend in the road, he looked back and waved. He might spend the money on a ball, a BIC pen. That wouldn't be so bad. Isabel had faith in him.

◆ ◆ ◆

Arriving in Nigeria, Nick and Isabel were picked up at the airport by one of Nick's colleagues and driven to the ancient city of Zaria, where they set up temporary housekeeping in an apartment. Immediately, Nick began training at the university for his assignment with USAID, the United States Agency for International Development. Isabel was left to discover her new world on her own. She began haltingly, making excursions by foot, down one flight of stairs and out onto the street. Small shops and kiosks abounded. In some areas, men sold their wares, and in other areas, women sold theirs. The men sold hatchets, flashlights, and radios while the women sold

cloth, foodstuffs, and even handmade pots. Isabel couldn't quite
make out what the dividing line was. She was happy one morning
to find a woman selling handmade leather sandals, and she purchased a pair along with several scarves to cover her head. The lively
colors called up her own experience as an artist. She could almost
feel the sensation of opening a new tube of paint. But that life was
over. At home, she stitched up wraparound skirts. Isabel had always
been a walker. She ventured even farther. One day a woman invited her into the family compound to partake of their repast of rice
balls dipped in a leafy soup. Isabel sat with the women and children
on mats. The next day, someone at USAID told Nick that his wife
needed to hire a young man to show her about the town rather than
going out on her own.

"I don't see why."

"It must be the custom."

"I thought we were here to meet people."

"Yes. But we have to respect how things are done."

"But you're introducing new farming methods. That's not how
things are done. Why shouldn't I meet women in the neighborhood?
I enjoy it. I'm sure they do too."

"Just go along for now. When we get an assignment and settle
into a house, you'll have more freedom."

So she had bided her time. Now they were set up in a house in
Kufana, and still she was limited in where she could go. She admired
Nick. He was good at his work. She felt sure she loved him, though
the bright flames of early passion had cooled. She supposed that was
normal. *And yet.* Nick was not coming home to take her to the party.
The boy had gone. The bird had flown. She was glad for its libera-
tion but perplexed by her own curtailed freedom.

What if she dared to take local transportation for the thirty-mile
trip to the party? Isabel could imagine herself climbing into an over-
burdened lorry, a goat at her feet and traders with their wares on
either side, swaying and sweating their way to Kaduna, as she sat
clutching her train case. Since her arrival with Nick, she had wanted
to get on a lorry. Beyond getting her clothes wrinkled, which had

happened on the plane, what damage could come to her or anyone else? Perhaps she would discover something.

It was two o'clock in the afternoon. Isabel turned the wedding ring on her finger. She ran her hand across her dresser. Then she turned on the fan and climbed into bed. Muffled sounds passed through the window: a mother's voice, a drum, a car horn—but not her husband's breath. She dozed and woke and stared at the ceiling. In watercolor, one had to know what portions of the painting would be white because white was not painted in. All of the other colors the artist applied, using gentle strokes of a soft brush. The more water one added, the lighter the pigments became. White was simply the bare rag paper. Once upon a time, she had loved to paint, loved it more than almost anything.

A bell rang, and Isabel knew that Daniel had entered the back door into the kitchen. He had a key, and she trusted him. In a moment, he would prepare hot tea and serve it to her with English biscuits. His last employer had been British, and Isabel could not dissuade him from this practice. She moved through the center of the house to meet him.

"Sannu," *hello*, she said. Blue flame licked the bottom of the teakettle.

"Sannu," he said.

She stood at the kitchen counter until the water boiled and Daniel poured it over the tea leaves. Moments later, she was blowing the hot liquid, served in one of the chipped china cups left by the house's last occupants. It featured a picture of a couple in Renaissance clothing standing in an English garden. The image reminded her of the tiny gardens she had created in the corridor of grass in front of her childhood home in the Oregon Hill neighborhood of Richmond—inch-wide paths, seedlings for trees, moss plazas.

"Do you think we can make our garden so lush?" she said. A coconut sat on the sink drain. She tried to remember if it had been there yesterday.

"It is not possible." Even with a negative response, Daniel smiled.

Isabel was down to her last English biscuit. She liked Daniel's honesty, though she could picture a tangle of big-leafed plants thriving outdoors if she could water enough. She smiled back before she let out a sigh. "I won't be going to the party in Kaduna tomorrow because Mr. Hammond will not be home to take us."

Daniel looked stricken. "But you have prepared to go."

"Yes, but I cannot."

Daniel Nenge was Tiv, his tall frame exaggerated by the vertical black-and-white-striped shirts he often wore, emblematic of his heritage. He had a broad forehead, a slender jaw, and one eyebrow arched higher than the other did. The Tiv were a minority in Nigeria, squeezed by the larger ethnic groups. Of all things, they produced sesame seeds, which Daniel used liberally in cooking.

When she and Nick arrived over a year ago, Isabel's first significant trial had been Daniel. Why, she asked her husband, did they need a servant, and why was the servant a man? Nick shrugged. "They want the work. They need to support their families. They're called stewards, not servants." "Steward doesn't sound much better. Besides, he's not married. A young girl would be more appropriate." "Men want the jobs." So Daniel stayed on and she called him the house manager, though she had come to think of him as something larger—the strong guardian of their bungalow. Sometimes he seemed more in charge than she.

At first, they tangled. She would come into the kitchen and correct the way he prepared an omelet or find him mopping the floor and question his methods. Finally, Daniel threatened to quit if she kept *disrespecting his work*, as he put it. "I do my job well, well." So she agreed not to interfere. But she wasn't accustomed to a man other than her husband knowing her life so intimately. When her period came, Isabel could not bear the thought of Daniel finding her bloody pads in the wastebasket. So she folded them in old sheets of the *Daily Times* and kept them in a covered pot behind the sink curtain and in the evening disposed of them outside in the burn drum. Later the drum would be emptied into the bola, the trash pit.

Then came the pregnancy in April, and she didn't need to take the pot to the burn drum. But at four months, she miscarried. Sadness set in until the rains ceased.

Isabel set the china cup on the kitchen counter. "Did you bring the coconut?"

"Yes."

"I must pay you for it."

When Daniel stepped out the back door, Isabel followed. He placed the coconut on the water tank and began to strike it with a kitchen mallet. It broke open, showing off its white flesh. Isabel wanted a bite but knew she must refrain. Daniel had already calculated how he would use this fruit, how far it would reach. Like Nick, he was orderly, a planner; he did not live in dreams.

At dusk, Isabel ate her supper alone in the sunroom, listening to the muezzin's call for prayer. Daniel sat just outside the kitchen door in the shade of the overhanging roof. In this arrangement, she felt she might be back in Virginia, living a life from decades earlier, when white ladies had servants, though not in her family. Her mother always said she grew up dirt poor, and her father immigrated as a child from Sicily. Nigeria was not Virginia, and Daniel was not like anyone she had known in the States. He had a whole world she knew nothing about.

♦ ♦ ♦

The next morning, Isabel woke before dawn. Her heart followed a piano scale up and down, from anger at Nick to longing for him. She walked about the rooms, the thoughts in her head too many and at odds with one another. She felt bruised, no; lost, no; like kindling, yes. She could sleep in Nick's absence but not in his indifference. As she wandered through the house, she touched a curtain, a bowl set on the coffee table, a sofa cushion. The walls seemed to breathe, but it was her breath. Once she knew they were moving to West Africa, she had imagined something magnificent would happen to her there. Nothing remotely magnificent had happened to her yet.

All at once, the sun was up. Isabel slipped into an old, shapeless dress. In the mirror, her long, dark curls rose about her shoulders and set off her blue eyes. Her skin had grown darker in the relentless sun. She should wear a hat. From a hook in the hallway, she selected one Nick had purchased, made of plant fibers, with an

exceedingly broad brim. So many things here were art without being
called art. Like the woven hat. Isabel could almost hear the thousand tiny shiftings of the fiber as she placed it on her head, stepped
out the back door, and inhaled the smell of cooking fires. A misty
haze covered the ground. In its faint, drifting movements, she imagined she saw people from earlier times. As always, the birds twit-
tered and sang. This was the best part of the day. It almost called
her to paint, but that impulse came from another lifetime—and she
put it away quickly.

♦ ♦ ♦

When had she first painted? In church of all places, St. Andrews
Episcopal in Oregon Hills. A fountain of living water after a Sunday
school lesson about a woman and Jesus. She used green, blue, and
lavender. The teacher selected her painting to put on the bulletin
board. Still, the girls from the Fan district looked down on her. Their
houses were nicer and their clothes smarter. She'd had mixed feelings about church from the beginning.

Then one Thursday when Isabel was twelve, restless at her parents' small pharmacy on South Pine, she walked to the notions store
and purchased a Mars bar. Back outdoors, the smell of tobacco surrounded her. She felt called by something. From Idlewood, she
walked to South Belvedere and turned left, up and away from the
James River, then zigzagged to Franklin and paused in front of a tall
row of brick houses. She started down First Street. The backs of the
houses were in disarray with laundry hung out and people gabbing.
Isabel scooted quickly into an alley where she hoped to pass unseen.
A robin hopped from a tree onto the cobblestone.

Other girls had mothers at home and didn't have to wander
around town or die of boredom. Halfway down the alley, through
an open door, Isabel spotted a seated woman. She wore her hair
plaited at the top of her head and her right shoulder rose and fell.
Isabel stopped and stared. The woman turned. Her face was dark
and warm. Her hand held a paintbrush. "Bella," she said.

"Yes," Isabel said, imagining she heard her name. "I was just passing by."

"Come in."

"I shouldn't. My parents." But the room smelled delicious, like vanilla but deeper.

"Come." The woman motioned with her brush.

Isabel dragged her shoe across the cobblestone. "I'm not allowed."

"You're not allowed to visit?"

"To go in any stores but the notions store near my house."

"But this is my home. Your parents want to protect you. But I am only a woman."

Isabel walked into the room. A large window opened high in the ceiling and darkness gave way to light. The woman wore hoop earrings pinned straight through her ears. She was painting a goldfish pond. The pond was placid, and Isabel could see the little golden fish. But turbulence filled the sky. "A storm," she said.

The woman turned the painting over, and Isabel saw that it had been upside down. Now the storm was in the pond and the sky was placid. Her mouth fell open. "How did you do that?"

"Always, I start with wet paper. The colors seep in and spread without hard edges. Your eyes expect to see sky on the top of the page. When you turn it, you can see another way. Now how about you? What have you seen as you came to my home?"

Isabel thought of the gabbing people and their laundry. "A robin," she said.

"Then let us paint your robin."

Angelica was from Cuba. She lived in the apartment with her son, who had installed the magic window in the ceiling. She spoke of "the turbulence." This turbulence had driven them from Cuba. "But I have not lost everything. I can paint anywhere. And I see better now."

"Did you get glasses?"

"No, child. Do you see me wearing glasses? No. Because the world has been turned upside down."

She showed Isabel how to paint her robin. The surprising thing was that the bird came to completion last. First came pale strokes for the sky. Then a wash of color called burnt sienna for the building to one side. Then the ground, an even lighter wash, followed by dabs of umber for cobblestone. Then came the robin. A curve of breast was already there in the white space. At last a stroke of darker wing, hint of beak, coppery breast, those dark, essential legs.

"You see, it's watercolor," Angelica said. "It is like life. Nothing can be taken out once it is put there. So you paint in washes and do the most detailed work last."

"Will you teach me how to paint?"

"Of course."

Isabel visited Angelica for four years, every Thursday when she bought a Mars bar at Carter's Dry Goods and Notions, until Angelica's son moved them to Washington, D.C. But the robin's curved breast stayed in Isabel's brain, along with Angelica's light brown hands.

◆ ◆ ◆

Suddenly, Daniel clattered into the backyard on his bicycle. Isabel looked down at her old dress, a little embarrassed. "What are you doing? You're not working today." A white letter glowed like a thin lantern in his bicycle basket.

"I have a message."

Had Nick been in an accident? Isabel took the envelope, stepping sideways into the deep shade of an avocado tree. She ripped it open.

Dear Mrs. Hammond,

Your cook has informed us that you need a ride to Kaduna for the party at the British guesthouse. We will pick you up by one p.m. Pack your things for an overnight.

> *Yours truly,*
> *Mrs. Van Dijk*

Isabel looked at the back of the letter as if some code might lie there. The British guesthouse operated as a private hotel with central areas and two wings with rooms. "How did you obtain this?"

"I sent a friend by motorcycle last evening. He found a man who knew the place where the woman lives. He brought the letter to me this morning."

"I must pay you for all that trouble. And your friend as well. How did you know to look for the Van Dijks?"

"There are not many bature there."

Bature. *White people.* Like Isabel and Nick.

"Mrs. Van Dijk and her husband have lived in this country a long time by now."

Isabel and Nick had met Elise and Hugo Van Dijk only once, at a Father Christmas party. They lived in Kachia, an hour south. Why did so many towns begin with K? A generation older than Nick and Isabel, the Van Dijks had come from the Netherlands after the war, he to teach and she to run a dispensary. From a mutual acquaintance, Isabel had learned that Elise had suffered during the German occupation, burying her first child. "Near starvation conditions," the acquaintance had whispered. In Nigeria, she and Hugo had raised two boys who were back in Holland in boarding school, and now they were semipermanent residents, living in an apartment above the dispensary, where Elise employed several Nigerians. They slipped so easily in and out of Hausa that Isabel thought of them as hybrids. Her house was on their route.

"How do we get word back to them?" she said.

"My friend will travel again."

"Tell them yes. I will be ready. Thank you."

"Bem," *peace*, Daniel said. He offered a flashing smile.

Isabel wanted to clap, but instead she hurried inside. She had to bathe and set her hair.

◆ ◆ ◆

Peugeots and Volkswagens, and a few Fords and Chevrolets, already filled the parking lot as Isabel and the Van Dijks pulled up to the red-roofed guesthouse where they would lodge and enjoy the evening's entertainment. It sat at the back of a wide yard surrounded by willowy casuarina trees. A few stray chickens wandered about the lawn. Down the street were the Kaduna swimming pool and Gamji Park, a shady corridor of towering kapok trees, destination for expats and well-to-do Nigerians alike. The Kaduna River flowed nearby. River of crocodiles, for Kaduna meant crocodiles, though Isabel had yet to see one. The river never looked dangerous. She had always liked to think that she would sense danger if it were near. As soon as she got out of the car, two young girls came running with cellophane wrapped chewing gum for sale. To please them, she purchased two packets from each.

Elise helped her settle into her room at the far end of the veranda. Isabel was delighted to find her own bath and two windows with sills large enough to sit on. She ran her hand across them. A vibration like a butterfly's flutter pulsed at the nape of her neck. She had never had a hotel room to herself, with starched sheets, a thermos of potable water, pull-chain lamps, and a single rose in a vase. She sat, looking out the window as more cars pulled in and parked. Soon, she slipped on the green dress and pressed a garnet clip into her hair. She reapplied her lipstick. Someone knocked. It was Elise, in a floral dress that amplified her width, her curls tamed by a headband, her deep hazel eyes aglow. Fleetingly, Isabel recalled that once this woman had been hungry.

"Wunderschön," Elise said. "Turn around for me."

Isabel did as she was told and felt she was sixteen again, ready for the prom, and in that moment, she longed for her reticent, far-away mother. "Really? It's all right?"

Elise lightly pinched Isabel's cheek. "More than that. Come along now."

They entered the dining hall and found seats around a table near the front. Waiters dressed in starched, white jackets brought drinks and bread. Just as Isabel wondered where the entertainment might be, she glimpsed a motion and there was Bobby Tunde onstage, beaming out over the crowd with his trim beard, wearing quite a different sort of white jacket, a sleek, modern one, and slender pants that flared at the base. Beneath the jacket, he wore nothing but a silver bangle necklace. His chest was smooth as water. Isabel was sure she heard alarmed gasps from other bature women. But before anyone could object, Mr. Tunde had picked up the saxophone and was jazzing his way through his first piece. He turned the instrument sideways, up, and back down. A Nigerian gentleman in a traditional

yellow robe stood and danced. Isabel felt bubbly. Elise elbowed her.
The main dish had arrived.

"Aren't you going to eat?"

♦ ♦ ♦

An hour and a half later, after a dinner of fried rabbit and curried
rice, Isabel sat by a window, drinking a second beer, listening to
Bobby, whose skin was the color of sand dunes at dusk. In the invitation to the party, she had read about how he had studied in London. During dinner, he had played Chopin sonatas. Now he was
serenading them with Perry Como. Many of the guests had moved
outside. Isabel had no wish to leave. This Bobby Tunde was magic
to watch. He left the piano and picked up a drum. At first, it seemed
Tunde merely fondled it, his hands delicate but firm. At last a sound
emerged. *Dada dada.* It filled her chest. Tunde struck a metal piece.
The vibration sounded like feet over tile, like pebbles rolling down
a roof. *Da da DA, dada Da.* Wood, goatskin, and a piece of metal.
How was he doing it? Isabel felt a crescendo coming. The mus-
cles in the man's neck tensed, and she felt electric at the tips of her
breasts. But Tunde let the sound go, the beat fading, as if he had
released a red bird, its heart flying out over the world. He seemed
a bit sad. She even wondered if he might have shed a tear, the way
he dabbed his eye with the sleeve of his jacket. *Who are you*, she
wanted to ask, *to have this effect on me?* Now back at the piano, he
took up a waltz number. The crowd flooded in from the veranda.
Hugo asked Isabel to dance. He was quite a good dancer, and Isabel
felt safe following his lead. Next came a pudgy Danish man Isabel
didn't know. He was clumsy as a bear. Still, the green dress flared,
and she wished Nick could see her. Nick, with his thick brown hair
and gray eyes and broad shoulders. But he did not appear, and she
wasn't sure he would like this party. He didn't like to dance. She felt
oddly happy in herself. Fortunately, the next man was a Peace Corps
worker named Jerry Frey. He was wirily built but cute enough, and
after the dance, Isabel asked him to sit with her. He talked about
how much he missed the Sunday paper and department stores and

a good hamburger. Isabel studied him. "But we have Kingsway here. It's a department store. And we have *Drum* magazine. I admire the stylish Nigerian women on the cover. Last week I read a fable about a man and a mosquito net and then a news story about the Lux soap factory in Ghana."

Jerry put a hand to her forehead, smiling as he did. "I believe you have the fever."

"What?" Isabel pushed his hand aside and felt for herself. "I'm fine."

"You're in love with the place," he said.

"I wouldn't mind being more in love," she said. "I want to get out. You know. See more."

A cake appeared along with several bottles of champagne. Isabel drank a glass and ate a large piece of cake, licking icing from her fingers, surprised by her ease. She did love the place. Her appetite seemed enormous. When the music started up again and the dance floor opened, she danced alone in the new style, conjuring Bobby Tunde's drum. She raised her arms and moved her hips. When she glanced up at the musician, who seemed to be watching, a wand of light passed through her. She threw a kiss to Elise. In a moment of overconfidence, she tried a twirl. She lost her balance and fell into a soft heap. The garnet clip fell from her hair and shimmied across the floor. She attempted to stand, but the hem of the green dress caught in her heel. The music stopped. She saw a flash of white suit and a hand before her face. Raising her head, she looked up into Bobby Tunde's eyes. He searched her face as if he knew her dreams. The silver necklace had broken; one link dangled at the end. "You," she said.

"Are you hurt?"

Isabel felt a flush begin in her chest, and its heat rose into her face. She focused her eyes on the man's throat. "I don't think so." He pulled her up. She took a tentative step, reeled, and reached for him. His temples bore a firmness that complemented his liquid movement and made him seem a masculine counterpart to herself, or a self she wished to be.

Suddenly Hugo Van Dijk was in front of her.

"Come my dear." He led her across the room. She tried to turn, to seek out Bobby's eyes again, but Hugo marched her toward their table.

"Did I make a fool of myself?"

"Nonsense. Let me get you a Fanta."

Isabel took a seat next to Elise. The woman patted her hand. "I've never seen an American girl dance as well as a Nigerian one."

The woman's eyes were full of a mischievous sparkle. Across the room, Jerry Frey leaned against a wall. She could have saved herself a spill if she had simply danced with him.

Twenty minutes later, the music stopped for good. Bobby Tunde packed up his instruments. Isabel tried not to watch, but she might never see him again. A shimmer seemed to surround him. She knew no other way to describe it, a faint tremble of the light. She wanted to ask if his music made him weep. But Elise said something, drawing Isabel's attention away. The next time she glanced at the stage, Tunde had disappeared, back into town to a Nigerian hotel, she presumed. Halfway down the hall to her room, near a door that exited to the courtyard, a silver crescent caught her eye. She bent to lift it from the red concrete floor. The open link from Bobby's necklace. She closed her hand around it.

Kaduna

•••••

Late February 1963

In her room, Isabel washed her face, took off her green dress, and slipped on a full-length nightgown; nights often turned cool. She turned off the lamps and opened the windows to moonlight. The silver link rested on the bedside table. She slipped it onto her right ring finger and closed her fist. Lying on her back, she thought briefly of Nick and how, if he had come, she would not have fallen. Then she thought of Bobby's strong temples, his fingers on the keyboard, that look of connection when he helped her stand, as if they had crossed paths before.

At age fifteen in Richmond, Isabel fell in love with a boy named Ian whose primary interest was fishing on a lake just out of town. He mowed enough grass to buy a dinghy and an outboard motor. Their romance took place in that boat. When the fish stopped biting, Ian headed for a shady spot on the far edge of the lake. Their kissing set them gently rocking as sunlight through leaves sent cascades of shadow into the boat. The still-living fish thumped against the side. After kissing, they lay in the bottom of the dinghy and slept. Waking before Ian, Isabel felt herself half-fish, half-human, rocking lightly on the water, emerald woods around her. It was an enchanted place and time, far from Pine Street and the concrete walls of the school building, and the muscular James River. Ian never pushed her for more than she was ready to give.

The spring and summer of their romance, they caught bluegill and perch and an occasional bass. They cooked them in Crisco over a lakeside fire. By then, her parents had purchased a house on Laurel Street, though still in Oregon Hill. When she got home late in the evening, she was relaxed and satisfied, and she fell asleep at nine o'clock, still rocking in the boat as she closed her eyes. Her Italian, Catholic father and Episcopalian mother, exhausted by a day at their pharmacy, appeared relieved by her wholesome romance. They didn't have to make plans for her. She was never out late. She didn't wear makeup or complain about riding the bus. Isabel had learned the power of affection and long, searching kisses.

In the Kaduna guesthouse, Isabel fell asleep thinking about Ian's boat and slept until a breeze came up that ruffled the large poinsettia bushes outside. Had she made a fool of herself? Or had she been bold? Would she be an object of gossip? Did Bobby Tunde shed a tear? The silver link circled her finger. Her legs felt light coming out from under the sheet, and she ran her hands up and down them. *I'm still a bit tipsy.* The concrete floor was cool beneath her feet. At the door of her room, she hesitated before pushing down on the lever-handle. She stepped through and pulled the door behind her. The sky was oddly light, though clouds covered the moon. How peculiar. The dry season should last until late April when strong winds brought dust storms riding on rainstorms, and more than once Isabel had had to dash home to beat the deluge. And yet away in the distance she heard rain. She breathed in the smell of damp earth that had already arrived, moved across the screened veranda, and took a seat in a white rattan chair. Before long, she saw a flash of lightning, followed by thunder. Heavy drops sounded one by one on the roof before the sky opened. Rain poured straight down, pummeling the path, the small frangipani trees, the towering palms, the caladium bed. A sudden wind moved through the screen, bringing a mist that wetted her skin. Isabel could imagine Nigerian children in their compounds, running out to stand on the elevated verandas that bordered their homes, clapping.

She pulled her knees up to her chin and tented the gown over them, holding herself in a ball, her bare toes sticking out in front. How would it feel to have Bobby Tunde hold her head as he had held his drum? Isabel considered Nick and wondered if the rain reached him and if the neem trees were being uprooted. Would he run out into the storm and try to hold them in place. Would he lie down in the mud and make himself a boulder against their destruction? Why wasn't he here with her, making himself a boulder against her wanton imagination?

Out of the corner of her eye, she sensed a movement, a figure in shadow. She grasped the arms of her chair. It was Bobby Tunde, in dark tunic and pants. Because of the rain, she had not heard the door open. Nor had she imagined him in the room next to her. She was grateful for her long, full gown and lowered her feet to the floor.

"You couldn't sleep for the rain?" he said, taking a seat beside her.

Now she saw him clearly. "No." She felt the way she did when she first learned watercolor, the swirling of paint on the page. She crossed her arms over her chest.

"It's very unusual. Anyway, it's hard to relax after a performance. I'm all jazzed up."

"I can imagine. I like your music." Should she look at him or at her hands? The silver band. She had forgotten it on her finger. She pressed her hands together.

"I put in just enough Yoruba sound that you white people don't notice but enough to keep me happy." He chuckled.

She looked at him. He seemed lankier than she remembered, his legs sprawled out in front of him, but the shimmer was still there, his face poised with intention that held her spellbound, though now she noticed a ribbon of flesh above his left eye at the outer corner, where it slanted downward as if at some point in childhood a nerve had been damaged. What could she remember about the Yoruba that might explain his magic?

"Unless I am playing for my own people. Then the equation goes the other way. Just enough English music to honor my mother but not so much that my brothers complain."

He spoke as if he had known Isabel for years, as if they were from the same hometown. She thought of Angelica, who had been from Cuba but started conversation right away. She and Bobby were already in the same river. The rain abated. Beyond the screen, an animal sounded. The Yoruba lived in the southwest. They were skilled artisans and weavers. Why was this man paying tribute to his mother with English music? What was this current passing through her? In the U.S. Isabel had been taught to avoid Black men. Like flash cards, she remembered the snippets of language that constructed this tacit admonition. Separation and segregation had seemed normal. Of course she would not have feelings for a darker-skinned man. But now that was exactly what was happening. A small wind stirred. She could make no connection between that past and this moment. What did it matter? The beautiful man beside her had no interest in her. Who knows when Bobby Tunde normally slept? He probably wanted to smoke. "You're quite versatile," she said stupidly, meaning his music.

"But not so versatile that you imagined I would be lodging in the room next to you? As you see, I am at the very end of the guest house, as far away as possible from the bature, except for you." He chuckled again, but a worried look came into his brow.

"I'm sorry. It's your country. It's a crying shame anyone would question your being here." Yet only hours ago, she had assumed he would lodge elsewhere.

"A crying shame? Is that something you say in America?"

"I suppose so."

Bobby chuckled before turning thoughtful. "It would make a good song. But such a pretty lady should not cry."

His tenderness was so unexpected, Isabel thought she would cry. "I'm not. The rain wet my face." A silence followed. If she were to do his portrait, she would start with the curve of his brow down to his square jaw, then his brows that seemed now to contract. "Something troubles you," she said.

"My mother is ill."

"Your mother is British?" Isabel felt suddenly bold and aware.

"Yes. And my father is a Yoruba man." He went on, as Angelica had, as if all thought for him was one continuous stream. "It's good you are not crying. I would feel responsible."

"I'm sorry about your mother. I pray she will soon be well."

"Indeed." He rested his hands in his lap.

She opened her fist. "I found a link to your necklace."

"Keep it," he said.

Her heart jumped. "When did you start making music?"

"Before I was born."

Isabel's hand went to her belly, as if she might feel an infant's kick.

"My grandfather was the lead drummer for the Oba of his town. I am actually Babatunde Ayanlola."

"Those names must have meanings."

"In essence, I am the reincarnation of my grandfather. It was my destiny to be a musician. Even my British mum discerned my true nature and taught me piano. I also stole utensils from my Yoruba granny to make music. Once I took her favorite enamel bowl to use as a drum after which she drummed on my behind." He smiled. "Anyway, in England I studied hymnology."

Flecks of green lit Tunde's eyes. Isabel's hand reached the sleeve of his shirt. "I'm a painter. Or I was. I worked in watercolor. But I never thought of it as my destiny." Work was hardly the right word. She dabbled. Or perhaps she had been told she dabbled. Only Angelica had encouraged her painting, and Isabel had painted for a time in college.

"But it must be. It is your underground spirituality."

She tightened her hold on his sleeve. "I once painted a fountain of living water," she said. "My first watercolor."

"Of course," he said as if this was no surprise. "What lies below the surface is your essence. Some of us musicians call it underground spirituality."

She thought of her fishy reverie in Ian's boat, that first painting composed in the basement of St. Andrews Episcopal Sunday School.

"We hear the rain, but beneath is the bird's heartbeat. My country has been covered in English, so my own tongue is below the surface. My ancestor is below the surface. The English cannot be taken out. It runs through everything. So I use it. But the aim is to bring the underground up. It may be the same for you."

Isabel felt herself being called from a distance. Angelica had said color could not be taken out of a painting. You had to use what was already on the page. "Why the bird's heartbeat?" was all she could think to say.

"The bird is a messenger between humans and deities."

They sat for fifteen minutes. Or maybe it was thirty, Isabel could never recollect, though she remembered the smell of earth, clouds rolling back to reveal the moon again, how her hand rested in the crook of Tunde's arm, how his face seemed to shimmer.

At last he spoke. "And Isabel. It must mean Bella, beautiful."

She sat up, alert. "That's what Angelica said, my first art teacher."

They faced one another. "But where is your husband?"

Isabel shook her head. Her dear Nick. Agricultural economist, planter of trees here for USAID. He loved her, but he did not comprehend her. "He's on a trip. Your wife?"

Tunde tapped the arm of the chair with his fingers. "She is back home."

For a moment, the moon disappeared again, and the night seemed very dark.

"Stay still," Tunde said.

Isabel looked straight ahead. A light slap grazed her cheek and she gasped.

"Mosquito." Bobby held the destroyed insect by one leg, then shook it to the floor.

The sting of the slap coursed through her. Moonlight reappeared. They sat back in their chairs.

"Moon once lived on earth," he said, "but water overwhelmed its hut and moon jumped for the sky."

"Did you just make that up?"

"No. It is a folktale. All songs are repeating." He ran a finger down her arm. "An hour until dawn. I must let you sleep."

Isabel's marriage vows shone in her mind like a small glass case. And yet. "I'm not sleepy," she said. Tunde offered his hand. Isabel placed her fingers in his palm. It was cool and she clasped it, as if a gale might move through and blow them off course. They stood.

We are leaves driven by wind. We are outside of time.

He pressed the door handle. A slight creak and they stepped from the porch, across the threshold, and into his room.

"Shhhh," she said.

Tunde pushed the door to and turned the key.

They faced one another. Tunde placed a hand on the offended cheek and kissed her there, his breath warm. He pinched the cloth of her nightgown at the shoulders, bent forward, and kissed her mouth. Isabel felt she had been plunged into a warm lake. She lifted her hair and Tunde kissed her neck. He stood back and turned his face from her.

"Ah," he said.

She saw him clench his jaw, saw his chest bend ever so slightly inward as if he were unsure, hesitating, withdrawing from her. "You teared up, playing the drum," she said. He faced her again, a look of surprise and gratitude passing over his countenance. He moved back into their embrace, and they held each other like they were the last survivors of a wreck. Tunde traced her shoulder blades, as if she were a new instrument he was warming to. A current ran from her underarms to her navel and spread down her abdomen, flooding the space between her legs. She pushed his hands aside and began to unbutton his shirt, staring fiercely at his smooth chest. He tried to put his hands on her again, but she slapped him away. This must not be. The silver link fell, and she heard it hit the floor. She held his face in her palms, his head sturdy and dense in her hands. She would kiss him once more and cease.

He seemed to read her mind. "We can stop."

She saw a line somewhere like a division between countries. But a wind erased the line. "No." They undressed and their clothes fell in a pile. His chest flowed down into his lean hips, so lean. His brown feet arched.

She took his hand and led him to the windowsill nearest the bed. It appeared deep maroon in the night. She turned the arm of the casement window to open the glass. "Help me," she said, and he lifted her so that she was sitting there, facing him, her head level with his, her legs a V, the night air sweeping her back. He sang into her ear, but she couldn't make out his words.

The smell of rain surrounded them. His fingers moved across her body. "Your skin is like silk from the kapok tree."

Her back arched, and she became a circle within circles, radiating out. He pushed into her, and she turned into a bowl, rocking. Suddenly she stopped. "Listen."

"What?"

"Drumming." She matched her movement to it, her hands pressed against the window frame. Did the makers of deep window-sills know this use of them? His thin hips, her hinged legs. What artful structure. Even in the night, she saw the green flecks in the dark discs of his eyes, sun sparking in pools of water. But now the drumming was drowned out because of their own drumming, the give and take, the perfect timing. He pulled her even closer, lifted her from the sill. Isabel grasped his shoulders and pressed her mouth to his forehead. She closed her eyes, and they broke open at the same time.

He set her back on the sill, singing something in Yoruba. He sang a bit and hummed and sang a bit, stopped, backed up, and repeated.

"What is it? What are the words?"

"Lovely lady should not cry. I'm working on the melody."

They lay on the bed.

An hour passed. "What do we do now?" As if they had any future beyond this night. "I can't be seen with you," she whispered.

"Nevertheless, I will find you."

"The silver link."

He searched the floor, found it, and placed it in her hand. The shimmer was still there in his face, on his arms.

Isabel slipped the gown over her head, opened his door, turned, went back, and kissed him once more. "Think of me. But do not weep." She walked onto the damp veranda. This must be a dream. The gray dawn was in her hands. She felt as wide open and un-defended as a person can be, yet full of bliss, as if Tunde had given her herself, not taken. She faced her door, opened it, stumbled to her bed, and slept.

◆ ◆ ◆

A rap on Isabel's door splintered her sleep. She flailed for her house-coat. She hadn't brought one. Was it Tunde? Had Nick come to get her? What had she done? Was there evidence? The broken silver band lay on her bedside table, and she scooped it up.

"Mrs. Hammond? Isabel? Are you joining us for breakfast? We must leave within the hour." It was Elise Van Dijk. Dear Elise.

Another rap. "Isabel? Are you there?"

The door handle jiggled, but Isabel had locked it. What day was she in her cycle? *Think. Think.* Day twenty, maybe twenty-one. "Don't wait on me for breakfast. Grab some fruit if you can. I'll be ready to travel."

"Are you sure? You aren't sick, are you?"

"No. I just overslept. I'll be right on time." Isabel clasped the band so tightly it left an indentation in her palm.

On her way out, she glanced at Tunde's door. Was he still inside? She wished for some sign of him. How would she know if his mother recovered? The grass on the front lawn had already dried and was back to its brown crispness. The sun nearly blinded her. She clutched the lapels of her light jacket at the center of her chest. This leaving was too hasty. Something seemed undone. She needed some subtle sign that meant, *Yes, we are joined, but we will never speak of it.* A drum sounded in the distance.

◆ ◆ ◆

By eleven o'clock, Isabel was back in her front yard in Kufana. Through her mind ran the lyric she had created to keep all the *K* names straight: Kaduna city, Kufana town, Kafanchan farm. If it had rained here, Isabel could not tell. The sun poured around her.

Daniel took her bag. "Barka dawowa," *welcome back.*

"Na gode," *thank-you*, she said. Was guilt written on her face? Or joy? Or any trace of Bobby's shimmer? During the drive, Elise had asked what was preoccupying her. "Nothing, really," she'd said.

"I suppose you're worried about your stumble last night," Elise had said.

Isabel had latched on to the suggestion. "Yes, I have worried over that."

"Only your radiance will be remembered," Elise had claimed.

On Isabel's porch sat a potted crown of thorns plant, blooming pink as watermelon. The thought made Isabel immensely thirsty.

"I have prepared egg salad for your lunch," Daniel said.

She had meant to bring something back for him, for arranging the ride with her friends, but in her delirium, she had forgotten.

"I'm starving. I'll eat right away."

"The party is good?" he said as they stepped into the house. Isabel's conscience stung more deeply, it seemed, at her forgetfulness of Daniel than her betrayal of her husband.

"Yes. Thank you for arranging it." She strode to the bathroom, nearly tripping over one of those leather stools called tim tims. She considered bathing, but she had told Daniel she would be right out. She combed her hair, brushed her teeth, and gulped water from the thermos.

As soon as she opened the bathroom door, she saw Nick midstride in the living room, heading straight for the kitchen. Isabel shrank into shadow. He was early, his skin flushed from the sun, and his wavy brown hair rushed up at the crown of his head. Isabel saw all of this, and the inside of her head burned. She heard the tap turn on, a splash of water, the close of the tap, the refrigerator door open. She waited until she heard a glass set down on the metal drainboard. How could she face him? Did she have an underground spirituality? Any spirituality? Perhaps once. But now? Laughable.

"Isabel?"

The metal coil of the screen door sounded, followed by a slam. Nick had walked into the backyard. She hadn't expected him for three days. She needed those days. What had happened? She put her nose to her underarms. There was no time to wash. With her palms, she pressed her head at the temples and closed her eyes. In a moment, she followed her husband. Through the screen door, she saw Nick squatted in the garden, a pinch of soil between his fingers. She pushed the door open and stepped down to the rim of concrete walkway and then onto the grass.

"You're home early."

He stood, and in that moment, she saw his beauty as utterly separate from her, something foreign. If she had only had time to get ready, to think about what she had done, to walk herself backwards in time, to clear her head, bathe away her crime, even paint a watercolor, to say a prayer, to turn back to herself, back to him, bury the silver link.

She ran to him, though in her mind she was running in the other direction, toward a maroon windowsill, and when she slammed herself against her husband's chest, it was as if she had thrown herself over a cliff.

"Are you all right?" Nick peered into her face.

"I'm fine. I missed you. You're here. But I'm not ready. I thought you wouldn't be home for three more days." Three was the number of something bad. A dark curl sprang from the knot she had made of her hair this morning, and she swept it back. Nick kissed her forehead.

"We worked through the weekend. We finished. I'm here. I'm all yours." He smiled broadly like a man happy over a hunting trip. "The Suburban needs a tune-up, though. I hit a pothole this side of Jema'a, and the suspension seems damaged. Lucky I didn't get a blowout."

Why did his speech seem like a row of boxes all stacked up against each other and nothing like a river? "Did you greet Daniel when you came in?"

"I didn't see him."

"That's odd." Isabel felt sure Daniel was watching them now through the kitchen window. He must have stepped into shadow as she had when Nick came pounding through the house. A sharp pain hit her temple. "He has lunch ready. You must be hungry." She pressed her pained temple and looked up at her husband. Did he sense how different she was? She felt herself to be in another country, as when they went to Matsirga Falls and she hid in the rock shelter behind rainbow sheets of water—she could see Nick, but he couldn't see her.

"I'm starving."

His eagerness was too much. She'd forgotten his American largeness, his volume, his decibel level.

Daniel had laid a green striped cloth across the dining table. In the center sat an orange Tupperware bowl full of egg salad. Next to it were six radishes sliced to look like roses and a plate of market bread cut into triangles. "How lovely, Daniel," Isabel said as she sat.

"Yes, madam."

He turned and she thought she saw disappointment in his back.

Perhaps he had hoped to hear about the dinner and the music. She had told Nick nothing. She would have to tell him about the party, about traveling with the Van Dijks. Daniel would expect her to say something right away. "I was able to go to the party in Kaduna without you," she said, mounding egg salad onto a triangle of bread. What was the bird that made its nest on the ground? Running through a field near her grandparents' farmhouse when she was eight, Isabel had glanced down to see a clutch of speckled eggs where she was about to place her foot. She was mesmerized by their color and shape. How odd that a bird would make a nest where it could be so easily destroyed.

"What's that?" Nick said.

A smear of yellow sat at the corner of her husband's lips, and she put her finger to it. He grasped her hand and gently bit her fingertip. She felt an unwelcome warming in her chest.

"I was saying that I went to the party in Kaduna. The Van Dijks were kind enough to come get me. You forgot all about it. I made a new dress. Daniel arranged for the ride. Just in case you wonder why I look so hideous. We came home in a rush." Was she performing well enough? She imagined Daniel's ears, finely made and close to his head, and sensed her words sinking into them. Unlike Nick, he noticed everything.

"You don't look hideous. I remembered the party after I sent the letter. I just hope you didn't have to endure too many dances with old Brits." There was mischief in his eyes, but she would not acknowledge it.

"Not too many. No."

"We'll have our own party. Maybe another trip to Matsirga Falls. You can hide from me again."

Was she wrong about him? Could he see into her? Her hand trembled, and she set her sandwich down.

Isabel's grandmother had explained that the bird she had seen was the Eastern Meadowlark. "I have a picture somewhere." Isabel had followed Gram into the living room, where she had opened a glass case and found the book. "See." She had pulled Isabel to the sofa and pointed, her hands speckled with brown spots. Isabel loved

---

her maternal grandmother deeply. The next morning she had run out to check on the nest, but she couldn't find it.

Nick scooted his chair back from the table. "Are you coming?"

"We haven't had dessert. Daniel made coconut pie."

"By all means, let's have dessert."

She couldn't stall forever. They always napped after the midday meal. It was what the bature did, lie down in the early afternoon, even when it wasn't hot and she wasn't tired.

"Delicious," Nick said when he had finished his pie. He pushed back his chair.

Isabel brushed her teeth for a second time. Nick was already on the bed, shirt off, shoes neatly placed by the dresser. She lay next to her husband on top of their double wedding ring quilt and closed her eyes. She had never found it useful to think of herself or anyone else as a sinner, but at the moment Isabel felt certain she was. Maybe Nick would fall asleep, nothing would happen. She needed time to come back to him.

The low buzz of insects filtered through the screened window. The curtain billowed, sending a breeze over the bed. Isabel relaxed and turned on her side. She heard the back door open and close softly. Daniel would not return until four o'clock. In a few minutes, Nick was snoring. What would the mother bird do if a plow were headed in the direction of her eggs? Would she fly away and allow the mechanical tiller to destroy them? Or would she stay? Nick was intelligent, a little aloof, a man who analyzed, who liked to be in the field alone. He could be charming. Did Isabel even have eggs? In three years of sex with her husband, there had been only one pregnancy, and that had failed. She dozed and woke in urgency, her hand between her legs. She turned to her husband, whose eyes remained closed, but the corners of his mouth rose slightly. She kissed his neck. His hands found her waist, circled her back, and shifted her skirt.

Good heavens. Look what I'm doing. Making love for the second time today and with a different man. But last night was madness and hallucination. Though there were signs of great clarity. The moon. The huff and sigh of greenery after rain. Tunde, who could see her for who she really was. And yet. Her husband. Isabel latched her legs around him, holding his shoulders as he bent to kiss her breasts. She tilted upward, as strong as the plow, her eggs safe, the nest inside her. She reached her climax as Nick rose above her, face heavy as he plunged into her. At last, his look turned to gratitude. He lowered himself carefully, her legs wide and throbbing.

That evening, fruit bats chatted noisily in the nearby trees. Isabel buried the silver link in the far back corner of her underwear drawer and banished the maroon windowsill from her memory. It had happened away from here, in some pleat in time that had now closed. It existed only for her and that luminous man.

Kufana

•••••

Early March 1963

Nick packed a lunch and left for his office in town next to the bicycle shop where he would write a report on his neem trees. Daniel had the morning off. Isabel dressed and pinned up her hair, determined to plant the lemon tree she had purchased weeks ago in the market. She had heard that the lemon symbolized commitment and adoration. With a lemon, one could clean windows, the floor, one's own adulterous face. Again, she borrowed Nick's straw hat from its hook in the hall. At the shed, she found shovel and spade.

In the center of the garden rose the water tap, giving the impression of a cobra reared up. She stepped around it. How surprised Nick would be when he came home to find she had dug the hole and prepared the soil herself. She selected a patch of earth that spoke of prior inhabitants with its hibiscus bush on a trellis and morning glories running willy-nilly. Her beloved Gram had given her space for her first garden when she was eight, taught her the use of a sharp spade, and helped her pick out seed packets. When Isabel told her grandmother there were fairies in the garden, she answered, "Of course there are."

Bobby Tunde was far away now, back in the Western region, Yorubaland. She hadn't even asked him where he lived but presumed Ibadan or Lagos. She pressed the shovel into the earth and lifted out soil. Isabel felt her own power, her thick hair piled on her head, her eyes discerning colors: burnt sienna, red oxide, yellow ochre. She could make paints from this soil. She wanted to talk about that, making paint, lying with Bobby again.

An evil burp came up her throat. She set the shovel aside. Indoors, she pulled the water jug from the refrigerator, poured a glass, and drank. Though she would never see Tunde again, he might speak of her. What if Nick learned of her infidelity? She could deny the story. There was no proof of a maroon windowsill. Only an open silver link in the back of a drawer.

Back in the yard, she knotted her skirt between her legs and labored in a rhythm, lifting soil, bending to scoop by hand, standing to breathe. The task became more difficult, a hard job of work as her grandfather would say. She set the shovel aside and reached for the sharper spade. A goat with a red cord around its neck moved into the yard and back out. She continued to dig. Finally, she thought she might be deep enough, the hole she had created two feet deep, maybe three across. The root ball of the lemon tree was smaller than that. She would loosen the roots that would begin to tunnel in the rainy season, twining around buried stones. Her hands were deep orange.

Something glittered. Isabel leaned into the hole and placed her finger on the protrusion. Some bit of reddish glaze. With her fingertips, she brushed away soil and then sat back on her haunches. A single cloud moved over her. She continued to dig until she uncovered the pebbly edge of something. Terra-cotta? Or it might merely be lava rock, a common occurrence here. In that case, she would have to find another place to dig. First, she would make a cup of tea. In the kitchen the clock registered eleven a.m. She sat in Daniel's chair beneath the overhanging roof, sipping her tea. She should have trained to be an archeologist or a serious artist. But after two years in art education, she left college to marry Nick. Women had so few choices. The ultimate success was to marry a good-looking man who was going places. She wanted to marry Nick. She was desperate to go somewhere, anywhere.

In the yard again, she got back to work, though it was even hotter now and not a cloud in the sky. The pebbly edge had a uniform curve to it and spoke of intentionality. Lava rock would not. It must be ninety degrees. But the work felt cleansing. Isabel's purpose was no longer to surprise Nick. Her purpose now was merely to dig. She scooped loose dirt to one side. In the distance, a drum started up. Bobby Tunde's smooth chest burst into her consciousness, and for a moment, she thought she would faint. "What if I pour water over whatever this is," she said, to fend off the intrusion. She meant never to see him again. But the world was more compelling with him in it. She raised the back of her hand to her face and inhaled as if she might catch his scent. The motion brought other images to mind: mist on her face, the slap to her cheek, the click of the door latch. She sat back, holding her legs to her chest. Her hands stained her blouse.

A car horn sounded. People passed on the lane. At the tap, Isabel filled a bucket and wetted her neck, then carried the rest to pour over the mystery object. The water cleared the hard curved surface before disappearing into the earth. A breeze came up over the bougainvillea hedge, smelling of manure. She continued the excavation. Suddenly a bit of dirt fell into a depression. Isabel leaned over. What seemed a black marble was a small and perfect hole in the curved surface of what must certainly be a long-lost vessel. Light seemed to move through her body. She could make out a definitive arch above the black hole.

Isabel seemed to ascend to a place of knowing. Somewhere close by a girl pounded yam, a mother called out to her child, an engine sputtered and died, a man set out three tins of palm wine for sale, two boys kicked a ball, a schoolgirl wrote her name on the face of a notebook.

Isabel moved to the opposite side of her excavation. Just as Angelica had told her, the world turned upside down reveals what we have not yet seen. Isabel saw. The object was some sort of sculpture. The strong arch was above, not below the hole. It was an eyebrow, and the hole was the iris of an eye. She could make out a faint upper lid. Isabel's hand trembled as she reached out to place her palm on what must be the curve of a head. She poured more water into the hole until the lower eyelid appeared in the shape of a new moon. Altogether, the eye looked like the eyes in ancient Egyptian drawings, almost extraterrestrial. Something in Isabel surged, recalling Bobby Tunde, her safe bed with Nick, her nest, the lemon tree. She would have to break the pot to set the roots free. The mother bird had hidden herself so well she could not be found, nor her eggs. Isabel must not break this sculpture. Already she could guess at its dimension. *The height of a table lamp.* Sweat poured down her face as she continued to dig. The second eye appeared: the forceful brow, a faint upper lid, the iris, the lower lid like a new moon. What Isabel had thought was the slanting shape of a pot was actually a long forehead. She could not see the entire figure yet and still Isabel knew that the eyes were its most potent aspect. They were huge, alert, and mysterious. *My God. She can see me.* For Isabel knew it was a female figure. In her pause, she confessed. *My name is Isabel. I had sex with two men in the same day. I didn't train for anything. I paint watercolors. Or I once did.* Her fingernails were ragged and full of dirt as she gazed into her interlocutor's eyes.

How long had this womanish figure been buried? All but a tiny bit of glaze had vanished. A thousand years? Two thousand?

She worked carefully, unearthing an expertly crafted nose with a lovely tip and finely wrought nostrils. Beneath that, the full lips of a mouth with the slightest opening in the middle, a tiny hole. *To allow airflow during firing.* What brilliant people had made this work of art? The lips did not smile, nor did they frown. They were of a piece with the mysterious eyes. A headdress topped the forehead. Isabel's fingers were thick with mud. She should rest, but that was out of the question. She dug until she had unearthed the figure's upper torso. Like the eyes, the neck was stylized, long and thin, decked in layers of sculpted beads. Arms emerged below the beads, raised in a spiral as if the woman were dancing, and yet they were close to her torso. *So as not to break off.* Below the raised arms were her tilted breasts, round and certain as the irises. A dancing woman. Not a thin ballerina but a rounded figure built to last. When Isabel looked up, the sky was pink. She sensed a presence and looked about, but no one was there, only the avocado tree and the bougainvillea, and the water tank and the house, with Daniel's chair under the overhanging roof, and the rack where pawpaws and oranges ripened.

The dancing woman, lying in the dirt, had danced even underground.

◆ ◆ ◆

At last, Isabel lifted the terra-cotta figure out of the earth. She was a sturdy Miriam, the female prophet, sister of Moses, dancing to timbrels, a governess, a diviner. Not quite lamp size; closer to the height of a man's forearm. One raised hand had been broken at the wrist. Otherwise, she was perfect, her body turned twenty-five degrees in her dance, wrists adorned in bracelets, a wrap furled down her torso. Isabel rinsed her off at the tap, rinsed her own hands, and then braced the terra-cotta at the base of the avocado tree. She seated herself before the otherworldly figure. The elongated head dwarfed the rest. The large, almond-shaped eyes were her strongest feature. She bore no weapon.

The dancing woman's eyes seemed to peer directly into Isabel's secret world. She studied the enigmatic woman, who had been resting in the earth, likely for centuries, and whose slumber she had disturbed, as Bobby Tunde had disturbed her own. She had felt the ribbon of flesh above his left eye with her tongue. Perfect beauty was never so enchanting as imperfect. "A stone from a sling shot," he had told her. "Intended for an aparo, bush fowl." She must tell Nick what had happened in Kaduna. Otherwise, there would always be a gulf. It was so tempting, to share the weight of what she had done. But, of course, she could not. It would cause him unending pain.

An African thrush scratched at the ground twenty feet away. Isabel touched her hair. She had not reclaimed the garnet clip she had worn just a few nights ago. Where was it? Would someone find it centuries from now, nestled in the corner of a buried building? She heard a female voice. It took a moment for her to understand that someone had stepped into her yard and was calling her. *What a sight I must be.* "Coming, madam." Isabel rested Nick's straw hat over the figure, quickly unknotted her skirt, and shook it out.

A woman with a yellow wrap stood just inside the bougainvillea hedge, a tray on her head. Isabel made the usual afternoon greeting in Hausa. "Barka da rana." Beginning in Hausa could be treacherous because Isabel couldn't go very far.

"Lafiya," the woman said. She was well. "Kuna jin Hausa?" Did Isabel speak Hausa?

"Ka'dan ka'dan." *Small, small.*

A slender girl with a slight widow's peak stood next to the woman. She might be thirteen years old, her skirt expertly wrapped around her chest, her head adorned with a long scarf in arabesque design. A daughter to the mother, no doubt. The women here took their children wherever they went. A sour odor entered Isabel's nostrils. It was her own smell. The visitor set down her headload, an enamel tray packed with newspaper cones full of groundnuts. She wished to make a sale. "Let me go for the house. I will return." Isabel rubbed thumb against fingers to communicate money. She forgot to ask how much. Indoors, she snatched up coins, along with a butter-scotch candy for the girl. Isabel returned to the yard to see mother and daughter resting on the grass, the woman adjusting the girl's hair beneath her headdress. Isabel halted in her motion. She could not remember her mother ever taking the time to fix her hair. Sunlight shifted on the ground.

"Mama!" Isabel called. "I have the money."

The woman gave a pat to the girl's head. She stood, retucked her yellow wrapper, and claimed her tray from the ground. The girl stood with her. Another woman had stopped at the hedge, and the two called to each other in Hausa across the yard.

"How much," Isabel said, "for the groundnuts?"

"Threepence each, or you have five for shilling."

Isabel knew she should ask for more and pay less. But the thought of her own mother distracted her. She motioned to the girl and slipped the butterscotch candy into her hand. The girl opened it carefully, handed foil to her mother, put the golden disk into her mouth, and gave it a serious suck. Isabel laughed. "Five for shilling," she said.

The mother huffed. "Give me the coin."

Isabel handed her the shilling, and the woman counted out four cones of groundnuts. The fifth she lifted slowly, as if it would kill her to hand it over. Finally, Isabel was in possession of five newspaper cones of groundnuts, held against her chest. "What is your name, please?"

"I am Amina."

"I am Isabel. Isabel Hammond. And your daughter?"

"Latifa." Small gold earrings sparkled on the girl's earlobes.

"Beautiful." Isabel searched her mind for the right Hausa word but couldn't recall.

"Okay, Mrs. Hammond. Good-bye for now," Amina said, surprising Isabel with her casual English. She gave her daughter a swift yank. The girl had to swivel her head around to wave back. In that instant, Isabel saw the slight press of young breasts against Latifa's blouse and considered that she might be older than thirteen.

The interaction pleased Isabel immensely. But why had she purchased five cones of groundnuts? The woman had got the best of her, making five sales in one to the crazy bature woman in her yard. She turned to spy Nick's straw hat sheltering the excavated sculpture and felt a sudden rush of affection for him. Still, she must find a place to hide the terra-cotta until she could figure out what to do. Otherwise, her husband would instruct her, or Daniel, who had more authority in such matters, would insist on some course of action that would require she give the dancing woman up right away. Isabel was sure she had found the sculpture for a reason, though she had no claim to a piece of art dug from Nigerian earth. Fine. She would keep her only briefly, being immensely careful that she come to no harm.

Across the living room from Nick and Isabel's bedroom, an anteroom opened. It could be accessed by an exterior door, but that door was kept bolted. Unlike the storeroom off the kitchen where Isabel kept a supply of tinned foods, china and crystal they never used, cleaning products, and light bulbs, the anteroom housed personal items: new underwear and t-shirts for Nick, new bras and slips for Isabel, toilet paper, toothpaste, and boxes of Kotex. It was the only room Daniel did not enter. In it, Isabel also kept a closed drum full of fabric and patterns from the U.S. After a year and a half in Nigeria, it was still two-thirds full. Except for the lime green dress, Isabel hadn't engaged much even in the art of sewing. And that art could at least be called useful. For now, Isabel would hide the sculpture here. She carried it indoors wrapped in a soft towel and lifted the lid from the drum. It smelled of the sewing section at JC Penney. She removed two patterns along with several yards of dotted swiss.

Oh! Here was that new bathing suit she had forgotten about. She set it to the side. She picked up the shrouded sculpture, so recently underground. Isabel removed the towel, placing her gently on four yards of lavender cotton. She layered in more fabric and patterns and set the drum lid back on, but she could not persuade herself to lock it into place. As if the woman needed air to breathe.

Isabel bathed and dressed. Her arms and torso seemed full of bees, humming like a hive.

When Daniel showed up midafternoon with a dour face, she covered her excitement.

"I cannot stay," he said. "I must carry my mother to the clinic. She has a pain in her leg."

"A recent injury?" Isabel worried about infections.

"No. It has been plaguing her for a long time."

That sounded worse. "Go to my husband's office. He will take you and your mother in the car." The dancing woman glowed in Isabel's mind, her raised arms, her large and knowing eyes. Daniel would not approve of her having it. And what about Bobby's British mother? Was her illness better or worse?

"I will carry her on my bicycle. You will see me in the morning by seven o'clock."

Isabel could imagine Daniel with his mother perched on the crossbar, weaving their way to the clinic. He was such a good care-taker. "Allah ya kiyaye," she said, *may God protect you as you go*. Why had the dancing woman been created? To honor a female leader, represent a goddess, immortalize a beloved who died too young, something else entirely?

Isabel was suddenly exhausted. She had become a woman with secrets.

Isabel's Virginia
· · · · ·

Growing up, Isabel spent her summers with her maternal grandparents on their farm thirty miles from Richmond. The summer she turned seventeen, she was tending the lemonade stand at the Fourth of July celebration in Chesterton's community park when some older boys drove up and parked. The driver got out and headed toward her. He was so handsome he frightened her. She glanced sideways, hoping to appear disinterested while the other boys rumbled out of the passenger door. The driver stood before her, and she turned to face him. He wore a faded blue ball cap and dungarees, but his hands were smooth and his face had the well-tended look of a comfortable life. He was not a regular farm boy. When she said, "Yes? How can I help you?" he said, "I should be asking you to marry me," and his smile tilted sideways.

She sought a retort—to distract him from the flush to her cheeks. She had broken up with Ian after she caught him sending notes to another girl, but she remembered everything he had taught her about what boys like: boats, outboards, cars, and trucks. "Where'd you get your F100?"

The handsome boy had dropped to his knee. "It's yours and so am I." He clasped his hands to his chest. He was bold as well as good-looking, and he had an air of goodness about him. She had the sense that wherever he went, he would be easy in himself, sure of what he heard and saw. She also knew that attachment to a successful man was her surest insurance against a life like her mother's, which might have been far worse if her husband, Isabel's immigrant father, hadn't been smart enough to land a scholarship that put him through graduate school and fortunate enough to receive a small inheritance that allowed him to open his pharmacy.

But then the pharmacy dictated their lives. Her parents could not take time off. How many times had her mother said, *We hardly break even?* Only once, when Isabel was ten, did the three of them take a vacation. They traveled to Clearwater, Florida, on the Gulf, and rented a little concrete house. They got hotter and hotter as they drove, and when they arrived, the house felt like an oven. Isabel's fastidious mother walked out to the yard, turned on the hose, and sprayed Isabel off in the clothes she'd worn from South Carolina, where they'd spent the night in a little blue highway motel. "Now go inside and dry off," she had said. "Antonio," she'd called Isabel's father, "do yourself."

"Whatever you say, Lil," he had said.

Isabel had never heard her parents say anything so funny, and the little trip suddenly seemed promising. From the window, she watched her tall, dark-haired father take out his wallet and step out of his shoes before sending a plume of water in the air and standing under it. When it was her mother's turn, she held the hose over her head and let it soak her. She seemed transformed, as if she had forgotten her family and the pharmacy cash register at 334 South Pine Street and the bowling alley, her only pastime, where Black men reset pins, had forgotten Richmond itself. For the first time, Isabel saw her mother completely enjoying herself. "She looks like a mermaid," Isabel had said aloud. This could not be her cool, practical mother. Not only was the world not stable, it could be made pliable. It was the only such moment with her mother, and Isabel held on to it, a reminder that the beautiful was always possible.

Her father stood in the yard watching her mother, his long arms clasped in front of him. He seemed as captivated as Isabel was but in a different way that she didn't comprehend. It was as if she had disappeared and her parents were in a movie.

The woman with the watering hose was altogether a different person. When she had finally finished, she didn't even bother to turn the hose off. She threw it on the ground where it flapped like a fish as she stood in place and shook out her hair until it fell in circlets to her shoulders. Isabel observed her mother's body. The exposed V of skin below her throat. Her small tight breasts and pelvic bones, a slight rise below her belt that Isabel instinctively knew had to do with birthing a child. The tuck where her dress clung to her private place. She held her arms to her sides, palms forward. And then the unimaginable happened. Her father, Antonio, walked to Lil, gathered her up in his arms, and kissed her for a long time. Isabel couldn't figure out why his large nose didn't get in the way of the kissing. Lil let her head fall back and her arms too. She didn't even wrap them around Antonio. He took her. When they stopped, they laughed.

But when they came into the hot concrete house, they were back to their normal selves. The next day at the beach, her mother read a women's magazine and Antonio swam in the surf. Isabel threw the beach ball back and forth with another lonely girl. She and her mother got sunburned, but not Antonio, who was darker skinned and never did. The rest of the vacation was hot and normal. When Isabel suggested they all hose themselves down again, her mother said, "Don't be silly." Isabel sometimes wondered if her mother was adopted. She didn't have her grandmother's soft fullness or bestow kindness in natural acts of generosity. What had pinched her mother back? *Was it I?* Whatever the reason, Isabel felt the same pinching in her life, no matter how she tried to shake it. Now she had gone and betrayed her husband, and that could not be the answer, not for more than one night.

Isabel had searched for the beauties in her life: her grandmother's quilts, lilacs on Laurel Street, the soaring arch at the entrance of Arents Free Library. But harshness was more routine: evenings when her parents were at work and she ate alone, indifference at school because Isabel wasn't lively enough to catch a teacher's attention, an empty coffee table. She looked for moments when the world might become something other than what it seemed, like the fishy dreams in Ian's boat and her mother beneath the hose and the fishpond that was actually a cloud. Isabel wanted the college boy to hold out his hand and release a parakeet, but he didn't. Still, she said yes when he asked if he could call on her.

Nick was between his sophomore and junior years at Virginia Polytechnic, in Chesterton for the summer, traveling to farms to do soil testing and diagnose plant diseases. The two of them spent evenings together, often in the swing on the front porch of her grandparents' house. He knew how to hold yarn for knitting, which endeared him to her grandmother, while his knowledge of what to do about fire blight on apple trees made him a favorite with her grandfather. Some evenings, Isabel felt she couldn't keep his attention on her, he was so taken up with explaining orchard practices with phrases like "reduced fruit bud initiation" and "mite management programs," phrases that seemed thick and square, not green and weaving like the world. She sketched in a notebook, and he peered at her images and squeezed her knee. Then he had to go back to college, and she returned to Richmond for her last year of high school. They wrote long letters. She wasn't sure Nick took her art seriously, yet she convinced her parents to invite him for Thanksgiving. Snow was in the forecast, but he boarded the Greyhound in Blacksburg anyway. The bus overheated outside of Lynchburg. He stood in the snow twice, hitchhiking to Buckingham. Finally, he caught a ride in a tow truck and arrived in Richmond eight hours late, soaked and grinning with those perfect good looks. His tardiness and subsequent arrival wound Isabel into a frantic love. On the Saturday after Thanksgiving, he won over her Catholic father by cooking a pasta dish with tomatoes and eggplant in full view of the crucified Christ and President Eisenhower, hanging on the wall. "You have family from Italy?" her father had said.

"No. I had good neighbors," Nick had said.

Isabel graduated from high school and applied last minute to Hollins College in art education. That put her an hour away from Nick, three hours from home. He came on weekends, and they made out in his truck. While she dwelled on the swirl in the tiniest snail's shell, he calculated how many apples might be harvested from the empty acre where they picnicked. Isabel wanted bowers of wisteria. Nick said it was invasive and ought to be yanked out wherever it popped up. One Wednesday in October of her sophomore year, Isabel suffered a much greater disappointment than her boyfriend not sharing her sensibility. She called Nick and asked him not to come for his usual visit.

"What's wrong?" He was always so in control, but at that moment his voice sounded lost. "I've had a bad day. I'm humiliated. I don't want to leave my room."

"What happened? Tell me. Tell me now." He'd regained his authority.

And so she did. The Famous Artist whose visit to campus people had looked forward to had come. Her watercolor of a northern cardinal was one of the works chosen for critique. In the auditorium, in front of every art student in the school, in front of the faculty and the dean, the visiting professor had found nothing good in her work. He admitted he did not care for "works on paper." "Facile," he had called her watercolor. "Predictable. This bird is never going to fly." Worst of all, he called it "soulless." She'd sat with face rigid while these words were branded into her, then ran back to her room, bumping and dodging other students, crying all the way. She had worked so hard to make the bird just right, recalling Angelica's instruction: "You paint in washes and do the most detailed work last."

"He's wrong," Nick said. "If anybody is soulless, it's that visiting artist. It's offensive that anybody would say that to you."

She fell in love with him more deeply.

"There's something I want to tell you too," he said.

"What? I told you my story. Tell me yours."

"I need to see you in person."

Friday evening, Isabel stepped out of her dorm. She had cut every class since that Wednesday horror and eaten out of the vending machines on the ground floor of the dorm. She asked Nick to meet her in the quad because she didn't want to pause in the weekend traffic in the dorm foyer. When she found him, he was holding a bright green Osage orange. He handed it to her. "It'll stay pretty on the windowsill for a month."

Isabel rubbed her thumb over the nubby fruit. It was perfect. When had Nick ever done such an odd, imaginative thing? The Osage orange was much better than candy or roses. When she looked into his face, though, she saw distances. "You look nervous. Is it bad? Are you breaking up with me?" She had just become passionate about him again.

"Let's walk," he said.

They found a bench. He took her hands, setting the Osage orange aside. For a moment, Isabel thought Nick was going to say, *I'm going into the priesthood.* Instead, he said, "I'm thinking of going to West Africa."

"You're what?"

"There's this new government project. It's called USAID. United States Agency for International Development. I can do agricultural work that makes a real difference."

"How long have you been thinking about this?" Isabel pulled back to get a better look at her boyfriend. She'd seen no hint of this coming.

"Since last spring. I didn't think you would want to go. It's why I haven't asked you to marry me. I couldn't decide what I would do if you said yes to getting married but no to Nigeria. That's where I would be going."

"And now you've decided?"

"I'm going to go if they'll take me. Will you marry me and go?"

For the first time she felt Nick might hold a miracle. She would have to take a risk, leave everything. She had always thought that was what she wanted. To start a new life somewhere, leave the past of inchoate inadequacy and invisibility, discover some means of expressing her soul, some wide connection that might begin in family but radiate out to rivers and plains.

At this moment, more than ever, she wanted an escape. "So you've decided, and if I say I don't want to go, you'll go without me?" She wanted him to say, "I'd be lost without you. Bring your paints. I love your paintings." He said, "I love you."

She believed him. Though what in her did he love?

Nick got down on his knee. He pulled a ring box from his trousers pocket. "Open it." She did. "It's a sapphire. It matches your eyes." The ring fit perfectly.

She tilted in his favor. "Yes. I'll marry you. I'll go." She believed she loved him. He was so earnest and solid and, lord, so good looking. Perhaps he was the visionary, not she.

By May, Nick had finished his graduate certificate in land management and Isabel managed to complete an A.B. from Hollins, taking education classes, no more art. Her parents weren't thrilled at the idea of Isabel traveling so far away, but Nick inspired trust. The wedding took place in June on the front porch of the farmhouse where Nick and Isabel had first courted. The Episcopal priest of the nearby church performed the service. Nick's parents came and brought the couple a set of Samsonite suitcases and a gift of five hundred dollars. Isabel's parents gave them an inherited set of Sicilian ceramic plates and stainless steel flatware. Her grandmother gave them the double wedding ring quilt she had made for the marital bed.

The first time they made love, Isabel found it painful and suffocating. The next night, when they tried again, Nick lifted her on top of him and she understood better what to do. A cord seemed to bind them as she moved with him, establishing a connection she had always known should not be broken. It was private and theirs. They rested and she slept and dreamed of hundreds of little fires burning in a large brown yard.

A week after Nick and Isabel settled into their three-bedroom, concrete bungalow in the village of Kufana, thirty miles from Kaduna, Daniel escorted them to the night market and Isabel saw her vision: a thousand small fires in a brown yard, market stalls illuminated by clay lamps lit with palm oil. She clutched Nick's hand. He was twenty-six, so wise to have brought them here. She had just turned twenty-one and had escaped from every ordinary thing that might have held her down to arrive at this exotic, fire-lit place of dreams.

Kufana

.....

March 1963

Fruit bats bickered and flapped beyond the window all night. Finally, Isabel slept. As the sun rose, she woke, dressed, and headed toward the kitchen. The dancing woman sat on the dining table in the sunroom, catching a ray of morning light. "What in the world?" Isabel moved toward the figure and stopped, overcome by déjà vu. What was she on the verge of recalling? It had been a week since she had uncovered the terra-cotta and hidden her in the drum. Nick was still asleep. Isabel slipped into the kitchen. There was no sign of Daniel, but the back door was ajar.

"Madam," he said, when he came back in. His tone was serious. Isabel steeled herself.

"Yes?"

"Where have you found that statue?"

"The one on the table? Where have you found it, I might ask."

"In your drum. A bat flew into the room where you keep your things." His voice dropped at the sideways reference to their personables.

Isabel shivered. "Surely the bat wasn't in the drum."

"Indeed, madam. By the time I fetched a broom, it was. I have disposed of it."

"So you dug through my things?" She felt guilty and incensed all at once.

"What's all the activity?" Nick's hair lay flat against his head, and he stretched his arms behind him. "You hear those fruit bats last night?" he said to Isabel. "Anyone made coffee?"

Isabel made the coffee, and the three of them sat around the table, the dancing woman a centerpiece. "You asked where I found her,"

Isabel said, facing Daniel. "She was buried in the spot I dug for the lemon tree. She must be very old. The glaze has almost vanished."

"Was anything buried with it?" Daniel furrowed his brow. There was no smile. Perhaps wives of bature men weren't supposed to dig up their backyards.

"Nothing else," she said. "No bones." She assured him she had finished digging. He could relax now.

But he did not relax. "It could be a deity," he said.

"A god?"

"A totem to an ancestor. But this one has no symbol, so I think not."

"What sort of symbol?"

"A fish, or a bowl, a moon perhaps."

Isabel was intrigued. She wondered if the broken hand might have held a symbol. "If a farmer found such a thing, what would he do?"

"It depends on the man. He may place it in the farm as a protection. If he is a modern man, he may dig it up for selling. Some older men would not touch it."

"What would a woman farmer do?"

"I am not a woman. I do not know. But you must show it to the Sarki."

"The Sarki? The chief, you mean. Why? I would like to keep her. At least briefly."

"The Sarki will say what can be done."

"I see." She would think about this. "How is your mother?"

"She is managing."

"She may need to see a specialist if the pain worsens. We can take her to the hospital in Kaduna." She meant to regain some authority.

Nick leaned forward to look more closely at the statue. "It's really quite something." He sipped his coffee. "I agree with Daniel. You need to take it to the chief. He likes you. Maybe he'll let you keep it." Nick set down his cup. Isabel didn't like the way he left dribbles on the lip.

"What makes you say the chief likes me?"

"He gave you that ivory necklace."

A necklace of tiny carved elephants, strung one after one, delicate as Queen Anne's lace. She had thought the gift customary, not a personal tribute to her. "I could wear it when I go to see him. Or should I invite him here? If I go there, I have to carry her." She pointed. "Everyone will see."

"What do you think, Daniel?"

"Madam must go to the chief. It cannot be the other way."

♦ ♦ ♦

"You don't care that he rummaged through the drum?" Isabel said when she and Nick were alone.

"He was trying to get a bat out of the house. He has never taken anything. When he shops, he returns halfpennies."

"I don't like it. He might rummage through my dresser drawers."

"Has he ever done that?"

"No."

"He has a key to the house. We trust him with everything. You just got caught smuggling a work of art."

The word *caught* pricked her skin. Heaven only knows what Nick would say if he found out about Tunde. "I did no such thing. I was just trying to decide what to do."

"I'm joking with you." He kissed her mouth.

♦ ♦ ♦

Isabel ransacked the house before she found her paints in the storeroom beneath the Sicilian ceramic plates. She had stashed the watercolors there for the children she hoped to have. Before leaving Virginia, Angelica had sent them as a gift. "These must go with you," her note had said, "as you depart for your own wondrous life." Isabel wasn't going back to painting, but she had to do a quick study of the dancing woman. She had to get her down in case the Sarki decided to keep her. A photograph alone would not capture the woman's essence. There was meaning in her and the possibility of revelation. To understand, she must keep the image before her. She applied quick strokes of pale Payne's gray for windows and a wash of burnt umber for the table. With a few strokes, she captured the figure's head, the body's movement, her upward arms. The feeling of a brush again in Isabel's hand made her want to laugh. She stopped to consider whether she would give the woman back her second hand. But what did it matter? She saw now that what she had done was all wrong, a mess. It had nothing of the feel of the figure. The body parts looked as if she had done them separately and pasted them together. She had not come close to capturing the woman's mouth, the suggestion that at any moment she would speak.

Brush loaded with black, she slashed a diagonal across the paper. And another. An X-mark. Bad work. Disgusted, she let it fall to the ground and sat, listening to the cars on the road, a radio somewhere, a drum. Briefly, she saw Bobby Tunde's hand and wanted for herself his ease with his art, his grace. Once she'd thought she had a tiny bit of that.

What male god could understand Isabel's secret heart? Not a single one. But the dancing woman might. Angelica certainly did. Isabel felt that the maker of the figure had seen the same pink sky she had seen in her digging and longed in the same way, but for what she could not say.

In fourteen months, she had not found her place here. When she and Nick first settled in Kufana, she taught a sewing class on the veranda of the Catholic Church. She had lugged her sewing machine and cloth samples and showed women how to make aprons. But they didn't want aprons. They wanted boys' shorts for school, a difficult pattern. That had been before her pregnancy. Then, for a precious few months, she had thought she'd be raising her own children. They would grow up with the taste of guava on their tongues. She would show them how to paint with their fingertips. They would wear sandals like Nigerian children and learn about Father Christmas, not Santa Claus. They would learn Hausa. But she had miscarried. She wasn't worthy of being a mother. Now look what she had done to her marriage.

♦ ♦ ♦

Isabel carried the dancing woman to the spare room and left her there. In the bedroom she shared with her husband, she sat on the bed with the double wedding ring quilt and contemplated absolution. She wanted to be free of guilt, but she knew confessing would cause Nick terrible pain and put a barrier between them that they could not overcome. He might want to divorce her. Could he do that here? He could probably send her home. She didn't know what rights she had as the wife of a USAID land management specialist. And what about Bobby Tunde? How would the story of their affair affect him and his wife and children? Why had she been so rash? How would she plead her case in a public hearing? How would she plead it to herself? She had no excuse. She had done it because she longed every day of her life for a larger expression of her inner world, to join herself with a sweeping unifying force, a river between the visible, the felt, and the imagined. Until she met Bobby Tunde, she did not comprehend that she did not have that, even the possibility of it with her sometimes tender but work-absorbed husband who didn't even see her nascent need for art and beauty, for an underground spirit that affirmed her being.

In the world that made the terra-cotta, what would happen to a woman found guilty of infidelity? Did she herself deserve stoning? Isabel closed the bedroom door and locked it. She lay down on the bed, opened her legs, and placed her fingers on the little mound of feeling. *Clitoris.* With one hand, she spread herself open and with the other, she entered herself with her fingers. Was she always this wet inside? She seemed at once yielding and muscular, hard and soft. How would a baby ever pass through this gate? She brought her fingers out and her legs together. Before the bathroom mirror, she unbuttoned her blouse, letting it drape behind her. She unhooked her brassiere and let it fall to the floor. Her eyes traveled from her unruly head of hair down her throat to her white breasts, and down to her slender waist. Tunde had said, "Your skin is like silk from the kapok tree." She dressed again, crossed the living room to the spare room, and looked upon the dancing woman. "Help me," she said aloud.

◆ ◆ ◆

The next morning, just before eleven, Isabel and Daniel left to meet the Sarki. They found the man seated in an open courtyard under the awning of his roof. Mud houses, both round and rectangular, with generously thatched roofs, comprised his compound, along with a squat tree for sitting under, a mango tree, and two hard-woods. Even in his voluminous white tunic, the man appeared wiry. Today he wore a red cap and eyeglasses. The glasses were new since she had last seen him and accentuated his round face. She estimated his age to be above fifty as a few gray hairs showed at his temple. Several men sat to his left, silent. Isabel had the terra-cotta in a leather bag with a pull closure at the top. In her American pocketbook, she carried her gift for the chief, a Kodak camera and several rolls of film. It was a precious item and she did not wish to part with it, but she and Nick had a larger camera. She must win the chief's favor.

Isabel wore her ivory necklace with a blue rayon dress and a small blue hat. She bowed deeply. "Ina kwana."

"Na kwana lafiya," he replied. *I slept well*. His eyes seemed to take in the necklace.

She resumed her posture and pointed to her own eyes. "Your glasses are handsome. Are they working for you?" Daniel helped to translate. A fly buzzed about Isabel's head.

"He says they are giving him a headache," Daniel said, "but he can now count every ripe mango in his tree. He will know if anyone is stealing them."

Stealing. Words were suddenly more dangerous. Was she becoming a thief as well as an adulterer? She might have claimed the dancing woman as her own if Daniel and Nick had not insisted she come ask permission. The chief motioned for her to sit on a nearby chair. Daniel remained standing. The fly would not relent.

"Tell him I hope he enjoys many delicious mangos this season and that his headaches end." She made a chopping signal with her hand.

The chief seemed to think she was asking for help. He motioned to one of the nearby men who came over and captured the fly in his hand. His legs were so dry they looked pewter. "Thank you." She turned to Daniel. "Please tell the chief that I have brought a gift to express appreciation for his hospitality since we arrived." Isabel opened her pocketbook and drew out the camera. Her parents had given it to her as she and Nick were leaving. She reassured herself that she could purchase a new camera at Kingsway in Kaduna. Glancing up she was surprised that the Sarki was sharing a moment of humor with one of his men, perhaps about the fly. She raised her voice. "I have brought you a gift of a camera and film. You can take pictures of your children or of your house"—she made a dramatic gesture with her arm—"or you may have pictures taken of yourself." She pointed to him. "The film can be sent away for the pictures to come back to you." This explanation by Daniel took some while, but it seemed to make the Sarki more appropriately interested in her gift. At last, Isabel placed the objects in the chief's hands. She was about to explain to him how he should look through the viewfinder, but he was ahead of her, taking his glasses off, putting the camera to his right eye. He looked all about, then lowered the camera, flipped open the film compartment, blew into it, as if bringing it to life, then he opened the box of film. Isabel had thought the Sarki would require a lesson. Now he had the film in place and was winding it forward to begin. Finally, he gave the camera a good sniff and started to talk. He seemed in a good mood.

Daniel translated. "He says this small one will do well for his little son who has been wanting a camera. The Sarki hesitates to let him use his own bigger one."

Isabel pulled back like a turtle into its shell. She remained quiet for several moments. "I see," she said. *What now?* "I suppose, then, that the Sarki knows how to get the film developed."

Daniel didn't bother to ask him. "Yes, he knows."

She had no gift for the Sarki himself. And she had imagined she was bringing him something he would look upon as a magic box. Embarrassing. Isabel stood. "I suppose we will take our leave," she said to Daniel.

"No, madam. You have the other item."

Isabel felt the trip was scotched, for now the Sarki would imagine that the Nigerian bag she carried held a gift for him, which she certainly did not intend.

"Please, sir, I have come with a request," she said, sitting back down. That seemed a word the chief understood. His brow knotted and he dismissed the other men.

Isabel opened the leather pouch. Daniel held it as she maneu-vered the terra-cotta out of hiding. A large redheaded lizard scuttled across the courtyard, just in front of Isabel's feet, and she hugged the treasure to her chest. The chief watched intently. "Your honor," she began, "while gardening in the backyard of our residence, I un-earthed this sculpture. It is very old. Daniel here says he has never seen anything like it. Perhaps I can find a specialist in your ancient arts who will examine it." That last was made up impulsively. "I wish very much to keep it in my home for now." She breathed deeply. "I admire the art of your country." That was true. "I myself am an artist." She wanted to make that truer. But the word "soulless," stamped into her brain, had stood in her way. Only recently had a man with whom she committed adultery insisted she was in posses-sion of an underground spirituality.

Finally she looked at Daniel. "Go ahead. Tell him."

She held the statue out, and the chief took it into his hands as Daniel translated.

The Sarki may have heard Daniel, but he did not respond right away. He ran his fingers over the dancing woman. He placed his thumb at her mouth and eyes. *He's going to want to keep it himself.* Now two redheaded lizards scuttled past, one after the other. At last the chief spoke.

Daniel translated. "He says it has no power for him. It does not speak of Kufana town or any people of this area. It may have been brought from another place and left behind. He says it has come to you for a reason."

Ah. He would let her keep it. Isabel took in a deep breath. She was about to pull the terra-cotta away from the chief and redeposit it in her bag.

"But," Daniel continued.

Isabel looked up.

"You must earn the right to keep this sculpture by learning what it has to say to you. It may be necessary to feed it, to bring it some gift, so that it will disclose itself. Then it may tell you something, even something you do not expect. It cannot be that you found it by accident."

"I see. I'll do my best." *Bring it gifts? Feed it?* Isabel took the figure back from the Sarki, nodding gratefully. It seemed heavier than
before.

Halfway back to the house, Daniel slowed his pace. "Please,
madam," he said, "One day I hope to go to nursing school."

He was asking for her help. Why had he chosen this moment?
Perhaps because he had just watched nurses at the clinic where he
took his mother. He was certainly good at looking after people. Isabel turned to him. "That would be a good career for you. You would
be a natural."

Daniel seemed perplexed by the idiom.

"You would manage it well."

♦ ♦ ♦

Isabel returned the terra-cotta to the spare room. How odd that a
Muslim Sarki had sensed her capacity and set her on a mission. Isabel thought of Bobby and felt the current he had created. But her
longing was larger than that. She had wanted to be a true artist, and
now the edge of that desire was coming back. Bobby had started
to rouse in her what she had held dormant. By turning a painting
over, a pond could appear as the sky. According to Bobby, the moon,
finding its house flooded, had jumped to the heavens. In creation,
everything depended on taking a leap, even before one knew where
one would land or where the paint would move or how the painting
would look once dry. How compelling to imagine that the Almighty
may not have controlled creation.

When she hung the bedsheets that afternoon, Isabel's fingertips
itched and the back of her throat felt full. Her breasts seemed lit
like candles.

Kufana

•••••

March 1963

Isabel asked Nick to help her plant the lemon tree.

On Saturday, she drank a second cup of coffee in bed and waited for him to finish shaving. She heard him slap his face with aftershave. He leaned into the doorway. "You ready?" She regretted having to break the earthenware pot to release the roots. But the lip was only half the circumference of its bulge at the center.

In the backyard, Nick lay the potted tree sideways on the ground. For the first time, Isabel observed an ornament near the bottom. A lizard pattern circled the base. "If only we didn't have to break it," she said.

"It's too bad." Nick tapped the earthenware vessel. "But the tree won't bear much fruit this way."

It was true. The little buds that had so beautifully adorned the plant when Isabel purchased it had fallen off. With rain, it would flower again. It needed to be in the earth.

"With luck, I might be able to break the pot in two. Not that we can mend it." He turned and smiled at Isabel, who drew back at the deeper suggestion in his phrase. Over and again, she felt how the connotations of words had shifted since the night in Kaduna. There was the fluidity of art that she loved, but this fluidity in meanings disturbed her. Tears came to her eyes.

"Are you okay?" Nick said.

Isabel pressed her hands to her face. "I'm so sorry."

"It's okay, sweetheart. You want to wait? We can think about it. Maybe you'd rather have the pot than the tree."

Nick pulled her into his arms, and she sobbed into the deep fragrance of his Aqua Velva. The cry felt cleansing after the past two weeks with the secret of Tunde woven through her every thought. But her husband was here now. He could make things grow. Gardening was one thing they could share. She turned her face up to kiss him.

"Is this a hint?" he said.

"Yes. I want the lemon tree. Better a broken pot than a barren tree." She spoke that last sentence before thinking. "What if we can never have children?" Her voice wobbled.

"We'll be fine. We haven't really tried."

"I want to plant the tree," she said, wiping her face with the back of her hand. Sunshine poured into the yard, hot and fierce.

Nick worked quickly, wedging the pot between two concrete blocks, raising the pickax, aiming straight for the center. The crack ran top to bottom. He moved the blocks, and the pot fell open in his hands with only one shard breaking off at the bottom. The root ball lay tight as an egg. Nick loosened the soil around the roots. Isabel put the little broken triangular slip into her pocket and picked up the two halves of the pot. She looked at her husband, who was the best thing she had and somehow not enough. At the spigot, she washed each half of the pot, running her fingers over the lizard images in their now broken circle. Nick got the lemon tree into the ground just as a swell of wind came up. Perhaps a needed, early rain. Isabel was sweating, but she planted the two pottery fragments upside down at the front of the garden as entry markers, the lizards on guard. She felt oddly happy with the two halves. They were a different kind of whole.

That evening, they made love, and Isabel prayed for a baby though it was too late in her cycle. Maybe next month. In any case, she needed practice praying. No rains came.

She spent the next week watering the lemon tree. Oddly, it seemed smaller now that it was in the ground. She prayed over it, that it would live, no, thrive, reaching for the sky. For Isabel, certain colors brought strong associations. March had always been yellow, as the lemon fruit would be yellow. Though it was the third month, she also associated March with the number two. At the moment, Isabel could find no correspondence for this idea. She made several watercolor sketches of the small tree. Not good, but not the hash she had made of the dancing woman. This wasn't really art. This was gardening. No real risk or commitment. She would mark the tree's growth by making new sketches after the rainy season.

When she woke in the middle of the night with the number two sitting in her brain like a Buddha, Isabel's mind turned. She should have started her period days ago. Briefly, she recalled Tunde's hesitation before their lovemaking. She went to the bathroom, and there was the familiar pink. She breathed deeply, reassured. She was surprised later when her period stopped so quickly. And yet, she reasoned, all was well. She had had short periods before. For several days, a skim of clouds kept the high temperatures at bay. Flame trees ruled the town. Driving with Nick on bush roads, Isabel spotted the occasional round fireball lily. More would follow. She had been in this country long enough to know.

Zaria, Kaduna, Kafanchan

• • • • •

May 1963

May arrived and Daniel planted corn. Isabel and Nick planned a road trip. First, they would go to Zaria where he had his monthly Agency meeting at Ahmadu Bello University. They would lodge with another USAID couple, Paul and Rebecca Ferguson. Coming back through Kaduna, they would spend the weekend at the eleven-story Hamdala Hotel, where they could order a hamburger and swim in the hotel pool. Isabel could get a proper haircut. Finally, they would drive to Kafanchan and visit Nick's neem forest. So that Isabel didn't have to stay in a tent as Nick had done on his last trip, he had accepted an invitation from an American missionary family he had met, the Parhams. The husband was also an agricultural engineer, though he spent half of his time in churches. The couple had two towheaded children and a spare bedroom.

"We'll have to pray before meals, but other than that, you won't be too awfully evangelized," Nick teased the morning of their departure. Isabel and Nick regularly sat through Sunday services given in Hausa at the Evangelical Church of West Africa in Kufana. USAID encouraged attendance at local houses of worship but didn't require more devotion than that. Luckily, Isabel enjoyed the women's melodious singing. She looked up from the breakfast table and smiled. Over the past several weeks, her mood had shifted from haunting regret to bouts of fantasy about Tunde to ecstasy over the garden and the lemon tree and gratitude for Nick's help in this arena. Together they had transplanted the sprouting cucumber and tomato plants that they had started in containers. She had made several quick watercolors, capturing the first tendrils. The paintbrush began to feel comfortable again, though these sketches were insignificant work. Still, she found joy in them even though Nick did not seem to notice what she was doing. No Famous Artist would critique her here. She felt sure she was pregnant. At first, she had panicked: could Tunde be the father? She thought on it long and hard. She and Nick had made love in the middle of her cycle, before Kaduna, before the neem forest planting, before the silver link and the maroon windowsill. She remembered calculating the early morning after she made love with Tunde. *Think. Think.* She had concluded it was day 21. Casting back, she was sure she could recall a sense of kindling with Nick, something sparking in her. Perhaps in some part of her mind, that knowledge had allowed her to lie with Tunde. She knew she was safe. Already pregnant. The period that came in March had not been a period at all. It was too light. She settled the issue in her mind and relished her newfound state. She knew for a fact that she would not miscarry. She was too strong now. When thoughts of Tunde arose, she carefully separated her pleasure from her pregnancy, like cutting a photograph in two. She was certainly not as good a person as she should be. One day, she would tell Nick. But at the moment she was grateful to be saved, to be expecting. In being a mother, she would become a better person. She could carry a baby in a basket, couldn't she? And still paint. Nigerian women did everything with children. She would love as her grandmother loved, with warmth and delight. Her grandmother had once jumped out of the hayloft into a pile of hay below, and Isabel had followed. They had laughed and hugged and rolled out, but then Isabel was all itchy, so Gram had made a warm bubble bath for her and soothed her skin with her own homemade salve.

The morning of their departure, she could hear Nick jiggling the change in his pocket. "I just need to finish packing my train case," Isabel called, tucking in a small paint case. "Ready." She met him at the door. They stepped out of the house. Nick turned the key.

♦ ♦ ♦

Isabel felt keener to learn about old Zaria than she had when they first arrived in Nigeria and the Muslim stronghold had seemed so foreign. By legend, the city had grown in greatness under a warrior queen, Amina, in the mid-sixteenth century. It didn't surprise Isabel that the woman who sold her groundnuts was named for a woman warrior.

The morning after their arrival, Isabel and Rebecca set out to explore, guided by Rebecca's Hausa steward, Danladi. Rebecca seemed all edges: sharp elbows, sharp nose, and sharp points in the patterns of her dresses. She appeared always to have been forty-five. Perhaps these qualities meant that she could keep Isabel safe in her light shift and sandals and headscarf. It had rained in the night, and the dirt road gleamed. Entering the ancient settlement, they passed a fragment of old wall and soon caught sight of the gateway to the emir's palace. Isabel stopped. The whitewash finish gave the impression that the gate was the hem of a dress, the dress of Queen Amina, no doubt, who strode high above them in the clouds. Isabel imagined her a goddess. The thought conspired with the dancing woman, and both images stirred her deeply, offering a sense of power and relief. A divinity in her own image, a divinity like her would understand, wouldn't she, her confusions and desires. *She* would shelter Isabel. The idea was so comforting, Isabel closed her eyes. *Let the baby be well.*

A bicycle clattered past. "This way," Danladi called. "We cannot visit the emir today."

Suddenly a camel came through the large gate. Rebecca reached out to catch Isabel's hand. They had to walk around a large mud puddle in the road. The murky edge lay clotted with trash and interfered with Isabel's sense of spiritual illumination.

Off Zage Dantse Road, they came to the dye pots that had been controlled by the same family for two hundred years. Farther on, they entered a cloth market where Isabel purchased four yards of a lined blue fabric. They moved into a brilliant section of town where clay houses flamed with low relief ornaments painted in yellow and orange. "This is truly stunning," Isabel said. She had recommended carrying a sketchbook, and now she slipped close to a housefront, pulled it out, and copied a geometric pattern onto the page. It contained a series of three vertical diamonds with space in between.

On each diamond appeared a cloverleaf design of four teardrops all pointing toward the center. Where the diamond points lined up, four teardrop shapes of similar sizes were placed horizontally, two at each intersection. All teardrops pointed toward the central line of the diamonds. The negative space between diamonds and teardrops looked loosely like two X's.

They entered an older part of the city. Here the house walls sloped up like smooth waves on either side. A gulley ran through the center of the lane. Isabel tried to imagine horses passing through this narrow channel. Small children backed up to the walls rather than running out to greet Isabel as Nigerian children usually did. A woman wrapped in red cloth came out of a housefront and moved past, her eyes lowered. A little farther along, two men in deep conversation approached. As they drew near, one of them made a point of stopping to spit at the base of the wall. Isabel wished Nick were with them. She pushed her sketchpad down into her purse.

At the end of the road, Danladi pointed soberly. "A station for slave trade was here," he said. Isabel clutched her chest. She turned to Rebecca. "Let's press ahead. Please."

"We must return as we came," Danladi said. "We are not welcome on the other side."

The other side of what?

They turned to retrace their steps. A strong wind flushed through the narrow lane, and their route was stunningly empty of people. Isabel held her scarf close and leaned forward, latching on to Rebecca's arm. A sound like a train filled her ears. "Hurry," she cried. The sound increased, not a train but hooves. Or was it people in an uproar? A crowd could enter from the other direction and they would be crushed. But the lane remained empty even as the storm of sound built, wave on wave. Isabel felt they were ploughing against a great current, and when she saw before them an exit into light, she began to run. Except for some trees, the space before her was empty. After all that roaring, why weren't the trees moving? Why no horses? Was the tumult in her head? Wasn't this the busy courtyard where they had just purchased cloth? Isabel bent down from her waist. The packed ground where her feet stood made her think of the dancing woman, made of clay. Wasn't Eve made of clay? Guilty Eve. She felt a hand on her back. Isabel straightened herself and the world went pink, the color that signaled some shift in her inner orbit. The next thing she knew, she was on the ground, Rebecca leaning over her. She felt the heat of the clay earth beneath her and smelled the water beneath.

"Here," Rebecca held a Fanta. "You fainted."

Isabel sat up. The hair on her arms held tiny particles of dust. "Thank you." She sipped the Fanta. It was the baby, she was sure, telling her to be cautious. But she could not tell Rebecca that. She hadn't told her husband. The person she most wanted next to her was Gram, in her apron and heavy black shoes. She would know exactly what to do.

♦ ♦ ♦

Back at the Fergusons', Isabel bathed and washed her hair. She tried to quell Nick's concern about her fainting by telling him it was merely the heat. She had gotten thirsty.

"You've got to be more careful walking around like that," he said, an edge to his voice. His tone and lack of sympathy tore like a shard of glass at Isabel's insides. Later, he caught her hand as she passed him at the table. He kissed her palm, and she forgave him.

♦ ♦ ♦

But, of course, Isabel considered when she woke in the middle of the night, it isn't only the pregnancy. I have turned back to my art. Now I feel the universe again, the way it speaks to me. I was overwhelmed by the glory of it. It caused me to fear. I must not fear. The dancing woman isn't afraid. Isabel got out of bed and found her notebook and a pen. In the bathroom, she flipped on the light switch. She sat on the toilet seat and entered a note: *I am Isabel. I am an artist.* Her thought was larger: *Thank God for Angelica, who taught me to see. And for Bobby Tunde, who saw the artist in me.*

♦ ♦ ♦

Friday morning, Nick and Isabel left for Kaduna. That afternoon, Isabel reclined next to the Hamdala Pool, drinking a Coca-Cola. The day was mild and clear. Nick left to play golf. She watched several

British mothers and their children on the other side of the pool as well as a Russian couple and some Lebanese teenagers. Nearby, two American families lounged. They were more modest than the British, who might change their children's swimsuits out in plain view. Nothing disturbed Isabel's pleasure but the occasional spray of some child's cannonball into the pool. Even that didn't really disturb her. As a girl, she fantasized she might fly when she jumped from the high dive into Byrd Park Lake. Isabel considered the decor for the baby's room. The pregnancy was a good secret. She would tell Nick soon enough, and then only the two of them would know until she was safely into her fourth month. She would use the blue-striped cloth from the Zaria market to make curtains. The child would laugh as they billowed in the breeze. She imagined a boy, named Patrick for her Virginia grandfather. She dozed until a welter of voices rose in the cafe. A group of young Nigerian men dressed in dark slacks and white shirts had found shade beneath the roof. She could only see their silhouettes, but their manner was unmistakable: lean figures, eager voices full of amazement. Someone turned up the radio.

She closed her eyes again. The music reminded her of high-life, that sound that poured out of every market stall and compound and filled the air with the energy of bounding gazelles. Isabel opened her eyes just in time to see a naked child run past. Catching the backside, she couldn't be sure if it was a boy or girl. She closed her eyes again, secluded by a pot of canna lilies. And then a ribbon of memory began in her abdomen and started up her chest, into her throat, and to the dark underside of her eyelids. Someone stroking her, tapping out a rhythm. The sensation was connected to the radio: *Lovely lady should not cry. Lovely lady, oh.* Tunde's words to her. She smelled chlorine and fried potatoes and lurched up from her reclining chair. Her drink turned over, and the plastic glass rolled into the pool, where it bobbed and tilted. It was Bobby's crooning voice. *But when she looks at me, oh brother, o dara ju.* The swimming pool blazed in the sun and an agony of joy flooded Isabel's soul. She looked down expecting to be naked. But she was not. A teenaged girl retrieved her glass and brought it to her like a trophy.

Bobby Tunde had found her. Just not as she had imagined before she stopped imagining that he would find her. She didn't wish
to be found. She touched her hair. Where was the garnet clip she
had worn that night? She looked around, expecting to be the center
of attention. No one paid her the least mind. Where was Nick? At
the golf course. He would be back for dinner. Isabel tried to settle
into her chair. The song moved into a saxophone interlude. At the
end, the lyrics returned, over and over. *Lovely lady should not cry.
O dara ju,* finally fading along with a low drumbeat that had been
there all along beneath the music. The bird's heartbeat. The radio
switched to an advertisement for Star beer. The naked child came
streaking back. Now she saw the little penis and heard the mother
shout, "Benny!"

In the hotel room, dressed for the evening and waiting for Nick,
Isabel paced back and forth. From the window, she looked down at
the hotel pool. She half expected to see Bobby out there. Again, she
longed for her grandmother, for the farm, that simpler time. The
affair was too large a secret to carry alone. She might have confided
in Elise. A flutter rose and fell in her abdomen. The baby? No. It was
too soon for quickening. She sat down and applied a second coat
of clear varnish to her fingernails. Outside the sun slanted over the
rooftops. She thought again of the whitewashed gate to the emir's
palace in Zaria and how it conjured the skirt of a goddess. She could
use an intercession right now, but the priest must be a woman. The
dancing woman glowed in Isabel's mind. In her era, might there
have been a council of women? Isabel tried to imagine what she
would say or ask for. Not forgiveness exactly. Understanding and
then forgiveness. She thought on this and hoped her heart was sin-
cere and felt she had come close to prayer, if prayer was serious
consideration about the state of one's soul, the spiritual core that
the Famous Artist had said she was lacking. With that thought, she
became frantic again. Just then, she heard a bag drop and the key
in the door; the door handle moved downward and there was her
husband.

"Sorry for the holdup," he said. "I showered off downstairs."

Isabel stepped forward and pressed her face against his shirt. "I'm holding a secret," she said. The words reverberated through her, and she cinched his shirt at his chest. Her fingers were thin and pale. "I'm pregnant."

✦ ✦ ✦

In Kafanchan, the neem trees Nick had planted were four feet tall, pale green flags waving in the wind. "They're glorious," Isabel said. Maybe it was okay that her husband didn't have an artistic temperament, that he would never discern her constant longing or sit with her listening for the heartbeat of the bird, that he spoke in square boxes and saw only blue in the sky.

Nick squeezed her hand. "They are, aren't they?"

At the home of the American missionaries, the two blond children, a boy and a girl, latched on to Isabel as if they could smell her motherhood emerging. She played pick up sticks and shared her paints. The little girl painted a picture of Isabel: a triangle for a body, stick legs and arms, and a head of hair that filled the sky. In the girl's rendering, Isabel was carrying a large spoon.

"Am I cooking?" she said.

"No. You're digging in the dirt."

"How do you know that?"

"I heard Mr. Nick tell daddy. He said you pulled a little lady out of your yard. I'm going to dig in my yard tomorrow. I'm going to pull out a baby sister."

Isabel's hand shook. The child had a sixth sense.

Kufana

• • • • •

May 1963

The moment Nick parked the car in their drive, Isabel flew into the house. Since last night with the Parhams, she had imagined someone breaking in and taking off with the dancing woman. But there she was, sitting just as she'd left her, in the extra room on the sewing table, gazing at Isabel as if she had been waiting for her return. "You're always about to speak. But what will you say?"

"You've started talking to that thing?" Nick came up behind and put his arms around her.

She turned, stood on tiptoe, and gave him a kiss. The scales of justice teetered. On one side was the secret of Tunde. On the other side was her pregnancy, which she had now shared with her husband. "I thought someone might have taken her."

"You mean like you did?" He smiled, but he was serious too.

"I didn't take her."

"You were hiding her away until Daniel found her." He pulled on a lock of her hair.

She was a little tired of his harping on this point. "But now I have an assignment." She stuck her finger at the center of his chest and pushed.

"What do you mean?"

"Didn't I tell you? The Sarki says I have to learn something from her."

He pulled her to him. Isabel heard his watch ticking. "What are you thinking?" she said, hoping he would ask if she had learned anything yet, and not as a joke, but seriously. Be interested in her underground spirituality.

"I want to take my shoes off and get in bed with you."

She would rather have talked first.

In their lovemaking, she felt the presence of another. *It must be the baby.* She and the baby made two. But two was March and this was May. Then dimly she sensed yet another. *As if we are three, counting Nick.* And while she had never thought much about the Holy Spirit, especially in the middle of sex, it seemed perfectly logical, as she opened herself to her husband's desire, that some divine energy would move over the waters of her womb, thus making them four, and the thought increased her desire. Somewhere in it all, there was a maroon windowsill. She did not banish it. She let it stay.

◆ ◆ ◆

The next morning, Nick brought her fresh-squeezed orange juice in bed. Isabel felt plagued by the secret of Tunde. Even if she deserved affirmation as an artist, she had wronged the universe, and she would have to pay. Little hairs stood up on her arm as she dwelt on this thought. If only she could see him briefly, make sure he would keep their secret. If anything got out about their tryst, her life would be ruined. Yes, if she could put a finger to that damaged place above his eye, feel his heartbeat, cement their understanding. But she must not. Could not.

Rain set in at midday. She and Daniel hung clothes indoors to dry. Isabel sat on the front porch as the rain pounded down, splashing the hedge, the trees along the street, the two palms on the other side of the road. Large brown puddles formed and grew. From east to west, the sky was gray. All of the goods in the roadside shops were tucked indoors. Occasionally, a child ran across a yard and an older one dashed out to fetch him by the arm and lift him back into the house. Why was it so important to have a husband? Nigerian women mothered in groups. They didn't live in a husband's house but in their own. Perhaps the dancing woman led a troupe of unmarried women. They met men and loved them, but they raised their children together rather than separately. Unlikely but not impossible. At last, Isabel went indoors and pressed their clothes, including their underwear. Nothing would dry in this weather. How much finer to share the task with a friend. Finally the rain stopped. Isabel wrote to Elise Van Dijk. *Please come for tea.*

Four days later, Elise drove up in a green Fiat. *So she does her own driving.* Isabel stepped onto the porch. She embraced her friend, who smelled like rose dusting powder and starch. "Come in. I'm so glad you're here. Now don't judge my tea-making skills too harshly." Isabel had made certain Daniel was out for the afternoon. Nick was in town where he was giving away the last twenty neem saplings that hadn't made it to the farm.

Elise laughed. "Being served is the most delicious part." She took a seat in the sunroom with her characteristic sense of belonging. Again, Isabel considered the privations her friend had experienced during the war. What could be worse than a buried child?

"Oh, let's go into the yard," Isabel said. "With luck, we'll catch a breeze."

"Right." Elise pulled herself up, and they found seats near the trellised hibiscus left by the former family. The squash plants were already big-leafed and bossy.

"One cube of sugar or two?"

"Three," Elise said.

Moments later, Isabel was divulging the details of her pregnancy, how she sensed the child's presence, how well she felt, how she had only lately told her husband.

"How splendid!" Elise's eyes sparkled. She took a sip of tea. "A baby." Another sip. "But don't you think Daniel knows? He works very closely with you."

Isabel touched her stomach. The bump was there.

"I would want to have Daniel in my corner," Elise went on. "I suspect he's looking for the freshest eggs in the market. And the best pawpaw."

"Now that you put it that way. But he has his own aspirations, you know."

"And well he should. Bature are bature. We come and we go. He has his life to think of."

"You're not going anywhere, surely."

"No plans at present. But we're talking about you. You're going to have a baby. So what do you think? A boy or a girl?"

"I think a boy."

"I'll have another biscuit if you don't mind."

"Of course." Isabel passed the tray of cookies to her guest. Elise's hair blew in the wind, and she laughed as she clutched two biscuits in her hand. "I gave up my girlish figure long ago." But Isabel heard the acquaintance who had spoken of Elise, *near starvation conditions*. Wasn't that it? And the Parham child said, *I'm going to pull a baby sister from the ground.* And her grandmother said the meadowlark nested in the grass and not the trees for better coverage, choosing fields where the acreage was vast. There was wisdom in their choices. Was there any wisdom in her own? Tunde had said, *We must bring the underground up.* Was he the great risk to her nest? Or was it she herself, her flyaway ideas about painting, her wish to conjure her own world, where perhaps babies wouldn't fit, nor husbands?

"Are you fine, Isabel? You look stricken."

"I need to tell you something. But you must promise never to tell. Never, never, never."

"Of course." Elise placed her hand atop Isabel's.

"You remember Bobby Tunde?"

"How could I not?"

"I made love to him. I feel I must confess to my husband."

Elise tightened her hold of Isabel's hand. She didn't look at her. She looked into the sky. Minutes passed. "You're very young. You don't know much about men. Leave it be. You will only hurt him. And that will turn him to anger. Unless." Now she turned to Isabel.

"Unless what?"

"Unless the child is Tunde's." Her hazel eyes were like searchlights.

"No. Nick is the father. I'm sure of it. It wasn't the right time of the month with Bobby."

"Then let yourself rest. It was a momentary slip."

Isabel relaxed. "Do you think less of me?"

Elise smiled, a little wearily. "In Holland, during the war, a woman betrayed my brother. He was a sympathizer with the Dutch resistance. He was sent to a camp. That betrayal cannot be forgiven. What you did was self-indulgent, even hurtful. Not evil."

"Did he? Did your brother survive?"

"He did. But he was damaged."

"I'm so sorry." *I must gain some perspective.*

"You make me think of the daughter I lost. She would be your age."

"I'm so sorry," Isabel's words sounded flimsy as tissue paper. "Was Hugh with you?"

"It was his child. But his family owned a windmill. He was allowed to stay with them and operate it. I was required to be with my family. We were hungrier there."

Isabel tilted her head sideways until it touched her friend's.

♦ ♦ ♦

Several days later, Amina, the groundnut lady, showed up at Isabel's front door. The daughter, Latifa, was with her, wearing a long scarf full of half moons. Isabel asked them in. Amina chose a straight chair, and Latifa leaned against her. In a moment, Amina brought out a fabric pouch and handed it to Isabel.

"Babe," Amina said.

"What's that? I don't understand."

Suddenly Latifa began to speak in English. "My mother has brought herbs for your baby's health. But you are the one who should take it." She picked up the pouch her mother was holding and placed it in Isabel's hands. "One half-teaspoon. Cook into your porridge."

"How kind," Isabel said, holding the gift gingerly. How did the woman know? Her husband hadn't even known. "Thank you. You're very thoughtful. Would you like a Fanta?" She set the pouch on the coffee table. How surprising to learn Latifa was so voluble, that she knew about half-teaspoons. She had hardly spoken at their first meeting.

Isabel poured the soft drink into her stemmed crystal glasses. Amina and Latifa drank daintily, and then they were ready to go.

At the door, Latifa turned and pointed at the pouch. "Don't forget. Good vitamins. The baby will be happy."

When they left, Isabel opened the pouch. It was full of small seeds. Carefully, she rewrapped it in torn pages of the *Daily Times* and placed it in the trash.

A few days later, with an earnest push against lethargy—easy to succumb to, the days were so hot and sticky—Isabel set out to surprise Nick at his office. She had used her small store of butter to make a fresh batch of oatmeal cookies. Her husband's office was no more than a room painted green with a pull-string electric light, a rotating fan, a broad hardwood desk, two chairs, and a bookcase. Nick liked being near the bicycle shop, stopping occasionally to sit outdoors, drinking black coffee from his thermos, and greeting passersby. He was out front as she approached, helping the shop owner change out a bicycle chain. She stopped to watch, admiring Nick's adeptness at things mechanical, his excellent back and legs, his face in laughter and seriousness. The two men finished the task. Her husband straightened, stretched, and went back into his office. How mysterious that she loved him more at a distance. She turned to go home, nibbling the cookies on the way until she had eaten every one.

Kufana

•••••
July–August 1963
•••••

A t five months, Isabel could wear only the tent-like dresses she had hastily sewn for her first pregnancy. With the lemon tree thriving, she considered bringing the dancing woman outside and setting her in the garden as a guardian, as Daniel had suggested some farmer might. After all, she had been underground for ages, subject to tree roots, water, and burrowing animals, but apparently not to building. No one had tried to lay a trench through her encampment. But with the rains, Isabel decided not to bring her out just now. Instead, she began a practice of bringing in birds' feathers, blown leaves, and frangipani petals to place around the sculpture in the spare room. Perhaps this was how to feed her. Such beauties as these fed Isabel's soul. Outside, the hard green lemons grew to the size of shillings.

Another month passed in furnishing the baby's room and writing letters to her mother and Gram and two visits to Kaduna—once to see the pediatrician, Dr. Eli, and another time to purchase some flats at Bata Shoe Store. August mornings could dip into the sixties, with daytime temperatures in the eighties. Occasionally there was a lull in the rain. Still, it was humid, and Isabel's clothes stuck to her. The garden was full to overflowing. Daniel warned Isabel to watch for snakes, which briefly pinched back her joy. But with cornstalks tall as Nick and okra plants spiking, she wasn't fearful long. They had more tomatoes than they could eat. Isabel and Daniel canned them, a fan blowing air through the kitchen. She sent shelled limas to Elise. Making love with her husband with a beach ball between them was not as hard as it should be. A maroon windowsill still hovered at the edge of her vision.

One afternoon when Daniel was out and Nick was at the farm or the office, she couldn't bother to remember, Isabel picked two ears of corn. In the kitchen, she shucked and washed the fatted fruit, closed her eyes, and ran a cool cob up and down one arm, then the other. The corn smelled lusty, like syrup and salt. She began to eat the raw niblets. They burst at the surprise of her teeth and juice dripped down her chin. She had never felt so hungry. In a state of delirium as if she had inhaled some exotic weed, she went to the extra room and picked up the terra-cotta. Outside, she wedged the dancing woman beneath the lemon tree. Her entire body swelled with generosity. She decided to throw a garden party.

Daniel returned to prepare the evening meal. He carried a basket of slender, yellow pawpaws and deposited some change onto the counter.

"They're gorgeous," Isabel said. "Where did you find them?"

"The woman who sells beside the Esso station."

Isabel nodded. "I was wondering, Daniel, if you might help me with a party. It would mean extra cooking. I would need you to stay late. I can pay you overtime."

"What is overtime?"

"In the U.S., if a person works beyond their normal hours, they may make as much as half again their hourly wage."

"I will do it." He smiled in his enigmatic way.

He's saving for nursing school, she thought.

◆ ◆ ◆

Isabel sent invitations to Rebecca and Paul Ferguson in Zaria; Jerry Frey, the wiry Peace Corps worker she had danced with in Kaduna, though he lived hours away in Bida; and the Van Dijks, of course; along with Nick's Nigerian collaborator, Peter Okwu, and his wife, Beatrice. She wanted to invite the American missionary couple, the Parhams, in Kafanchan, but she also wanted to serve beer, so she held back.

The sunroom offered a perfect setup for serving. They could spill out to the garden to eat. Music from the record player would waft outdoors. In the back of Isabel's mind, a thread of music played, but it was not American music. It ended with *o dara ju*, notes flitting like fireflies.

The day of the party, Daniel fried chicken while Isabel made pimento cheese sandwiches and sliced pineapple. Nick invented outdoor lights by nailing empty tin cans to thin stakes, hammering the stakes into the yard, and centering a candle in each. At six p.m. guests began to arrive, Beatrice and Peter first. They were Igbo, originally from the southeast. A soil scientist, Peter wore a European suit, and with his square face and glasses, he struck Isabel as ordinary looking. Beatrice radiated style with her coiffed hair under an elaborate, gold headdress, a lace blouse over a short trim skirt, high heels, and a gold necklace with matching earrings. She handed Isabel a gift wrapped in brown paper and tied with a string. Isabel opened it to find two boxes of Callard & Bowser's butterscotch candies. Immediately Isabel felt drawn to her. "Thank you. How thoughtful," she said.

"You are welcome," Beatrice said, still holding her black patent leather handbag with the gold clasp, like the queen of England.

Nick appeared through the kitchen door, looking too large next to the Nigerian couple, and once again, Isabel felt clumsy in their Americanness. Hugo and Elise Van Dijk were suddenly just there in the garden, seated and waiting to be served, and their appearance sorted everything out, for they had the blowsy look of people who have chosen comfort over fashion. Daniel escorted Jerry Frey through the house. He had a woman with him.

Jerry gave Isabel a hug and stepped back, apparently admiring her rounded form. "May I present my colleague, Kate Munroe? She works in the south of the country, in Akure, but she's up for a conference. I assured her you would welcome an extra guest."

"What a nice surprise." Isabel felt her defenses go up like a drawbridge. Kate was just the sort of pretty girl American men admired: chiseled features, long, straight hair, narrow hips, a dusting of freckles across her nose; all of this made more appealing by her blue jeans and tailored white blouse. It seemed Nick would fall over himself as he got a drink for Kate, who took it from him and wandered out to the garden. She squatted in front of the dancing woman, placing her fingers at the enigmatic mouth. Isabel hurried after her. Would she ever again be able to squat? "Who's this?" Kate said.

"Apparently she's not a god. But she's very old. Coil built," Isabel said, not certain at all that she was right. Yet it seemed important to have some authority here.

"Where did you get it?" Kate looked over her shoulder and up at Isabel with her glowing, symmetrical face. If she was with the Peace Corps, she had finished college, which Isabel had not.

"I dug her up in the garden." Isabel's envy grew as Kate took her time admiring the sculpture. The envy made no sense. She had wanted someone to share her fascination. It was her own doing, spending the night with Bobby Tunde. She had introduced jealousy and doubt into her own mind.

"How amazing," Kate said, standing back up. "Jerry, come here." Jerry loped forward, a look like hope on his face. "Isabel dug this up in her garden. What do you think?"

"Reminds me of Miriam dancing in the desert. She has something on her mind."

Exactly. Miriam with something to tell me. Isabel felt someone's eyes on her and looked up to see Daniel at the back door. "Excuse me." Daniel wore one of his handsome Tiv caftans of black and white stripes.

"The food is ready," he said when she reached him.

Isabel rang the bell. "All right, everyone. Serve your plates and find a seat. The Fergusons will be here soon, I'm sure."

The guests flowed inside, leaving Isabel behind. The green swirling world of the garden filled her with expectation. When she heard someone say, "Watch your step," she looked at the dancing woman. Of course, the figure had not spoken. It was Hugo. The baby kicked and kicked again, like a drumbeat. "Oh," Isabel placed her hands on her middle.

"The wee one," Hugo said.

"Yes," she answered.

He offered his arm and she took it.

"You go ahead," she said once they were indoors.

Isabel stood to the side, sheltering the sensation of the baby. She thought dimly of Bobby Tunde, at the same time making a note to herself to tell Nick how the baby joined in the rush to the table, how their child was already responding to laughter. She conjured her most recent attempt to paint. Corn in the garden, and sky. An okra blossom and a bit of a tomato bush. She had not been ready to attempt the dancing woman again. She might never be.

Rebecca and Paul appeared around the side of the house. Isabel ushered them into the sunroom, pushing them to fill their plates.

"I hope you haven't had any more fainting spells," Rebecca said curtly, as if she didn't know how to begin in kindness.

"No. I feel wonderful." With the babe in her womb, Isabel had more company than she had ever imagined. Rebecca would not diminish her joy. At last, she served herself and reentered the garden, looking for Nick, but he was in deep conversation with Kate, leaning forward, an eagerness in his body she hadn't seen for a while. The only available seat was next to Paul. Her buoyant heart sank. She tried to shake the feeling, but it lingered through the evening, even as she danced with her husband. He held her hand too loosely and let go of her too soon. At the end of the party, he leaned toward Kate at the door and said something, and Kate smiled. It put a dagger in Isabel's heart. She had imagined a tender night with her husband, the baby between them.

Isabel and Daniel cleaned up the kitchen, and he left for the night. Nick snuffed the lanterns and pulled the stakes out of the ground. Isabel's skin felt heavy with sorrow as she changed into the girlish nightgown her mother had sent for the pregnancy, large enough for two. "What were you talking with Kate about?"

Nick sat on the bed, his back to her, taking off his shoes. "She teaches photography at the high school in Akure. Built a dark room by herself. Does the developing for the student paper."

Isabel shook her head. These were irrelevant details. "You seemed very engaged."

"She's had some trouble with the men. They don't want to learn photography from a woman. They think she can't possibly know what she's talking about. So she's invited girls in, and now the boys are up in arms."

"What did you whisper to her before she left?"

"What?"

"You whispered something to her as she was leaving."

"Really? I might have said 'nice to meet you.' I was trying to be polite to everyone. To make you happy."

"You thought you would make me happy by falling all over yourself with another woman? Whatever you said made her smile."

"Good Lord, Kate." He turned to her. "I did everything you asked me to do for your party and now you're going to berate me?"

"It wasn't my party. It was our party. You abandoned me. You should apologize."

Nick grabbed a pillow and started for the door.

"Don't you dare leave."

"Okay. What do you want me to say? I found her attractive. That's not abnormal. Haven't you found any man besides me attractive since we married? Let's go to bed. We can talk later."

"No," Isabel said. "No."

"No, what?"

"I have not found anyone else attractive." Isabel's forehead burned. What possessed her to say such a thing?

"Honestly, that's a little scary." Nick put his pillow down and got in bed on his side.

Isabel clung to the edge of the mattress. "Don't touch me," she said when Nick tried to hold her. The baby kicked. She should turn to her husband. But at the moment, she hated him. He had flirted. Others had witnessed it. Yet he had confessed and she had not, and what she had done with Tunde was much worse. In fact, there was no comparison. Far off, she heard what sounded like a gunshot. She thought of the mango tree: green leaves so dark they were blue. The lemons had grown large and nubby, and she had not had time to show anyone. And who among her friends would care about the shape of the lemon, the shadow thrown by the okra plant, the wells of ochre and Venetian red in the dancing woman's eyes, or the hum she felt beneath everything when she painted?

Isabel rolled onto her back, her center bearing down on her. The ceiling was blank. At the top of the wall, two geckos slept, the harmless house lizards. Nick breathed rhythmically, beside her yet far away. Whom did Tunde lie next to? What if she ran into him the next time she visited the Hamdala Hotel? Would he approach her? Would he say, "You are with child"?

◆ ◆ ◆

Isabel woke to the sounds of Daniel in the kitchen and the smell of toast in the oven. She dressed and brushed her teeth. She hated a standoff with Nick. It always left her exhausted. She should just apologize. In the living room, the tim tims were tipped and set before a fan. She reached the kitchen. "Why are the tim tims like that?" she said.

"They are molding. I have wiped them down," he said.

"Thank you. I hadn't noticed."

"It happens quickly." Daniel snapped his fingers.

"We're very lucky to have you," Isabel said, feeling her words were far from adequate. Though she had tried to make Daniel a coworker in the house, she knew he was still a steward and she was still the madam. It was a crying shame, as Bobby Tunde sang. She fingered the pleats at the front of her dress. "Thank you for all you did to make the party a success," she added. "We couldn't have done it without you."

"You are welcome," Daniel said, but he did not look at her, and she wondered if he had some concern in the back of his mind.

She turned around, and there was Nick with a cup of coffee. A smile wobbled across his face. She followed him into their bedroom. "It was all my fault, my stupid imagination," she said. "Where were you just now?"

"On the front porch. I'm sorry too. I wasn't very thoughtful of you. Okay. I complimented her blue jeans."

"I wish I could slap you."

"You can."

"No, I can't." They sat next to one another on the bed. "I don't have a purpose. What am I doing besides tidying the house? And planning meals?" She might get her paints out again, but again she might not. She asked herself if the corn and okra paintings were soulless. How would she ever know? What they were was amateur, hesitant, and unsure. "Pregnancy isn't my best look."

"It is your best look," he said, and kissed her mouth. "Kate said she could never compete with you. I suppose being my wife isn't quite enough."

He seemed genuine and her heart opened to him. "No, honestly, it's not. I think it would do me good to go on a little trip, maybe with Elise, catch the little dry season." She wished she could say, *And listen for the bird's heartbeat, learn what the dancing woman is saying, find my underground spirituality.*

"Where do you want to go? I'll take you."

"I was thinking of the Kagoro Hills." She held her rounded belly. "But if you don't mind, I'd rather go with Elise." Elise, her mentor and friend.

"Are you punishing me?"

"Yes, a little."

He smiled bravely. "I'll find a driver to take you two in the Suburban."

"I'd rather go with Elise in her car. Just the two of us. We'll spend the night with the Parhams in Kafanchan."

He wavered.

"Elise has been driving around on her own in Nigeria for twenty years. The Parhams will baby me. You know how they are. I want to do it."

"Okay," Nick said, giving in.

But did I really have to have his permission?

They ate breakfast in the sunroom. Light through the windows sent shadows dancing on the walls.

♦ ♦ ♦

Elise estimated when the little dry season might fall—a week without rains. Isabel scribbled a quick letter to her mother. It was easier when she could be practical. She could picture her mother reading the letter, standing in the pharmacy office with that tiny rectangle of window to the outdoors.

Nick and I are well, though I've ballooned like a sail in high wind. You asked what we might need. A friend has offered a pram. We don't have a bassinette. Diapers cannot be found here so do send. And a pacifier (or two; we're sure to lose the first one). I can make all the clothes we need, though a pair of first leather shoes would be lovely. White, I think. Maybe two pairs, as they will soil so quickly here with the red dirt. I must rush to get this note to the post. A friend is taking me on an outing.

With love, your Isabel

Kufana

•••••

August 1963

A week later, Elise drove up in her green Fiat. Isabel was ready with a picnic, a thermos of coffee, her overnight bag, an extra pillow to wedge beneath her heavy belly, and her paints. She had decided to take them, though she wouldn't let Elise have a single glimpse of what she did. "You chose the perfect day," Isabel said, raising her hands to the sky. Nick bounded down the steps in that way American men have of showing their vigor. He kissed Isabel's cheek and helped her into the car.

Elise knew the way to an open roundhouse at a small station near the Kagoro Hills sometimes used for clinics. The scent of frying yams filled Isabel's nostrils as they drove out of town. Once in the country, she dozed. In a moment of waking, she saw, in the scrub brush, a group of Fulani herders in red shawls and conical hats, grazing their cattle. The men were thin and young and looked with disinterest at the passing car. An hour later, Elise pulled onto the grassy shoulder.

"Are we there?"

"No, but I need to use the bush. Open the glove box, would you?" Isabel did, and Elise reached for the toilet paper.

"Wait, I need to go too." They picked their way across the edge of a farm and headed to a cove of trees. Not a soul anywhere. Or at least none they could see.

They were in the plain and the Kagoro Hills rose around them, a slow green crescendo and then the joy of a sudden apex and outcroppings of rock. The hills were blue, now green, and now yellow, as clouds rolled across the sky. Here and there, a sudden hilltop appeared like a pyramid. Isabel took in all that she could see. Meanwhile, Elise was a silver movement up ahead. *She doesn't know I'm not behind her.* A band of turquoise sky opened beyond the hills. Isabel turned in a circle and wind doused her face. Suddenly she had to go. There was no waiting. She attempted a squat behind a bush, but her large stomach made it impossible. Her flow wetted her ankles. It smelled like boiled eggs and went on and on. Without as much as a tissue, she pulled several leaves from the bush. When she stood, she was still wet.

"What happened to you?" Elise held her hat on her head with one hand and the toilet paper in the other.

"I was admiring the landscape. And then I couldn't wait." She laughed.

On the way back to the car, crossing a field, she saw it. A little man like the dancing woman. He sat atop a mound of earth, smashed between several cornstalks, his gaze out before him and across the expanse of farm. So there were two of them? A man and a woman. Perhaps more? Suddenly the world seemed a mirror. Isabel had her own double, this self she was becoming with Elise out in the hills, laughing, smelling her urine, dreaming of pyramids, the same Isabel but also not. She had felt a double, making love with her husband, and then triple, maybe quadruple, if she counted the Holy Spirit.

"Look." She pointed, for Elise had not seen. This terra-cotta was the same size as the sculpture she had unearthed, with the same large head and almond-shaped eyes with deep pupils and distinctive brows, though the man's nose flared and he wore a triangular goatee. The fellow sat, arms crossed and rested on knees, his chin perched on the upper arm. One leg was broken off. He looked like a philosopher.

"A match to your dancing woman!" Elise said.

"Yes! Each is a book in clay. I must paint him." She grabbed her painting pouch from the car and returned. She could do this. She must try. Elise sat on a mound, the cornstalks splayed by her backside. Isabel handed her a jar of water. In a few minutes, she had a firm beginning. The tilt of the figure's head, the eternal eyes, chin rested on arms, the look of the thinker. She added a blade of cornstalk, a figment of sky.

Elise stood to get a look at the painting, but Isabel stopped her.

"You can tell me about Bobby Tunde, but I can't look at what you've painted?" Elise said. When Isabel, silent, continued to work, Elise went on. "What do you suppose it's doing here? Family totems aren't left in fields."

"No. But he was put here intentionally. Perhaps to inspire the farmer whose land this is. Perhaps the figure feeds the farmer's soul. He's a kind of spiritual anchor."

"You're eloquent this morning. What do you suppose he means to say?"

"That's what I want to know. Both of them are poised to speak, as if they have a secret."

"As you do," Elise said.

"Yes. I suppose." Isabel might have argued that her secret was consequential but not spiritual. The figures' secrets, the dancing woman and now this philosopher, were about something deeper, something much larger. For now, they were keeping their counsel.

"Come along now. Let's leave the fellow in peace." Elise cleared her throat and continued. "But, Isabel, if you're not going to show your work, why do you paint? What's it about anyway?"

Isabel pulled up short. "I once thought I knew."

"I expect your musician friend might know and that's what attracted you to him."

◆ ◆ ◆

The Fiat passed through fallow land and then through a thin forest before banking up an incline. "Almost there," Elise said.

Suddenly, they had arrived at the open roundhouse. Elise insisted Isabel sit as she unloaded the car. A path passed by just on the other side of a fence, and as they enjoyed their sandwiches and coffee, they watched the occasional passerby. Which of them, Isabel wondered, had the ancestor who had made the philosopher and the dancing woman? Or had the makers been of some other race who disappeared without a trace? Out of the corner of her eye, she saw the groundskeeper come out of his guard station, toss down a grass mat, kneel, and begin his prayer to Allah. Perhaps high in the hills, a great spotted cuckoo flew close to a cliff, veered, and disappeared.

Heading toward Kafanchan and the Palmers' compound, windows down, Elise smoking, Isabel watched the road ahead. She felt a new zeal for life, an intense longing for what was to come. Yet she felt pulled back to the mysteries of the earth, the hills, the flood plains, and the open roundhouse where they had picnicked and could see in every direction. She wanted to tell Nick about her longing, her underground spirituality, to open her new awareness to him as she opened her body. It would sound silly. Her words could not convey what she felt. Only painting could, but she still wasn't good enough, though the watercolor sketch of the little philosopher did have some feeling. She coveted her new solitary watcher, the self within, who examined herself. Soon enough, she would literally be two. The child would come. This jewel of time before that advent rested at her breastbone like a locket that held her own image. She was in her story.

Somewhere someone was grilling corn.

Kufana

•••••

Mid-September 1963

O ne overcast afternoon the heat bore down so intensely that Isabel stepped into a cold shower for relief. The moment she stepped out, she heard the wind. She dressed as quickly as she could. Out the window, wind gusts flattened the grass. She heard a crack. Across the street, a large limb of the flame tree bent downward like a letter flap. In a moment, it fell, sending a shudder through the ground. Isabel pulled on a dress.

"Mah." It was Daniel.

"I'm here."

"I am closing the windows."

She heard him pass through the rooms, tilting up the louvered panes. The dancing woman! Isabel had left her outside. What if a limb—or an entire tree—fell on her? Isabel flung the back door wide, ran down the steps and into the yard. Wind blew her dress up her thighs and whipped her hair. She bent to grasp the sculpture, holding her tight as a child. Wind blew into her face now, stinging her skin with sand. She ducked and ran, up the stairs, into the house, and nearly into Daniel.

The rain poured. This was the turning, when the wind came and announced the change of season. At last, the storm passed. It was cooler now. The sun came out. Isabel stepped onto the front porch. The world seemed polished to a shine. She could see the gentle rise of land and adjoining countryside miles away. Water droplets clustered on the leaves of the crown of thorns. Down the road, a woman reopened her fabric shop and hung out four dresses to display. Isabel sat with her legs spread beneath her skirt. After a while, she moved indoors. Through the sunroom windows, she saw Daniel in the backyard, picking up limbs. She moved to the storeroom. The jars of canned vegetables sat on the shelves in careful array, and they seemed to her like samples of eternity. She ran her fingers across them: green beans, red tomatoes, yellow corn. She hated to open even one. In the kitchen, she set a can of green beans out with a fresh onion and some potatoes from the market. She wrote: *left-over baked chicken, fried potatoes, green beans with sliced onion, banana pudding.* Daniel had made the pudding that morning.

Two days later, Isabel looked out the back windows and there was Amina, named for the Zaria warrior. She stopped by twice a week on her way to market. Sometimes she only called Isabel to the hedge and offered her a gift: a single tomato, an orange. Sometimes the woman came into the yard and sat down under the avocado tree, the daughter, Latifa, imitating her mother, sitting erect with her legs out straight in front of her. There seemed no clear purpose to these visits unless Amina was exercising a right gained through her gifts to relax and gather her strength in the bature's yard before she went home and fixed the evening meal.

Isabel went out to greet her visitors. She was fetching a chair for herself when she saw Elise in the side yard. "Bring a chair," Isabel called. She went back indoors and claimed a bowl of fried plantain left from lunch. She introduced her visitors to one another. Amina smoothed her skirt and tipped her head before extending a hand to pick up a plantain slice. She nipped off a piece for the daughter before gracefully reaching for another slice. "Your mother dances with her hands," Isabel said to Latifa, who explained to her mother. Elise took a bite. The four of them took turns eating the plantain, shaking their heads in agreement at the deliciousness of the fruit, licking their fingers and laughing, until Latifa rolled over onto her side in glee. The girl's hips were rounding. Elise could converse better in Hausa than Isabel, and she and Amina enjoyed an exchange. Before leaving, Amina allowed Isabel to give Latifa one golden nugget of butterscotch candy. Just as Latifa unwrapped the sweet, Isabel thought perhaps she might like a girl rather than a boy. And then Amina said "da sannu," and that was a Hausa word Isabel knew. *Soon.*

That night, Isabel couldn't get comfortable in bed. Nick was up writing reports for the D.C. office. Along with the neem project, he had toured surrounding villages, meeting with farmers and encouraging them to compost and fertilize their soil. It was slow going. The men had been farming the same way for ages and the women too, though Nick didn't meet with the women. If he was going to direct a workshop, the village elders introduced him to the men. The cassava that filled so many stomachs was sacred as corn in Nebraska or tobacco in North Carolina, and it was the men's crop, but it had little nutritional value. Still, no one was likely to give it up. On the other hand, Amina grew lots of tomatoes; those were nutritious. All of the women in the market sold oranges in season, and bananas too. Isabel wondered if Nick's mission was a little catawampus since women were already doing more things right and had more to gain through the changes USAID might bring since they were further down the economic ladder. But she wasn't prepared for that conversation, which wouldn't do any good anyway. Right now it seemed important to get two pillows positioned just so beneath her belly.

The next morning, a courier from USAID delivered a package from Isabel's parents. Diapers, pacifiers, and two pairs of baby shoes. The arrival of these necessities offered Isabel a sense of intactness. Her heart filled with gratitude. Elise came by and left two silver teaspoons her boys had used. Sewing garments for the baby, Isabel found herself making two of everything. After all, once she mastered a pattern, it was easier to sew another. She would always have a clean one, while its mate was in the laundry basket.

That afternoon, she and Daniel went to the market. She had offered to purchase school notebooks for his younger brother. The family didn't have money for supplies after paying for the child's school uniform. Suddenly Tunde's song came pouring out of a shop front. *Pretty lady should not cry. Moon jump for the sky.* His music was now in Kufana. "That song," she said, catching at the air as if she might seize the lyric like a kite's tail.

"Yes. It's very nice," Daniel said.

Isabel stood absolutely still as the melody continued. Her heart felt so exposed she wondered if a window had opened in her chest and a passerby could look in and see it red and knocking. The lyrics faded. Isabel picked up her step, arriving at the first vendor feeling warm and tremulous. The man waiting on her seemed to observe her dishevelment. She hurried to the next vendor where she searched furiously for notebooks.

"There, madam," Daniel said, pointing.

Isabel paid for six exercise books and two pens and handed them to Daniel.

"Thank you," he said.

"You're welcome."

What Isabel herself needed but didn't expect to find was elastic for gathering cloth around tiny wrists and legs. "Do you have elastic band?" she said to the merchant in front of her. Miraculously, he pulled out a cylindrical carton, brown from dust. "How long have you had it?"

"Since last month."

Isabel laughed, spread her feet, and let her belly extend even farther in front of her. She was beginning to master the ways of the marketplace. "Since last year, I think."

The man sucked on his teeth, put the cylinder of elastic back in its hiding spot, and looked away.

"Zan iya ganinsa?" *May I see it?*

The man's mouth settled into a scowl, and he waved her off.

"Don allah." *Please*.

Without looking at her, he handed the item across his countertop, covered with oil lamps, alarm clocks, machetes, and flashlights. She tried the elastic. It was dingy but usable. She held her hands out as far as she could. "This much, please. What is your best price?"

"One shilling, sixpence," came the answer.

"Ah! Too steep," she said. "Sixpence."

"One shilling, threepence."

"Ninepence," she said.

"One shilling."

"One shilling. Okay." Isabel was feeling hot. Her midsection seemed to grow heavier by the minute.

The man cut Isabel's elastic and tied it up. "Take, go," he said as she paid.

"Na gode," she said. *Thank you.* She turned triumphantly to Daniel.

At home, she lay in bed, clutching the package of elastic. She dozed and woke. She thought she heard Bobby's song outside her window. She sat up, shook her head, and searched her lingerie drawer for the silver link. Not finding it, she pulled out her things until at last it fell from a bra she could no longer wear. She scooped it up before returning it to hiding. Nick wouldn't be back until five, and then he would join her for tea in the garden. He had become solicitous in her pregnancy. His thoughtfulness almost frightened her. What if, with his greater attention, he guessed about the affair? How could she have been so unwise? In the market, another lyric from Bobby's song had penetrated her consciousness. *Skin like silk from the kapok tree.* Had he slept with her to get the song? Or had she inspired him like a goddess? What ridiculous ideas. She closed her eyes, and there he was in his white suit, pants close against his thighs, flaring at the ankle. His lean hips. The open jacket. The feeling of his head between her hands.

Kufana

•••••

Late September 1963

Several days later, Daniel didn't show up at four p.m. to begin the evening meal. He had never been late. He wasn't there at five when Nick got home. Around six, Isabel made toast with cream sauce and boiled eggs. "I'm worried about him. Could you go to his compound?"

"It's almost dark."

"All the more reason. I'll go with you."

Nick looked at her belly. "You should stay home."

Isabel was already pulling on a sweater. "I'm going."

They drove toward Daniel's compound. Isabel's center felt tight, and it wasn't the pregnancy. "His mother might be worse. She had some kind of leg wound." Someone else's mother had been ill. Bobby Tunde's.

Nick didn't reply.

By the time they arrived, they needed their flashlights. Several elder men sat on benches at the compound front, a fire glimmering at their feet. Two recumbent dogs completed the group. No one seemed pleased to see them. Perhaps Isabel should not have come. Nick addressed the man who held a carved walking stick between his knees. "Barka da yamma." *Good evening.*

The man replied in kind.

"We're looking for Daniel Nenge. He works for us." Nick paused as if suddenly awkward about how to express their relationship. "Well, he helps my wife. He comes in the evening to prepare food." He turned to Isabel as if her condition might explain why they needed help doing what any Nigerian family would do for itself. He turned back to the man with the cane. "When he didn't show up today, we became concerned." Nick exhaled like a schoolboy who hopes his story holds up.

For several moments no one spoke. At last, the man shook his head. "He has left this afternoon."

"Do you know where he went?"

"He has gone to the family compound."

"I thought this was his family's compound," Nick said.

"He has traveled to his father's homestead. There is trouble there."

Isabel couldn't restrain herself. "What trouble? Is he well?"

The gentleman observed her. "He was well when he left." He turned back to Nick. "There is some dispute. Some Jukun men have encroached on the father's land. It is an ongoing battle."

"What do you mean?" Isabel imagined bloody sabers, Daniel wounded and dying.

"You don't know? Only three years ago, we Tiv people pushed against the Jukun for terrorizing our markets. They came to slaughter us. Many were killed."

Daniel had told her, but she had thought the event was further back, settled in history like a stone in the earth, before Nigeria gained its independence in 1960.

"Where is the homestead?" Isabel felt like an idiot. She knew little about Daniel except that he made great fried chicken, wanted to go to nursing school, and looked after his mother and brother.

"Near the Benue River."

Nick put a hand on Isabel's shoulder. "That's half a day by car. But surely there's no battle now," he said.

"Muna rokon Allah," the man said. *We pray to God.* A log settled in the fire and a host of sparks flew up and disappeared. One of the dogs stretched and turned on its side.

The world seemed suddenly uncharted.

◆ ◆ ◆

Daniel did not return the next day. Isabel took out her paints. She had no thought for a subject until she looked up into the mirror and there she was. To right of center, she applied a wash of green. Thin dark lines for the frame of the mirror. A pink of diluted aliz-

arin crimson for the left side of her face. White space left for the
cheekbones. The right side, near the window, she painted in curves
of yellow. With three broad strokes, she began to shape her hair.
Her nose emerged where the facial planes met. She used a wash
of burnt sienna for her arched brows, paler on one side. Pink lips,
lightly closed. A stroke of reddish pigment brought out her chin.
Eyes, a pale blue touched with lavender at the edges. Isabel observed
the painter, herself, in the mirror. She came back with a second pass
of pink for one cheek. The hair billowed out and up. "There I am,"
she said. Of course, she was backwards, a mirror image.

Three days later, Daniel showed up early in Isabel's kitchen.

"I'm so glad to see you. Are you well?" Isabel wished she could
give him a hug.

"Apologies, madam. I was called away to the family farm. Some
trouble is there."

"We heard."

"It is an old grievance. We Tiv will not lie prostrate before the
Hausa and Fulani or the Jukun. We are our own people. But they
run over us like dogs."

There was something Old Testament sounding about Daniel's
language, and it sent a shiver up Isabel's spine.

"Are things settled?"

"The local authority required the man to pay my father. It is not
enough, but, God willing, he will not come again."

"I'm so sorry. What can I do for you?"

"Madam, you can help me find a road to nursing school. As a
nurse, I can support my family."

But I need you. Immediately Isabel chastised herself for being so
selfish. "I will talk with my husband. I'm grateful you're safe. Would
you fix tea in the English garden cup?" She smiled, but he remained
grave.

Kufana

* * * * *

Early October 1963

Isabel sought more knowledge about the Tiv. In a new book just out from London, *The Federation of Nigeria*, she read, *At the confluence of the rivers Benue and the Niger live the Tiv.* The sentence was so poetical that Isabel found it hard to think of the Tiv as being in *an old battle by now.* Reading further, she learned that the Tiv had long been pressed, first by the Fulani, then the British, then by the Hausa. There was a Tiv uprising.

Isabel thought of the old men at the compound front when she and Nick went to ask after Daniel. They were Tiv standing against anyone encroaching on their way of life. What did she and Nick represent? Though Daniel was solicitous of her, he didn't act as if they were a "we." She had thought he helped her out of sympathy when he arranged transportation with the Van Dijks to Kaduna. But she had once overheard him in the market say "nothing is for nothing." His request for help with school was his calling in the debt.

Later, Isabel wandered into the baby's room. Nick had painted it blue. She sat in the rocking chair, rested a hand on her enormous middle, and let her swollen feet splay. The striped curtains hung softly in the windows, made from the fabric purchased in Zaria on that frightening day that turned inspirational when Isabel understood that her artist's sensibility had resurfaced.

A butterfly mobile created by her own hands danced lightly above the crib. A bookcase held the few children's books they had inherited from the Parhams—Little Golden Books, some absurd in their surroundings, but they would read them anyway: *Frosty the Snowman*, *Winky Dink*, and *Surprise for Sally*. To soften the floor she had put down her grandmother's handwoven rag rug.

The back door opened. Daniel was here to prepare dinner. She stayed in the rocker until she heard Nick arrive. They ate dinner. When Nick asked for coffee, she excused herself. "I'm so tired." She crawled into bed. Through the wall, she heard Daniel clearing the table. In her dream, she washed clothes in a stream where orange and blue fish darted. Other women washed nearby. Children swam and jumped from a rock into a swimming hole. She was surprised to touch her hair and feel the garnet clip. Now she was in Angelica's pond. But, no, she was in a stream, washing the baby's clothes, Nick's white shirts, and her nightgown, the one she had worn with Bobby Tunde. A circle of blood stained the front. She rubbed the spot against a rock, but the stain grew larger. Suddenly she heard cries, mothers calling to their children, a gunshot. She tried to turn the gown so the bloodstain wouldn't show.

A mother ran back to the stream, holding her son. "They have killed my child. Ya, Allah, they have killed my child. They are killing us." Isabel was on Daniel's farm where *many were killed*.

Isabel woke to a sharp pain in her belly. She reached for Nick, but he wasn't in bed. She needed to relieve herself. With a flashlight, she found her way to the bathroom. On the toilet, her water broke. Impossible. She was at thirty-two weeks, eight months. They planned to go to Kaduna for the delivery but not yet. The last time she had seen Dr. Eli, he had frightened her, listening for the heartbeat. "There seems to be an echo," he had said, and she thought he meant an imperfection and surmised she had brought this on herself. "Is that bad?" she managed.

He listened again. "Ah, Nothing to worry about. It must have been yours, following the child's."

But this pain would not do. "Nick," she called and tried the wall switch. Nothing.

She moved into the living room. In the dining room, a spike of pain hit her belly. She put her hand against the wall, leaned forward, and moaned. When she could right herself, she turned to the kitchen. The door to the backyard stood ajar. Cool air moved in through the screen. She shown the light into the backyard. "Nick?"

"Honey?"

"My water broke." She began to cry. "We're going to lose the baby."

"I'll drive us straight to Kaduna."

"What were you doing?"

"Checking the generator. I think I got it fixed."

A spasm twisted her center. "There's no time to get to Kaduna. Go get Elise."

"That means leaving you here, and it will take as long as going to Kaduna, longer."

"Get Daniel first. Ask him to bring a midwife. I can't get into a car."

"I can't leave you here with Daniel."

"You have to. Go."

◆ ◆ ◆

Isabel quivered beneath the double wedding ring quilt. Why was she cold? What if Nick couldn't find Daniel? Or Daniel couldn't find a midwife? The night outside pressed dark and hard. Something seemed to roll over her, a typhoon of weariness, and she dozed. The pain came back, not terrible but insistent, a threat of worse to come. Isabel turned onto her side, holding her belly. What if the baby came and no one was here? At least the electricity was back on. She heard a loud thump against the outer wall of the house, as if a large animal had run into it in the dark. Why wasn't Nick back? How long had he been gone? She looked at the clock. Only fifteen minutes. It felt like hours. A sense of absolute aloneness enveloped her. She would drown in her own blood. Then suddenly, there was Daniel in the doorway to her bedroom.

"I have brought Amina."

Amina the warrior, though the woman beside him seemed smaller than Isabel remembered, perhaps because she wasn't wearing her usual headdress. Yet her face was self-assured. "Show her the kitchen. Have her wash well, well. Boil some water. We need scissors."

Amina returned, bearing the smell of Lux soap. From somewhere, she pulled out what looked like a long wooden spool and placed one end on Isabel's belly and the other end to her ear. She listened. Isabel tilted her head back until she was looking at her headboard.

Amina's hands were cool and firm. Isabel let out a deep breath. "Is the baby all right?"

"Eh," Amina said, nodding her head *yes*. Then she went to the bedroom door, opened it, and called Daniel. A few minutes later, he was back with clean towels. Amina shooed him away. She stood beside Isabel and held her wrist. When the next contraction hit, Isabel rocked up, and Amina leaned into her with her own chest. Isabel knew she wasn't supposed to push yet.

"A'a," Amina said and made a downward motion with her hands, then fluttered them out. Down and flutter. Down and swish. *She means I should breathe.* The next contraction turned Isabel into a corkscrew. It was too much. A month too soon. What was happening? Where was Elise? She heard Daniel in the kitchen and imagined him boiling pots of water, water bubbling until the walls wept. The pain stopped, and she slumped in the bed. Amina fanned her face.

"Yaranki nawa?" Isabel said. *How many are your children.* Then she remembered it was an impolite question, the kind Americans asked but not Nigerians. Well, too bad. She was in a tough spot right here and could not be expected to remember every damn thing.

Anima answered, and Isabel caught the word *seven*.

"How wonderful. Seven is an auspicious number," Isabel said, pressing back a wand of hair. Amina may not know auspicious, but what did it matter.

"Allah is great," Amina said.

There was a lull. Isabel fell into half sleep and felt the pull of a wave. She should swim, but the waves invited her to float. This must have some good meaning. Something began to churn in her. The next pain arrived like a hot knife. She leaned forward with a howl. "God!" She fought against the quilt, nearly coming out of the bed. "Let me out. I need to squat." She heard the Suburban, the slam of the car doors, feet across the porch, the open and close of the front door. Elise and Amina nodded to one another. Isabel groaned.

"You go on," Elise said to Nick. She closed the bedroom door, pulled off Isabel's covers, and eased her back down. "Let me take a look." She released a puff of breath. "You're further along than I would have thought. This little one wants out." She stationed the chair next to the bed, and Amina helped Isabel to the chair. "When the next contraction comes, stand up, put your forearms on the bed, and push. You'll need to push hard," Elise said.

Isabel closed her eyes. She conjured the redheaded lizard moving in and out of the great philodendron that clung to the side of the house. The lemon tree hovered in her mind with its lemons large as melons. Harmattan mist filled the screen of her closed eyelids, followed by the crown of thorns, pinker than all pinks. Finally, she summoned the dancing woman in the garden, arms swirled upward. Someone must refresh the flowers at her base. Patas monkeys followed, picking at one another on her living room floor. A train broke into her consciousness, moving straight at her. Except it was inside her, trying to get out. She opened her eyes. Amina held her wrists and pulled her up, leaning her over the bed. Isabel panted, fisting the bed covers. The train turned and went behind a hill. It emerged, enlarged, engorged, galloping, a horse big as a ship, incalculable, crimson. Nothing had prepared her for this. "God," she screamed and fell forward.

"No, stay on your elbows. Now push. Push!"

"I can't."

"You must."

Isabel threw her head back. She was the roaring train, running over herself. The next thing Isabel saw was Amina, kneeling on the floor. For an instant, Isabel thought of the well at the farm, how her grandmother pumped and she, Isabel, held her hands below to catch the cool water, how in the spring, crocuses sprang up, purple buds not yet open. Something slipped.

"Mah. I have it!" The gray-pink head and little ball of body rested in the woman's hands.

Isabel collapsed forward. Elise turned her over and pressed her back into bed until her head was on the pillows. Amina held the child up and thumped it as someone back home would thump a watermelon. The child wailed.

"It's a girl," Elise said. "Your very own girl. I'll clean her in the basin and give her right back to you."

Within moments Elise had the bright pink child on Isabel's chest, a wisp of light hair sticking straight up. Isabel massaged her tiny head, touched the small nose, the mouth like a fairy cup, eyebrows so perfect they looked painted with a brush. "You will be Sarah. Just because," Isabel said. *And you are Nick's. I see you are.*

Amina was busy between Isabel's legs, her strong hands massaging. Suddenly, she stopped. "Please mah," she said. "Su biyu." *They are two.*

"What?" Isabel said.

"Two," Elise said. "There's another one."

Two two two two two two 2 2. "What?" Isabel said.

"Twins."

This time it wasn't a train, but a furious bird, beating against the delta of Isabel's blood and bone. Elise placed the first baby in a bassinette. She joined Amina with the second birth.

"It's another girl," Elise said. "She's you all over. Amina is cutting the cord." She held the child up, and again Amina thumped and the infant wailed. "My goodness," Elise said, "but she's so different from the first. Lucky you."

The babe nestled on Isabel's chest, the smallest kitten. *She's breathing. Her color is lamplight. She has my dark hair. See the wave in it. Her fingernails are the smallest shells. No wonder I sewed two of everything.* In the far distance, Isabel caught a glimpse of Bobby Tunde's suit, like a white egret rising in mist from a lake. But this child in her arms now. She was Isabel's own twin. She would be Catherine for her grandmother.

"Where is my husband?" she said.

Kufana-Kaduna Road

•••••

Mid-October 1963

ater, when Isabel thought about the accident, she wondered if a bush dog had witnessed it, or a monitor lizard high in a tree, or a hawk in the air. On the way to Kaduna to register the births of his twin daughters, Sarah Marie and Catherine Archer, Nick's Suburban skidded, turned over, and lodged in a tree on the other side of the road. Someone who examined the area later and saw the tracks thought the vehicle hit a drop-off at the edge of the pavement and when Nick tried to correct his course and regain the road, it flipped. Certainly, the state of the Suburban suggested a flip. There may have been another vehicle, a lorry, perhaps, that ran Nick off the tarmac. If so, someone must have seen the American car in its wild motion, skidding and barreling. But if such a person had cried out to the lorry driver, would he have heard? If the pavement was not broad enough to allow the passage of two vehicles, was it the responsibility of the lorry driver if another car turned over? Or was it the responsibility of the prime minister of the region? Or the engineer who planned the road?

Isabel played the scenarios over and over in her head, an abstraction against the horror of her husband's beautiful body raked and compressed by metal and glass.

Did sunlight play across Nick's bloodied face when he was discovered by the driver of a Peugeot station wagon, a young mathematician, Shaibu Abubakar, who taught at Ahmadu Bello University in Zaria? He said he had checked Nick's pulse and seen the rise and fall of his chest, but he didn't want to risk pulling the man out of the vehicle alone. He knew what USAID, painted on the side of the Suburban, stood for, knew there was a headquarters in Zaria. But he also knew he should get the white man to a Kaduna hospital. In his moments of pondering, a bicyclist came by and stopped. Together the men lifted Nick into the back seat of Abubakar's Peugeot. "No," he said later to Isabel, "I did not see a snakeskin folder with a zipper closure that held your family's passports and papers."

At six o'clock the evening of the accident, Daniel prepared dinner. Isabel rested after bathing the girls one by one and placing them in a single bassinette. Elise folded clean clothes and diapers, because she had come for the day, to help with the girls. That was when the car of the vice counsel must have entered the outskirts of Kufana. In half sleep, Isabel's throbbing nipples seemed to press her deeper into the bed. She smelled curry, and from some recess of memory, a bed of marigolds on Grace Street in Oregon Hills rose up and filled the sky. She heard the approach of a motor and its cessation and felt the sound as a wave.

Kufana, Kaduna

* * * * *

October 1963

That was how Isabel thought back on it. In fact, she heard the vice counsel's car. Vaguely she considered that a bigwig from town was coming to congratulate Nick on the birth of the twins. If only he were here to greet them. Elise would do it. Isabel turned onto her side and glimpsed the girls, asleep in the bassinette. She was not allowed, it seemed, any time for rest herself. Her body thrummed with exhaustion. In her half dream, everything doubled: two cars, two brown goats, two voices, two vines, or was it a single large snake?

"What are you saying?" she heard from Elise. And then "On the road." Isabel fell back into slumber. A loud *twak, twak* interrupted her rest. Daniel's sandals. Something was wrong with Elise's husband or the dispensary or a patient. Poor Elise. Nick would be home any moment. The sweetest time of day was evening, when he held the girls and she showered and then fleeced herself with lily of the valley talcum powder and put on a clean dress and sat for a cup of tea. She felt a boundlessness then, as if in motherhood she had opened all the doors.

Elise stood in the door to the bedroom, her hands clasped at her waist. She looked suddenly old, her skin pale. Isabel sat up, her head wobbly with vertigo.

"Is Hugo all right? Come. Sit down." Isabel patted the bed beside her.

Elise sat. She took Isabel's hand. "Nick is in hospital in Kaduna. There was an accident."

Isabel felt ice cold. She pressed her head with her palms and felt the throb of her heart. "Is he all right? Were there others?"

"There were no others. He's not awake, Isabel."

"What do you mean?" She released her head and held her hands out in entreaty.

"He's unconscious. He hasn't come to yet. They're keeping him stable."

Isabel smelled smoke—from a burning car or a woman's fire across the way? She looked at her sleeping girls and then at her friend. Why was Elise on her bed? Nick wasn't even thirty.

"Vice Consul Gerald Linderman's wife is here, Mary Linderman. She's brought with her the man who found Nick on the road, Mr. Abubakar."

Nick was slipping away, down a long alley. Isabel stood and picked up Catherine. Catherine always wanted holding. There was Mary Linderman standing in her doorway, a petite woman with brown hair and a declining chin. She had bright green eyes. She took a step forward.

"I'm so sorry to carry this news, Mrs. Hammond," she said. "But your husband is in the best of hands at Kaduna Hospital."

"Thank you for coming, Mrs. Linderman." Isabel didn't want this woman here. She must get back to fifteen minutes ago when she was napping in the assurance of her husband's return, inhaling the scent of curry from the kitchen. She just needed to reach for Sarah and get both girls out the kitchen door and go far enough back in time to tell her husband about her infidelity. Then this would not be happening. It was her fault. She had split them. She had pushed her husband away. What a stupid woman she was.

"Your husband has a broken arm and a leg. The break in the leg . . ." She didn't finish the sentence.

"Yes? What about it?"

"They had to do surgery. The fracture punctured the skin. The doctor thinks the Suburban turned over. Your husband must have broken some ribs because a lung collapsed. The doctor inserted a tube. This wonderful man in your living room—he's the one who stopped on the road and took Nick to the hospital."

"But what's wrong with my husband? When will he wake up?" *And come back to me and these babies?* "A broken arm and a leg don't explain why he's unconscious." How cruel that this would happen. It was her fault. She had made Nick vulnerable.

"There are lacerations on his head. I haven't seen him, mind you. I'm telling you what I was told. If the car rolled over. Well, you can imagine. His head would have hit hard surfaces."

Isabel summoned a fierce look and directed it at Mary.

"The doctors are hoping it's a subdural hemorrhage." Mary's eyes did not waver.

Isabel took a deep breath. She clutched Catherine. "Will my husband survive?"

"We're hopeful," This small Mary held her ground, alert as a snake. "The doctor may attempt to lessen the pressure."

"What does that mean?" Isabel pumped Catherine up and down in her arms as if the child were wailing, though her daughter had decided all was well and had closed her eyes again, though her little hand clung to the fabric of Isabel's dress.

"They would have to do surgery."

"On his head?"

The electric lights flashed and went out. In a moment, they came back on. "Open the skull to see if there is bleeding. You can understand how that would cause swelling."

Isabel felt a piercing in her ears, bright and hard as a needle. "He won't leave me." She shook her head as her mind lurched forward. "I must dress and go to him. Take the babies." She held Catherine out precariously. Mary and Elise both rushed forward. "I'll need clothes for a few days. We need to pack for the girls too. Mary, you can take care of them, can't you? I'll need a clean nightgown, maybe two. Underwear." She started to open her top drawer.

"Isabel, please. Sit down," Elise said. "You can't go tonight. There's nothing for you to do. Wait until we hear from the doctors in the morning. Nick is getting the best possible care. Vice Counsel Linderman has been in contact with London just in case Nick needs to be flown out. Your job is to stay well and take care of the girls."

"I have to go to my husband." Isabel searched among her bras and slips. The silver link sparkled in the back of the drawer. She slammed it shut. "I'll stay tonight if someone promises to carry me to the hospital tomorrow." She looked to Elise, not Mrs. Linderman whose husband, no doubt, was relaxing in their fine Kaduna apartment, sipping brandy and watching television.

"I'll take you and the girls tomorrow," Elise said.

"I don't see what good you can do your husband at this point. He needs rest," Mary said.

Isabel wanted to hit the woman. "I will speak to the man who found my husband." Yes, Mary was the dreaded snake in her half dream. Isabel swept past her.

Mr. Abubakar stood in the middle of the living room in his gray robe and red cap.

"Thank you for stopping to help my husband. He might be dead if you hadn't."

"You are welcome." His eyes met Isabel's. "I pray to Allah he will be well."

"Please be sure Mrs. Linderman knows how to find you. So we can thank you properly when my husband comes home. I'm sure it won't be long."

"Yes, Mrs. Hammond."

"Did my husband say anything? Anything at all?"

Mr. Abubakar wiped his forehead with his hand.

"I see."

♦ ♦ ♦

Elise spent the night. In the morning, she helped Isabel pack while Daniel prepared a lunch for them to carry. Sarah spit up and had to be changed twice.

"I can follow you," Daniel said.

"I would be so grateful if you stayed here and kept an eye on the house and the garden. I'll send word about how long we'll be away."

Daniel's eyes seemed to gaze upon something beyond the house.

"Don't worry. We'll be home soon. All of us."

♦ ♦ ♦

On the road to Kaduna, the truck ahead threw up dust and smelled of diesel. Grasses near the road had begun to brown in the onset of the dry season. Just yesterday, Nick had been here, and here, and here. Suddenly Isabel wondered if the Suburban had been towed. Or would it be there on the road, crushed like a tin can? She closed her eyes. The bassinette wedged next to her in the back seat held her daughters. Already the girls had developed personalities. Second-born Catherine held on to Isabel intently, even scratching her with her little nails. She kicked her legs when put down. First-born Sarah studied everything with her eyes. When Isabel held her close, she pushed away.

Isabel's stomach churned. She had indulged her whims and taken her eye from her husband. She was a fool. Now he was broken. All she wanted was her husband and their girls back at home. She was seduced by her own ideas, her hungers. She would shave her head to get him back. *Lord help us. There is no one else to do it.*

♦ ♦ ♦

Mary met them at the hospital. The hallways smelled sharply of cleaning solution. Nigerian nurses, all of them men, moved smartly in their white uniforms. Isabel imagined Daniel back in Kufana, looking after the house, anxious about their breadwinner and his own future. Elise kept the girls in a waiting room. Isabel followed Mary to the intensive care ward, clasping her purse against her abdomen, her back cold with fear. Twenty-four hours since the accident. Surely Nick would be awake.

The man in the bed could not be her husband. He lay crumpled on his back, a leg sticking out awkwardly in a cast, a casted arm hoisted in the air. The upper portion of the other arm lay covered in some sort of dressing. His eyes were so swollen, it didn't seem he could possibly open them. Lesions abraded his face. Black stitching pulled harshly on a shaved area of his head. Nothing about him moved but his chest, up and down in quick breaths. Isabel opened her mouth, but no sound came. She clamped a hand over it.

"Sit down, Mrs. Hammond," Mary said. "I'll get the doctor."

Dr. Meyers towered over Isabel. He was balding on top, skin splotchy from too much sun, though he didn't look old. Isabel imagined him as a tennis player and could picture him later that day at the Lawn Club. He spoke things she didn't understand: *sternal rub; contusion to the heart—probably the steering wheel; fractured tibia; edema of something or other, skin graft.*

"When is he going to wake up?" Isabel said.

The doctor's head dipped infuriatingly like one of those drinking bird toys. "He won't be on the up and up right away. He seemed to respond to light in his eyes this morning." The doctor took a deep breath and released it through his mouth. "We can let him rest and see if he improves. Or we can do a craniotomy to remove pressure on his brain."

The man's lips were chapped. If Isabel had any other choice, she would fire Dr. Meyers and go in search of someone else. She looked at her crumpled husband, his slightly open mouth, the gold wedding ring on his undamaged hand.

"There is almost certainly blood either inside the brain or out-side, between the skull and the brain. One sort will drain on its own through the stomach. The other sort will not."

"What are we waiting on?"

"You, Mrs. Hammond. You must decide. In my professional opin-ion, it might be best to wait another day and see if anything changes. We want to defer the skin graft because that requires moving him. We'll take skin from the back of his thigh for his arm."

"What is the downside of waiting?"

"Pressure builds on the brain."

"That's your best advice? Wait and see? But waiting could also be damaging?"

"Yes."

Isabel looked again at Nick's contorted form, his sutured head, the bandaging around his chest where they had inserted a tube to inflate his lung. Just yesterday, he had held the girls in the garden, one in each arm. She stood beside him and placed her palm very lightly on the least bruised side of his face, then leaned over. "It's me, Isabel. I know you're there. I'm right here beside you." She squeezed his hand. He didn't squeeze back. Instead, his face seemed to de-scend more deeply into sleep.

She stumbled out of the room. "A lavatory, please." She vomited into the sink, hunched like a sick animal. Sitting on the toilet, she saw fresh blood on her menstrual pad. Elise said it was common with twins, for the bleeding to go on. Isabel put her hands over her eyes and pressed her lids. Everything was on her now. She pressed her lids harder, gaining an even deeper darkness. Someone coughed outside the bathroom door. Isabel changed out the pad. In the nurses' station behind a half curtain, she nursed first Catherine and then Sarah. Elise helped her burp them and change their diapers. *If only I could unspool the past two days, hold Nick back, even for five minutes, the crash may not have occurred. What was the rush? Why were we ever in a rush?*

"The Agency has a nearby chalet for our use," Elise said. "I'm staying here with you. Hugo and my midwife will cover the dispensary."

Isabel leaned into her friend's embrace. "Thank you." How would she take care of two babies and a disabled man in a foreign country? Her joints hurt, even her teeth.

"There now, that's good." Threads of silver highlighted Elise's short hair. "One hour at a time."

On the street, Isabel felt herself tossed like old newspaper. A great black-and-pink pig stood in a doorway across the way. Elise held the girls in the bassinette. Their need to nurse several times a day would not change, though their father languished between life and death. Someone brought the car around. Bicyclers passed with loads of cloth strapped on their rear racks, street vendors sold food, men in business suits clipped past. The world had not paused for Nick.

Kaduna

* * * * *

Third week of October 1963

sabel lathered her hair. The smell of Breck shampoo took her back to the farm in summers, and she was wrapped in the memory of fresh peaches. But when she left the shower and the mirror reflected her slack belly, her mind flew to Nick. At levels she could hardly comprehend, she had decided against surgery. She could not allow anyone to drill into her husband's skull.

The chalet was close enough to walk to the hospital, but Elise insisted on driving them and waiting. The swelling on Nick's head was worse, and the sutures pressed staple-like against his scalp. Isabel doubted her decision. In moments alone, she pulled at her hair. In the presence of nurses, she sat tight as a lidded jar, felt her heartbeat, and willed it to her husband. On the third day, Nick moaned. Isabel leapt to his side and squeezed his hand, but he turned his head away. On the fourth day, he slurped slices of orange popsicle, but Isabel was out of the room and only heard about it. She scolded herself for not being vigilant. How careless she had been and still was. Finally, on the fifth day, Nick opened his eyes. Whether she imagined it or not, it seemed the room itself revived. The wilting roses brought in by the consulate stood back up. A breeze swooshed through the louvered windows and set the papers on a clipboard stirring. She leaned over her husband and held his face gently in her hands. "I knew you were there." A look of confusion crossed his tightened brows. What if he woke but didn't recognize her? "Do you know who I am?" He didn't respond. She put her hand in his. "Nick, honey. Squeeze if you know I'm Isabel." The slightest pressure. Or was she imagining it?

"Madame. Please. He needs to rest." It was the nurse from the hall.

Outside the room, Isabel wept in great bursting sobs, holding herself up by the wall.

The next morning, she rose early and nursed the twins as Elise made coffee. "Do you mind keeping them? The walk to the hospital will do me good." She passed a man selling bread and bought a loaf, along with a warm Coca-Cola. At the hospital, she had to wait. Nick was receiving a bath. It took a while with the way he was hoisted and bandaged and casted. Then she had to wait for Meyers to come. The nurse didn't want Nick over-stimulated before the doctor could examine him. She sat in the hallway, ate the bread, and sipped the Coca-Cola. Finally, around eleven o'clock, Meyers arrived. Normally, Isabel would be curious about a middle-aged American doctor living and working in Kaduna and ask his story, but the days were not normal. Dr. Meyers seemed to spend forever with Nick before coming out to report that his vitals were stabilizing. He had opened his eyes briefly, eaten some mashed banana, and uttered a word: *pain*. "That's good. He's with us. He's communicating. We'll do the skin graft tomorrow. It's better if you let him rest. Have you had breakfast?"

"Some bread."

"Come back this afternoon. Go to the Swim Club. Get yourself a nice lunch. Where's your friend?"

Just then, Elise came down the hall with the girls in the pram borrowed from Mrs. Linderman, who certainly was not a snake, but rather a reliable ally.

"Ah, there she is. Just in time." Dr. Meyers waved his clipboard. "Take this woman to lunch. Her husband is progressing. A mother of two needs more than bread."

Isabel felt her first affection for the doctor and his splotchy skin. Just as she was walking out, he had one more instruction. "When you come back, stop at the business office. They need to see your husband's passport for recordkeeping."

Isabel looked at him blankly.

"You don't have your passports with you?"

What came to Isabel's mind was blue sky and a dry plain, a hawk, the smell of a cooking fire, a flag of pink fabric flowing out of a trundle sewing machine. The vision collided with an enormous propeller and was shredded to bits.

"Mrs. Hammond?"

"I think my husband had our passports with him in the Suburban."

"Before the accident?"

"Yes."

"And where is the car now?"

"Towed? I don't know. Nick carried everything in a snakeskin folio. Our passports were in it. He was coming to Kaduna to register the babies' births and then going on up to Zaria to fill out some form. It had to do with our request to stay another two years on this assignment."

"Who brought your husband to the hospital?"

"A man who found him on the road. Mr. Abubakar."

"Do you know how to find him?"

A yawning abyss opened. "I can't think about it right now. I don't know." She stumbled toward Elise and her children.

◆ ◆ ◆

They waited beneath an awning beside the pool while the infants dozed. Isabel didn't feel hungry. She had come because the doctor insisted and she had nothing else to do until midafternoon. She was plagued by the question of passports. A branch extended over their table and appeared to descend of its own will. In a moment, a green chameleon made its slow way down the branch and onto the tablecloth. He was a young one, perhaps ten inches long, nose to tail.

"I'll remove it," Elise said.

"No. Let it be." Isabel watched as the reptile moved one leg and then the other, its eyes rotating, its tail a curl. In amazement, she observed its color lighten to pale yellow. The French fries and hamburgers came. Suddenly she was starving. As she and Elise ate, the chameleon made his slow journey across the table. Isabel dipped her finger in her water glass and tried to get the creature to drink. He climbed atop her finger and onto her hand. The prick of his claws sent a delightful tickle up her arm and over her scalp. He looked at her with his protruding eyes, dark orbs rimmed with multiple lids, colors moving from yellow to orange to aqua. She laughed. "I must get one of these and keep it at home." Chameleons were ancient creatures, surviving eons. If she were a flower, she could welcome him into her bower. Her thought-rhyme delighted her, and she recalled the portrait she had made of herself. Yes, she liked it. The last evidence of her life before she was split into two or three or four. It was hard to know how many. She was an orange with a dozen segments. Isabel wondered if a chameleon could be the hand of God. The creature had given her her first relief in days. A group of rowdy children ran past their table. She placed the reptile again on the limb but higher up. Suddenly she remembered Daniel. "Elise, we must send word to Daniel. Now that we know Nick is mending."

"I've already done so," Elise said.

Isabel thought ever so briefly of Bobby Tunde and his mother.

They were preparing to leave when Rebecca Ferguson, who had toured old Zaria with Isabel, arrived and spotted them. She rushed over.

"You poor girl. How are you holding up?" She pulled up a chair, hardly acknowledging Elise except with a tip of her head. She clasped Isabel's hands. "You must be worried to death."

Isabel bristled at the effusive claims of concern. The chameleon had seemed kinder than this jarring woman. *You might have come to the hospital. It's been a week.* Vaguely she remembered someone named Tessa coming and perhaps Alisa, both related somehow to the Agency. But not Rebecca. Isabel applied her napkin to her lips. "You remember Elise, from the garden party? She's been my constant companion. Nick's been squeezing my hand so much, it's about to fall off." With that, she hoped to be free of Rebecca. But no.

"Wherever have they put you?"

"I'm at the nicest chalet. Elise is staying with me."

"But look at you. It's not any good for you to be out in such heat."

What did she mean, *look at you*? Isabel's hair had come out nicely this morning, and she looked rather well considering her husband had just about been crushed to death and she had given birth only weeks ago. "Our summers in Virginia were much hotter than this. My grandmother worked her garden and kept her babies in boxes by the field when they were small and stopped to nurse them under the pecan tree. But what are you doing in Kaduna?"

Rebecca looked momentarily stumped. "Paul has some business. I talked him into a long weekend. Zaria is already parched."

"I would ask you to join us, but we're just finishing," Isabel said. She smiled at Elise.

"There must be something I can do for you," Rebecca said.

"I'll let you know if I think of something," Isabel said. She looked back at the limb where she had placed the chameleon, but she didn't see him. *Good. Stay hidden.*

♦ ♦ ♦

From the Swim Club, Isabel, Elise, and the twins headed to the telegraph office. The roadside was thick with walkers, many stopping to look at the girls and comment. "Ah, Mama, you have done well," Isabel heard over and over. She glowed in her reproductive power.

The telegraph office sat adjacent to a three-story, concrete-brick building, but because it had been constructed when mud and plaster were common, it was ten degrees cooler than the street. A calendar ornamented the wall, with an image of a man at a table with tubes and glass cylinders and the legend, VACCINE PRODUCTION. Isabel hadn't wanted to send a telegraph to Nick's parents before she had something good to report. The last letter, sent less than three weeks ago, had announced the birth of their twins. Now she wrote, *NICK IN CAR ACCIDENT. EXCELLENT CARE. PROGRESSING WELL. YRS. ISABEL.*

Somewhere out in the bush, their passports were being picked up. They were being nudged under a woman's mangos. Or a bird was tearing out the pages for a nest. Or someone was rolling the pages into wands and lighting the ends to start a fire.

♦ ♦ ♦

Back at the hospital, Isabel walked into her husband's room to see his head elevated and his eyes wide open. He looked at her with recognition and offered a weak smile. "Isabel," he said.

Her heart brimmed over. All else forgotten, she moved to him, carefully touched his forehead with her fingertips, kissed his abraded cheek, leaned back, and peered into his eyes. "Thank God," she said. "Oh, Nick." Tears poured down her cheeks. He raised a hand to wipe them. She clutched his hand and held it. "How do you feel?"

"Sore," he said, and tried to smile again.

"I've been so worried about you."

"I'll be home in no time."

"You must be patient."

"I don't have much choice."

"Do you remember anything?"

"Nothing."

"It doesn't matter. Don't worry."

He closed his eyes again.

She sat beside him for a good while until Dr. Meyers appeared. He was all business.

"Go home, Mrs. Hammond. Your husband is out of danger. I cannot say exactly when he will be mended, but he will mend. There's no need for you to be here in Kaduna. In fact, Mr. Hammond will do better with less stimulation."

Isabel looked at Nick, still in two casts and a back brace, the skin graft angry and red. The entire day of that disastrous trip was stripped from his memory. But not from hers. She saw it repeatedly. Nick getting into the car, turning to wave back at her, his sunglasses, his hair blowing up like a wing.

♦ ♦ ♦

Back home in Kufana, pieces of Isabel seemed to slough away. She weighed less than she had when she got pregnant even though her breasts were twice their normal size. She was just so tired. As soon as Catherine slept, Sarah woke. As soon as one nursed, the other demanded the same. Twice a week, she gathered the girls and Elise drove them to visit Nick. By the fourth visit, he seemed to look younger, somehow, more innocent, while Isabel felt ancient and porous. Her breasts leaked; she still bled. Nick spoke to the girls but couldn't show them much affection.

After each trip, Isabel came back to Kufana more exhausted. If

their passports weren't under a woman's mangos or burned or softening a nest, perhaps they had been crushed in the metal. It hurt
her to think of that, as if their lives had been canceled. Or perhaps
some passerby had found the leather folio and taken it to sell. She
wondered if she and Nick really existed in this country if they didn't
have official papers. And what about the girls? They couldn't obtain
official birth certificates without their parents' passports.

Elise plied Isabel with cake: coconut cake, chocolate cake, fruit
cake.

And then Isabel's stools were off. They came in hard pellets.

Kufana

✦✦✦✦✦

Early November

Three weeks after Nick's accident, the Sarki called for a report on his bature man. Fortunately, the girls were asleep. Isabel invited him in while his escort sat on the porch. She asked him to take a seat. In a moment, she placed an unopened Coca-Cola and a glass in front of him. He gestured for her to open it. Isabel heard the back screen door open and shut. Daniel must have been watering the garden with the dishwater.

The chief smoothed out his white robe. He sipped his drink and listened to Isabel's report on Nick's progress, how miraculous it all was, how his head was healing and he would be home soon, though Isabel was conjuring Nick in Virginia when he was perfect, unscathed, standing on the front steps of her family home in Oregon Hills that snowy Thanksgiving.

"Your husband's bones must sit quietly like a cat," the chief said. "They will become stronger than before."

It occurred to Isabel that this wise man might know how to find the missing folio. The pink that had escaped a sewing machine in her dream vision floated at the edge of her perception, and she saw the passports hovering somewhere outside Kufana.

"Ah," the chief said when she told him about their disappearance. "I will alert my people. We will find your passports. After all, nothing disappears. Not even your husband."

Isabel looked up to see a young child on the other side of her front window, hands cupped around his face, looking in.

"Is that one of your children?" she said.

"Yes. That one is Rahman. It means kind. He is always concerned for me." The chief stood and nodded his head. "He is the one who received the camera you gave me."

"Ah." Isabel rose to open the door.

"I will return with your papers," the chief said as he left.

Isabel waved at the boy, whose face was open as a hibiscus bloom at midday. She recalled a painting she had made of a pink dogwood in Oregon Hills, the four-petaled flowers open like hands. A stream of joy had passed through her when she showed Angelica and she had said, "You are a true artist, Isabel." She hoped her gift had helped the boy in some small way.

When the infants were a month old and Nick was still in Kaduna and Daniel on his afternoon break, Isabel opened her door to see Bobby Tunde, the actual man, standing before her. He wore a sky blue Nehru suit and a tight, round, yellow cap. Across the way sat a car with a driver. Bobby had stepped across her yard in his lovely shoes, and she hadn't heard the motor.

"I felt someone calling me. I thought it might be you," he said.

The man in front of her was more beautiful than she remembered. His voice reverberated under her tongue. She extended her arm across the doorway, meaning to block his entry or fasten her heart. "It was not I," she said.

"I learned about your husband's accident. Soon he will return to you. It is not his voice I heard." Bobby looked like a man who had already been in her house, and Isabel supposed that he had been, given how often he was in her mind. Her eyes went to the damaged place above one eye. She meant to be stern and unyielding. After all, her infidelity had led to misfortune, and he was her coconspirator. "How is your mother?" She would at least be polite.

"You remembered." He sounded happy as a boy. "Health has returned to her."

Against her strong intentions, Isabel saw a mauve windowsill lodged high in a baobab tree. Her defenses fell. She withdrew her arm from the doorframe. "My friend, Elise, is in the sunroom with the babies. Since you have come all this way, I must invite you in."

His eyes lit up. "You have children? Ah! Before you had none. Now you have at least two? They must be hatchlings." For a moment, Isabel saw that shimmer on his skin. He might be famous, but he was not damaged by it. His humanity seemed almost a liquid element.

"We are thriving on milk and cake," she said, surprised by his

swift calculation and her delight. How fortunate that she had told
Elise about Bobby. "Would you like to see them? The children, not
the cakes. I have eaten all the cakes." She had not said anything witty
in weeks. Now here she was, liking herself better. They moved to the
sunroom. Bobby nodded at Elise and then crossed to the bassinette
and looked down at the infants. Wind billowed the curtains. A dove
coo-cooed. Tunde placed his hand lightly on Catherine's back. He
stroked her hair, her cheek, her tiny eyebrow. It felt good to have
him in the room. Isabel wondered about herself, how she could contain such contradiction: Nick, Tunde. She was some species of chameleon herself.

Catherine's eyelids fluttered as Bobby massaged her head. "Even
she knows," he said.

"What's that?" Isabel said.

"It was her voice I heard. She is my child. You can see."

Isabel was too stunned to speak. "They're twins," she said at
last. "So I'm afraid that's impossible." She started hiccupping, then
coughing. She moved to the kitchen and poured a glass of water.
Her heart beat high in her chest. She rapped lightly on the drain
board as she drank the water. Who was this enigmatic man, tender
yet taut as a guitar string, stalking her in Kaduna? She sensed not
only her heart but also his heart beating. She must not let him throw
her off. Look what had happened to Nick.

"It's not impossible," Elise said, from her corner of the sunroom.

For a wild moment, Isabel detested her friend's frowsy knowing-
ness. She moved back to the sunroom as milk rose in her breasts.
The light shifted, and the shadow of a tree branch netted the interior wall. Isabel steadied herself, clasping the edge of the table.
She had dreamed of Bobby Tunde, but not in her house. Her eyes
burned. *I must make this man leave. I must get him out of my house.*
She raised her head. "I don't know why you came, Mr. Tunde. You've
disturbed me. Isn't it enough that my husband was nearly killed in
an automobile accident? Now you want to make up some story
about what? Your paternity? Do you want to write another song? Is
that why you've come?" She had not meant to say all of that. It just
came out.

"I'm sorry to have disturbed you. You know I would not harm you. Yet the child has called me. This summoning is one a father cannot refuse." The intensity in his eyes conveyed his sympathy. Yet he was unmoving as a mile marker on the road.

Isabel turned to the girls. She stared at Sarah, her cheek pale as the interiors of shells, and then at Catherine, whose skin was like lamplight, her dark hair curled more tightly than her own. She would not believe him. Her life was already impossibly complicated. Tunde looked at her for a long moment. A clamor of alarm rose in Isabel's head.

Elise rose and came to Isabel and placed a hand on her arm. "Let me get some drinks."

The three of them sat in the living room.

"Fraternal twins can have two fathers," Elise said. "I had already thought of it when I saw them, and especially over the last week as Catherine's skin has darkened a shade. And because of what you told me earlier. It's rare but it happens."

"My father is Sicilian. His skin is as dark as Mr. Tunde's is. I inherited his dark curly hair." Isabel pulled out a strand and let it spring back. "Catherine's skin is like mine. Just because something is possible doesn't make it so. I thought you were my friend."

"I'm only offering my observation, Isabel. I could be wrong."

"And you have said nothing before, why?"

"I thought you might discover it yourself."

"How exactly do twins have two fathers?"

"Do you want me to describe that to you right this minute?"

Isabel stretched an arm toward the center of the room and looked at Tunde, to entreat him, to beg if necessary. "You have other children?"

"Yes."

"And you can't leave this one to me?"

"She summoned me. I must respond. Among other things, I must give her a name."

"She has a name. It's Catherine Archer."

"She must have a Yoruba name as well. She is a daughter of the soil. Even my mother accepted this truth. It is why I am."

"Why you are what?"

"Myself."

Isabel stood up. Tunde also rose. The room darkened. A long wire of lightning appeared far off beyond the front window. Rain in November was rare. Apparently, rain accompanied this musician. The wind increased. Isabel began walking through the rooms, closing the louvers. She paused in the storeroom where the windowsill appeared oddly pink. When she returned to the living room, Tunde and Elise were waiting for her. Again she sat. What would Nick say if he were here? Tears started in her eyes, and she buried her face in her hands. No one came to comfort her, and no one asked her not to cry. The smell of rain was present now and underneath it, she smelled the Ivory soap she had used to wash her hands and beneath that the smell of water in her own skin. Her crying ceased but she continued to take in her watery smell. There was a deep comfort in it for it connected her with the earth itself, Matsirga Falls, water in the bucket placed in the garden overnight to pour over plants later in the week, water pouring down the faces of children in their compounds even now.

She lowered her hands. She had heard of other expat American children being given Nigerian names as an honorific. "I suppose it can't hurt for Catherine to have a Yoruba name," she said. "But she's my child. She cannot be taken from me."

"I would not take a child from her mother. I came because she called. Every child must be blessed in the appropriate manner. As she grows up, you must tell her she is a child of this place. Her father lives here. Otherwise, she will float in the world like a ghost."

If Nick were here, he would boot this man out. How stupid she had been. "All of this—your coming here—is just between us, the three of us," she said.

"No. It is between four of us because the child is included." Tunde's voice was magisterial, and again Isabel felt the power of his attraction. He could have been a prophet.

Isabel looked from him to her watch. Daniel would be back to prepare the evening meal in an hour. The girls would want to nurse.

"Do you have a name then?"

"I will have three. But not today. Now that I have seen her, I must reflect. Whatever her road in life, she must have a good name, not one pulled out of a bag. I will return tomorrow."

"Not tomorrow. I will be in Kaduna, visiting my husband. The girls will be with me."

"Very well, the day following."

"If I agree to that, you must agree not to come here again." She meant what she said though it hurt her to say it. Her thought turned. Maybe he could come occasionally, greet the twins, and be a friend to the family, a friend she need not fear. There was peace in that thought.

"I will not upend your life. Whether I see my daughter, God will decide. You know, Isabel, the only constant in life is change." He kissed her hand.

When he left, Isabel still felt his presence in the billowing curtain. He was movement, like the wind, but he was also fire. Now that she was safely out of his presence, she felt intensely how he spoke to her, body and soul. She knew that eventually she would long to have him back, privately, for a moment, for a single touch.

◆ ◆ ◆

The rain stopped and the sun came out. Daniel returned to fix the evening meal. Late in the afternoon, Elise bathed the girls. Isabel sat in Daniel's chair under the overhang of the roof. Was that a civet cat at the opening in the hedge? She held still, squinting her eyes, trying all sorts of ways to pin the animal with her sight. It was half-way in shadow, half in sun. Did it have the telltale spots? She wasn't sure, though she could make out a large tail. Then it slunk beneath the hedge and crouched. What else could it be? It was too large for a regular cat. Was it a mother? Did it have babies somewhere? Or was it Tunde's spirit, come back to inhabit her world? Now it was just a dark shape. Isabel rested her eyes. When she opened them, the animal was gone.

In a deep wordless place in herself, Isabel had known Catherine wasn't Nick's. This was why she could not throw away the silver band. Would Tunde keep his word? *I will not upend your life.*

She needed to believe him, or she would never feel safe. It was one
thing to be pregnant, quite another to learn she was in the process
of giving birth to twins. Now she knew with certainty—yes, she was
now certain—that one of her children had a Nigerian father, or a
Nigerian-British father. Isabel crossed her arms in front of her and
held onto her elbows. What was her prayer? *In everything give thanks,
for this is the will of God.* Was it God's will that she had lain with
Bobby to create Catherine? Or that she came home and slept with
her husband hours later? She recalled her sense of twoness at the
Kagoro Hills. How naive she had been, imagining it was only herself,
a new adventurous Isabel who was going to paint again. Instead, she
had literally tripled, and now two new beings occupied the world
and one of them came from the betrayal of her marriage. She hardly
had time to paint.

Isabel pulled up her dark curls and felt the wind on her neck. A
fragment of prayer came to her. *We have not loved you with our whole
heart; we have not loved our neighbors as ourselves. Forgive us, renew
us.* Was Catherine the mending of some ancient separation? Wasn't
that a little lofty? *We have sinned against you in thought, word, and
deed.* She supposed she was an adulterer, but surely she was not
merely that. *By what we have done and by what we have left undone.*
She had conveniently forgotten that part. Left undone was a confession to her husband. The impossibility of that, the crime it would be
to tell him, just to ease her pain, meant she was permanently alone.
Before her, the lemon tree reached upward, the plant that symbolized commitment and fidelity. Indoors, the dancing woman waited.

◆ ◆ ◆

Isabel asked Daniel about his Tiv names.

"Boseda Terhemba," he said.

"What do they mean?"

"The first means born on a Sunday. The second means God is
supreme."

"Very beautiful. And do they help you?"

"My name is my holy of holies."

"Daniel. Born on a Sunday. The Lord exceeds. You are very fortunate." Isabel gazed upon her girls, Sarah trying to get her right hand into contact with her left foot, Catherine pressing her entire fist into her mouth. Was there a Yoruba name for Catherine that meant, "She will taste the earth?" Perhaps one even for Sarah that meant, "She will meet the challenge?"

Kaduna

· · · · ·

November 1963

On the next visit, Isabel found Nick propped awkwardly like a praying mantis on its back, but his eyes sparkled. She clasped his hand. An internal fog seemed to have broken. The skin graft on his forearm looked tamer than last time. A month and a day had passed since the accident, six weeks since Sarah's and Catherine's births. The two-year anniversary of their USAID contract had rolled around, and their renewal request had been granted. Still, Isabel suspected that if Nick couldn't return to work full-time, they might be sent home on leave. The hospital room was air-conditioned. She pulled on a sweater. "Would you like to hold them?"

Nick looked doubtful.

"I can wedge pillows around them." Isabel propped Sarah close to her father. The infant tried to focus her eyes, and they grew large when a wand of cool air hit her forehead. Nick and Isabel laughed, and that felt good. Next, she lifted Catherine from the pram and wedged her into the crook of Nick's elbow. She looked like a baby owl safe in a nest. "Has Dr. Myers given you a date for coming home?"

"He thinks I can move to the Lindermans' in a week. There's an elevator in their building. Home two weeks later if I'm lucky."

Isabel's eyes brimmed with tears and spilled down her cheek. "I've been so afraid."

"I know. But we're all going to be fine."

Sarah whimpered. Isabel picked her up and bounced her lightly. "Daniel is anxious to have you back." She herself needed him back, to keep her focused on her marriage.

"Tell him I'll be there soon."

Catherine's eyes lifted at Nick's voice. Then she moved her head and snuggled down even tighter into the V of his unbroken arm. Had Isabel imagined that Bobby Tunde came to her house and declared Catherine was his? Surely she had because here she sat with her husband and children in the hum of the air-conditioning like a family in a snow globe, complete and untouchable. Nick shifted slightly and knotted his eyebrows.

"What?" Isabel said.

"Is this our baby?" He nodded toward Catherine.

Isabel felt a strike to her heart.

"Of course she is." She pressed Sarah too tightly against her breast, and the little girl cried in alarm.

"I just wondered," Nick's voice rose over Sarah's cry. "She's very calm, given how bold and passionate her mother is." He grinned at Isabel.

"Things are going to be different now. I can't go traipsing off."

"But I like your traipsing. You come home stirred up."

"I only meant." A shiver ran up Isabel's arms. If only Nick had spoken such sentences before her dalliance, seen her life's mission as enlivening and essential, equal to his own.

"You're cold. Call the nurse. She'll turn the air-conditioning off and open the windows. I like hearing the horns blaring. Don't you?" Nick smiled more broadly at his second joke. Neither of them understood why Nigerian drivers used their horns so much.

Isabel felt something tacit pass between them. Could it be that he knew, that he understood that she had been unfaithful and was telling her he loved her anyway?

"Yes." She smiled. "I'll be right back." How glorious it would be if she could know that he apprehended how she had, for an hour, stepped out of their marriage. At least suspected. And that he had already decided to forgive her. Rectangles of light fell through the windows and illuminated dust motes in the air. She had almost lost a husband, but he would live. If only her illicit affair would not count against her. She wanted safety. Then she could do normal things: carry the girls to Elise's dispensary for an afternoon, visit again with Amina in the yard and eat plantain. She could paint. She could talk further with Daniel about *Kwaghalom*, the rabbit stories, and how large groups of Tiv folk gathered around the fire in the full moon telling them. "They must be linked to Brer Rabbit," she had said to him.

She returned with the nurse, her secret lodged in her like a bullet.

Of course, Isabel had no time to paint at present. When Dr. Meyers came, she had some minutes in the hallway, and as the girls were asleep, she pulled out her notebook. From memory, she sketched the meadowlark's nest as she had seen it years ago, the woven grass tightly fitted and snug in the ground, the dappled eggs so vulnerable, grass growing up around the nest, some canopying over it. She must hold that nest.

◆ ◆ ◆

Home in Kufana that evening, little Catherine started crying and would not be soothed. Isabel picked her up, and the child wailed. "Oh, my darling. You're warm." She crushed half a baby aspirin, added sugar to a tablespoon of hot water, and fed it to her daughter. In thirty minutes, Catherine had settled. Isabel put her down, but she could not sleep. At last she did, only to wake to Catherine's cries. It was seven a.m., the sun fully up. As soon as she picked up her daughter, she knew the fever had spiked. Sarah began to whimper. The back door opened and closed. Daniel had arrived. Isabel set Catherine down, pulled on a dress, and flew to the kitchen. "Thank goodness you're here. Please boil eggs and pack them with bread and bananas. Catherine has a fever. I have to get her to Kaduna."

"You have told me a visitor is coming."

She stared at him. Bobby Tunde! "I forgot. I have to take care of my daughter."

"You do not have a vehicle."

Heaven help me. Nick's crushed body in that bed when she first saw him, her guilt over what she had done, the impossibility of setting things straight, all of it raked through her.

And suddenly, there was Tunde, standing in her living room.

"Do you have need of a lift?"

"Yes. Thank God. Catherine has a fever. Can you carry us to Kaduna?"

"Of course. We are leaving now. Find the other child."

Isabel scooped Sarah up without changing her and handed her to Tunde. "We'll put her in the bassinette. I'll carry Catherine. We must find Dr. Eli. Hurry."

She looked back at Daniel. "Pray for us."

In the car, Tunde kept his hand on the stick shift. Isabel held Catherine in her lap and placed a hand on his, as if somehow this connection would return health and well-being to the child of their union. She did need this man. He alone knew everything.

Dry vegetation lined the road. Here and there, Isabel spotted huge anthills. Women walked on the shoulder carrying firewood. A man stood casually under a tree with a long pole. Something hung from it. An enormous dead bush rat. Isabel closed her eyes.

"Do you pray?" she said.

"Of course. I am praying now."

"What are you praying?"

"I don't use words."

"Then what?"

"I imagine Catherine sitting in the sun. I picture her face when she learns to read music."

"Good."

Catherine fussed, trying to get a hand to her mouth. That seemed hopeful.

♦ ♦ ♦

At the clinic, Isabel cradled Catherine like her own heart. Dr. Eli entered the private room. He took the child from her. A young doctor with a bright face, he looked into Catherine's eyes and ears, placed a stethoscope to her heart, and pressed her abdomen. Isabel didn't know if he was Hausa or not. He exuded pure goodness, as Jesus must have.

"Has she had chills?"

"I don't think so."

"It's not malaria then. It could be an infection. We'll give her penicillin and watch her. Your other daughter is in the adjoining room." He placed Catherine in a child's bed with high metal rails, then steered Isabel toward the door. She opened it to the room where Sarah lay sleeping in a similar crib. Dr. Eli pointed to a day bed. "Give yourself a rest."

Isabel slept. She woke, tiptoed to the adjoining room, and checked on Catherine. The girl no longer felt so hot. In her bare feet, Isabel left the room and padded down the hall. She found a young girl in a blue uniform. "Is there coffee?" The girl led her to a large, open area with a kitchenette and a few toys: a rocking horse and building blocks. The girl showed her the teakettle, Nescafé, and sugar cubes. "Biscuits are here." She opened a tin full of malted crackers.

"Thank you."

Waiting for the water to boil, Isabel gazed out the window. Schoolchildren in brown uniforms filled a courtyard. A large hardwood tree reigned over them like an umbrella of the gods. Girls held hands. Boys kicked a ball. With her coffee, she slipped back to Catherine's room. The girl stirred. Isabel sat beside her, praying. She had never prayed so sincerely before. *Make her well. I'll do anything.*

♦ ♦ ♦

Midafternoon, Dr. Eli returned. "No more fever. Luckily, your other daughter has no symptoms. But we don't want to take any chances. You will stay with us tonight."

"I think that's a good idea."

"I can't help but notice," Eli said, "how different these two look."

Isabel felt like a slot machine with gadgets whirring and stirring, and who knew what might pop up next? She cleared her throat. "They have very distinct personalities. Isn't it contrast that makes anything beautiful? Like the inselbergs that arise from the green plains in this region, every one different from the other? My father was Italian. My husband's family is Irish."

"Beautiful," Dr. Eli said. "I love family stories. Europe is so fascinating. All of those tribes."

Isabel had never imagined European nations as tribes, but Dr. Eli was exactly right. And he had just explained everything in her favor. She and her husband were a tribe of Irish and Italians. Nick would be well and come home and their family life would begin. Only two more weeks. Right now, she should search out a telephone and ring Mary Linderman to ask if she might bring supper. Back in the hallway, turning a corner, Isabel found Tunde slumped in a chair. It appeared he had sat there all day. He was surrounded by covered enamel bowls and several bottled drinks: Coca-Cola, Fanta, and Sprite. "What's all this?" she said.

"A few of my fans found me. They are plying me with food." He looked chagrined.

"You didn't speak of a daughter?"

"I said I was visiting a friend. The truth. Yes?"

A little hope started in Isabel's center. She remembered how this man had delighted her, how his poetry had drawn her in, how he prayed. He had shown up at just the right moment to help them, and in that moment, she thought, *Yes, yes, we share this child.*

Bobby Tunde looked up at her.

"Catherine is fine," Isabel said. "She's going to be fine."

He stood and took his hat off and ran a hand back and forth across his head. His hair had grown since they first met and little ringlets framed his forehead. He looked into her eyes. "Isabel," he said. "How will you return home?"

"I can call the Lindermans. You don't need to stay."

"Very well. I will find you at home two days from now."

He looked sad as he lifted her hand and kissed it. Then light came back into his eyes. "You are a bowl collecting water in the rainy season. You will never be empty." His coat glinted like silver foil as he stepped out of the hospital and into the sun.

◆ ◆ ◆

Mary Linderman brought chicken and dumplings for Isabel's dinner. She had never been so grateful for a meal. A young Nigerian girl was with her, carrying a container of lemonade on her head. The girl was curious about Sarah and her light hair. "What's your name?" Isabel asked. "Oma," she replied, touching the downy wisps on Sarah's head. As Mary was about to leave, she pulled two Raggedy Ann dolls from her large bag. "For your girls," she said. Isabel laughed and took them. They looked so absurd in this country, like little clowns.

Kufana

✦✦✦✦✦

November 1963

As promised, Tunde called on Friday afternoon, carrying a leather satchel. This time he wore a traditional Yoruba agbada: a tunic with embroidery around the neck, voluminous sleeves, and loose trousers. He matched it with a jaunty cap that featured two upward flaps on either side, like perky dogs' ears. Isabel had determined to be disinterested, but the cap was too amusing, especially with the ringlets of hair peeping out. She felt her warmth for him return.

"Mr. Tunde," she said, gesturing with her arm to let him in. Elise was in the kitchen preparing tea. Clothed in tiny smocked dresses that had come from the U.S., the twins lay on the sofa, bolstered with pillows. Tunde moved to Catherine. He rubbed her head.

"Don't let me catch you causing more trouble for your mother." He looked at Isabel. "Where will we have the ceremony?"

"Ceremony?"

"Of course. We don't spit out names at our children and hope they will catch, Madam. How long have you been in this country?"

He was enjoying the performance, not that he wasn't also deadly serious about names. Isabel added to his possible career paths: dramatist. "Two years, thank you. But I have not attended any Yoruba naming ceremonies." She hoped she didn't sound too lighthearted. She must control her emotions around this man.

"Today is a new day. We can hold the ceremony in this room." Tunde cinched his robe from behind, pulled the bulk of fabric around front, crossed his feet, and nimbly brought himself to sitting on the floor. He opened the bag and pulled out a richly embroidered, gold cloth. "Please, Mrs. Hammond, bring Catherine."

"Are we having tea?" Elise stood at the doorway.

"Ah, Mrs. Van Dijk. We will celebrate after the naming."

Sarah began to fuss. Isabel handed her to Elise. She brought Catherine to Tunde, who had added several layers of bunched white cotton to the embroidered, gold cloth. He placed Catherine there like a crown. The child looked up at him and kicked her feet. From the corner of her eye, Isabel saw Daniel watching from the door of the kitchen. She had explained to him that Tunde was in Kaduna and when she ran into him and told him about the girls, he had offered to give them Yoruba names, as was the custom even for bature children born in Nigeria. Daniel didn't seem surprised. Rather, he seemed happy that he might meet Tunde. "Come," Isabel motioned. Daniel stepped forward, leaning a bit shyly to one side, still holding a dish towel.

"Bobby Tunde," she said. The man looked up. "Please meet Daniel Nenge. He manages the house for us. Daniel Nenge, please meet Bobby Tunde."

Daniel bowed. Bobby kept a hand on Catherine and nodded in response.

"You are welcome," Daniel said.

"I'm glad to know you're here helping Mrs. Hammond."

"Your music is very fine-o."

"We thank God," Tunde said. "Please join us."

The ceremony began. Tunde held up a pound note and waved it in front of Catherine. She appeared to observe the motion but didn't reach for it. "Ah, Mrs. Hammond, she will not be wealthy. Let us hope for other blessings." He opened a small jar. "This is only water." He dabbed Catherine's face with it, and she made little fists and raised her arms. "It is the cleansing force of life. You see, she likes it." From a small pouch, he pulled out another bottle. "This oil will help her in times of turbulence." *Turbulence, that word.* Tunde pressed a small amount onto Catherine's forehead. "I will leave the kola nut rather than feed it to her as I can guess she will not like it and you, Mrs. Hammond, will worry over germs. But the kola nut must make its appearance. For good health." Tunde leaned over the child and after some time, he sat back.

"But what about the names?" Isabel said. As he turned to her, the shimmer returned.

"I have told her."

"Yes. Well, tell her mother."

"As second-born twin, she must be Kehinde. Even so, she is considered the senior because Taiwo, the name belonging to Sarah, went out first and cried for Kehinde, who quickly followed and then took the lead. This child will be attached to the earth, while Sarah will reach for the sky. The second name is Funmilayo. It means 'she brings joy.' Kehinde Funmilayo."

"It's fitting," Elise said.

"But the most important is her oriki name," Tunde said.

"What is that?"

"The name only her senior family members may call her by. It is a name of endearment. When a parent calls a child by her oriki name, she knows she is loved."

"And what is this name for this child?" Isabel said, wondering why Americans didn't have such names for their children, what it might have been like to have had one, whether her life might have been different if she had had an oriki name in Virginia. And whether Daniel might glean that Tunde was the parent here.

"Aduke," Tunde said. "It means someone intensely loved. Loved like a waterfall."

Catherine looked golden. She gazed up at Tunde and blinked. Isabel felt a tide flow over her. Tunde sat back on his haunches.

"And now the other child," he said.

There was a clatter in the back of the house. Daniel stood. "Ah, Mrs. Hammond, the water for stewing chicken is boiling over." He hastened to the kitchen.

Isabel thought Bobby went a little too quickly through Sarah's naming, but she was also grateful because there was no oriki name for her and Daniel would certainly wonder why. She became Taiwo Ibukun, the second name meaning *blessings*. Oddly enough, when the ceremony was over, the twins seemed more connected than they had been before, as if the ritual had awakened them and they had understood when Tunde said that twins were most revered among children. Each turned her head to the other and whirled her arms.

At the door as he departed, Isabel clasped Bobby's hand. She had not given much thought to his predicament. What did it mean to be father to a daughter who was twin to an American child, and whom he could not speak to as a daughter, at least not now and not for many years, if ever? Like a series of lamps illuminating long library tables, she dimly perceived a future in which Tunde and Catherine leaned over a book, walked down a road, sat at a piano. It would only be fair for Catherine to know the truth at some point. Then Isabel thought of Tunde's wife, petite, no doubt attractive, in high heels and carrying a black pocketbook and wearing gold jewelry. At the moment, though, Isabel was on a craggy bluff, her feet ill shod, trying to hold a world together. She could not think too long on these things. "Thank you."

"You are welcome,"

Just as she heard his car drive away, Isabel saw the man's perky dog-ear cap on a side table. She lifted it to her lips as if she might drink from it before she saw the slip of blue paper. He had left his address. She touched her hair, recalling the lost garnet clip. She would never find it. She looked up to see Elise watching her.

"He's a lovely man," Isabel said.

When she put the girls to bed that night and sat on the floor beside them in the dim light, she felt that bliss that sometimes came to her, a euphoric feeling of having no boundaries, of being a crossroads through which all time flowed.

Kufana

•••••

November 1963

That evening, with Daniel long gone, the electricity went out. The girls were asleep. In the bedroom, Isabel lit a kerosene lamp and turned on Nick's battery-powered radio. Static filled the space, and then a voice that sounded like Tunde's but wasn't came in and out. *Burning shops,* she heard, *rioting,* she heard, *thousands... state of emergency in the West.* The Western Region was south of Kaduna, below the Niger, where Tunde lived. *Premier of the Western Region . . . Awolowo, guilty of treason,* she heard. *Sentenced to prison . . .*

The danger was not close. Yet what happened in one region always affected the others, and violence could be catching. Nigeria's major regions weren't sealed off like Tupperware containers. Was there anything she should do? Isabel imagined crocodiles bunched in low water on the banks of the Kaduna River. They would outlast everyone. She thought about the work of naming, the ingenuity of Kehinde and Taiwo, the one who arrives second becomes first. What did the name Awolowo mean? Could a different name have shielded him? She had never asked her own husband where his name came from. She burrowed her head in the pillow.

In the morning, she gazed out the window. Everything looked normal. There sat the Peugeot sedan the Agency had supplied until their new Suburban arrived. That particular vehicle was aboard a freighter somewhere in the Atlantic. Last week, she had driven out to one of Nick's projects in order to report back to him. She had spoken with an assistant and taken notes. Where had she put them? The electrical outage and news of the West had scrambled her brain. Daily, her thoughts scattered like paper torn by birds.

Isabel smelled of baby spit-up. Her clothes were a muddle. The bliss of Tunde's visit had evaporated. How had she gone from sexy to dowdy so quickly? She was silly to dream of Bobby Tunde. If he had been interested in her once, he was now only interested in Catherine. That thought would take some getting used to.

The bell at the back door sounded. Daniel was here. She hurried to greet him, to ask about the West. He brought more complete news into the house than the radio delivered. "Awolowo would not make a government with the North. He wants an alliance with the Middle Belt, including my area. He is determined to resist Northern domination. He is falsely accused."

"And what of Kaduna?" This story was getting too close, close enough to start a fire. "Is Kaduna North or Middle Belt?"

"It is between."

That didn't sound reassuring. "Are people worried?" Somewhere Isabel had read about the plague in medieval England, how it crept into towns and once there, spread like wildfire.

"We Tiv are worried as we always are." Daniel flicked the light switch, but the power was still out. Thirty minutes later, he had it going again. Isabel remained on alert.

◆ ◆ ◆

Three days later, Isabel was up and dressed when Daniel arrived. "I am going with Mrs. Van Dijk to Kaduna today," she said. "My husband is being released from the hospital. He will move to the Lindermans' flat to continue convalescing. In two weeks, he can come home."

Daniel turned to acknowledge her. "It is good."

"I have not forgotten your request about nursing school." It seemed important to reassure him in these uncertain times.

"Thank you," he said. He did not smile.

◆ ◆ ◆

Elise arrived, but they took Isabel's car. Once she had snuggled the twins in their bassinette in the back seat of the Peugeot, they were off. The tiered casuarina trees around the Catholic Church offered a singular vision of green as they passed. Coming around a corner at the edge of town, Isabel almost hit a goat standing in the center of the road. She honked. The animal bleated but did not move, and Isabel drove around it. The girls slept.

"That business in the West," Elise said, "it's not good. I only hope something can be worked out, for all those people caught in the middle."

"I haven't heard much more about it. I thought it might have blown over."

"Nothing blows over here. Or anywhere. You know, I was a middle child."

"I did not." Isabel looked briefly at her friend. "I was an only. I longed for a sister."

"Being a middle means you never get your way. You appease the older one and take care of the younger. I came to Nigeria to escape after that awful war. I was also escaping my family. My only regret is leaving my younger brother. He was never the same after the war."

An unwelcome thought came to Isabel. *Did I come here to escape my lack of direction after the blow dealt by the Famous Artist and use Nick's offer because I had no other plan?*

She redirected her brain to Elise. "You and Hugo came."

"Yes. We wanted a new life, and we wished to be useful."

"You have succeeded brilliantly." Isabel adjusted the rearview mirror to catch a glimpse of her sleeping children. Was she useful? To them, yes, but in general?

Suddenly they were in Kaduna. A new banner declaring THE GOOD LIFE claimed pride of place across the windows of Kingsway Department store. Isabel deposited Elise and the girls at the Lindermans'. Ten minutes later, she found her husband practicing ambulation with crutches on a garden path in the hospital compound. The arm cast was off, but the leg cast remained. He looked like an overgrown high schooler learning a new sport, but that was better than the praying mantis or the crumpled tin man she had first seen after the accident. Something in her hesitated, but then he glanced up and saw her and she moved to him and took his face in her hands. The abrasions were largely healed, and his skin glowed from his morning exercise. She kissed him. "I wish you could come home today." She did love him. His eyes were steady and clear. She saw again his essential goodness.

"Me too. But Meyers doesn't think a ride on Nigerian roads is the best remedy for my brain." His smile was a little crooked, and the skin graft shone pink and smooth on his arm.

"Did you hear the news about Awolowo and the West?" she said.

"Of course."

"What do you think?"

"I don't know yet. It's not likely to settle down right away."

"But will it affect us here?"

"I hope not. I'm sorry you've had to worry on your own."

"It's okay." She touched his shoulder. "It's just that the power was out when I heard, and it sounded distressing." She gave his sleeve a gentle tug. "Do we have to check you out?"

"I've already done it."

They walked to the car. Nick folded himself into the passenger seat. They passed the beautiful white, two-storied Lugard Memorial Hall with its arched windows and magnificent blue dome, a Shell station, Barclay's Bank, Bata Shoe Store. Young boys sprinted across the street. Bicyclers wove in and out among the vehicles.

"The world is still here," Nick said. "I'd almost forgotten after six weeks indoors."

At the Lindermans', they found the girls, squirming like ladybugs on their backs. Nick angled his way to them. Isabel stood back and watched. Her husband laid the crutches aside, sat on the divan, and tried to hold back his tears, but he cried in great spasms. Suddenly, Isabel felt exhausted. But she could not lie down now. She still had to hold them together.

♦ ♦ ♦

Back in Kufana while her husband recovered at the Lindermans', Isabel at last felt a rhythm returning to her life. She wrote to her grandmother:

Nick is out of the hospital and will be home soon. I longed for you throughout his ordeal, but I had little to convey but my worry. Forgive me for not writing sooner. We are in the dry season, but the girls don't know that. They grow and flourish like ducklings. From one day to the next, they develop new expressions. You and granddad would laugh to see their funny faces. Remember how we laughed, the two of us, making a tent under the dining table, making faces with a flashlight? I wish I could be with you to help with Thanksgiving. I would do all the work and you and grand-dad could babysit.

She wasn't sure how to ask after their health, if they were mobile and alert.

Are you still doing the daily crossword puzzle? And please tell me you bought that new electric washing machine you mentioned when you wrote in September. Love—

◆ ◆ ◆

One afternoon Isabel and Daniel traveled out to a rabbit farm, leaving the girls with Elise. Isabel never purchased rabbit, but she did purchase fresh bread and eggs. On the way home, she spotted an inselberg. "I'm going to stop. I'd like to do a painting." Isabel now carried paints and paper on any errand. "It won't take long." Daniel took the opportunity to cross the road in search of a snack from a vendor. Isabel spotted a path around the rock and took it, looking for the best perspective. Gaining the other side, she saw a group of women. Behind them stretched a Guinea corn farm. Two-thirds of the field was flattened. The remaining stalks were enormous, three times Isabel's height. She hesitated, thinking she might be trespassing, and just as she was about to retreat, she heard her name. It was Amina calling. She sat on the ground with a number of other women, and Isabel surmised they might have been harvesting. At the moment, their hands worked over something in their large enamel trays. Latifa was with them. She wore a dark blue skirt and white blouse. Her hair was tucked under an ivory scarf dotted with red roses. She looked ready for high school, not a Guinea corn farm.

Isabel noted that her breasts had grown, and something switched in her brain, some concern, something she must come back to.

"Ina kwana," Amina said, standing, shaking out her hands, and adjusting her skirt. She came to Isabel and looked behind her, as if the twins must appear from somewhere. "Baby?"

"Ina kwana," Isabel said. "The babies are home with my friend." She pointed vaguely. A good Nigerian mother would carry one girl in front, the other on her back. "I'm only gone for a short time." She showed a thin distance between fingers. "Latifa. She isn't working in the farm."

"No." Amina seemed to find this quite funny and laughed. Apparently, a good Nigerian mother shielded her daughter from the hardest jobs.

Isabel tried to recall a Hausa word for "wonderful." She came up with "yayi kyau," *nice.*

Daniel stood against the tree and spoke Hausa back and forth with some of the women. "What are they saying?" Isabel said.

"They say you should be speaking better Hausa by now."

"Tell them I agree. I will work harder." Away in the distance, she saw hills. Perhaps they were the beginnings of the Kagoro Hills. She didn't know her geography well enough. But her spirits rose. She cobbled together some English and Hausa, hoping Amina would understand. "Have you walked into those hills?"

No, Amina had not. Yet the hills meant good rain and cool air, so she praised the hills.

Isabel shook her head, trying to loosen an idea from its hidden place in her brain. Then it flew to her, and she spoke it, "I will lift up mine eyes to the hills from whence cometh my help." Amina seemed to catch the gist of her words and agreed, raising her arms. What a lovely connection. Like the dancing woman. Isabel felt bright as a bird, lighter than she had in months. Perhaps the terra-cotta had been made in the hills and a flood had carried her along creek beds until she was at last deposited in Kufana. Isabel pointed to the enamel trays. "What is that?"

"Kayan mata."

"What is it for?"

Amina answered in Hausa, and Daniel translated. "Woman potion, as the one she already gave you, and love medicine."

"Really?" Isabel looked from one to the other speaker. She had thrown her potion away. *Please, God, don't let Amina ask me about it.*

"She says you may have some to try," Daniel said.

Was he about to smile? Isabel blushed. "Na gode. Tell her I'm fine. We've spent too much time now for me to get a painting." She put her arms around Amina. "Barka da rana."

"Okay, bye," Amina said, in her disarming way, as if Isabel was an interesting diversion but not the true business of her life.

At home, Isabel felt cowlike, nursing the girls. Maybe she did need a love potion. Was it possible that Amina was happier than she was in her American life with a Suburban on the way and a faithful husband and a nice home? In the back garden, the lacy strips of old sheeting that Nick had strung for the green beans blew gently in the air, and the lizards on the broken pot seemed to shimmer. Like Tunde. Did she love him? A man she had spent one night with? When he was in her home, she was too distracted and on edge to let herself feel. But there had been that moment in the car when Catherine had a fever and she placed her hand on his and he seemed almost like her twin, the person most like her, the light and dark of them.

◆ ◆ ◆

Isabel woke the next morning to someone knocking at the front door. It was Daniel, who always let himself into the kitchen at the back. He carried a transistor radio in his arms. "Please, Mrs. Hammond," he said, "your president has been killed."

"My president?"

"Yes, madam. Your President Kennedy. He has been shot in the head, in his car in Dal-las, Texas. He is dead by now."

Isabel shook her head sideways as if water blocked her hearing. "You can't mean it." She stepped back from him, looked toward the twins' room, then back at Daniel. She spoke her words slowly. "President Kennedy. Has been shot? He's dead?"

"Yes, madam. One man has killed him. The announcement is on

BBC and Voice of America." Daniel moved through the living room, set the radio on the table in the sunroom, and turned it on. A voice filled the space, repeating everything twice.

"President Johnson took the oath of office on Air Force One at Love Field, following the assassination of President Kennedy in Dallas, Texas, yesterday. He was flanked by Mrs. Kennedy, who was beside her husband in the limo when he was struck by a bullet at twelve thirty central standard time as their motorcade made its way through the streets of Dallas. The former president's casket was on the aircraft. Mrs. Kennedy would not leave without it. We are told that Mrs. Kennedy was still wearing the pink Chanel suit she wore in the motorcade. President Johnson took the oath of office on Air Force One at Love Field" and on and on.

"Oh my God." Isabel leaned against the table. She looked out the window at the bright morning world, and when she brought her eyes back to the room, she was momentarily blinded.

Kufana

◆◆◆◆◆

December 1963

Ten days later, Isabel looked up to see Nick with his crutches in the frame of the front door. "Oh," she said and moved to him, opened the screen door, and embraced him. They breathed together. Isabel felt perfectly, soundly in place. Beyond their yard, the Lindermans' car idled. "Have you dashed the driver?" Nick looked puzzled. "You know, tipped."

"Yes." Nick turned to wave, and the car took off. "Funny how words don't always register right way."

"I still can't believe Kennedy is dead," Isabel said to change the subject.

"I know. I can't either. I keep feeling as if my lung is punctured again."

"Then we mustn't talk about it. Not now." Was any subject safe?

◆ ◆ ◆

Isabel felt the strain of a rearranged household. She had been living with the babies as a family of three with Elise as great-aunt and Daniel as chief associate. Now her husband, still swinging crutches, took up space in the kitchen making coffee when she was cutting up grapefruit. When she was ready to bathe, he was taking a shower. Normally, Elise helped dress the girls, but she was no longer here. One morning as Isabel wrestled Sarah into a frock, Catherine pulled out of her diaper. Nick sat on the bed, legs extended, and pale from his morning exertions. The skin graft on his arm looked bone white. He needed to read a report, he said. Could she look for it in his satchel? And how was she to do that carrying a baby in each arm? She walked into the backyard for air.

Lunchtime approached. For the past several weeks, Isabel had eaten at the counter in the kitchen and worked with Daniel on her Hausa. Now she must go back to the sunroom and a formally set table with her husband. Except that Nick had developed a headache after studying his report, so she sat at the table alone. The girls were already down for a nap. Later she found Nick on the sofa, his recovering leg up on a tim tim, his head against the wall, reading again.

"Isn't that just going to make your headache come back?"

"I have to try."

"Very well. Thirty minutes. That's it," She was becoming a scold.

By the end of the first week, Nick was better at maneuvering. But the headaches continued, and he spent an entire day in bed, curtains closed. On Thursday of the second week, Isabel found him with the twins on the sofa, tickling their stomachs as they wound up their arms, occasionally landing a fist against Nick's cheek. She felt a deep satisfaction watching them.

"I missed the first two months of their lives," he said.

"But you're here now. That's what matters."

"I could have been here the whole time if I hadn't been watching that guinea fowl."

"What do you mean?"

"I mean I wasn't watching the road."

"You remember now?"

"I remember that far."

"You can't blame yourself." *Because I will too.* "There was almost certainly a lorry in your lane. The driver was reckless." She went to him and embraced his shoulders and head, feeling her still-lax belly against his head. "There's no sense reliving it."

"I can't seem to help it. These thoughts just pop into my head. I'm in the Suburban again, and I look up to a blank windshield and then I feel this terrible blow."

Isabel held her husband as the girls kicked and blabbered. At last, she released him and sat on the rug, her back against the sofa. Here they were, the four of them. They remained so for a good while. The girls' kicking lessened. Nick adjusted his position. Out the window, a bicycle bell rang. Isabel rubbed a thumb across her ankle. For the first time, she wondered what might have happened to her if she had been in the car with Nick. Would she have lived? "Do you mind terribly if I go outside to paint? I feel like I'm losing my mind." She ran a hand through her hair. "I thought it was all the worry over the girls and you, but now we're fine and I feel crazier." Nick didn't answer. She turned to him. He was asleep with the babies.

The hibiscus bush on the trellis had grown, creating a bower. She set her easel up there. If only she had the chameleon for her model. Could she remember him well enough? The bulging eyes, the color change. Could she recall the tail? How many claws did the reptile have?

She started with pale leaves. The slightly off-kilter angle of the trellis. Off to the side, one hibiscus flower bloomed. She moved it to fit her composition and brought down a slender limb. There she found the curve of the chameleon's back, the greater curve of his tail, the essential eye, the noncommittal mouth. She had him, reaching out to claim the next branch. Her brush seemed to move of its own accord, inspired by a force beyond her but also part of her. She seemed to vault to a new level of capacity as she added shadow, curvature, texture to animal, leaf, and sky. But who could celebrate with her, or understand? She walked about the yard, ecstasy in her arms. Her chest expanded with her power. The maker of the dancing woman would understand. Isabel carried the painting inside, tiptoed past her family, and entered the extra room. The terra-cotta seemed to be waiting for her. She laid the painting at her feet. Then in a squat, hands clasped, elbows between knees, Isabel lowered her head and sobbed.

◆ ◆ ◆

On Sunday evening with the girls in bed, Isabel sat with Nick in the living room, listening to him talk about the neem forest. She painted her nails as he described how he would plant the next acre. It seemed too large a task to undertake just yet. Isabel thought he should postpone, though he was much better, his speech clear and strong. His gait had improved. "I need to go over there and check on things anyway," he said. "Maybe after Christmas."

She looked up from her nails and at her husband. "It'll be awfully hot. And with the babies."

"I would go alone."

"Oh."

"There's one thing I would like right now."

"What's that?" Isabel imagined he might want lemonade, or an oatmeal cookie, or perhaps a back rub.

"You."

"Me?" She fanned her hands. After nursing and holding the babies all day, she thought she would scream if she had to touch another human being.

"Is it okay for you?"

"I think so." Right now, she had no desire for this large man.

They were tentative as if it were their first time, and Isabel felt raw between her legs. Nick kept asking if she was okay, and she kept saying yes, though really she wasn't. She sensed she might be bleeding but was too self-conscious to stop. Nick hesitated.

"I'm sorry," she said.

"It's okay. I don't want to hurt you."

Isabel felt embarrassed and feared her husband's disappointment. She was slick with sweat, and Nick had a kind of stink about him that she didn't remember from before. One of the girls cried. Revulsed at their failure and relieved, she left the marriage bed.

◆ ◆ ◆

Isabel turned down invitations to Christmas parties. She wanted Nick free of scrutiny until he was fully himself. She made a Christmas tree of casuarina boughs and decorated it with red silk balls her mother had purchased at the five-and-dime and sent with a note, *guaranteed not to break*. "This must be a terrible time for Mrs. Kennedy," Nick said one day at lunch.

"You're right," Isabel said. She had failed to think about the former president's wife and her children. What would they do about Christmas a month after the president's death? There was little she and Nick could do to help them. "We should deliver a gift to Mr. Abubakar who took you to the hospital." Daniel was able to locate

him at the family farm just north of Kaduna. Isabel wasn't sure how
Nigerian networks of communication and discovery worked, but
they seemed to operate better than telephones. On Friday morning,
Nick and Isabel packed up the girls and started out. They found Mr.
Abubakar sitting in front of a spacious, blue house that stood at the
entrance to the family compound. He rose to greet them.

"My friend," he said to Nick. "You are reborn."

"Not quite." Nick smiled almost shyly, and Isabel felt a pang of
love for him.

"Most certainly you are. I saw with my eyes. Your wife has called
you back. Praise God."

In Mr. Abubakar's living room, Nick handed him the box of pawpaws, oranges, and bananas Isabel had selected, covered by a floral
tablecloth she had made with fabric from the U.S. "My wife will love
this," he said. "She is always telling me she needs to go to America to
shop. One day she will succeed in making me take her."

The man served them orange squash in glasses embossed with
green and gold stars. "Everyone has gone to the mosque. I stayed
back to watch a newborn."

"You have a newborn?" Isabel said.

"A newborn calf." He laughed. "Come and see." He led them to
a shed at the center of the compound, beneath a flame tree. In the
stall was the mother and her offspring, fast asleep.

Back in the sitting room, Isabel pondered Mr. Abubakar's life, the
way he spoke of his family, the cunning way he mentioned a newborn, the cows at the center of the compound.

"If you need to take care of the children, please use the guest
room." He showed Isabel a lovely suite behind a curtain. It contained a bed and bedside tables and a settee. The curtains were
pulled, giving the space a cozy appeal. She nursed the girls both at
once and rejoined the men. Still the rest of the family had not returned from the mosque. Isabel turned the twins over to her husband. "I believe I'll lie down a minute." Nick hardly looked up. He
was in deep conversation with Mr. Abubakar. Isabel wasn't sleepy.
She simply wanted a moment to herself. Her life had become so
practical. She missed seeing the world through eyes that perceived

not merely surfaces but what lay beneath. She wanted to paint. Was she trying to escape her life? Or had the dancing woman inspired her to pour out more paint? Was it Nigeria that rekindled her need to hold a brush? Or Bobby Tunde? She wondered if her own mother had had an artist's inclination but had been forced to smother it at the pharmacy cash register. She did sleep after all. In her dream, Nick was digging up the lemon tree, symbol of commitment, and throwing it into the bola.

On the way back to Kufana, Isabel sat in the back seat with the girls, the heat pricking her skin like a fever. What had brought on that horrid dream? She must not put any stock in it. Rather, she must find a time to talk with her husband about assisting Daniel with nursing school. But when they stepped out of the car in their own yard, Nick looked suddenly pale.

"I guess I'm not fully recovered," he said.

"Let me help you in. I'll come back for the girls."

"You must be getting tired of this."

"Now listen here." She took his arm. "You lean on me. We are in this together. I am not going to give up and you aren't either. Meyers said it would take some time."

They spent the next two weeks in seclusion. Isabel mulled over Daniel's request. She didn't have her own money or a bank account to hand over to him. Nick handled all their finances. Paul Ferguson had given her cash to spend while Nick was in the hospital. She would inherit thirty acres of her grandparents' land. Perhaps they would sell five acres now and send her the money. But wouldn't they be miffed? They had loved her so bountifully. What right did she have to ask for more? She tapped a pencil against her head. Why was she so keen to pay for Daniel's schooling? Was she hoping to gain grace in the moral universe where she hung in limbo because of her infidelity? Or because she thought it would make up for all the times he'd been at their beck and call?

One afternoon, she waited for Daniel to finish watering the back-yard plants. He had his method: a Dutch Baby milk powder tin full for each hibiscus in the ground, two tins full for the lemon tree, a smaller amount for caladiums in pots. The croton and bougainvillea were left to survive on their own. Finally, he set the tin down by the tap and entered the kitchen.

"May I ask you something?" she said.

"Yes."

"If you had the money for nursing school, when would you begin?"

"Ah."

"I don't have a contribution yet. I'm trying to understand."

"I can begin when you go on leave."

"That will be two years from now."

"I am building my own fund. Bit by bit. If you can help me by that time, I will be ready." He smiled, and there was no worry in his brow.

Now she had to find some money.

◆ ◆ ◆

The next morning, the harmattan dust was so great, Isabel could hardly see out the front door. She set about closing the northern-facing windows. This dust coming off the Sahara had been arriving for eons, bringing cool temperatures and foreshortening the horizon. It suddenly occurred to Isabel that the dancing woman might have to do with seasons. She moved to the spare room and looked in on her. Was it her imagination, or had the figure been moved just a bit to the right? Had Daniel done this? Perhaps the figure was turned in various directions depending on time of year. Isabel peered out the sunroom windows toward the lane beyond the hedge. She could barely make out the shapes of people, all of them draped in cloth from the head down.

She must paint this scene. It would be difficult, nearly impossible to capture the shrouded figures, houses and trees bathed in dust, the air a desert mist. How would she accomplish it? Her paintings had always been vivid, full of color and curves, but also marked by distinct edges and sharp lines. She might make a mess of it, overwork it. If she did, she could lose the confidence she was regaining. All of her hope destroyed. Regardless, she must try. This was the moment on which all else depended. Stepping forward into the abyss with nothing but brush, paper, and paint. No map. No directions. Only herself. She taped the paper onto the easel, mixed her colors, mak-

ing sure she had enough browns, grays, yellows, and purples, filled
a lidded jar with water, put on a painting smock, filled her pockets
with brushes and a scrap of towel, and in one swift movement, she
bolted out the screened door and let it slam behind her. Though
the dust was thick, there wasn't much wind. She followed her heart
to a spot beside the lemon tree, the source of the dancing woman,
for in digging to plant the tree she had found the figure. She set the
easel down, set the water jar on the ground, tossed her hair back,
and looked before her. People still passed on the lane. The houses
beyond were just as she had seen them from her window, muted
squares and rectangles. The trees had the look of a backdrop for a
play in which great distances were implied. Yet for all of the blur and
half erasure of the world, a sense of holiness hovered. *God is here.*
She thought that thought and knew it to be as true as anything she
had ever known. She wetted the entire paper, then came back with
a wash of brown, wetted the brush again, and slathered the color
across the page. Now she must wait. She held the brush and walked
the perimeter of the yard ten times. When she returned to the paper, the paint had dried. And low and behold, the page held infin-
itesimal grains of sand. Isabel felt a thrill so great she could hardly
contain herself. With a slightly darker brown, she shaped houses
and trees. Again, she walked the perimeter of the yard several times.
When she returned, there was yet more light sand in her painting.
She selected a smaller brush. Quick quick. With a pale gray, she ren-
dered several figures passing by. She made some up. She included
a goat that wasn't there. Another several loops of the yard. Back
now to detail the various figures: a soft turn of a roof, the muscle
of a tree limb, the bend in a torso, a touch of yellow to the goat's
horns. Another several laps. There were no hills, but she decided she
must have some. Ever so carefully, she arced a distant hill beyond
the trees. The color was so mild, the form so subtle that a person
might look at this painting for a dozen years and never know for certain if the artist intended a mountain or a low cloud. Isabel walked
about the yard one more time. When she returned, she loaded
the brush with a pale brown-gray and spattered the color across the
foreground. What she had created looked like something out of the

Sahara, a mirage, a morning from a thousand years ago at least, a country before time as she, Isabel, knew it. Leaving her painting, she ran indoors. She scooped up her girls. "I did it," she said. "Come see." They looked at her in expectation. She backed through the screen door. "Now look here," she said, standing before her work. Catherine gazed at her mother. Sarah raised her hand. "There's nothing you can't do. Remember that."

Kufana

January 1964

Aweek into January, Isabel still had not made love to her husband. Now one of his colleagues was driving him to the neem forest for an overnight. Isabel finally wrote to her mother. She had found in letters a closer correspondence with Lil than she had ever felt before. She could be more vulnerable, which was odd. She began: *How long after I was born did it take for you to feel comfortable with Dad?* Far too obvious and embarrassing. She tossed the paper aside. *Nick isn't quite himself yet, still having headaches. He seems to relive the accident, and that makes him irritable. I almost feel as if I have a grown son to look after.* That was so subtle her mother might not understand that she was writing about sex. She felt guilty revealing too much about her husband, so she switched to the positive. *He is a wonderful father though. He bathes the girls and gets them to sleep. After missing their first two months, he is really claiming them now, both of them.* That last bit was for herself. Nick said nothing about the contrast in Sarah's and Catherine's appearances, and Isabel was certain she had dreamed up that tacit look of forgiveness in the hospital. He had no idea about Bobby Tunde, so he couldn't possibly forgive. He simply took each girl as his own. If anything, he seemed partial to Catherine, who responded so eagerly to touch and loved to be cuddled. Of the two girls, she was the most twin-like, always seeking contact with another body, while Sarah, whom Tunde had said would reach for the sky, appeared detached, interested in her own exploration. She rolled over to look out the window while Catherine rolled over to look at people in the room. In the first two months of their lives, Isabel had favored Catherine too, knowing that she would be less favored in the U.S. than the fine-

boned, fair-haired girl who already seemed full of self-confidence.
Now she tried to move in the other direction because Sarah needed
someone on her side. *P.S.*, she wrote, *Please send two notebooks of
heavy art paper and a box of cotton rag. It would also be wonderful to
have some new paints. I can use any color you send.* Isabel had never
been soulless. The Famous Artist was a cranky old man. Perhaps he
feared that she would outdo him one day.

   That evening alone in bed, Isabel's thoughts moved from one
concern to another. She felt sure that some good sex would help
her husband. Perhaps more important, it would bring her back to
him. She thought about kayan mata, Amina's love potion. If only
she could get some but without anyone knowing, not even Amina.
Though Amina would understand that after birthing, a woman
might need something for herself and the man she bedded with.
Then it occurred to Isabel that she wasn't yet sure whom the potion
was for: did it enhance the man's pleasure, the woman's, or both?
Then she felt annoyed that she had to think about this on her own.
Why shouldn't Nick figure out a way to seduce her? She wanted to
think about painting. She wanted someone to share that passion
with. Finally, her mind jumped to the missing passports.

◆ ◆ ◆

The moment Nick returned from the neem forest, she started. "We
must get the girls' birth certificates."

   "I've just gotten in the door. I need rest."

   When he was up, bent over the sunroom table, looking at a slur
of pages, she pressed her case again.

   Nick seemed to stiffen. "I need to write up this report. My notes
are hardly legible."

   "But we need new passports to get the birth certificates. Even if
the old ones showed up, we need a new passport for the girls and
me. You know, they do the mother with the children."

   "Yes. I know. Okay. Get a picture made with them. We'll have to
go to the embassy in Lagos." Nick kept his head down.

   When will that be?" Isabel hated the sound of her voice.

   Nick didn't respond.

"Can you hear me? Please answer."

He jiggled his foot up and down. "I have loads of work to catch up on. Can you just leave it alone? The Agency has a record of our paperwork. There's no rush."

"But what if there was some reason we needed to travel quickly? I want the girls to be secure." She wanted him to feel as upset as she did. Not just about the girls but his still present limp and the confusion in her heart and the painting she could not do because there was no time.

"They're secure. Believe me. They're children of American parents. Stop."

She fixed her gaze on her husband, who now seemed her combatant. "I want it taken care of. Besides, we're due a vacation. I want us to plan a trip to Lagos."

Nick finally looked at her. "You told me you hated Lagos. It's so humid. You don't like Bar Beach. The traffic is terrible."

Isabel clinched her fists. "I want to go."

He gathered his papers and moved to the spare bedroom. She heard the lock turn.

Isabel felt a constriction in her marriage that she had not known before the accident. In Nick's absence, she'd become accustomed to fending for herself, making her own decisions, figuring things out with Elise and Daniel. Now here she was with an American man suffering from headaches, telling her she would have to wait until he was ready to get a passport for herself and her girls. She considered the possibility of seducing her husband to gain influence. She felt certain someone had done it in the Bible.

Kufana

•••••

January–February 1964

ry, dry, crackling dry. Isabel walked to the market. On her way home, violent noises broke around her. She imagined a tree exploding and crouched. Across the street, women gathered children and headed indoors. A dust cloud rose over the houses. But there was no wind. Still, she held her scarf as if it might fly off her head. All at once, several men ran from a side street onto the main one, where she stood in wonder. They wore thin white robes and waved their hands before them in warning. "Move back." "Make haste." The cloud approached, the roaring increased, and a barreling herd of rams appeared, hundreds of them. Young men flailed at the animals with their long sticks, running alongside. One animal fell but regained his footing and rejoined the others. A minute later, they were gone. The street was mute.

Isabel looked at her arms, covered in dust. One of the men who had appeared first and warned her stood nearby. "What was that?" she said.

"For Ramadan," he said. "They go for market. You don't know?"

Morning and evening the muezzin called for the beginning and ending of the fast.

•••

Several days later, Isabel put the babies in the pram and stationed herself with several shillings and a cup of coffee at the edge of the yard. A cock scratched the ground, scattering the red earth, his neck and feathers dusty. Amina hailed Isabel before she could see her. When the woman was close enough that Isabel could touch her tray, she blurted out, "Kayan mata?"

"Ah," Amina said. She untied and retied her wrapper, but she didn't lower her tray.

Oh no. I've exposed myself, and she doesn't even have any this morning.

The woman reached into the neck of her blouse and pulled out a pouch. Her slender fingers opened it and pulled out a small knot of sticks tied with twine, or perhaps they were dried roots. "Take water," she said. "Soak. Three days. Make a tea. Drink."

"Me or my husband?"

"Baba." *Husband, father.*

Isabel nodded her head *yes*. She held the packet of roots gingerly. Amina opened her skirt to reveal a private purse below her outer wrap. From it, she produced a powder wrapped in newspaper. She pressed Isabel's arm.

"For you. Mix with milk. Drink."

Isabel relaxed. Amina understood her, woman to woman. "How much?"

"Half pound." Amina appeared confident. She placed a palm on Sarah's head and then Catherine's as one might in a blessing.

It was a steep price, and Isabel knew it. She was an American and expected to pay more. She pulled out her coins and placed ten shillings in Amina's palm. As soon as Amina had her payment, she released the pouch to Isabel and continued on her way. Isabel gazed across the road to see through the dust a series of lovely white crescents like upstanding homes bent in the wind. She pushed the pram a bit to the right and continued to gaze until she understood that what she was seeing was homes, but they weren't bent. They were painted with great bands of white like canoes. The thrill of this vision ran along her arms, and before she could stop herself, she thought of Bobby Tunde who was the only person she knew who might understand her excitement over white paint on a brown wall.

Isabel spent the morning in excited confusion. She must rekindle her passion for her husband. She must find a way to soak the roots for three days without his noticing. She resorted to her usual spot, the curtained area beneath the bathroom sink. She found a lidded enamel bowl from the market, placed the twigs in water, and scooted it back as far as she could. How she would get Nick to drink it in tea was another matter. He seldom drank tea. Perhaps she could convince him it was chamomile. She would think of something.

Three days later, after the girls were in bed, Isabel prepared her own concoction with milk and shaved ice. It didn't taste bad; in fact, it tasted a little like honey and chewing gum. How odd. She drank it to the last drop. Then she prepared Nick's tea, warming the water from the soaked roots and adding a Lipton's tea bag briefly, just for the color. She warmed some milk to add to the brew and stirred it with two heaping teaspoons of sugar. Nick was curved into the light of the living room lamp, reading a new book on farming systems in the tropics.

"What's this?" he said.

"Something to make you sleep better."

"Morphine?" His face held a half smile. Nick had refused to bring home the bottle the doctor had offered.

"Everyone knows a warm drink makes you sleep better."

"I thought I was sleeping better."

"Some nights you still thrash around."

He shrugged and drank the tea. "Funny taste," he said. "Almost like a chewing stick. Did you put vanilla in it?"

Why hadn't she thought of that? "Only milk and sugar," she lied.

When Nick didn't come to bed, she tried to coax him. "All that reading is just going to give you a headache. I'll give you a back rub."

He finally relented, but then fell promptly asleep. The milk had relaxed him but not stimulated him. She sighed and turned over. Isabel hadn't thought she wanted sex. She wanted to seduce Nick so he would do her bidding on the passports. But now that he'd fallen asleep when he could have made wild love to her, she did want it.

Later, she felt herself enter a warm current. In the dim morning light, she saw Nick's face, perplexed and urgent. "Baby?" he said. She felt his hand on her leg, the cause of the current, and turned to him, and in swift, well-rehearsed maneuvers, he moved over her and she let her legs fall apart and he pushed into her, and she was ready. She wrapped her legs about his back and raised her mouth to meet his and they rocked in brilliant motion, again and again until she was all the way there and he was too and she raised her legs to the ceiling and cried out.

After their passion, they slept late and only woke when they heard one of the girls squeal. Sarah was rocking back and forth on hands and knees in her crib while Catherine exclaimed her encouragement. Soon they would be crawling.

◆ ◆ ◆

Isabel didn't really believe in kayan mata. Or she only half believed. Her grandmother, after all, had made spring tonics. Her standby came from boiling sarsaparilla root and dogwood bark and adding a little rock candy and whiskey for fevers and chills and sometimes, Isabel believed, just to make a child sleep.

Isabel waited until Wednesday to ask Nick about a Lagos trip.

"Why don't you write to Green Garden Hotel, find some dates? Maybe closer to April." He was much sweeter than before. Sex did make men happy. It made Isabel happy too.

She wrote to the hotel. It wasn't as nice as the Hamdala, but there was a pool and it was close to Ikoyi with its fine modernist houses, left by the British and now occupied by important Nigerians. Her stomach still sagged. She must start an exercise program, make a new dress. She needed to write to her grandmother about selling some of the land and helping Daniel.

Isabel had become unruly. Her deepest secret—her great sin— was not infidelity. It was her self-interest. At times, she resented her children. She wanted to live in her imagination. She wanted to take off spontaneously. She wanted to experiment with life. A mother with twins was not going to have much time for such indulgence. She longed for and feared this side of herself. She had hardly painted in the past three months. Somewhere out there was Bobby Tunde, still singing *lovely lady should not cry*. The Kagoro Hills were singing with wind, and Latifa was putting up her hair. Isabel missed Elise, the one person she could be honest with. But she wasn't sure even Elise would understand this hunger for herself. Elise *gave* herself, which was why Isabel loved her.

◆ ◆ ◆

From her front porch, Isabel could see it, a red stream flowing out of a compound and into the street. She didn't want to get closer, yet she wished to get closer. She called into the house. "Daniel, please keep an eye on the twins for a moment. I'll be right back."

Before she could change her mind, she crossed the road. In the first compound, two rams lay slaughtered, heads back, necks slit, blood oozing out. She went on to the next compound, and the picture repeated itself. She kept walking. The next compound had no rams. So it was not a Muslim household. She walked on until she got to a familiar baobab. She had passed seven houses with slaughtered rams. She held her own throat, crossed the street, and started back home.

At last, fasting was over and the feast day arrived. All about Kufana, families paraded, showing off their new clothes and smart shoes and accessories. The children were especially proud. They went door-to-door, including Isabel's, asking for treats. The new Suburban arrived, a peculiar addition to the festival. A festooned horse would be more appropriate. Still, families stopped and admired it and had their pictures made with the American vehicle. The whole town bustled like a carnival. Even Christian families seemed joyful. Everyone could sell more. But the Muslim children were the most happy. They kept looking at their parents and fisted their treats, as if they were first at the banquet and angels had fed them.

◆ ◆ ◆

Isabel was relieved that Valentine's Day came and went and Nick didn't mention it. All she could think about was Bobby Tunde a year ago. His coming to her house had frightened her. Now she wanted him at her door again. She felt sure that if Nick looked closely, he would see what was running through her mind like a newsreel. On their next trip to Kaduna—a final checkup for him—they took some time to shop, starting out early, after leaving the twins with Oma at the Lindermans', the young girl who had carried lemonade on her head and accompanied Mary when she brought chicken and dumplings to Isabel that day Catherine was ill in the hospital. "You're going to need more help later," Mary had said. "Oma is just right for you. I'll stay here with her to supervise." Mary had become a reliable friend.

They stopped first at a CMS bookshop. A display case held pencils, ballpoint pens, and paintbrushes. One wall held several shelves of notebooks and account books. Behind a row of Bibles, Isabel found a sampling of compelling titles: *A Christian Looks at Polygamy* and *Is Bribery a Sin?* Further back, she discovered Latin grammars and books on African midwifery and, even further back, a few stray encyclopedia volumes, copies of *Oliver Twist, Hamlet*, and *Jane Eyre* and, on the top shelf, Darwin and Aristophanes. Finally, at the end of a dusty row, she found a book on butterflies and another on orchids of West Africa. She claimed both of those along with *Jane Eyre*, which she had never read but understood had something to do with a man and two wives. Back at the front, she added to her collection several new paintbrushes, and she selected two notebooks and several ballpoint pens for Daniel's brother. Nick, meanwhile, had found a book on the making of northern Nigeria and another on agriculture in semiarid geographies.

Feeling light with the discovery of her books and brushes, Isabel stood on tiptoe and kissed her husband on the cheek. The young man at the register wrote up their purchase on a receipt pad, took their money, and tied the books with paper and string.

Off they went to Kingsway. Isabel hoped to find a new set of dinner glasses. Nick was looking for film and a briefcase, though what they both most desired was a luxurious stroll through the grocery section. Kingsway sold blue tins of Australian cheese, little hotdogs (also in tins), tinned hams from England, jellies and marmalades, teas and coffees, British cookies, cans of asparagus, pimentos, and green peas. They arrived at Kingsway just before ten. Plenty of time to shop. Just as they were getting off the escalator on the second floor, they were met by a Nigerian man attempting to come down. Nick tried to urge him away and Isabel slipped by, but somehow he and Nick got tangled up. Nick's damaged leg gave way, and he fell.

"Ah, sorry; have patience with me," the man said, his white caftan gleaming under the store lights. He tried to help Nick up, but Nick waved him off. "My apologies, madam."

Nick rolled sideways and gripped his leg.

"Honey?" Isabel leaned down. "Are you hurt?"

"Just startled me is all."

The gentleman left and came back with a chair. Nick was up, trying out his leg. "Please have a seat."

"I'm fine. Really." Nick looked sideways.

"You are so kind. We're fine. Thank you. You can return the chair." She turned to Nick. "You're sure you're okay?"

The man uttered one more apology and left.

Nick bent forward, his face down. Isabel took her husband's hand when he permitted it. "Let's go to the café." She felt exposed and frightened. How could her athletic husband still be at the mercy of an accident that occurred months ago? She needed him to be a rock because she was not. Oh, she was physically strong, but her heart moved all over the place. And because of that, she was nowhere and felt the gap, a vacancy, dark and whistling.

They drank their coffee and shared a bun. "Are you sure you're okay?"

"Good as new." But Nick winced when he put weight on the damaged leg again.

They returned to shopping and were headed to the luggage area when Isabel saw Bobby Tunde on a poster, just behind her husband, advertising a new album, *Golden Like the Sun*. "You go on. I'll be right there." Isabel found the LP in the bin and scanned the song titles on back. "Wonderful Traffic," "Birds of Paradise," "Lion Power." The title, "Baby Mine, Golden Like the Sun," seized her. She turned the record back over to the photograph of Bobby in the blue Nehru suit he had worn to her house.

Though she had never heard Tunde sing it, she could imagine the lyrics.

She clasped the record before returning it to its place in the display. A pain settled in her chest, and she realized that her heart hurt. She was two people, with two lives, pulled in two directions. She hurried to catch up with her husband. "We have to go."

"We just got here."

"I have to go. The twins. They're with people they don't know at all. I should not have left them."

"The twins are fine. What about the groceries?"

"I'm worried. They may be frightened."

"You're awfully temperamental today."

"I'm temperamental?" In the car, Isabel leaned forward as if she could make the Suburban move faster. At the Lindermans' apartment, she jumped out of the car before Nick could park properly. She dashed upstairs and through the door without ringing, into the living room, and only stopped to catch her breath when she saw Sarah and Catherine fast asleep. Oma sat in a straight-back chair, fanning them. "Any trouble?" Isabel whispered.

"No, madam. Good babies."

Isabel slumped onto the Lindermans' wicker divan.

"What's gotten into you?" Nick held his thigh and lowered himself onto a chair.

"I don't know. I was seized with a terrible fear that they would go missing. I haven't left them like this, you know." Her scalp tingled with the thought of Tunde singing about their daughter, *his* daughter, *Baby Mine*. He had promised not to upset her life. This was damned upsetting. He wouldn't kidnap Catherine, would he? Of course not. But in some way, Catherine would never be just hers, just hers and Nick's. She held in her tiny body the revelation of another attachment, deep as the sea.

It had been over a year since the party in Kaduna, since she lost to Bobby Tunde her garnet hair clip and something else, a view of herself as incorruptible. Unlike the female meadowlark, she had exposed herself unnecessarily. She couldn't say she would not do it again. Some part of her was released that had been on hold since the Famous Artist had dismissed her work. Between Tunde and the dancing woman, she had found the most precious part of herself, and it wasn't the girls and it wasn't Nick. It was Isabel. She thought of her past year as a completion of her education at Hollins. She had learned so much more about what she could do with paint, but more than that, she had learned to give herself to it, to immerse herself, to love it. Painting was loving. You could not possibly do it without loving. That was what Angelica had shown her without telling her. *If you have some light, you can see anything, you can make the world your own.* Without Tunde, how would she have seen the

particular pink light that was her guide, that told her something important was happening, and how was she going to keep herself and
her girls and Nick together with this singing man out in the world
making art of her crime?

And yet neither Tunde nor the dancing woman was truly hers,
though she was bound eternally to Bobby through Catherine just as
she was bound to her husband eternally through the promise of her
marriage and Sarah. Still, if there was a God and God was the Cre-
ator, surely that God would understand that painting was her most
soulful expression, her very being.

♦ ♦ ♦

Isabel's family got back from their Kaduna trip just as the chief entered their yard. They were hardly out of the car before he made
his announcement. "I have your passports." He wore a red turban,
matching his red-and-gold Babban riga. Beside him stood his umbrella man and beside him a young boy. Before Isabel could speak,
the youngster blurted, "Bature!" and lifted the lost zip folder out from
under his shirt. He pointed to Nick. "He is the man in the vehicle."

Isabel's hand flew to her mouth.

"This boy has found your passports," the chief said.

Everyone entered the house, including Oma, who had come back
to Kaduna as their new nanny. Isabel got the town's dignitary seated
and brought him a drink. Nick seemed stunned, holding his right
arm over his chest. Isabel introduced Oma to the sunroom and left
her with the twins. At last, the chief instructed the boy to tell his
story.

"I saw the big American car roll over like a buck shot in the side
before it rammed its head against the tree. Birds flew. I was carrying
food to my father on the farm. I always cross the road that way. A
small river runs close by, and I like to look at that river. On a market day, no one is there. It is very peaceful. But the large American
vehicle was wedged in the tree. The driver did not emerge. No one
came from the other direction. I did not wish to get close. What if
someone came and found me with a dead man's body?"

An exaggerated shiver went up the boy's spine. His eyes seemed about to roll back, and Isabel thought he would faint. He regained himself, and she saw that he was being dramatic. One day he would be in Lagos onstage.

"It would be very bad. The police would come for me."

The boy shivered once more, to great effect.

"I wanted to flee. My head told me I must look on the driver. I crossed the road. The man in the car had wounded his head. Blood covered him."

The boy stopped and looked at Nick. "Baba," he said. Then he went on.

"Even so, I saw his breath. I pressed his arm, but he did not wake. By that time, I heard a vehicle advancing. I was afraid. I began to run. I did not drop my father's food. A short way and I found a man's purse with a zip. The oncoming vehicle had stopped. I ran for the river with the purse. Again, I did not drop my father's food. I opened the case. It held two green books with photographs and stamps. My father would not like me to carry this thing. I closed it and found a good rock for hiding. Many market weeks passed. I crossed on that road and saw the injured tree. I passed by the river, but it gave me no peace. The man's purse remained beneath the rock. No one found it. Then the Sarki called to my village to ask someone to find those green books. I took him there. Now I give it to you, I can be at peace again."

"Thank you," Isabel said. The snakeskin folder was a little warped, and she held it in her lap like a tray bearing full teacups. "You must have been frightened to bring them here."

"Allah protects me."

At last, Nick spoke. "Isabel? Aren't you going to open it?"

The zipper resisted for a moment, but then it gave. The folder fell open, and the passports slipped out like flowers flattened in a book. Isabel leaned forward to pick them up. "Here." She handed Nick his passport and flipped through her own. Her image was faded, and she looked grayish and thin. She prayed briefly that God would keep her secret about Bobby Tunde and knit her heart to her husband's and bind them safe with their daughters, now and forever, amen.

She glanced up at her guests. The young boy looked sealed and hopeful as a newly addressed envelope. The chief stood. He shook his head up and down. *Yes, yes, yes.*

"How can we thank you?" Isabel said.

The chief pointed in the direction of the boy. "He is already happy."

"Surely there must be something." She looked to her husband, who had brought himself to standing but seemed flummoxed. He must speak. "Nick?"

"Thank you," he said finally. He stepped up to the youngster and placed a hand on his shoulder. "You've given me something to think about."

Isabel ushered her guests out the door. She turned to Nick, standing in the middle of the room. "Are you okay?"

"Hearing that story. I remembered."

"Remembered what?"

"Skidding across the road. The car turning over and I thought, this is it. I'm going to die. I don't remember the tree, just the impact, like concrete."

She sat beside him and held his hand.

"The boy didn't see a lorry. I just ran into that tree. I watched the stupid bird and ran into the tree. God."

"Don't blame yourself. We all make mistakes."

"I damned near killed myself and left my children fatherless."

"But you didn't. We're fine now." Isabel was sure she felt the rush of blood in her husband's hand. It seemed to her she had just stepped onto the porch of her grandparents' house in her wedding dress and Nick was laughing at how his truck had backfired, how it had frightened him. Tears had come to his eyes, and he had said, "I guess I'm nervous."

"We all make mistakes," she said again and pulled his hand to her face and kissed it. Out of the corner of her eye, she saw Oma.

"The babies sleep," the girl said.

Kufana

. . . . .

Late March–May 1964

Reservations for the Green Garden Hotel arrived as the girls reached six months. Mangos ripened and more fruit bats arrived. Isabel found housing for Oma with a middle-aged Hausa couple she had met at church whose children were grown. But a niece lived with them and helped with the house. Oma would be surrounded by her own culture.

With a nursemaid, Isabel had newfound freedom. This morning the rising sun gilded every leaf. She meant only to go to the vendor's shop where she could purchase batteries, but the day was mild and she felt adventurous. After purchasing batteries, she headed down an open lane with a few tall hardwoods. Goats wandered here and there. Two young boys came up to tell her she was bature. "Yes," she said. She glanced into a compound to see a woman weaving on a stately loom. In a bit, Isabel heard music and sweet singing. She turned down another lane, between two compounds. It was curious how few people were about, but then again, men were at the farm or hunting, women were out trading. At last, she turned a corner, and around a bamboo enclosure, she caught a glimpse of half a dozen girls dancing in a circle. Another girl danced in the center. They were the music makers, their voices accompanied by a young boy on a drum. Had Tunde once looked like that? The girls were dressed as if they had just fetched water or helped their mothers pound yam, but for this moment, they were lifting their head ties aloft like flags, circling and circling. Had they finished grammar school? Was there no more education for them? Occasionally the girls closed their circle and placed their hands on the head of the girl in the center. They seemed to chant something over the one in the center. Then they moved back, and the girl danced by herself. Her dance became more muscular. Suddenly, she flicked her head back and began to shake her breasts and bottom. She turned, bent at the middle, and then straightened back up, all the while continuing the shaking. This was serious business. Just as suddenly as she began, she stopped. She threw up her hands and laughed. The other girls tossed in, bringing their scarves down upon her head. All of them laughed and fell upon one another in glee. It was like cheerleaders practicing or the pep squad or something. A stern woman appeared from under a tree and began to instruct the girls. They put their head ties back on. Isabel moved back behind the bamboo. When she peeked next, the girls were stroking one another's arms, and then they broke up like dandelion seeds, this one picking up a pot and calling back to say goodbye as she left, another picking up a basket of foodstuffs, and so on.

"What were they doing?" she asked Daniel back home. "A bit of fun between chores?"

"They are practicing for a wedding. The girl in the center is the bride."

"That can't be. They are too young. They could hardly be twelve."

"They are not too young for Hausa land."

The next morning Isabel enrolled Oma in the local school. She could be a nursemaid in the second half of the day.

◆ ◆ ◆

The dancing woman had grown a fuzzy coat of dust. One afternoon, Isabel took her outside to rinse her off. It seemed more appropriate that the figure should be under sky for such a ritual, not in a bature's sink. The lemon tree had grown so tall that two people could sit in its shade. Isabel looked on it with pleasure. Just then she heard a car drive up, a door close, and, without notice, Elise came walking into her yard. Isabel sat the statue on the water tank. "How nice of you to drop by," she said. "Have a seat." Elise did just that, adjusting her skirt and bringing out a fan. "I'll be right back with refreshments."

Thirty minutes later, Isabel filled a basin with water and sat it beside the water tank for the ritual cleansing of the statue that had become her icon. Across the yard, Oma had the girls in the pram next to the bougainvillea hedge. Elise had joined them. The twins watched the passersby, and Oma got to visit. Everyone was happy. To Isabel's eyes, her daughters' differences had become normal, and when anyone remarked on the uncanniness of one blond- and another dark-haired daughter, she felt the knife's edge of her secret kinship and only smiled. Men could have a fling and not end up with babies to show for it. Well, she had babies, one by a fling, one by her Nick, and she would not trade them for anything. But it simply was the case that women were treated more harshly and thus judged themselves more harshly than they should for such infractions. When would men be judged so? Never. Most American men would not claim a child conceived out of wedlock, but Bobby Tunde had. She contemplated this, and it came out in his favor. Her mind tumbled on, and she recalled her desire for a goddess who understood women's hearts and their fears. Isabel did worry about Catherine because of her darker skin tone and dark, dense curls and larger frame. Her American friends picked up Sarah first. She fit the type of the Gerber baby ads.

Isabel pressed her pursed lips to one side as she lowered the dancing woman into the water. Elise came back in her direction. "So your passports are restored," she said.

"Yes. It's a big relief. But I want to talk with you about Latifa."

"What about her?"

"How we might save her from an early marriage."

"What?" Elise cupped her ear as if she hadn't heard. She sat on the water tank and fanned her face.

"Save Latifa from an early marriage," Isabel said more loudly. She wasn't sure why her friend had stopped by.

"There are thousands upon thousands of girls to save if you're going to start this up. Will Oma be next?"

"I already enrolled her in school. It was only right." *And why not save women? Women needed saving.*

"Don't you think Amina knows how to take care of her own child?"

Elise was always direct, but Isabel wasn't used to her being snappy.

"Perhaps you should talk with Nick. About your own daughters. About Tunde."

Isabel nearly lost her grip of the terra-cotta. Her ears burned. She wanted to express her belief that women were judged more severely than men. "I thought you said I shouldn't tell him, that it was pointless and would only wound him."

"I did say that. But your impulse to save Latifa seems misplaced. She's practically an adult and well taken care of."

"An adult?"

"Sixteen, I'd guess."

Isabel pressed her hair back and returned to bathing the dancing woman. She was going to have to be shrewder. "But since her mother already works with herbs, you could let her spend time at the dispensary learning modern medicine." She pulled the dancing woman from her bath and set her on the water tank to dry.

"When you say herbs, you mean kayan mata?" Elise said.

"What? You know about that, about *women's things*?"

"Of course I do. It's been going on for five hundred years. I suspect Egyptians were purchasing it from the Hausa about the time the Portuguese landed in Lagos. Men sell it too, next to their cloth and incense. You just have to know how to spot it." Elise fanned with greater vigor.

"So intriguing, don't you think?" Isabel put her hand on the dancing woman's head. She had to be more careful. "Do you imagine it works? I mean, does it lead to better sex?" It occurred to Isabel that women might have been paying Elise with herbs at her dispensary.

"I thought you wanted to move this girl beyond kayan mata, not become her customer."

"Of course. You're right." She touched the dancing woman's lips. "Are you and Nick?"

"Things could be better, to tell you the truth. But I'm getting sidetracked." In some future world, Isabel could imagine kayan mata being sold by Avon in its winsome little bottles shaped like peaches.

"I'm not against having Latifa at the dispensary, but you must ask Amina. I can teach her to take temperatures, ask questions of patients, clean wounds. If it goes well, we might go further into basic medicine."

When Elise left, Isabel carried the dancing woman to the spare room. She placed a hibiscus blossom at the figure's base. "What *is* it that you have to say?" she murmured.

◆ ◆ ◆

The next time Amina stopped by, her daughter was not with her. Isabel tried to inquire about Latifa's future plans, but she didn't get far, so she squatted next to the woman and asked about the kayan mata on her tray. "What is this one?"

"Camel's milk and herb."

"And this?"

"Silky kola."

"And young girls learn about this so early?"

"Yes. Cooking and this one," she said, pointing to her potions. Isabel thought it sounded about right: the kitchen and the bedroom, women's places. She conjured her Virginia grandmother. How had she been prepared for sex? Probably not at all. She hoped her grandfather hadn't been prepared either and that the two of them had had to figure it out, haltingly, over a series of nights until they got it right. She hoped they had laughed and that they had become creative out there on the farm before they had children, doing it in the hayloft, in the creek. And then she wondered if Bobby Tunde had used a potion to seduce her. No. He hadn't needed one.

"I wonder," Isabel said, "if I might do a painting of your hands."

"What is this?" Amina said.

"Wait, please." In a moment, Isabel was back with her paint box and a piece of cotton rag from a brand-new supply her mother had sent, taped to her board. "If you would just place your hands on your knee, anyway you like."

Anima humored Isabel by crossing her legs and clasping her hands lightly. Isabel laid down a pale wash of thinned cobalt for the woman's skirt, leaving the center white. She used a fine-tipped brush and a diluted ivory black paint to sketch the hands, giving detail to the top hand. She thought of Bobby Tunde's tapered fingers, and her brush jiggled sideways, leaving a wavy line. Now what would she do? She would carry on. She gave a light brown wash to the top hand and a deeper one to the lower hand. Now back to the upper hand. She created dimension through shadow and light until the skin looked like antique brass. Back to the fabric of the skirt and its folds, the darker planes almost purple. Isabel looked at Amina. "I have always admired your hands," she said, and she wondered how they stayed so lovely when the woman did such hard labor. She came back to the fingernails, their oval shape. What color? She used a watered-down crimson for the upper hand. The wayward line she had drawn was now obscured. The knuckles required finer work. Suggestion of lines drawn in with a thin brush. She touched the dome of the upper hand with yellow ochre, working wet into wet. Isabel was particularly pleased with the way the pointer finger of that top hand had turned out, lifted slightly, as if it had its own brain.

"Now," she said and turned the painting around. "What do you think?"

Amina furrowed her brow and then slowly relaxed it. "I would like to have it."

"Of course. It needs to dry."

So they sat and waited for Amina's hands to dry.

♦ ♦ ♦

The next day after lunch, Isabel asked Daniel's advice on getting Amina's permission for Latifa to work with Elise at the dispensary, explaining that the girl might get a real education.

"In Arabic or Hausa?" he said, and she thought he sounded sarcastic. It was not a tone she had heard coming from his mouth.

"In English."

Daniel placed a washed glass on the drain tray. He washed another, rinsed it, and set it down. Isabel crossed her arms and drummed her fingers against her elbow. Daniel seemed ready to speak. He hesitated and then looked at her.

"I have told you some time back, I need money for nursing school. Why are you putting this girl in front of me?"

"I'm not. I won't be paying. Mrs. Van Dijk will instruct her at the dispensary for free. I'm just hoping to save Latifa from an early marriage to some old goat."

"An old goat?"

"An old man."

Daniel turned and walked out the back door. Isabel followed him.

"Why are you leaving?"

He swung around. "You are wrong to meddle in the girl's life. Why are you here? To impose your belief? If the girl wants school, she can tell you. Or the mother can tell you. Why Latifa? You have Oma working here. You just decide with your finger who you will favor? You close your eyes and choose? Are we toys to you?"

Isabel's insides quaked. Elise had made the same point. *Will Oma be next?* She had worried all this time that she and Bobby would be found out. Daniel seemed to feel she had committed a different crime. Her face burned. "I must think about what you have said. I must think about it seriously," she said. "I am very sorry to have offended you." She must write to her grandmother about the land. She needed some money. Though she wished she could go in person and help clear the garden for summer planting before making a request.

◆ ◆ ◆

With the passports restored, Nick insisted there was no reason to rush off to Lagos with the girls for a new one. "We'll wait until there's some other reason to make the trip. When the twins are a bit older. If we take their picture now, they won't look the same in a year." He was deep into a storage container project he had initiated, having expanded it into a community undertaking in an area thirty miles away where several villages abutted one another. It was a Hausa area, and maize farmers had banded together long ago to keep out Fulani herders.

"I thought we had agreed." Isabel needed to tread softly. Her husband never questioned the girls' appearance, never once expressed anything but devotion to them. He was getting stronger. After the self-blame and fright that followed the boy's report about the car wreck, he seemed to have put down the load of regret and self-recrimination.

Isabel bided her time. She wrote to her grandmother about Daniel.

Five hundred dollars would pave the way for him. You once told me I was in your will, that you had acres of land that would come to me. Could some of that be sold now? Might I ask for the proceeds for this worthy man? The girls and I would not have survived the period of Nick's ordeal without him.

She posted the letter, and when May arrived, she heard back.

Our intention was to give you the land when we died and then you could sell it as the value increased. Your grandfather says it will be worth much more ten years from now. Even more in twenty years. Because you have asked, we are exploring possibilities. We'd like to sell to someone who won't put up a filling station or cut all the trees. I will write again once I know more.

Isabel couldn't say anything to Daniel. She didn't have answers. He seemed less warm toward her, but there was nothing to do.

Sarah babbled. Catherine turned her head and babbled back. Isabel studied Catherine's face. Was she imagining it or was the tyke developing Bobby's cheekbones?

◆ ◆ ◆

One morning a dog began to bark. The sound seemed far off and then close. Daniel was at the market, Oma was at school, and Nick was working on the container project. The twins paid no mind, and Isabel continued to sit on the sofa as they played on the living room floor. She was hemming a new dress. But the dog kept it up, barking and then howling. Any Nigerian owner would have slapped its head by now. She set the girls in their playpen and went to investigate. A lean brown dog paced on the other side of the garden. It barked and then nudged something and barked again. Then it growled and pawed at the ground. If she raised chickens, Isabel would think the dog had killed one. Perhaps the canine was rabid, though it looked healthy enough for a bush dog, its tail marked with the familiar white tip. Now the dog seemed to plead as if the object of its interest should do something. She couldn't make out what it had cornered.

Perhaps something in a hole. Someone near the fence threw a stone, but the dog only ducked, waited a moment, and began to bark again. Its yip went from high-pitched to full-throated. Isabel had no idea what to do except stay indoors until Nick came home. If the dog were still in the yard, he would shoot at it with a BB gun and run it off.

The dog ran in circles, nipping at its prey, and now Isabel saw. The dog was intent on killing one of the Raggedy Ann dolls that had been left outside. She opened the back door. "Shoo." The dog raised its head and yawped again. At least it wasn't growling. She walked into the yard. The dog shook its head and ran back and forth beside the doll, turned face down in the dust, one leg oddly bent beneath its body, making it appear almost human. Isabel felt a fierce protectiveness rise up in her. Couldn't it happen that one of her small daughters would be attacked? She fought off an image of Sarah's small leg caught in the dog's teeth and advanced into the yard. The animal stood with its chest forward and raised its snout, its throat silver as doves. Isabel pulled out a tomato stake and held it before her, hand to hand, and didn't move. Her heart beat wildly. The dog was interested in the doll because it smelled of the girls. Suddenly, the animal lunged at the doll, closed its jaws around it, and began to carry it off. A liquid fear poured through Isabel, and she charged after it. The dog reared back, established its feet, and pitched forward, coming so close to Isabel that she could smell it. The doll hung from its mouth like a dying bird. "No!" she shouted. She hardly thought as she lifted her arm and threw the tomato stake as hard as she could. It turned over itself twice in the air before coming to rest near the hedge. The dog let go of the doll and ran for the stake, snatching it up and then running parallel to the hedge before darting through an opening and passing out into the lane. Isabel picked up the Raggedy Ann doll and walked backwards to the house and through the kitchen door. She collapsed in the middle of the sisal rug of the sunroom, listening for her cooing girls. She was safe. They were safe. Then without warning, a wail rose from somewhere in her, and she cried deep sobs from her belly.

Kufana

• • • • •

June 1964

The girls ate the finger-sized bananas Isabel purchased by the stalk. Nick rigged up a double swing for them in the backyard and built a canvas canopy over it. Isabel cautioned everyone—her husband, Daniel, Oma—about the dog. "The girls must never be left alone in the yard. Not for an instant."

One morning, she moved the dancing woman to a corner table in the sunroom, out of harm's way but in a location where she would see her daily. How long ago it seemed since she had dug her up and felt the ecstasy of discovery. Isabel was no closer to discovering her message now than she had been when the Sarki gave her the assignment. She purchased two clay pots, filled them with philodendron, and placed them on either side of the terra-cotta. Perhaps with the figure closer by, Isabel stood a better chance of making sense of her. "You're the Mona Lisa of Nigeria, aren't you?" she said.

Elise came to visit and brought a box of English biscuits.

"Latifa's father has given permission for her to work in the dispensary. She already knows how to write English. She will stay with me three days a week but only until he finds her a husband," she said. "He says the experience will increase her bride price in the new world."

"What new world?"

"The one you and I brought here."

"Then we must work fast."

"To do what?"

"To get her educated enough so that she can actually go to school and delay marriage." If Isabel was going to fail at the riddle of the dancing woman, she wanted to succeed with Latifa and Daniel.

"We can't force her decisions, or her father's."

"Well, what are we going to do?" Isabel had not heard again from her grandmother about the land.

"Give her some nursing skills and a rudimentary knowledge of medicine that may help her have a better life along with the excellent sex she's going to enjoy." Elise sat with a huff.

"Surely we can do more." Lately, Elise had not been her usual self. She was always direct, even stern on occasion, but tender too. Today she was short-tempered. Isabel wondered if she'd just gotten over a bout of malaria but said nothing. No friend can always bring the perfect temper to meet another's need. "I'm glad she can learn from you. I'll try to find the patience you have." But her brain darted. She needed purpose. Or forgiveness. She wasn't sure which. And forgiveness for what? An hour's affair or her use of people? Wasn't there some pure light in her?

Isabel smiled faintly.

The night brought rain. Nick woke Isabel, they made love, and there was some rich maturity in it, as if they had found the familiar path, yet it was lush with flowering.

◆ ◆ ◆

The next morning, Isabel got her paints out and set up her easel in the garden. Her intention was to the paint the vegetables that were beginning to ripen and make a gift to Mary Linderman, who had been such a help during Nick's crisis. She started with a circular wash in the right corner of the page for the large tomato that would be her center of interest. It was amazing how many colors revealed themselves in the curve of a green tomato. Like water, the translucent skin reflected sky, ground, and surrounding growth. The spiky okra made a good contrast to the tomato globe. Large yellow bursts of squash blossom filled the left-hand side of her page. Just then, a man on a camel appeared in the lane. She worked in a frenzy. Raw sienna for brown hump, neck, head. The pull of muscle in the animal's shoulder, in its leg, then the man's figure, his robe, suggestion of face. She hardly thought what she was doing. In the foreground, she placed the upper portion of a tomato plant. Back to the man, who was gone. Yet she had the image in her head. She gave him a cap, detailed his clothing, tufted the camel's fur, filled in the blanket across the animal's back, and shadowed its flanks. More squash blossoms, cadmium yellow, the very yellow of yellow. She sat back. It was a good painting. She had never meant to have a camel in it. The camel simply arrived. And oddly, camel and tomato seemed to belong together.

When she finished, she felt happier than she had in months. Full of light. Transcendent. As if she could walk through walls. Her success with the harmattan painting was not a fluke. She was truly becoming an artist. Isabel wondered if this was how a ballerina felt. She took off her sandals and danced by herself in the yard, grass tickling her feet. She would have to do another painting for Mary. The camel was hers. And she saw like a window opening that the incalculable gift of art was that it could not be a crime and it never required forgiveness. Immersed in painting, she left her narrow confines and stepped into the spinning excitement of what was not yet, of life being made. For a moment, she slipped back to the dance in Kaduna, Bobby's music. She had held back so much.

Kufana

·····

July 1964

A letter for Isabel arrived from Rebecca Ferguson, asking if she might visit. The days were miserably hot and humid, and Isabel had diapers she must iron to get them dry. But the expat community required hospitality. "Please come," she wrote back. She had never liked the draperies in the sunroom, so she purchased cloth in the market, a bold pattern of cocoa pods and banana leaves. With her hair up and a fan at her back, she stitched them right up. The drapes created a rich glow in the morning and made the dancing woman seem even more at home. Nick's tan had returned. His hair held the hue of the sun. He poured himself into her at night, and Isabel rang like a bell. The next day her secret compartment throbbed lightly with the reminder of her husband's presence, and she thought of Bobby Tunde and his drum.

Oma was now firmly in control of Catherine and Sarah, using a double stroller Nick's parents had shipped. On the day of Rebecca's visit, Isabel sent Daniel to Kaduna to inquire at the new nursing school. She made cucumber sandwiches and pulled out a hidden bag of Lay's potato chips purchased from the commissary. Nick had flown to Ibadan in the south of the country for a two-day conference, but he would be home the following evening, and Isabel looked forward to gossiping with him about Rebecca and whatever stories she might bring. She could not quite say why she disliked Rebecca. She told herself it was because Rebecca seemed insincere but wondered if it was truer that she was the one at fault for not seeing Rebecca's worth.

The girls were down for a nap when the woman arrived. She was not the effusive presence she had been in Kaduna when she tried to convince Isabel of her deep sympathy over Nick's accident. Instead, she sat like an Episcopalian in a Baptist church, with her back straight and her legs bent slightly to the left as she drank her tea. She talked about the pool being closed for repainting and about a recent James Bond movie she had seen. Isabel had no interest in James Bond. Then she spoke of her husband and how dedicated he was to his work, just as Nick was, she said. She gave Isabel a look of required confirmation, but Isabel wasn't sure what it was she ought to confirm. She wished the girls would wake up. Rebecca would become bored, and with any luck, she would leave. Instead, she leaned forward in her seat.

"Are we alone, Isabel?"

"I told you. Nick is at the University of Ibadan."

"No. I mean him." She pointed toward the kitchen.

"Daniel is in Kaduna."

"The thing is, Isabel, there's been gossip. I think we should nip it in the bud."

The phrase had always annoyed Isabel. Buds were meant to bloom. Why would anyone want to nip one? "Really?" The woman's condescension infuriated her.

"There's been some talk that Nick isn't the father of the twins. The girls are so unalike. Little Catherine, with her coloring." She trailed off, and her mouth bent down at the edges, giving her the look of a displeased nun. Isabel tried to hold back a laugh, but it sputtered out anyway.

"I see that this amuses you," Rebecca said. "I'm only trying to be your friend. No one else had the nerve to come."

It took a moment for Isabel to recover herself. "How many of you are placing bets on who the father is?" Suddenly her head swam with vertigo. Was she supposed to issue a public announcement? "Why not ask Nick? Wouldn't he be the one to question?" She dared Rebecca to continue her inquiry.

Her guest stiffened. "No one has asked Nick for the very obvious reason that only a mother knows. Men are in the dark. They are always in the dark. Haven't you figured that out?"

Isabel's vertigo dissipated. Not all in Rebecca's life was going as well as she pretended. She might like the woman if she would share her own struggle. "I don't think Nick is quite that dense. But you still haven't told me how many of you met to discuss my case." A chill crept in now. She could picture the wicked delight of those discussing her, her marriage, her babies. Who were they? She would bet it was only Rebecca.

"Alisa Dunn and Tessa Smith and me. You remember they came to see you when Nick was in the hospital, or maybe you don't. So much was going on. But if three of us are talking, don't you think someone else has considered it? The girls really are so different and neither of them looks anything like Nick. They hardly look like you." Rebecca seemed to have no hesitation in betraying Alisa and Tessa.

Isabel's moment of sympathy evaporated. "Don't be ridiculous. Babies change by the day. They are unformed creatures. They're a bit like fish. Lovely, funny little fish, but fish nonetheless. Their character has emerged sharp enough. But if what you came here for was to question my marriage, it's time for you to leave."

Rebecca's voice shrank, and she seemed to speak to herself. "The expat community can be harsh. I slipped up once, and I haven't been forgiven since."

Isabel's flicker of kinship with Rebecca awakened again. "What happened?"

"I had the slightest flirtation with a Lebanese man. Nothing happened. An innocent kiss at a party. It was the slightest thing. You would have thought I was trying to bring down the British Empire, which, by the way, had already been brought down. Can you give me your word that Nick is the father? You didn't slip up and have a brief affair with an Egyptian did you?"

"Of course Nick is the father. I didn't know we even had Egyptians here."

Rebecca smiled weakly. "I feel silly. I hoped to find you had committed a graver sin than I. And if you had, I would hide it for you. Honestly, I just wanted some company."

Isabel ended up showing Rebecca how to do a finger painting. They even put paint on the tips of their noses, and Isabel made handprints of the girls. Rebecca left happily with her painting. For thirty minutes, Isabel felt fine. She had cured Rebecca of her suspicions, even made a friend of her. Still, Isabel knew the truth. The creamy blossoms of the frangipani that she had placed in a bowl suddenly stank, and she gathered them in anger and threw them into the bola. Her heart seemed to miss a beat. She wanted to tear the clouds out of the sky. Let it be blue blue blue. What if some colleague at Nick's meeting had heard the gossip and said something to him? She picked two pans of green beans and cooked them up. Then she plucked tomatoes, took the imperfect ones, stewed them, and stored them in the refrigerator in clear jars. The girls crawled about and played in the sunroom. They seemed to read their mother's mood and only cried once. Isabel plied them with Elise's English biscuits that turned to mush on their tongues so she didn't have to worry that they might choke. She started cleaning out the storeroom, wiping down the shelves, arranging the canned goods. She checked the seals on the Tupperware that housed flour and sugar. She refilled the salt and pepper shakers. She got out her recipe box and resorted it.

Finally, the girls had had enough. They started howling in unison. Isabel fed them. She ate toast. Then she drew a shallow bath and got into the tub with the girls. She washed their wispy hair and soaped them all down, and then she got them out, dried them off, put the twins in her own bed, crawled in, and slept.

Two days later, Nick returned. His meeting had lasted longer than expected. Should she suspect him? She fought off the impulse. It came from her own behavior, not his.

♦ ♦ ♦

At ten months, the girls' private language had deepened, yet neither child had attempted "mama" or "dada." Sarah continued to cast a sharp eye on the world. Catherine pressed her face into any part of Sarah that was handy. The twins really were one life, one being, two halves of a whole. Bobby Tunde knew this as a Yoruba man. It was why he would not assert more claim on Catherine. Either girl would be lost without the other, no matter how different they were.

A drum, a drummer, a flash of white, a silver necklace, a white

egret, a kiosk with women's dresses billowing in the wind, the pink
flower that made the crown of thorns, the dancing woman's forehead warm to the touch, Amina's hands, the golden glow of sunset,
the granite precipices of the Kagoro Hills, rain pouring down the
louvered windows, a camel in the lane, the maroon windowsill, fog
on the ground in the morning like the hem of a dress—all of this will
come back to Isabel for the rest of her life.

Kufana
•••••
August 1964

Two weeks later, a knock came at the front door.

A man in slacks, a white shirt, and a tie stood before Isabel on her porch. "I am Gabriel Igede from Ahmadu Bellow University." He informed her that she was in possession of a Nok and asked if he might see it.

"My name is Isabel Hammond. I don't know what you're talking about. Come in. I'll call my husband." She asked Oma to take the girls to the backyard and then she called Nick into the living room. "Perhaps you can explain to my husband. Did you say Igede?"

"Yes. Gabriel Igede. How do you do?"

"Welcome." Nick extended his hand.

"Thank you, sir. Good day. I hope you are well."

"We're fine, thanks. Have a seat. What can we do for you?"

"I have been sent by Mrs. Ferguson. You know her?"

"Yes," Nick said.

Mrs. Ferguson? Rebecca? Isabel felt suddenly weak. *Had she sent this man to tell Nick that Catherine wasn't his?* "Wouldn't you like something to drink?" she said. "Nick, see if you can find a cold Coca-Cola in the refrigerator." Her husband cocked his head, and she thought he would tell her to do it.

"Okay," he said, lifting himself out of his chair.

"Mrs. Ferguson is my friend, not my husband's. You can tell me what she needs."

"I can wait for your husband."

"Please, go ahead."

"She told me."

Isabel could hardly hear for the hammering in her head.

"She said you have a sculpture of interest to me and my research team."

The hammer rested. It was the dancing woman he was after. Her fury at Rebecca slowed from a gallop to a canter. Unable to find Isabel guilty of a crime, she had apparently determined to complicate her life in some other way. Nick returned. "Mr. Igede is interested in the terra-cotta," she said, imagining a man in a white coat putting the dancing woman under a microscope.

"I have a letter from my colleague at the university requesting it for study. I have no legal authority to make you give it to us, of course. If only the Nigerian government cared that much about our cultural heritage. I'm afraid they are much more interested in the next census and votes for the coming election."

"I see." Nick turned to Isabel.

Of course, she should let him take it. She had told the Sarki that if anyone wanted to study the sculpture, she would offer it to them. But she was digging in against anyone who would challenge her hard-won revival as an artist and so-called friends who gossiped about her for their own relief. The terra-cotta would still be lying deep in the backyard if she hadn't pulled it out with her own hands. That didn't make it hers. She understood that the yard was not hers. This was not her country. Its ancient art was not hers, though she might learn from it. She would have to give the sculpture up at some point, but did it have to be today? She stalled.

"Explain to me about the census, Mr. Igede."

"Ah," he said. "In 1959, a census was taken to determine the divisions of the country as we now know it. North, West, and East. But at the heart of the census is power." He talked for some minutes about this. "Now as to the sculpture."

Isabel took a deep breath. "Yes. Of course." She needed the dancing woman for the duration of her sojourn in this country. The man before her would not want to wait for years. She was sure her husband's friends saw her painting as a hobby, Isabel's little pastime, her indulgence. She could imagine more gossip: *She hires a nanny to look after her children so she can roam around the countryside and do watercolors.*

She let the breath out. "I've grown attached to the figure, spiritually attached. It seemed to come to me, the way I discovered it in the garden and dug it out of the earth." She looked to Nick for support. His eyes were on her as if he expected her to do something brave and generous, like give the sculpture to this man in their living room. Why did Bobby Tunde understand her underground spirituality while her husband did not?

Finally, Nick did speak, but he didn't exactly shield her. "We've been through a rough year," he said. "I was in a bad car accident."

"Ah, I praise God you are healed."

"Mostly," Nick said. "Some pain here and there. I've got a bit of a limp." He looked at Isabel.

She wanted to shout, *That's not the help I need! That's not it at all! It's not about you!*

"But you are looking very well." Mr. Igede kept eye contact with Nick. "The sculpture is one of many that have turned up since 1940 or so when a British official found several during a tin mining excavation near the village of Nok. That is why we call them Noks. Many more have been discovered in that vicinity and elsewhere in these parts. Some of these works are thousands of years old. You can understand why it is so important to study them. I wonder if you would allow me to look at the one you have."

Nick and Mr. Igede stood up. Isabel must oblige. "Of course. You wish to see her." She led her visitor to the sunroom. The dancing woman struck her as she had the first time Isabel laid eyes on her, mysterious and essential as the Rosetta Stone.

"So you have created a shrine? I can't blame you. This one is quite rare." The man stood close enough to the terra-cotta to breathe life into her or, more likely, to draw strength and courage from her. "There are very few female Noks and almost none in such good condition. You did an excellent job in your excavation."

"I had endured some difficulties when I found her. She seemed to restore my soul. The Sarki has told me I must discern her meaning."

"It is quite interesting that you should put it that way. We are trying to imagine what these sculptures were for. We have found nothing else of the people who made them. No tools. Not even bones.

Yet as you say, they are powerfully made and seem to carry a divine energy. You can feel it, can you not? What has it said to you?"

Isabel put her hands on the table. Did this guy know Bobby Tunde? They spoke in a similar way. "I believe she has something to say about the importance of women in culture. After all, we raise children. But I also believe a woman made this figure." None of this had quite distilled in Isabel's brain before this moment.

"It is likely there are others in your compound, still in the ground. They are congregated where people long ago built settlements." Mr. Igede finally stepped back. He was ignoring her observation about the significance of the sculpture for women in particular.

Isabel had a vision of an archeological dig in the backyard, a discovery of pavers laid out in a circle, one Nok, if she must call it that, set in the center, the others facing in. For surely, they were meant to be in conversation. A sky, pink as a guava, had opened before her that day as she dug. There was a second world reflecting on this one, a second Isabel who observed her life even as her daughters clamored for her attention and her broken husband banged around the kitchen and she stumbled with her Hausa. She felt a presence emanating from the dancing woman, as one might from a true mentor, a kindly god. She felt purified, her outer coarseness lessened. This feeling was compounded when she practiced her own art, which was not nearly as profound as the terra-cotta, but somehow her paintings existed in the same stream. She wished she had a name for the stream. She felt a great need to tease it out, to understand what she was trying to do in her paintings. She could not live in her parents' world or Nick's world. She had to create her own world, her own nature. Painting took her there. Right here in this place some woman long ago had felt the same need and created the dancing woman.

Isabel crossed her arms across her chest. "That question you just asked me—what is she saying? As I said, the chief told me I must learn exactly that and report to him. I have only begun to discern an answer. Perhaps sometime soon, my husband and I together can bring this Nok to you and your colleagues."

Isabel's visitor seemed to grow stouter. "Mrs. Hammond. This figure will correctly be in our possession. You are only a visitor, whereas this terra-cotta is from our ancestors."

She needed to talk with Bobby Tunde. He was the only person she knew who might understand and be sympathetic with her. What she wanted was to go find him. Somewhat to her surprise, this Mr. Igede left without the dancing woman. She'd half expected him to seize her by force.

♦ ♦ ♦

Carrying several ears of ripe corn, Isabel called on the Sarki. An older boy led her to an inner courtyard where the chief sat in a chair, his feet propped up as a lad read a book to him. A fire glowed a few feet away, and several children were gathered around it, not because the morning was cool but because fire was coveted. Isabel wondered if the book was the Koran and felt foolish with her corn. She turned to go. Catching her movement, the chief hushed his reader, and the lad left. Isabel felt sure that the chief pitied Nick for having received two girls from her and no sons and probably thought she was a rather poor excuse for a wife. Still, she believed he held her in some esteem. Perhaps because she treasured the Nok?

The Sarki asked after her household, and she offered the standard reply. At least her Hausa was better. She asked after his household, and he replied with enthusiasm. The rains were good. His crops were doing well. His children were growing. The reader returned with a chair. Isabel sat. The chief said something that Isabel didn't understand, but it acted on the youngster as a change in channels on a radio because he was suddenly speaking English. "The chief wishes to know what messages you are receiving from your Christian god. He says there is a yellow cloud in his dream, and he cannot perceive what is behind it. He fears there may be a great trouble."

Isabel's insides grew chill. Was the Sarki going to test her and find her grossly underprepared as the Famous Artist had? She was still holding her corn in a knit bag on her lap. She did not pray regularly, only when she was desperate. All she wanted to do this morning was solidify her friendship with the Sarki, who had allowed her to keep the dancing woman, but on the condition that she discover some message in it. She was not a diviner—though she had seen those lights in her dream long ago in the U.S. before she saw them here in the night market. In addition, she had sensed a twoness in herself when she visited the Kagoro Hills with Elise, and then she had produced twins. She had no idea what to make of a yellow cloud. She was such an indecisive Christian that she could not competently convey the major tenets of the faith. Nevertheless, she had snatched up that Psalm about lifting mine eyes unto the hills from whence cometh my help, and Amina had responded to it.

"Tell the chief that I find comfort in looking upon your inselbergs and hills. Their sturdiness tells me that God is with us and will not abandon us, even in heavy storms. We must believe in his promise, even if trouble should come."

The chief shook his head as if in understanding, and Isabel hoped she could now deliver her corn and report to him about the terracotta. How she believed the dancing woman was an image of women's strength, their connection with children but also their own self-making, their inner light or underground spirituality, as Bobby had said. She hoped the Sarki would approve if she spoke these things.

"The chief says that enemies can also hide in the hills. Will your God smite them dead? And if not, how will he protect you?"

Isabel was still pondering how she might report on the terracotta. Now she was stuck in a theological tangle. The Psalm came from the Old Testament where the smiting God dwelled. How was she going to shift to the sympathetic Jesus who raised people from the dead and seemed to have a handy parable for every seeker? Whoever had made the Noks had perished, or they had moved, and why would they move unless pushed out? This land was too rich and yielding to leave it by choice. What had smitten them? Perhaps she should come up to the present moment and try another angle.

"Is there some news on the radio or from the surrounding towns that causes the chief to worry? Sometimes what we hear in the daytime troubles us at night." *Or the other way around.*

"The chief hears these big men vexing to govern the country. He doesn't think they will care about his own town. But this is not new news, so it cannot trouble him now."

Isabel didn't wish to ask about the chief's private life, whether an ambitious son might be pushing up from beneath him or whether he suspected a wife of poisoning him. The question of poisoning seemed to preoccupy the minds of many men. Good thing Nick hadn't had that thought when she served him his aphrodisiac. "Tell the chief I must think." She closed her eyes and tried to put herself in the chief's place. It was impossible. First she would have to become a Nigerian, then she would need to be a middle-aged man with fragile power, then she must be alone in that power because no one shared power with the chief, then she would need several wives and lots of children, and she would need to have lived in this compound with all of these people and townsfolk coming all the time to ask favors or report crimes. Not only that, she would have to have lived here all of her life so that there really wasn't much new except for more powerful people pushing you around. *What would worry me now if I were the chief?*

It was no use. She could not enter the chief's life as he knew it. Instead, she must assume that she and he were not so unlike that they could not sympathize with one another. She must focus on their commonality. She continued to sit, her eyes closed. The smell of the fire curled around her. She recalled how the chief had found their passports. Finally, two answers came to her. What would most trouble her was death or nothing changing—no growth, nothing new, no discovery—which seemed like death.

"Perhaps," Isabel said, "the chief needs some change, something to liven him up and bring him joy. The yellow cloud may be a feeling of, how do you say it? Boredom. Deadness in the heart. He may need to find a new interest." *As I have rediscovered painting.* For the briefest moment, she saw the little garden beside St. Andrew's in Richmond blooming with camellias.

This took some while to translate. Isabel picked at the rickrack on her skirt. The day was warming, and she raised her hair off her neck. The corn sat heavy on her lap. From somewhere, a child appeared and started fanning her. She smiled at him.

"The chief says you have given him something to consider."

"I'm glad." Isabel let out a sigh. "I have some corn. That's really why I dropped by." She handed the knit bag to the chief. "I wish to thank you again for your generosity." She expanded her arms as if showing the size of a large fish. "You remember the sculpture you allowed me to hold in my house? I am beginning to understand what she is saying."

The lad shored up Isabel's Hausa. The chief spoke. "What has she said to you?"

Suddenly Isabel felt inadequate to express what she had apprehended. It seemed rather lame or ordinary. "It may be," she began, "that the sculpture represents a woman who is a leader of women's affairs. She may be pleading for a woman in her community." The chief had ceased to look at Isabel. He seemed to stare at a stack of baskets under the awning. Isabel needed to conjure something loftier. "Or she may be singing the praises of the women in her area, for their power as mothers." The chief shifted his gaze back to Isabel. Still he did not speak. She might as well tell him what she really thought. "I believe that the person who made her was also a woman. In creating the sculpture, she elevated women and appealed to the men in her area to allow women to express themselves, to bring their inner spirit out." Now she had said it.

The chief looked again at the baskets. How could she back up what she had said? "I have seen in your own town that women are very industrious. They care for children, but they also sew, weave, and sell their products. They create medicine. They are also very fashionable." The chief appeared to scrutinize his hands. Isabel had never met any of the chief's wives, though she had seen them on special occasions. She knew he had an elder daughter and had seen her walk beside him during Ramadan.

Finally, the Sarki spoke. "You observe well. My mother was a powerful woman. She was a great healer. Once when my father was on his deathbed, she pulled him back to life. I have sent one of my daughters to Lagos to school. She is on Victoria Island."

Isabel had had no idea. Just then, a variable sunbird, about four inches long, landed on the baskets. Its colors were purple, green, blue, and black—purple near the beak, a blue stripe across the head, green at the neck, and black to the tip of its tail, but white breasted. It flashed its head side to side, showing off its long beak. "Will your daughter go on to college?" Isabel said, almost absently, before she fully realized her question.

"This I have not decided," the Sarki said.

"I see," Isabel said.

"It is well what you report," the Sarki said. "But you must continue to listen. You have the beginning of the story but not the end."

"The sculpture is telling a story?" she said. She looked about. Sooner than expected, the Nok would not be hers. Other things would disappear. She had today. She must get home to kiss her children. They must remain.

"Of course," he said. "Thank you for the corn. I salute you."

Isabel didn't have to wait long to learn the influence of her advice on the Sarki. The next time she went to the market, she saw him glide by in a new Peugeot sedan. His driver wore a red fez and drove carefully to avoid large puddles. The chief himself was dressed in a lavish yellow robe, as if he had decided to conquer the yellow cloud by wearing it. She waved but couldn't tell if he saw her from behind his sunglasses. She wondered if he might have his driver, at some future time, teach his daughter to drive the Peugeot. Isabel would like to see that.

Kufana

· · · · ·

September–October 1964

Petite Oma experienced a sudden growth spurt, and Isabel spent a week stitching up five new dresses with cap sleeves and soft belts. By September, Nick had pulled up the tomato plants and thrown them into the bola. The okra still bore some fruit, but the green beans were finished and so were the limas. Nick and Isabel might yet harvest a few more yellow squash, and there were still lemons ripening on the tree. The dry season approached.

One afternoon a sudden windstorm swept through, ripping clothes off the line. When it was over, Isabel wrested several pieces of underwear from the bougainvillea hedge. The winds came twice a year, and still they caught her off guard.

The Sarki was still making his rounds in the new Peugeot, allowing various children to accompany him. She'd even heard from Daniel that the chief had taken a trip to Jos. Isabel had said nothing to Nick about her interpretation of the chief's dream. Her husband worked with Nigerian men all the time, but he did not seek the locals of Kufana for camaraderie and knowledge nor, Isabel thought, did he discuss their dreams with them. If a knock came to the door, she feared it might be Mr. Igede again, this time with a legal document requiring her to turn over the dancing woman. Time pressed her for an answer. But there was only so far she could go in seeking counsel from the Sarki and Amina. Her last few encounters with Elise had left her feeling chilly. One day she pulled Bobby Tunde's address from her dresser drawer and looked at it. It was just a post office box in Ibadan. It would not lead her to his home. Still, she could write to him. She could offer a report on Catherine. They shared an underground story.

Dear Bobby, she began. Her handwriting sloped downward. She crumpled the page and began again. *Dear Mr. Tunde.* That looked sturdy.

After that scare with Catherine that required our rush to Kaduna.

"Our" wouldn't do.

After that scare with Catherine that required an emergency trip to Kaduna, the girls have been healthy. They grow like weeds.

Comparing children to weeds didn't seem like a Nigerian way to praise their good health.

After that scare with Catherine that required an emergency trip to Kaduna, the girls are now growing in health and expression.

Finally, she had a start.

They talk in their own way and crawl about with alarming speed, seldom parting ways but always moving and speaking together like dancers or musicians.

He would like that. Now she should give more detail on Catherine.

Catherine is the more experimental and takes risks first while Sarah follows. I believe this pattern supports your notion that she would become "firstborn" and the leader. They are natural collab-orators. One day they will overthrow their mother!

Catherine is comely, her hair falling in ringlets. She has large eyes. When she opens them wide, her brows shoot up and create a delta of small lines in her forehead that seem more expressive than any language.

Speaking of which, I have in my home a sculpture that is more expressive than language. I dug it up in the backyard. A man from ABU came to ask for it and informed me that it is thou-sands of years old. He wants to study it. However, the Sarki is allowing me to keep it for the time being. He has even given me an assignment, which is to discern its story. I feel that you might have some insight.

I hope you are scratching out new songs or perhaps, I should say, tapping them out.

For a moment, she felt again her anguish and distress when she saw his album in Kingsway and the phrase "baby mine." So far, he had done nothing to interrupt her life. He was not a rash person, as she was.

I wish you well in all of your endeavors. May good health sustain you.

> *Your friend,*
> *Isabel Hammond*

Isabel addressed the letter, stamped it, and walked to the mailbox. An orange hibiscus flower blazed in a neighbor's yard. A good sign.

◆ ◆ ◆

The following day, stirred by her letter writing, Isabel decided she should paint the girls' portrait. Their birthday would arrive soon. It had been nearly a year since Nick's accident. She dressed them in soft blue gingham dresses. Catherine's curly hair needed no ornament, but Sarah's fine hair required a clip. Isabel set up her easel and paints. She put the twins down in the sunroom with two toys for each child and a tim tim.

First strokes made all the difference. Isabel mixed a pink wash to create rectangles in the top left edge of the page. Windows. She moved to Catherine because she was in front, rubbing her hand across the leather stitches of the tim tim. Isabel applied a blue puddle of dress, suggestion of pinkish-brown face and neck, crown of hair, arms and legs, high cheekbones touched with yellow. Now to Sarah, sitting on the floor, staring straight at the dancing woman. Isabel's brush captured the tilt of head, an arm lifted, pale blond hair. She added strokes of pale green to suggest a curtain before she began with the terra-cotta, off-center between the girls. First, she mixed burnt sienna with a touch of aquamarine blue. A few swift strokes to capture her face, the eyes with their dark centers, the mouth just before speech. Then the turn in the body, the suggestion of cloth across her back, arms raised. A spree of light came through the window. Using a rag, Isabel lifted some color from the paper to reveal the almost white of the paper, then threw a slash of yellow onto the bottom of the picture, dabbed a bit of yellow on the wall, and a touch at the back of Catherine's dark hair. She used flowing movements, creating a dreamlike cast around the girls. Then hand, wrist, shoulder blade, neck, swoop of Catherine's lifted leg, Sarah's forehead. The billowed curtain stirred by wind. A dab of red to the top of the dancing woman's forehead, Isabel's first glimpse of the object that had beckoned her.

Oma returned from her lunch break. "It is good," she said of the painting. Then she pointed at the dancing woman in Isabel's rendering. "This lady is very powerful."

"I agree." Isabel was surprised by Oma's comment and confounded in herself that she had not thought to ask the girl her opinion. "Can you tell me more?"

"Ah!" Oma said. "You see her. She has lived a long time. First she was born. Then she married and bore children. She danced. She spoke in the town symposium. Then she became a seer. Even the men had to listen to her." Oma put a hand over her mouth to smother a laugh.

Town symposium? My goodness, Oma was learning fast. In a flash, Isabel saw that this Nok was every age, girl to old woman. She saw her own girls in their oldness, after Isabel was gone. They would never change and they were already changed. The curtain swayed. The dancing woman was the singular bookend, holding women's stories not yet written. She was all mothers who wished to hold their children and dance or paint or write or weave. Angelica, Elise, Amina, Beatrice, Lil, Mary, even Rebecca, and of course Miriam, who had no children of her own but helped lead the children of Israel out of bondage. If only the men of the world would be silent long enough to hear. "I believe you're right," she said. At some point, the dancing woman must reside in a great Nigerian museum for girls like Oma to witness.

✦ ✦ ✦

The next day, a letter arrived from Isabel's grandmother.

> *We have put five acres on the market as you requested. We will not sell unless we can get a good price. We intended this invest-ment for you.*

Kufana

• • • • •

October 1964

sabel licked her thumb and index finger, moistened and twisted the end of the thread, eyed her needle, pulled the thread through, made the ends meet, and tied a knot. While sitting with Nick at the dining table where he was writing invitations for the girls' birthday party, she would finish the seams in a new dress. He had insisted on sending the notes and had made a list of everyone he could think of: Rebecca and Paul, Elise and Hugo, Beatrice and Peter, the Parhams with their blond children, the Lindermans, Dr. Eli the pediatrician, Jerry the Peace Corps volunteer from Bida, and even the Sarki. It occurred to Isabel that Bobby Tunde might show up on his own. He seemed to hear voices inviting him all sorts of places. Perhaps she should anticipate him. He had not replied to her letter about Catherine and the dancing woman. All the more reason to expect a surprise. Nick lingered over the last envelope. He would soon be up and preoccupied with something else. "You remember when I went to Kaduna with the Van Dijks for the party last year?"

"Hmmm. What? Not really." He made a stack of the envelopes.

"Surely you do. You were off planting your neem trees."

"Oh, right." He began to lick stamps for each one.

"I met the musician. He's British-Nigerian. It might be fun to have live music for the birthday party. He heard about your accident and stopped by when you were in the hospital. I think he would come if we asked him."

"Not for free, he wouldn't." Nick pressed each stamp twice.

She had not planned for that rebuttal. It was a bad idea. Besides, she wasn't at all confident that she should write Tunde when she had not received a reply to her first letter. And why would she invite possible discovery? Because she wished he could be here.

✦ ✦ ✦

The Parhams and Dr. Eli sent regrets.

The day of the party, Nick blew up balloons and hung streamers from the front porch. Long after most folks had gathered, Isabel kept an eye out for Bobby. Finally, she gave up. Then she heard a commotion and ran to the window. It was the Sarki. She could see him off in the afternoon haze, proceeding down the middle of the road with several umbrella carriers. Though he walked beneath the brightly colored brollies, as the British called them, a young boy led a horse fitted out in colorful attire.

"The chief is coming," she whispered to herself. She moved onto the porch, searching for any of the chief's wives, but she didn't see them. The sun was beginning to slant low, and for a moment, Isabel lost the procession in the glare. When they reappeared, they were much closer.

She ushered the chief and his entourage into the backyard where Daniel rearranged chairs to make room for the town leader. The Sarki's escorts took seats on the ground. Isabel's guests rose to greet the chief. When everyone was again settled and lemonade poured, conversation resumed. Various guests picked up the twins, held them, and passed them on. No one commented on their difference. Isabel felt the undertow of Bobby's absence like a sadness whose origins she could not remember. The chief asked to see the dancing woman again. Isabel feared he meant to take her. But he seemed happy to find the terra-cotta ensconced in the sunroom amid plants and Nigerian cloth. "You have done well," he said. "I expect another report soon." Then he sashayed out of the room and back into the yard where he asked Daniel for a beer.

Beatrice helped cut the cake. "Do you play tennis, Isabel?"

"I used to. It's been a couple of years."

"Why don't you come to Kaduna with Nick one day and we'll play."

"I would love that." Isabel felt lifted by the gesture of friendship from a Nigerian woman of her own class who doubtless had many friends already and did not need her.

An hour later, when she had seen the last guest to the door, the energy went out of her. She felt flat. Tunde had not come.

◆ ◆ ◆

Two days later, when Isabel heard Nick open the front door followed by Tunde's voice, her first thought was to run out the back. Amidst her guests at the birthday party, she could have held her composure. Today Nick would surely read her face and see that something was wrong. She wasn't cool enough to escape his scrutiny with no buffer.

She walked into the living room. Nick wore shorts, knee socks, and a short-sleeved shirt while Bobby sported the blue Nehru jacket, fitted slacks, and leather shoes. The contrast was almost comical. However, this was not the time to laugh. This was the time to keep her head. "Welcome," she said.

"Thank you, madam."

Bobby was not going to help her.

"Do you know my husband?" she said.

"We've just met." He turned to Nick. "I met your wife when I played at the British guest house in Kaduna. I believe it was February before last. She expressed some interest in my music. On another occasion, I passed through Kufana after your accident, to extend my concern, and she introduced me to the children."

"Yes, she told me."

"Good, good. I have come today to salute the twins. They must be a year by now."

Once when Isabel was ten, the pond at the farm froze. She put on her skates without asking and went out on the ice, dark and shiny as blackbirds. She skated across several times before she heard the crack behind her. She pressed forward wildly, shearing the ice, the crack chasing her, propelling her to the shoreline but not quite in time. Her legs sank and her breath snapped like a tree in the icy water as she clung to the frozen grass of the pond's edge. She looked up, and there came her grandfather, who had, miraculously, witnessed her desperate leap. He pulled Isabel out and carried her into the house, stripping the wet clothes, no care in either of them for the propriety of it or not, and he put an afghan around her and set her in front of the fire. There was no grandfather now.

Nick moved some papers from the sofa. "Have a seat, Bobby. Or do I call you Tunde?" He picked up one of the Raggedy Ann dolls. *Danger*, the doll seemed to signal.

"Bobby is fine. Thank you."

Nick looked for somewhere to stow the papers. Isabel took them and the doll.

"Sit. Sit," Nick said. "What instrument do you play?"

"Quite a few of them. My grandfather was a drummer. I started on the piano. But I like the saxophone and am working to master the guitar. It's what you Americans like, isn't it?"

Nick laughed. "I tried to learn guitar in high school but failed miserably."

A small wicked hammer seemed to knock at Isabel's temples as she lay the papers and doll on a side table.

"Cut any records?" Nick said. *Men, always taking the measure of one another. If they bore children, their offspring would be one of their productions.*

"As a matter of fact, I have. I have brought one to give to your wife."

Isabel brought a hand to her throat. "Let me bring the girls in. They're out back with Oma." When she returned Bobby and Nick were drinking Fantas and eating groundnuts. She placed Catherine and Sarah on the rug in the center of the room. "Now, can you remember which is which, Mr. Tunde?" It was a dangerous game, but she was angry and intoxicated all at once.

"Let me see now?" He squatted in front of Sarah, then moved on to Catherine and ran his hand back and forth over her head. Both girls reached for him, for his blue jacket and his goatee and the shiny ring on his right middle finger and his golden cap. Isabel had almost forgotten about the dog-ear cap he had left before and which she had lied to Nick about, saying she had purchased it for its whimsical design.

"They are quite distinctive, aren't they?" Bobby said, focusing on the girls. "Quite lively. Yes, I believe I remember now. This one," he pointed to Sarah, "is Taiwo. This one," he touched Catherine's forehead, "is Kehinde." He explained to Nick. "Taiwo is firstborn, but Kehinde is actually the elder, as Taiwo sent her out into the world before deciding to venture forth."

"Interesting," Nick said. "Quite a lot of twins among the Yoruba as I remember."

But not in your own family, or mine. This conversation must take another direction.

"Yes. We are blessed with Ibeji, or twins, as you say. All children are magical but Ibeji especially so. They share the same soul. Even fraternal twins."

Lord help me. But Isabel could think of nothing to divert these men.

"I was given a sort of general introduction to the country when we arrived several years back," Nick said. "Though I have to say, it was far too general. I would need a year to begin to comprehend the complexities of Nigeria."

"You would need a century. I don't understand my own country." Bobby chuckled. He picked up his daughter, and Isabel could hear that black ice breaking as she recognized a likeness in the two. Then the house seemed to breathe, and Isabel sensed the danger passing. Nick would not see a resemblance because it would never in a million years cross his mind that she would sleep with a stranger, nor that she would betray him. Nor would he ever believe that his daughter was actually Bobby's offspring. He would as soon believe that Isabel could fly. Bobby crooned a song. It was the golden song. *Baby's skin golden like the sun.* Isabel felt an intense pain in her soul at the impossibility of her desires. Painting, like song, really was the only means of expressing and resolving the heart's contradictions.

Catherine reached for Tunde's ear, pulled it close and put her mouth on it. He kept singing. Nick watched in apparent amusement. "You're a natural. You must have children of your own." Isabel's pain increased.

"Yes, indeed I do. Two boys and two girls."

Isabel wondered at their ages, wondered about their mother with the black pocketbook, who could doubtless also cook up a savory soup. Was Catherine one of the girls in his count? Were there aunties and cousins in the house helping to care for this brood? Did the oldest child put on a blue uniform and walk to school? She could imagine brown sandals lined up at the door. Catherine had half brothers and at least one half sister. Bobby had already thought of this. Isabel recalled a recent dream in which she discovered her house had rooms she had never opened.

Bobby handed Catherine to Nick. He opened his satchel, pulled out his record, and handed it to Isabel. "For you, madam." The LP was indeed the one Isabel had seen at Kingsway months ago. She pressed it to her chest. Then Bobby went searching again in the satchel. "I have something for your girls." He brought out two small dresses, made from Adire cloth. "For the next time you go to Lagos."

Nick accepted the dresses. "You're up here all the way from Lagos?"

"Lagos has the recording studios. But I live in Ibadan." His eyes found Isabel. She saw a softening, the kindness just behind the brassy exterior he projected. She placed her palm at the center of the record. She knew Bobby would like to stay and spend more time with Catherine.

"Thank you for the gifts," she said. "They're beautiful. We'll enjoy the music. Why don't you stay and eat lunch with us?"

"I have to run to the office for a couple of hours," Nick said, "I'm meeting some men who own a peanut farm. I'm trying to talk them into adding nitrogen to the soil." His words seemed tossed out like hopeful seeds, and Isabel recalled those days when he could not speak, could not open his eyes, hovered somewhere semiconscious, and her heart flamed.

"Well, run off, then, and come back." She gave him a smile and pressed the heel of her hand to her eyes against the tears that wanted to come.

"Excellent. I'd like to hear more about the recording studios." Nick nodded at Tunde.

Isabel watched her husband leave, his tall frame folding into the

Suburban. She turned back into the room in time to see Bobby holding both children, carrying them through the sunroom out the back
door and into the garden. On her way through the house, every object glowed and demanded her attention. The mahogany table in
its solidity, the English teapot from Chellarams sitting on the side-
board, the rolling pin waiting for Daniel to return to make chocolate
pie, the curtains in the sunroom.

She passed through the back door and across the yard, to where
Tunde stood with the girls in the shade. She looked at the pale flats
on her feet. The girls chattered. Her hands shook, and she tucked
them under her arms. Was another time with him what she had
been seeking? She heard an airplane high in the sky. From up there,
a person would look down and never know she was standing in
the middle of a conundrum that could never be solved because any
solution would bring disaster, and therefore she must live in the
knowing without acting on it. She must know Catherine's secret
but not tell her. Not now. Not for a good while. Because Isabel was
married to Nick and loved him, and she could not break that tie. Nor
could she tell her girls they were half sisters. By blood, Catherine
was as close to Tunde's other children as to Sarah.

"You look too sad. I have told you I will not disrupt your family,"
Bobby said. "The girls must remain together. At the same time, I
cannot ignore Catherine or pretend she is not my daughter. I wish
I could embrace you and know I must not." He set the girls down.

She raised her head and gazed at him. He took her hand and
clasped it lightly.

"You know what drew me to you? I sensed you were reaching out.
Not for me, but for life. I was attracted to the passion pent up in
you." He paused and looked to the girls, gabbing with one another.
"It's been a struggle. It's been a struggle."

"Why do you say that—it's been a struggle?"

"Being two people, English and Nigerian. Not entirely one or the
other. Though I am largely a Yoruba man. But I have memories,
you know, of Devonshire. My mother was from Exeter. I remember
the neat house with its rose garden and my mother's piano and the
smell of bread baking. No one shares those memories with me."

The slanted ribbon of flesh above Bobby's eye seemed to quiver. The girls fell against one another in the grass and pushed themselves back to sitting.

"But you seem so at ease," Isabel said, "as if you have magic at work in you."

"That is the result of great effort, to appear, as you say, at ease."

The girls crawled a few feet and looked back over their shoulders.

"You're an accomplished musician, a cosmopolitan man. I am only a bature mother, dabbling in paint." She looked into his eyes, afraid she might not be able to hold back the tears this time. She wanted to tell him about how she worried that in America, Sarah would be preferred to Catherine.

"Why do you say only a bature mother? No person is just one thing. You yourself are becoming a Nigerian." Bobby had picked up a stick and was stripping the outer bark, exposing the lighter wood beneath.

She laughed and wiped her eyes. She wanted to stretch out time, to be here in this moment with the girls, with Bobby Tunde. She gave a brief downward nod. "Sometimes I have imagined myself two people. I may merely be a fool, but I must follow the thought to its end."

"Indeed."

They paused in their speech and watched the girls, who were now patting the white stones lining the flowerbed.

"Ah, they are drummers." Bobby laughed. He looked back at Isabel. "At some point you will have to leave and take the children."

"Yes."

"I can find my way to the U.S. I will come to record an album and to see Catherine."

Across the way, a young boy with a long stick herded several cows down the lane. When Tunde spoke next, it was about his love of oat porridge and how his mother had fixed it in Britain, with warm milk, and he ate it with strawberry jam and how comforting it had been to eat on a winter morning. "The happiest event has permanence only in recollection," he said.

Of course, her first thought was of the hour she had spent with

him. Was that what he was thinking too? "I grew up on cold cereal."
She reached up to touch the ribbon of skin above Tunde's left eye.
"Maybe that's why I am searching."

"For an alternative breakfast food?" He laughed.

Isabel laughed. The wind caught her hair, and it blew into her
eyes. Tunde brushed it aside and let his hand remain at her cheek.
His thumb brushed her lip. That shimmering was there again, on
his skin, radiating from his clothing, his cap. His touch was not an
overture, though. She knew the difference.

"We're forgetting something," he said.

Isabel felt her heart rise and fall. "What's that?" He took his hand
from her face. She couldn't help it. She felt bereft.

"This sculpture of yours."

She had forgotten because Oma already helped her understand
the terra-cotta. But this man was here as she had wished him to be,
so she must consult him.

They picked up the girls. Indoors, Tunde held his hands behind
his back as he studied the dancing woman. "Quite distinctive. I am
surprised the Sarki has let you keep it this long. He must not believe
it belongs to his clan."

"I found it just there." Isabel pointed out the window to the
lemon tree.

"Ah," Bobby said. "The chief doesn't see a resemblance to himself.
Or perhaps because it is a woman, he doesn't feel its power."

"There's no resemblance to anyone. The sculpture is stylized to
show what was important to the artist, the eyes especially, and her
forehead. Though the woman is moving, she is also perfectly balanced. What do you think she was made for? The man who came to
ask for her says there are hundreds of them, or even thousands, but
very few women. They don't know what they mean."

"Who can say? Perhaps they marked a grave. Or adorned a palace.
Or distinguished various trades. You can see she has some knowledge she is holding." He pointed to the broad forehead. "She must
have been highly revered. Perhaps she was a leader who rose up by
her own merit. If one were made today, she might be a premier."

"I have wondered what her story is. Could a woman be a premier?"

"Why not? Didn't you say that it was your assignment to tease out the narrative?"

"Yes. And you are helping me with my research." She smiled.

"In that case, I would hazard that she is giving birth to herself. She is rising up."

Isabel looked again at the sculpture. "I had thought she was speaking out for women everywhere," she said.

"Why limit her? Perhaps she speaks to anyone who will listen." Bobby leaned toward Isabel and kissed her on either cheek, as if they were in France. "I must depart."

"I thought you were staying for lunch."

Suddenly Sarah crawled by, clutching one of Isabel's high-heeled shoes that she had last seen in her closet.

"Where did you get that?" Isabel said.

"O dabọ, Isabel. Help me to say farewell to your husband." Tunde squatted to catch Catherine and gave her a hug. He seemed to hold no sense of apology or awkwardness toward Nick.

"Be well," Isabel said at the door, suddenly very afraid that Tunde's car would crash, his airplane fall out of the sky.

"Don't worry," he called back as he got into his car, the driver waiting. "I am destined to live a long time."

As if he could read her mind.

◆ ◆ ◆

Nick returned for lunch. "Where's the musician?"

"He had to leave early."

"Just as well. I've got a hell of a headache. I'm going to lie down."

"Don't you need to eat?"

He waved his hand and, listing to one side, disappeared into the bedroom. Isabel ate her lunch alone in the sunroom. Her shoulders felt heavy. She tried to remember what she had planned for the afternoon, but she could not. She drank her iced tea and ate the lemon slice. Still, her brain felt fuzzy. Angelica used to say, *painting will keep you company.* That wasn't always true enough, not when you couldn't cross entirely to one side of your life or the other. On the one hand, Tunde. On the other hand, her husband. Or perhaps that was not it at all. Perhaps these men were only markers, not that she didn't love them or care for them. But perhaps she had to decide which of her selves to cross over to. Who was she? Isabel couldn't remember. Even with Oma's nannying, her mind still seemed split. She had forgotten something crucial. Dimly she recalled an early Bible lesson about Jesus in the desert. The point was that even holy men were tested. Then she recalled the story of the brilliant philosopher, Hypatia, how she was skinned alive because of her mental and personal powers. Isabel shivered. She must believe that she would find her way without such awful punishment. She had a galloping need for her own life.

Daniel left for the afternoon. Isabel took her flats off and padded to the front door to look out at the world. In the heat of the day, life had paused. The dresses at the shop across the street hung limply. Children were indoors in the shade or under the eaves at the backs of their houses. A lone bicyclist rode past. The crown of thorns bloomed as always on the front step.

Half an hour later, Nick stepped out of the bedroom in his t-shirt, a hand at the back of his neck.

"Are you better?" she said.

"I guess so." His bare feet were large and strong on the tiled floor.

"Daniel fixed a plate for you. It's in the kitchen."

Nick didn't seem to hear. He walked into the living room and picked up Tunde's record, studied the man's photograph on the front, and turned it over. "I wonder what he wants."

"What do you mean?"

"You don't just stop by a stranger's house with gifts unless you want something."

"We're not entirely strangers." Isabel forced herself to look at her husband. "Would you like some iced tea?"

He didn't answer but headed toward the kitchen. Isabel found him with the refrigerator door open, staring at the contents. "The funny thing is I felt like I'd met him before." Nick pushed a pitcher aside and kept staring into the refrigerator before pulling out the covered plate.

Isabel sensed a bristling in her husband. Likely it was only the internal repair his body still labored under. What he had just said was a small thing and wouldn't worry her if he said it about anyone else: Bobby Tunde wants something. Yes, everyone wants something. But he said the words thoughtfully, as if reading unwanted news in a letter. She felt like a small animal in danger. She supposed it was her fault that her husband often seemed a stranger. He took the pitcher of tea from the fridge and said nothing more.

Kufana

◆ ◆ ◆ ◆ ◆

November 1964

Isabel had never played on a clay tennis court, but it looked exactly right, set down in a green field and bordered by hibiscus and mango trees.

"Let's volley to warm up," Beatrice said.

"It's been years since I played. I hope I don't disappoint you." Isabel thought briefly of the girls in Nick's care at the pool. She had been weaning them. It was going better with Sarah than with Catherine. Beatrice sent her an easy ball, and she hit it back. The court took some getting used to. Her tennis shoes tended to slide. The ball bounced higher but also came slower.

"We don't have to play a real game if you don't want to," Isabel said.

"I like keeping score," Beatrice said. Isabel admired Beatrice. She felt happy in her company. They might become true friends.

By the time they started the first set, Isabel was sweating. Beatrice looked cool and springy. She won the first set six to two. They sat for fifteen minutes, drank water, and resumed. Beatrice won the next set six to three. But Isabel felt less drained than she had after the first. She was finding her stride. It helped that her breasts were no longer as large as they had been before she started weaning the girls. She was making good on her serves. Her arms felt long as bamboo. Why hadn't she been playing tennis for the past two years? No one had asked her. She met Beatrice at the bench.

"Do you want to stop?" Beatrice said.

"I must look frightful." Isabel laughed, pushing her hair back. Her white cotton shirt was soaked through, and her white tennis shoes were now brown. Except for a skim of sweat on her forehead and at the base of her throat, Beatrice looked just as she had when she walked onto the court. "No. One more set. I'm having fun." Beatrice won the last set six to four. Still, Isabel was exhilarated. "You're very good. I don't know when I've had more fun."

"The court has been here. Why haven't you been playing?"

"One thing or the other. I tend to go to the pool. The girls, of course, and I haven't had anyone to play with. I had no idea you might play."

"You didn't know Nigerian women play tennis?" There was something refreshing about Beatrice. She was disarmingly direct.

"Honestly, no." With Beatrice, Isabel felt safe admitting this ignorance.

"Girls are learning at the mission schools. Maybe it is also your pastime of painting that keeps you so occupied and unaware of what is going on."

My pastime? Beatrice's tone was definitely dismissive. Isabel felt hit in the stomach. "I've enjoyed today immensely. Thank you," she managed.

"Yes, of course." Beatrice paused and they stood facing one another. "I hope I didn't sound too didactic. I'm sure you find some pleasure in your art. But there is so much of great import going on in this country just now. Serious work that needs to be done. It seems too bad. Well, you know what I mean."

"Yes, I think I do." Of all the people for this attack to come from. Isabel's skin stung as she walked to the pool.

"Are you okay?" Nick asked as she joined him with the girls.

"No, I'm not. Maybe I overdid it on the court." That was an odd way of putting the hurt she felt in Beatrice's words, which were true in Beatrice's mind and thus even more painful. But was art an indulgence? Whoever made the dancing woman thought it was essential. She wished she could talk it all over with Nick, who would be sympathetic but not indulge her conversation for long. There was so much workaday living in marriage.

She slipped into the pool.

◆ ◆ ◆

The next morning, Elise showed up at Isabel's door. Her eyes were red.

"Hugo has taken a Nigerian woman to bed."

It couldn't be that her friend had just spoken that sentence. "No. He's devoted to you."

"He has done it. I had my suspicions." Elise cried in jagged sobs.

This was why Elise had been irritable. "That's terrible." Isabel couldn't imagine being in bed with Hugo. She hadn't even considered that her older friends still had sex. Was she so self-absorbed that she couldn't see the complexities in her friends' lives? Nigeria's independence wasn't merely an experiment for Beatrice; it was her children's future. And through wartime and to this very moment, Hugh was Elise's soulmate.

"I suppose it could be said that she has taken him." Elise plopped down on the sofa, dabbing her eyes. "I think she connived to get him. If I knew where they were meeting, I would set fire to the roof. Perhaps she hopes to get pregnant. Then he will have to support her."

"Can he still? Get her pregnant I mean?"

"Of course he can. Men can impregnate women into their eighties. It's an awful fluke of nature, a great mistake in the order of things and proof there really is no god."

"I'll talk to him." What was she doing, making such an offer? Preposterous. Isabel had never exchanged more than pleasantries with Hugo.

"You're welcome to try. It won't do any good. He pretends he is helping her with her lessons, but he admits to going to her dwelling. He's out late. He hums and tidies himself up and is trying to lose weight." Elise held her hands to her face.

"What sort of girl is she, Elise? Nigerian families protect their daughters so closely. What is she going to do with a mixed-race child?"

A silence opened between them. Catherine was a mixed-race child. What would she do at some future date, even if Nick never guessed about Tunde, when Catherine asked why her appearance differed so from her sister's?

"She is a widow. Young but not that young. I think she's also trying to avoid being pushed into her brother-in-law's harem. She'd rather sleep with my husband, bear his child, and take his money. I have no idea what she expects to do after that. Go to Lagos, I suspect."

Isabel had her doubts. It seemed much more likely that Hugo had lured the girl with money, that she was desperate, that he was taking advantage, not the other way around. "Well, it has to stop. It's not good for either of them. A scandal will unfold. It will ruin your husband's reputation. He won't be able to teach at the high school."

"He's beyond reason. All he can see is the moment. He thinks he's twenty-five years old again. That's how he feels, he says. Though he claims his renewed health comes from dieting. He won't admit it's the girl. I think it's time to go home."

"Go home? What do you mean? Kachia is your home."

"Not any longer. I mean Tilburg, the Netherlands. I'm weary. I should have gone earlier, to attend to my younger brother. Let's see how Hugo likes it alone. He doesn't favor Nigerian food. I've ironed his shirts, made his favorite dishes, and kept his house all these years. Maybe he can learn to roll yam balls and scoop up the goat stew his new lover will prepare. Though I doubt she will take care of him once she has what she wants."

"I would miss you." That was a huge understatement.

"I'm sorry, Isabel. I have to think of myself for once."

◆ ◆ ◆

It was tricky business, but Isabel felt she had to consult Nick about the Hugo problem. He didn't leap at the chance to help her. "It's not our business," he said. He was looking for a mate to his sock and not finding it.

"Let me look," Isabel found the matching sock almost instantly. "I don't know if I can survive without Elise. She's been my sister here, my best friend. I depend on her weekly."

Nick looked at the sock and then at his wife. Isabel continued. "I know it sounds selfish, like I want her here for me. But she should not be pushed out. She's built her life here. Others depend on her.

She's an entire industry. It would be one thing if she was retiring and there were a proper send-off." ·

♦ ♦ ♦

Isabel sent word to Elise that she and Nick were coming for a visit. When her friend didn't write back to discourage her, she took the opportunity. Perhaps if Hugo were reminded of the deep well of friendships he shared with Elise, he would be less likely to risk the life he had with her. She recalled the dance in Kaduna, how she had fallen, how Tunde had come to her rescue first and then Hugo. He seemed so safe and reliable. People really were unpredictable.

When they arrived, Elise prepared tea. She seemed girlish, almost ebullient, as if she too believed the visit might set Hugo straight—or perhaps she had already booked a flight home. Her cheeks glowed. Locks of her wispy hair fell onto her forehead. Even Hugo acted glad to see them. He kept rubbing his hands down the tops of his legs, telling stories of students who were winning scholarships to the University of London.

A fan oscillated in the room, clicking each time it turned back in its half circle. They finished their drinks.

"Hugo," Nick attempted.

Yes, go on, Isabel thought, for something must be said. It was why they had come. She was grateful her husband was taking the lead.

"Elise tells us you've been distracted lately. It's not really our business, except you are our friends and have been such a support to us, especially to Isabel and the girls. We hate to see you lose what you have here." He's handling it well, Isabel thought. As well as Tunde could have done it.

Hugo grew sullen. He turned in his chair. Elise wept. The world seemed crumpled, ruined even, as Isabel watched her friends suffer, for they were both suffering in this new entanglement where before they had always seemed so happy.

"I can't say that was successful," Nick said on the way home.

"No. But it's the best anyone could have done. It's as if they can't move, either of them. They can't go forward and they can't go back."

Isabel felt a dizzying relief, talking about the other couple and Hugo's infidelity. But she knew her feeling was treacherous because she was taking refuge in her friend's pain. She was no better than Rebecca. She was worse than Rebecca. When would her girls learn that their mother had not been faithful? As she and Nick passed a roadside kiosk, its thatched roof bright in the sun, she caught a glimpse of two women and a stack of root vegetables. She longed for such camaraderie on a daily basis, a friend next-door, a sister. Her girls would have that. The maker of the dancing woman must have had a friend, a cocounselor. A woman could not birth herself alone. Men had built-in help with this. In Nigeria as in the U.S., societies were designed to give men what they need. Along a wooded stretch of road, a gazelle leapt in front of the car, tawny with short black horns and a white rump. Nick braked. Along came another, smaller one, and another. A mother and two young ones disappeared into the bush.

♦ ♦ ♦

Ten days later, Elise came to tell Isabel good-bye. They sat on the front porch. "How did you leave Hugo?"

"He got teary and said he was sorry, that he would try to stop. But that he hasn't felt so alive in a decade. He's very torn. All that sort of thing. Nevertheless, it will continue. It's been going on longer than I thought. I cannot believe the woman doesn't already have a child. Perhaps Hugo is all dried up, and there is some justice after all. But I can't live this way."

"But you will come back? Because it will blow over. He will see he's lost his way. As soon as you leave, he'll be writing, begging you to come back." Across the street, dying palm fronds hung limply down the stem of the tree, but the crown was still bright green. "Of course, you will return only if you wish. If it's what you want," she added, meaning to be less selfish.

"I don't know, Isabel. Something has broken."

"But what about the dispensary?"

"I've turned it all over to a Nigerian nurse. She's quite brilliant. Just up from the South with a brand-new degree. Latifa will con-

tinue her training." She rummaged around in her voluminous handbag, pulling out a small, carefully wrapped package. "Open it."

Isabel untied the string and unfolded the brown paper. In it lay
her garnet hair clasp.

"I picked it up when you fell at the dance, with the intention of
returning it to you. But I kept it. At the time, I was envious of you,
so young and daring and beautiful. My Hugo fancied you. I could
tell by the way he went to your rescue. I wanted something of yours,
to deprive you of it and to make me feel more glamorous. I wore it
on occasion when I knew I wouldn't see you or Hugo. Out in the
villages. I felt a little richer, a little more wicked. Then when things
began to go wrong for you with Nick's accident and then learning
about the girls and the danger Catherine's identity could pose if anyone ever found out, I felt things had leveled. I had my Hugo even
if I was old and dumpy. You had your beauty, but your husband
was broken and you held a heavy secret you could never let out. I'm
ashamed of myself. Of course I am. But I have loved you as a true
friend, and so I have to set it right between us. I hope you can forgive
me, Isabel." Her chin trembled and she began to weep.

"Of course I forgive you. Don't you want to keep it? It may give
you some strength yet. Take it for now and bring it back later. You
must come back. I can't manage without you."

"No, dear. You must have it now. I'll write to you. I'll write every
week."

Isabel wept and hugged her friend. Elise was a truly noble soul.
She had offered grace when Isabel confessed her infidelity. Now her
husband's infidelity had broken her will. Isabel spent the rest of the
day full of heaviness, a heaviness so great she felt like an old woman.
It surprised her, looking in the mirror, to see how young she was.

Kufana

November–December 1964

Nick's latest project, a series of trial farming plots, was floundering. He had a report due and little good news. Much of the seed hadn't sprouted. The fertilizer had burned some rows, likely because the farmers hadn't distributed it properly, but it was his responsibility. He was still working on the storage units for corn, but after getting concrete bricks delivered, the project had stalled when he couldn't find zinc roofing and the rainy season came early. One afternoon Isabel came into the sunroom to find him bent over the table, studying his notes. He looked rail thin, and his face was the color of untouched canvas. How had that happened? This could not be. "Wasn't it Einstein who said that when you fail, you've successfully learned one way not to solve the problem?"

He looked up and smiled weakly. "I believe it was Edison. Go on. I'm listening."

Isabel smiled back. "Write the report from that angle. What did you try? What didn't work? What do you know about how to do it better?"

"Good thinking. I guess I'm lucky only to be trying to grow better vegetables and not save souls."

"Except that better crop yields may save lives. Don't underestimate the importance of what you're doing."

They sat up two nights working on the report. Isabel offered to type it. Wednesday morning, Nick had it ready to carry to Zaria for the bimonthly meeting with his Agency colleagues. In the emptiness of the house when he left, the girls napping and Daniel at the market, Isabel felt for the first time the absolute loss of Elise. She turned a circle in the living room. She walked into the sunroom and

looked at a painting of the garden she had done last growing season. She stood at the window gazing out onto the backyard and the
shining lemon tree. Was she going to let Beatrice's comments deter
her from painting? This was the time to paint again, even though
she didn't feel like it.

She headed outside and plucked lemons from the tree. She arranged three on the dining table before gathering her paints. Values
of light and shadow were everything when one painted an object of
such unvarying color. In turns, she mixed yellow with white, with
gray, with red, with blue, adding water, diluting, then dipping the
brush in water and scooping it over to the paper to model the ob-
long shapes. She layered gray and yellow on the paper itself to work
out the softly pointed base. She needed something else in the composition, so she retrieved a particularly lovely porcelain cup from
the kitchen, decorated with blue and yellow vertical lines, and set
it off-center. She framed the lemons with an open window, pink
blush of light beyond. Each time she painted, she met a presence,
her awakening to truth. It wasn't about her place in the creation but
more about her witness to the world. She became one with something larger than herself.

◆ ◆ ◆

Dry season set in for good. The grass in the front yard crinkled like
paper when Isabel walked on it. Only the green and yellow grass-
hoppers offered color. The heat was unyielding. Isabel wore cotton
dresses and tennis shoes. She called once on the Sarki to take him
half a dozen lemons. She filled a large zinc tub with water and put
the girls in it to play. She served tuna fish salad because it didn't require the oven. Nick's report received mixed reviews. Some of his
colleagues felt he might be trying too many projects at once. They
suggested he delay the concrete storage units, but that made no
sense as the bricks were already on-site and moldering, having sat
through the wet season. Others thought he was trying too many
new varieties of seed, though he had only tried four. "Try one. Show
the men the results. Stick with it for two years. That's how they're
convinced to change," he'd been told.

"Make the same demonstration to women," Isabel said when he told her. She was in the bedroom sorting outgrown baby clothes to give away. He stood in the doorframe. "They are less intransigent. They're the ones who have to feed the children. They're the ones who get nothing to eat if the crops are low because the men and boys eat first. You'd have better luck with them."

"You may be right, but the Agency model tells me to work with the men."

"It makes no sense. You'd make twice the progress with women." She glanced up and saw frustration in his face. She must keep him looking forward. "The negative comments always weigh heavy. You've hit a bump. We'll figure it out."

"Come here," he said, and she went to him and he held her tight against him. He felt solid, even in his doubt and leanness, and she pondered that strength in him.

◆ ◆ ◆

Isabel pulled her clean sheets off the clothesline. Inside, she left the basket in the sunroom, pulled down her *Better Homes & Gardens* cookbook, and located the recipe for chicken pot pie. Nick would not look poorly fed. She was in the midst of cutting up the chicken when she heard Daniel's footfall outside. It helped to have him here, to balance out the house. But he came indoors looking like a thundercloud.

"Prime Minister Balewa has sent his army into Tiv land. An entire battalion has entered."

"What? Why in the world?" Isabel rested the knife.

"Joseph Tarka was detained. You know him?"

"No. I'm afraid I don't." Beatrice was right. She was out of touch with what was happening here.

"He is our leader. You know we still want our own region, or we can join with the West as Awolowo proposed. We cannot live with these northerners ruling our homeland."

"Thank you for reminding me about Tarka." She didn't remember anything about him.

"These politicians will not allow us to live. The people have risen up. They are being met by soldiers. I must go to my family."

"Now? Today?"

"Yes."

"How will you travel?"

"By lorry."

"Will you be safe?"

"Only God knows."

Isabel set the chicken in the refrigerator. "There must be some way we can help you. Can you bring your family here?"

"You do not understand. We are not refugees. We are at home in our own country. But Balewa has turned us into goats."

Daniel ducked his head on his way back out the door. Isabel felt something tear right through her middle. She loved Daniel and yet was so limited in what she could do.

◆ ◆ ◆

By early December, the girls were able toddlers, chatting up a storm, occasionally using words their parents knew. Oma could hardly keep up with them. Nick built a sandbox. Isabel worried about snakes and scorpions, though as far as she knew, no child of Kufana had been bitten since they had lived here. The worry seemed to come with the territory. One worried intensely for a week and then gave it up because, after all, this was where one lived.

Gone were the days when she could invite Elise over for tea and conversation about all the concerns that filled her mind, though her friend had been true to her word and wrote often, describing her various family members and the *poffertjes* she had made, slathered in butter. She did not mention Hugo. Instead, she went on about her brother and his garden and how he had found healing through it. Isabel's concerns no longer included kayan mata, and she thought little of Bobby Tunde. She worried about her husband's success. She worried about Daniel, who had not returned from Tiv land. She worried about how to raise her children. Sarah pinched Catherine. Did that mean she was mean-spirited? Sarah fell in love with Isabel's high heels and shuffled across the tile floor in them. Catherine took her dress off and ran about naked. Nick was preoccupied with work. He had never failed at anything. For the first time, his capability was questioned. He was no solace when it came to worrying about the babies. As far as he was concerned, the girls were healthy, beautiful, and relatively peaceful. The latter was due, of course, to a nanny and Isabel.

◆ ◆ ◆

Daniel finally returned one morning, carrying a bag of oranges from the homestead. Isabel stood at the door to the kitchen watching him wash the fruit and set it in the dish drain to dry. "Is your family well? I've been worried about you."

"The family is well. The farm is well. However, these military men sit in the street smoking cigarettes, even ganja. They are a blight to our happiness."

"Ganja?"

"Marijuana."

Isabel tried to imagine American soldiers strolling by her grandparents' Virginia farm and setting up roadblocks. Her grandparents. She felt an odd pain at her breastbone and wished she could be back in Virginia helping them instead of asking for money. "Do you think they will leave soon? If there is no trouble, why should they stay?"

"They will not leave. Balewa will not move them."

Balewa, the country's prime minister and a northerner. "Why do you say that?"

"He is practicing."

"For what?"

"For trouble."

"We must pray there is no trouble. We must pray your family and your farm and all of Tiv land are safe and unmolested."

"Yes. But these people are not listening to God."

◆ ◆ ◆

A Christmas package arrived from Isabel's mother with dresses for the girls, nylon slips for Isabel, and two shirts for Nick, along with a windup music box that played "Fur Elise." Isabel was stunned by the music box. When had her mother purchased something so frivolous? And the name: Elise, *for Elise*. A throb of love filled her chest. She did not show Nick. She would wrap everything to put under the tree. Her husband worked compulsively. He left the lid off the sugar jar and ants invaded. He lost the cap to his fountain pen and the ink dried up. Isabel felt his distress as a new phenomenon, different from the accident, which made him helpless. He was not helpless now, but he doubted himself. On Christmas Eve, she got the girls to bed early. She adorned her hair with the garnet hair clasp and put on her green sleeveless dress, the one she had worn so long ago to the party in Kaduna. Nick had never seen her wear it. "Now bathe and dress," she instructed him. She lit candles and served Nick oyster stew from cans she had purchased at the commissary in Kaduna. She had saltine crackers too and Gouda cheese. She even had a box of Whitman's chocolates and a bottle of champagne. Little trail marks like tiny birds' feet marked Nick's face where the skin was abraded in the accident. In the candlelight, a deeper wound glowed darkly at his hairline. He kept his left hand balled on the tabletop. "Relax," Isabel said. "Eat slowly. Let's pretend for the moment that it's just you and me. Like it used to be."

After dinner, they slow-danced in the living room to the sound of John Coltrane. A cool breeze came through the window, and they walked onto the front porch. Stars filled the sky. Even in the dry season, there was a scent of damp earth in the air. Isabel shivered in her dress.

Nick put an arm around her. "Teach the women, you say?"

His comment startled her. "Yes. I do say. Though it's not the romantic sentiment I was hoping for."

"It's quite romantic. It means I listen to you."

She remembered their first meeting in Virginia at the Fourth of July celebration, when she had said, *Yes*, and he had said, *I should have asked you to marry me*. How could it be that he did not discern anything of her split nature? He still didn't. Perhaps it was simply that she was so busy with the girls that she appeared perfectly normal, a good mother. Whatever was odd about her he attributed to her art but without understanding what her art meant to her. *My wife is an artist*. How many times had he said that by way of explaining to colleagues her desire to drive out into the countryside and just look?

They made love in the bedroom. Out the window, Isabel could

see Sirius, the Dog Star. Nick had taught her to look for it. Later, he slept while Isabel remained wakeful in the glow of her own darkness.

◆ ◆ ◆

Two days later, Isabel meant to catch up on correspondence but wrote only one letter.

Dec. 26, 1964, Boxing Day
Dear Elise,
Forgive my late Christmas letter. Be assured, I think of you every day. We kept our celebrations simple this year, not even throwing a party. I wore the garnet hair clip on Christmas Eve. Last week, I visited your dispensary. Everyone asks when Mama Van Dijk will return. Patricia, the nurse who replaced you, is working to get the children vaccinated against measles. I have seen Latifa there twice. You would be quite proud of how your team of women is pulling together.

I have not seen Hugo since you left, though Daniel tells me he is still in your apartment. I am of a mind to go see him and tell him again what I think. You could return on your own, you know. We could find a place for you to live, an apartment. Your skills are so essential to this country. Please tell me that you are at least considering it. If you wish to return, that is. Whatever you decide, I am devotedly yours,

Isabel

She looked in on the girls as they napped. Sarah's leg lay atop Catherine's. Catherine's fingers had slipped into the armhole of Sarah's baby dress. Their hair flowed together on the pillow. Isabel's heart grew as she watched them. How delicate, how perfect they were. Yet how boisterous, how brilliant. Little monkeys, she sometimes thought. For all of her dreaming, she could never have dreamed these two. They had come like swallows out of their own distance.

Kufana

✦ ✦ ✦ ✦ ✦

February 1965

February arrived as Ramadan ended. Daniel's demeanor remained subdued as the occupation in Tiv land continued. Nick lined up four ballpoint pens in his pocket, and Isabel had to remind him he had forgotten to shave. At fifteen months old, the girls had separate beds, and now they slept through the night, a miracle Isabel celebrated. It had been more than two years since that early morning of the maroon windowsill in Kaduna, but the memory still held power for her. She could think of it and conjure that shimmer that had surrounded Tunde. But that was behind her. She suggested to Nick that they travel with Daniel to his hometown. "As an expression of concern," she explained. "Nigerians don't just say, 'I'll pray for you.' They *call* on you. With gifts. We can take the Suburban. Take Oma."

"Not a bad idea," Nick said. "How about March? We're about to finish up the containers. And I've got to finish this pamphlet on peanut farming with nitrogen. Next week, I'm running up to Zaria to get it to the printers."

That boxy talk again that Isabel so disliked. But it was her husband's job. He did sustain them. They were here because of him. Meanwhile, the girls were getting second-year molars. One evening, Sarah developed a mild fever. Isabel spooned cream of wheat into her mouth, gave her a baby aspirin, and put her to bed.

The next morning, Catherine called out first as usual. Isabel turned over, hoping for ten more minutes of sleep. She dozed but woke again to Catherine pushing her shoulder. The girl turned and ran back to her bedroom. Isabel found her clutching Sarah's bedcover.

"No, baby. Your sister is still sleeping." She observed the perfect oval of Sarah's head on the pillow, her light hair spread across her face. "Come."

Catherine whimpered.

Isabel picked her up. "Are all of your toes still here? Did any run away in the night? Let's count." She sat with her daughter on her bed and counted, five on one foot, five on the other. "They're all here!" She began to count the youngster's fingers when she sensed something wrong. She put her nose to Catherine's head. It smelled like fresh laundry. She looked at Sarah. Something was wrong with the angle of her head. "Sarah?" she called. "Sarah, baby?" The child didn't move. Isabel set Catherine on her bed.

"No, no," Catherine said, hitting Isabel, scurrying to her sister.

Isabel knelt beside Sarah. "Honey?" She turned the child. She was hot, hot, hot. Her cheeks flamed. Isabel screamed. The sound stretched out of her mouth and hit the walls.

"Oh my God. Nick. Come."

In ten minutes, they were in the Suburban on the way to Kaduna. Isabel held Sarah. Catherine sat in the back and kept repeating, "No, no," while hitting her fist against the leather seat.

Isabel saw only a blur outside the car window: brown, blue, green, a tail of white. "Can you go faster?" How had she misread last night? She felt the back of her head grow large and tight as if her hair were tied back in a cruel bun. Catherine's chant continued. Isabel felt her kick the back of her seat. At last, the child grew silent.

"Meningitis," Dr. Eli said.

"She had a slight fever last night." Isabel swayed back and forth, looking at her small daughter, hooked up to tubes. Nick stood at the window, holding Catherine, who sucked her thumb, her eyes full and empty at once.

"We're giving her liquids and an antibiotic."

"She'll be okay?"

"We hope so."

"No, no," Catherine chanted. Nick carried her out of the room.

Isabel sat in a chair beside Sarah's hospital bed. She was so tiny, a little boat in a great sea. Isabel touched her forehead with her thumb, combed her hair with her fingers, spreading one pale curl across her own palm. The air stank with threat. Isabel rose and pressed the window open. Where had she erred? Sarah was a bit fussy yesterday but nothing out of the ordinary. She had run in the backyard until her white socks were brown. She had fallen once. Oma had picked her up and brushed her off, and she had gone off again in search of the green canna lily seedpods that she could squeeze and pop.

Nick returned to the room. He looked bent like a book that has stood too long on the shelf. "Hold her feet," Isabel said. "Stay just like that. Don't let her go." Isabel closed her eyes. "Who has Catherine?"

"Mary Linderman."

"Okay. Just hold Sarah's feet."

She leaned over Sarah until her head dipped down into the swale of her daughter's abdomen. She could sense something coming, but she would not let it come. She was in the narrow-walled cavern of houses in Zaria. She would press through. She would carry her daughter. They would get out, come horses, camels, or armed men. She was prepared to fight. *Please,* she prayed.

The hours crept by. Nick remained, occasionally placing a hand on Isabel's arm. Dr. Eli returned. He checked this and that. Isabel would not look at him. What if he frowned? What if he screwed up his lips or fiddled with an instrument or any other thing that spelled disaster?

"Is she better?" was all Isabel said, her head still tilted down. Her husband was silent.

"She's not worse. Hold on to that," Eli said.

An evening and a morning, Isabel thought. She seized on things that lived and set them side by side in her mind: the gloriosa lily, minnows at the creek, the newborn calf at Mr. Abubakar's house, orchids hanging from a tree, the red-eyed dove. She would gather life and pour it into her daughter. In the heat of the afternoon, Isabel allowed Nick to leave for lunch. She sat, examining the bottoms of Sarah's feet. They still had their baby roundness and were marked by tiny, curving lines. "These are the paths you will take," she said, squeezing one foot and then the other. She must help the blood flow. She must keep Sarah breathing. In, out. In, out. A small crease

formed between Sarah's eyebrows. "That's right, you can hear me.
Now listen to Mama. Come back into the room. Come to me. Catherine is looking everywhere for you."

Evening came. Still Isabel held her vigil. Dr. Eli stopped by again.
"We can bring in a cot for you."

"No. I must sit next to her. She has to feel me."

"I can sit with her," Nick said.

"You stay too. I won't leave. She has to know we're here. That we expect her." Isabel thought of her garden, last year's abundance. All she
had given to both daughters, every nursing and rocking and soothing
and blessing. Had it not been enough? She had thought herself cunning to bring forth two children, an entire family at once. Was it her
pride that caused this disaster? She promised to do better, to be hum-
ble, to take nothing for granted, and never to take her eye from either
girl. She would tie them to her with twine. She lowered her forehead.

Deep in the night, Isabel started awake. Nick held her shoulders.
He pulled her back from Sarah.

"She's gone," he said.

"No!" Isabel caught the fabric of Sarah's gown. "Call Dr. Eli.
Quickly. Go. Go."

"Isabel."

"No, I won't." She lurched upward, hitting her husband's chest.
"You let go of her."

"Isabel, there was nothing more we could do."

She hit his plaid shirt over and over. "Be quiet. Leave me."

She turned back to Sarah. The child's lower lip lay perfect as a
petal. Isabel bent her head and touched the lips, the nose. Sarah was
paler, but that was because the fever was gone. She would not place
a hand on the girl's chest. The weight might hurt her. Should she
knead Sarah's palms? Or was it her temples? She must bring water
to Sarah's lips. She moved to the water pitcher, dipped her finger,
and brought a bead of water to the girl's mouth where it sat like
a pearl until it ran down her cheek. Isabel had worried too much
about Catherine and not enough about Sarah. Now look what had
happened. She would have to right things. She breathed into Sarah's
face, touched her collarbone.

The door opened and shut. Isabel saw Eli's white coat, saw his stethoscope move like a snake toward her daughter's chest. She was not quick enough to stop him. He said the same thing, "She's gone." Stupid men. How could Sarah be gone? She didn't know how to un-latch the door. She didn't have her shoes on. She hadn't eaten. She would never leave without Catherine.

"I'm so sorry," Eli said. He said other things. Isabel supposed Nick was listening. She closed her eyes. She was walking away with Sarah, headed for the Kagoro Hills where Elise and Catherine waited. A breeze passed over them, and they beheld a crest of white egrets rising like a wave. Blue rock shone out of the hills, and a long pink cloud shielded them from the sun. The violent screech of a car horn brought her back to the present. She was still in the room with Dr. Eli and Nick. Nick had an arm around her shoulder. He was crying. How could she do this? Maybe her fair daughter would only sleep a little. Because where would her voice go, her gaze? Perhaps she was dead only for this day. Isabel could bear it for a day. She picked Sarah up, righted her head so it lay against her chest, and carried her to the window.

◆ ◆ ◆

The interior of the church was blue as a robin's egg. Pink, yellow, and purple crepe paper hung between the interior columns that buttressed ceiling and roof. Was it Easter? Isabel had thought it was late February. Perhaps she had been drugged. Her head felt funny. She touched her hair. She had a hat on. Now she remembered. Nick had helped her dress. He had dressed Catherine. She couldn't seem to keep two thoughts in her mind at once. One was so large, larger than a country. It was Sarah. An image of the lifeless girl came into her mind, and she gasped. Nick tightened his hold of her elbow. He carried Catherine in his other arm. If Catherine was here, Sarah must be close. Why the crepe paper? Was it a birthday party? A sign above the baptismal read, BLESSINGS OF THE NEW YEAR.

Near the front, a small pocket of white people turned to look at Isabel and her family. *Those are our friends*, she thought. *How small we are.* Nigerians filled most of the pews, wearing traditional clothes

in red and black. The pianist struck a chord, and the women's choir
began to sing "Nearer My God to Thee." Their voices were sweet and
pure. The notes held in the air and alighted on the congregation and
in her peripheral vision, Isabel saw people swaying. The dance was
not a celebration, but an ode to sorrow. Her eyes fastened for a moment on a man who stood like a weeping willow. She was struck by
this kindness for her, a stranger.

Isabel's diminished family drew close to the small casket. It was
the size of the box her wedding dress came in. Isabel wanted to re-
mark on this to her husband but thought perhaps she would tell
him later. It sat on a brown table draped in white and covered with
green palm fronds. Isabel smelled the fronds, and for a moment, a
tiny hope flitted through her brain. What they would do is gather
Sarah and all go home together. But that hope met a black wall,
unyielding as the hull of a ship. She pushed Nick aside and moved
forward, gazing at the baptismal before her, Jesus in a river. At least
she had been able to bathe Sarah at the hospital. She had washed
the last bit of dirt from her neck, trimmed her fingernails, created
a tiny plait to curl up on her head, and kissed the swirl of her ear.
Jesus looked much too small to save the world. Poor man. Such a
burden had been placed on him. She was suddenly furious. "Why
couldn't you have saved her?" she blurted. No one spoke. Not even
Catherine whimpered. *Pull yourself together. What you do now will
stay in Catherine's mind even if she doesn't recall it. You can fall apart
later.* She moved to the tiny casket. She took off her shoes, the ones
Sarah had loved to try on, and set them under the table. She walked
on her bare feet back to Nick. Daniel was there with them, in his fin-
est Tiv clothes. He reached out and pulled Isabel into her place on
the pew.

◆ ◆ ◆

Isabel thought she was hallucinating when she turned to walk out
and saw Elise. Her friend embraced her. "Dear girl, I came as soon
as I heard."

"From Holland?"

"No. I've been back at the dispensary for a week. Not back to

Hugo. But that can wait. Now we take care of you." She linked her arm through Isabel's.

They walked out to the children's cemetery with its concrete fence and iron gate, a young palm tree in the corner, sandy soil all around. The slender brown arc in which Sarah would sail into eternity was already there, covered with the same green palm branches that had graced it in the sanctuary. Someone handed Isabel her shoes, and when the casket was lowered, she filled each shoe with soil and poured it into the slash of open ground. She dropped the shoes in too.

Back in their home before their friends arrived, Catherine claimed Isabel's hand and pulled her through the rooms, one by one. "Where Sawah?"

"She is all around us."

"Where?"

Catherine climbed into Sarah's bed, newly made with clean sheets. "I sleep Sawah."

"Yes, you may sleep in Sarah's bed."

"No!" Catherine said. "I Sawah."

Isabel sat with her living daughter. Her wild, scared heart leapt and buckled. Catherine slept. Wind rustled the light blue curtains. The familiar sounds were there: an engine, a hawker calling his wares, a bicycle bell. But beneath all of that was silence. A stone had fallen into water. It lay somewhere dark and still. Nick came into the room. He pulled Isabel up and held her, his large hand against the back of her head. "It has been three days," she said. "Three days and she is still dead."

◆ ◆ ◆

The Sarki arrived to express his condolences. The room was already crowded with the small band of friends who had come for the service at the church: Paul and Rebecca, Beatrice and Peter, Mary Linderman, Rev. Parham the missionary. But they made way for the chief, though the chief didn't sit right away. He spoke to Isabel, and though she could not understand all that he said, she saw in the way he moved his hands that he expressed sorrow. Then he knelt on the

rug and began to chant. It sounded like a lament. Isabel decided to
join him, kneeling as well. The rest of the room receded. She closed
her eyes. Again, she was walking with Sarah, who was now miraculously five years old, up into the Kagoro Hills. The sun was out.
A wonderful hum entered her ears. She held a peeled orange and
fed bits to Sarah as they walked. The smell of oranges filled the air.
There, her daughter said, without speaking, and pointed to the red-
roofed roundhouse where Isabel and Elise had picnicked and now
Elise and Catherine waited for them. A bird settled on Isabel's head
and she opened her eyes, but it was the chief's hand. He helped her
back to standing.

◆ ◆ ◆

Isabel's heart was bound in chains. She woke to grief, moved with
it, and lay down with it. Nick held her when she wept. Poor Daniel.
His eyes avoided hers. His shoulders slumped. He loved the girls.
Finally, she spoke to him. "What are you thinking?"
    "We cannot know the ways of God."
    "But a child's death is not the way of God."
    "No, madam."

◆ ◆ ◆

Isabel found Nick in the girls' room. "What should we do about Sarah's things?" he said. "Don't you think it's confusing to Catherine?
Elise sent word that she can help."
    "We do nothing. It's too soon. Catherine would be more con-
fused by the change. Do you know that I can distinguish every item?
This cup is Sarah's because there is a dent in the bottom where she
banged it on the water tank. This brush is Sarah's because the handle is smooth whereas Catherine's is rough where she gnawed it
when she was teething. This bow is Sarah's because it is lighter and
would stay in her wispy hair." She demonstrated by placing the bow
in her palm. Isabel stepped to the closet and leaned over, then stood
back up. "This set of shoes is Sarah's because they are smaller. Her
feet were hardly bigger than your thumbs." She placed a shoe up-

side down on Nick's thumb. "I cannot have Sarah dead," she said. "I must have help."

◆ ◆ ◆

Elise arrived. She made tea and the two women sat in the girls' room. "Speak of her," Elise said.

"She was slightly pigeon-toed, and when she ran, I was afraid she would trip. Her eyes were blue-gray, but you know that. She loved to try on my shoes. She cocked her head when she was thinking. She was particular about her socks. They had to be pulled up so-so. She liked for me to stroke her face with my softest paint brush." How could she ever have grieved losing painting to the Famous Artist? That was not grief. This was grief.

"What if we push the two beds together to make one?" Elise said. "Put on double sheets. That way Catherine isn't looking at an empty bed. You can lie with her until she sleeps."

"I think I can do that."

"I washed this set with chamomile tea. The smell is soothing."

"What about the Raggedy Ann dolls? They've been washed."

"Keep both of them. Put them on the bed."

Isabel heard a struggle. A cry. Palms against the door. Catherine appeared, dressed in a white-bibbed romper, streaks of mud across her face. She threw herself, wailing, against Isabel. "Mama, mama." Her mouth bubbled with sound and sobbing. "I my bwoke. I my bwoke."

"Your eye is broken? Let me see, darling," Isabel held Catherine, pushed her hair back, dampened the hem of her skirt with her own saliva, and cleaned the girl's cheek. "I don't see anything. Your eyes are fine."

Catherine pointed to her lost sister's bed.

"She means she can't see Sarah," Elise said.

"Oh, darling." Isabel felt her heart split in two again.

Catherine pressed against her, looked into her face. "Bwing back." She rocked on Isabel's lap, tears running down her face. Isabel stood, held her daughter, and walked into the backyard. She saw Daniel out of the corner of her eye. "Come with us, please," she said. They walked the perimeter of the backyard several times until Catherine quieted. A dove landed on the bougainvillea hedge and cooed. Catherine pointed. Then she pointed to Daniel, leaned toward him, and poured herself forward like water from a pitcher into his arms.

◆ ◆ ◆

The night was dark as the inside of a glove. Perhaps, Isabel thought, her eye was also broken. She held her hand in front of her face and saw nothing. She looked toward the window. Only the slightest illumination. Clouds must be covering the stars and moon, an ocean of clouds. But it was the wrong season for clouds. Isabel sat up and moved from bed to window. Someone had pulled the curtains. Why? She got back in bed. She had sinned. Was she required to give up one of her loves? She had been allowed to keep Nick so one of the girls was taken? Was that it? If she could go back, would she turn in Nick for Sarah? What a terrible tunnel of thought, dark on all sides, walls slick with mud. Could she trade her own life? Part of herself? The self she loved the most?

Kufana

•••••

March–April 1965

On a morning in March, Nick stood before Isabel, hands pressed against the door header leading to their bedroom. "I had the portrait of the girls framed. Your watercolor." He swung slightly forward, then back, then forward again. "I thought it might be good to hang it in the girls' room, for Catherine."

"Yes," Isabel said. "You're right." But she could not get out of bed, could not move to him or embrace him.

Nick turned and crumpled like a puppet whose strings have been cut. Isabel watched in horror as he collapsed onto the floor. A shoulder rose and fell. He must stand again. He must regain himself. Instead, his howling enveloped them like one of those rainstorms that changed direction with every gust of wind. The house seemed to quake. Isabel pulled herself up. She moved to him and knelt. She turned his shoulders until he faced her. She sat between his splayed legs and pulled him close and held him. He shook like a tree hit with the ax.

♦ ♦ ♦

Later, Isabel found herself in the kitchen, making tea. She could not remember when she had bathed or combed her hair. She wore the same clothes she had worn when Elise was here. When was that?

"You are the mother of Catherine," Daniel said. He polished a drinking glass.

"Yes," she said. "What are you saying?"

"You are yet the mother of Catherine."

She wanted to hit him. She was also the mother of Sarah. But he was right. Catherine was here now. Catherine, the dark-haired child, the one so bonded to the world, who loved touch and texture. Oma had been sleeping in the girls' room, caring for Catherine with little help from Isabel. She found them in the backyard. Oma had filled a bucket with water, and Catherine was slapping it. Isabel sat and watched them. Catherine kept looking sideways. She spoke, but no answer came to her. In a little bit, she simply let her legs go limp and landed hard on her bottom. She seemed startled but didn't cry. Instead, she clapped and waited, but no sound came back.

Isabel scooped up her daughter, and they cried together. *How many times will we do this?* Isabel must act. Her husband was breaking. She must pay a penance. She must restore them. But she was as broken as Catherine, who had lost half of her soul according to Bobby Tunde. Bobby Tunde. Over and again, Isabel condemned herself. How could she not have seen that Sarah was at risk? Catherine pulled her mother's hair. "Yes, I'm here." But Isabel was not.

♦ ♦ ♦

One afternoon, as Nick rested and Catherine napped with Oma, Isabel entered the bathroom, closed the door, and cut her hair. She used the blade from her husband's razor, holding out strands of her hair and lopping them off. The locks rebounded into her palm, and she let them fall into the sink. She made no attempt at form but took great interest in the sound of the cutting. It sounded a bit like fileting raw fish. Doing the back, she nicked her neck. She felt the prick, but it didn't seem bad and she wasn't finished, so she kept going. Her hair stuck out at odd angles. She sawed a bit more near her crown. The cut hair seemed to smell now, like smoke, and she stepped away from the mirror. Then she looked at her wrists. Very, very carefully, she set the razor down. She set herself down between the toilet and the bathtub, brought her knees up to her chest, and lowered her forehead onto her knees.

The bathroom door opened. Isabel raised her head to see her husband.

"Baby," he said. "What have you done to your hair?"

Isabel placed an index finger at her clavicle. "Here's the thing. A chair bottom sits on four legs. If you take away a leg, the chair falls.

I keep thinking this. It's the same for a table. A house has four walls. Think about it."

"What's that got to do with your hair?" Nick picked up the blade, put it in the razor, and placed the razor in his pants pocket.

"It has to do with holding up."

"I'm going to fix your hair," he said. "Sit on the edge of the tub. I'll be right back."

He came back with sewing scissors. "You nicked yourself."

"I know."

He placed a damp washcloth on her neck and then touched it with iodine. It stung, and she was happy that it did. He pulled up batches of hair and trimmed. He massaged her scalp. "Okay. Look," he said.

She looked at her head, blooming oddly from her shoulders, hair short as a boy's but soft because of the curl. The bangs were not too bad.

"It's not your fault, you know," he said.

"I went back to sleep. Who knows what difference those ten minutes might have made?"

"It's not your fault."

"Sarah's head wasn't right on the pillow. I didn't pay enough attention. I thought Sarah was safe while Catherine was at risk. I always worried about Catherine."

"Why did you worry about Catherine? She's so strong."

"I've done everything wrong."

♦ ♦ ♦

In April, Nick traveled to Kaduna for the day. Isabel sat in the garden. Green shoots of something were sprouting in nursery pots. Daniel must have planted seeds. She couldn't remember. A spade sat wedged in the dirt. A small shovel rested next to the lemon tree. A snail moved over a leaf. Without forethought or plan, Isabel began to dig.

"Why?" Daniel's shirt billowed

"There may be more terra-cottas. There may be at least one more. You can help if you like."

Daniel walked into the kitchen. Isabel used an ice pick, a hammer, a spade, an American shovel. By noon, she had dug a trench three feet wide and a foot deep but found nothing. After lunch, Daniel joined her. "Isn't it time for you to go to your compound?" she said.

He didn't reply. They worked together, and the progress was greater. When she got tired, Isabel sat back and looked at the sky above the avocado tree. Clouds bunched like dogs fighting in muslin, but she knew it would not rain. Every once in a while, a blue space of sky opened. *Above are stars, even if I can't see them. Taiwo is firstborn, but Kehinde overtakes her.*

Isabel returned to digging. Daniel brought water for her to drink. She dared not look at the lane where passersby may have stopped to observe her. Likely, they knew she had lost a child. They might run past her dwelling out of fear of her bad luck. She would run if she could, but she could not. So she dug. There must be more. That man who had come for the dancing woman had said there would be a congregation. She had heard no more from him. She almost wished he would show up and help her. She needed help. Midafternoon, Oma brought Catherine out. The toddler sat on the side of the hole with a spoon and imitated her mother.

Should we go deeper or wider? "Deeper," Isabel said.

Daniel motioned to Oma to move Catherine aside. With a pickax, he took to the center of the hole.

"You'll smash it!"

"It is only earth. There is nothing."

"I won't give up yet."

He sat down and watched her, his knees belted by his arms. Isabel worked from inside the hole out. She was the meadowlark in its ruined nest. Still she dug. Her leg cramped up, and she walked it off.

"Mama," Catherine called. Isabel picked her up and gave her nose a kiss. "Now back to Oma," she said, but the child wouldn't let go. She clung to Isabel, sucking her thumb furiously. She twisted a strand of hair. Isabel watched, mesmerized as Catherine twisted it until it turned on itself in knots. Then she yanked on it, as if she meant to pull it out. When that didn't work, she leaned into her mother and bit Isabel's arm. It burned like a lick of flame. Isabel gripped the girl's shoulder. "No!"

Catherine wailed, tears streaming down her dusty face. Isabel stared at her, furious and frightened. She felt a terrible desire to bite the girl back. She glanced up to see Oma watching. "Now, now," she whispered to her daughter, rocking her back and forth. Isabel's head pulsed. She tried to remember a favorite melody, but nothing came to mind. "It's okay. Shhh," she said. She paced with her daughter up and down the yard until she felt Catherine relax.

Daniel went in to make dinner. Isabel carried a sleeping Catherine back to Oma. She dug with the pointed spade. Dirt flew around her with the velocity of a sporting event. At last, she heard the Suburban and sat back. The clouds were gone. The sky ran pink with a dark ribbon of purple beneath. She sat, watched, and waited, her heart heavy with the familiar pain.

◆ ◆ ◆

Two days later, Elise came again. She looked at Isabel's hair. "It needs a good wash," she said and led her into the yard. Isabel leaned back in a chair as Elise ladled water. She lathered Isabel's short, dense locks and massaged her scalp with her strong fingers. She rinsed and repeated until Isabel was lost in the smell. Elise sat Isabel up, combed out her hair, and brought tea. Later, she fed her banana pudding. Once Isabel's hair was dry, Elise made a ribbon headband and told her they were going for a walk. Oma had Catherine ready. The girl had sucked her thumb so hard it was raw. They headed to the lane beside the house. A brown lizard darted out and ran in spurts just ahead of them. Its antics delighted Catherine, who pointed and laughed. Isabel already felt better. The lizard disappeared into the grass. At the edge of town, they came to a field, a small creek, and a footbridge. A young girl filled a calabash. Isabel greeted her. The girl smiled briefly as they passed. "Have we had rain?" Isabel said. The grass beside the path hinted at greening. "Yes, two rains by now," Oma said, in a stately voice. Oma had changed with Sarah's death. Before she had seemed like a child herself, wearing her American-style dresses. She now wore a traditional blouse and skirt and kept a small leather purse around her neck at all times. Isabel did not ask but wondered if it carried some potion.

A whiff of wet earth touched Isabel's nostrils. She took Catherine from the nursemaid and set the child on the trail beside her. Catherine held her arms out to take in the wind as she pressed forward. "Glee," she said. "Glee." It had been their word, hers and Sarah's, for wind. They came to an outcropping of rock. A patas monkey, with its funny peaked ears and mustached mouth, sat watching them. "Monkey," Isabel said, pointing. Catherine' laughter came in honks. The monkey scampered away. Here was the world: rain showers, monkeys, a girl with a basin of water, a stream, her daughter laughing. Yet as they returned to go home, Isabel felt her spirit failing. It wasn't right. How could they be joyful without Sarah? She could not bear this much light. "Oma, please," she said. The girl picked up Catherine. "I have to get home. Elise, I'm sorry." She stumbled forward. In the house, she returned to bed.

♦ ♦ ♦

Several days later, the chief arrived. He asked Isabel if she would give art lessons to some of the town's children. "Are you trying to dispel my yellow cloud?" she said.

"Yes. I am."

"I will try."

"That is good. By Muslim law, the children are not allowed to draw people. But anything else."

When she arrived in his compound the first day, carrying only pencils and paper, she saw that he meant boy children. "Ah, Baba," she said. "I beg you. Find some young girls for the class."

The next day, she arrived to find ten boys and four girls assembled for lessons.

She rewarded the group by pulling paper, paints, and brushes out of her bag, supplies that she had put away since Sarah's death. She paired the students and allowed each pair two colors. The results were blue and orange trees, a red and yellow lorry, and best of all, a pink camel with black stars in the sky. For the period of her class, she forgot her pain. It simply vanished. On her way home, the weight of agony descended, and she veered onto a road she had never taken. She kept her head down. Once she almost stepped into a cooking fire. Her chest burned with her exertion. She must come out to a field. In a field, she could remember the way back to Sarah, she could gather up the threads, reweave her family, and reunite them in this season. Jesus had raised the dead. What was prayer but a request for wholeness and repair? She looked to her right and saw a young boy gazing at her. He held a wand of dry grass in his mouth.

"Sannu," she said.

"Sannu," he said.

"I hope I didn't startle you. I took a wrong turn," she said. Her arms hung like weights by her side.

♦ ♦ ♦

Isabel asked Nick to write to her parents. She had not done so and could not bear to do it. In the last letter she had sent, she had included photographs of the girls together and had at the time very much believed in goodness and joy. *Dad, look how Catherine favors you. And how Sarah favors Nick*, she had written.

♦ ♦ ♦

Nick's clothes hung on him, and he fastened his belt to the last notch and then had to drill out another. Often, Isabel heard him under his breath, "Lord, have mercy." His colleagues helped him bring the storage containers to completion. Catherine latched onto a horrible pink doll she had never before paid any attention to but now carried around like an essential organ. Amina came to visit. She sat with Isabel in the afternoon shade, stroking Isabel's arm. "Ah, ah," she said. Finally, the stroking subsided, but Amina didn't let go of Isabel's arm for a long time.

Kufana

· · · · ·

April–June 1965

I
sabel turned the dancing woman to the wall. She covered her with a veil. "She's in mourning," she said when Nick asked.

"You're getting a bit pagan."

"Why shouldn't I?" Isabel felt heat rise in her head.

Nick leaned toward her as if there was some chasm between them and he might not be able to span it, but he found her hand and pulled her into his chest. He smelled of Old Spice and she felt the slightest stirring of desire, but it flickered and died like a wet match. If only they could lose themselves in each other. They had tried a week ago. It hadn't worked.

Isabel had little interest in the garden. She spent days sitting or lying in bed, looking out the window. Her husband seemed spectral. Only at Catherine's demand could she rouse herself. She wept over the smallest thing: a sound like Sarah's step, one of her own shoes turned upside down. At last, Nick planted the garden with Daniel. It wasn't until May, when the seedlings were up, that Isabel began to spend time outdoors with Catherine and Oma. All of the things that had worried her before—Bobby Tunde, Rebecca's gossip, saving Latifa from an early marriage—seemed far away. The only thing that absorbed her was teaching art to the children in town. For the hour or two she was with them, she forgot about Sarah. She even forgot about Catherine. She always offered a demonstration first: here is how you might paint a palm; here is how you might paint the sky, a pot, a goat, a lorry. Then she offered the children paints, brushes, and paper and let them do as they liked. She wove between the mats, where they leaned over their work, the girls daintily settled on their knees, the boys sitting cross-legged. Isabel admired and commented. She never criticized, though occasionally she might use a finger to suggest how a student could extend a line, a shadow, sharpen a contrast. The boys included Arabic designs: moons, spirals, tendrils. All of the children favored red and yellow pigments and sometimes mixed a purple-brown for calligraphy, colors they might have drawn from the earth of northern Nigeria.

Though it seemed impossible, life went on. Catherine reached eighteen months. Oma napped with her. Indoors, they built towers of wooden blocks and toppled them. Outside, they collected leaves and seedpods and set them afloat in pots of water. But in the middle of play, Catherine would wander off, looking for Sarah. *Sawah, Sawah,* she called.

One afternoon, Isabel picked up her daughter and discovered raw spots on her scalp. "What are these?"

Oma was just beyond the sunroom door. She swiveled into the threshold. "She twists the hair. She pulls it out. The hair will grow back."

Isabel's stomach turned. "You're not watching her carefully." Her arms trembled and she tightened them around her daughter. "You must stop her from doing it."

"You cannot make her stop. No one can make her stop."

Startled, Isabel studied her nursemaid. Oma didn't smile as Daniel did. She rested her lips noncommitally. Who knew how many children she had observed growing up on her family's compound? "Try to keep her hands busy." Isabel's head pounded.

That evening she rinsed Catherine's head in the tub. She hummed, but her voice bent and broke. "Soft, soft," she said over and over as she put the child to bed.

In the middle of the night, Isabel woke herself screaming. Her roar seemed to come from the center of the earth. Even after Nick woke her and turned on the light, she roared, inconsolable, until she exhausted herself.

For the next several days, Isabel woke early, but she stayed in bed, cycling through the maze of terror. Something must be done. She must make amends, atone. She had indulged her passion, sought her own desires, believed in the holiness of her own artistry, which was nothing, nothing of consequence compared to her daughter. How could she have been so stupid? She had imagined her interior life a source of insight, even revelation. Idiocy. She must make a sacrifice. Surely then she would find relief from the open wound of her heart, the daggers in her brain—and the sagging horror of all hope gone, which scalded her chest and burned her tongue and left a black mass at her center. In such a state, she could not live, her brain bedeviled with the most horrid thoughts: she would exchange Catherine for Sarah; or Nick for the girls; or burn down the house and kill them all. No. It was herself she must obliterate.

The next morning before dawn, she suddenly knew what she must do, and the awareness filled her with power. Her mind became clear, and her arms, prone on the sheets, rippled with intention. Silently, she slipped from bed, inched to Nick's side, and found the flashlight. She shut the bedroom door behind her, moved to Catherine's room, and checked her breathing.

A proper sacrifice might be a hand cut off. As the dancing woman's hand had been destroyed. Isabel would do the closest thing she could imagine. In the sunroom, she opened the cabinet where she kept her portfolio of watercolors. She was surprised to see how many there were. When had she painted all of these? The pungent smell of pigment wafted up to her nostrils. She let the scent fill her body. Her mind skipped to Sarah's body, slack in the hospital bed. Isabel scooped up the stack of paintings. She carried them to the kitchen. They were surprisingly heavy and gave out a soft sound like a child turning in sleep as she lay them on the drainboard. She returned to the living room. In a moment, she was back with a candlestick and a taper. Where did Daniel keep matches? Her mind rushed and her heart leapt like a hare across a moonlit field. The drawer to the right of the sink? No. The windowsill above the range? Yes!

Isabel wore her nightgown. It didn't matter. She needed shoes. She couldn't go back to the bedroom. Nick kept his boots in the storeroom. She thrust her bare feet into them. He had left his socks in the toes. The lock on the back door sounded as she turned it. She must hurry. She had taken too long already. The morning felt soft against her skin, and she recalled the soft velvet of Sarah's cheek. A sob escaped her mouth. "No," she said, for she must act. She took the step down to the concrete path next to the house, holding the paintings. They bulked in her left arm. The lit candle blazed in her right hand. Earliest dawn was breaking, gray and soft as a cat.

The crescent moon hung over the avocado tree. Isabel reached the burn drum. It would hurt more to burn them one by one. She placed the paintings on the ground and held the flame.

The first was a painting of the garden. She liked the sturdy ambition of the climbing beans. Before she could change her mind, she dipped the corner into the flame and threw it into the drum. For a moment, the climbing beans came alive, paper twisting and curling. She closed her eyes, though still she saw the orange flame shoot up. Quickly now. The next painting was of the front of the house, completed soon after she returned to her art. The perspective was off, though there was a nice mango tree in the background, plump in deep green. It was easier to give this one up. She watched it flame, the mango tree turning red like a maple in fall. A breeze caught fragments of paper and billowed them skyward. Isabel's heart beat erratically. Yet there was terrible joy in the violence. How long she had worked on her portfolio. How quick and easy to destroy. Her capacity to obliterate bloomed magnificently.

In the next painting, an inselberg rose in the savannah. Isabel had painted it on the roadside when they stopped for lunch, years ago, it seemed now. She pushed the memory aside. The fire caught. Bright red embers lifted and fell as she tossed the lit painting into the drum, a fragment of ash floating out over the yard where it died. The next painting was the camel. Isabel set it aside and went to the next. The crown of thorns. She hated to part with it. She had captured the flower exactly. But she must. She moved the painting toward the candle flame. More quickly now: a painting of dresses hung in a market stall; a duiker by the road; a woman on a mat beside stacks of tomatoes; a termite mound with a human figure dwarfed beside it; yet another and another and another. Lit. Consumed. Gone to ash. She came to her own portrait. She held it and looked up to see the moon again. It had slipped down into the branches of the avocado tree. She thought of the horrible lullaby of the baby falling from the treetop. Her grandmother had taught her a different version, her glasses slipping down her nose as she sang. Isabel had sung it to her daughters, when she had two.

Hush a-by baby on the tree top, When the wind blows the cradle will rock, When the bough breaks the cradle will fall, Into the haystack, cradle and all.

The song had been an assurance of soft landings even in hard times. It had been as close to a religion as Isabel had known. Once when she was very small on the farm, she had awakened from a dream of falling into a swirling pit. Her grandmother had picked her up and rocked her. "Gram will never let you fall, darling." She had held Isabel's head close, tucked beneath her chin, her body yielding to Isabel's.

Isabel pulled the self-portrait and the camel painting to her chest. "No," she said. "No. This is not right."

She sat in Daniel's chair. Before Nick woke, she gathered the remainder of her paintings and returned them to the cupboard.

♦ ♦ ♦

In the late afternoon, Isabel looked out the sunroom window. The light across the yard was oddly green, as if filtered through green glass. She apprehended something coming but couldn't remember exactly what it could be. She walked out the back door. Heavy clouds bagged in the sky. She walked into the middle of the yard, past the garden. She thought she heard a train, but there were no trains here. A man scurried by on the lane. A woman followed, market goods on her head. Here came a dozen people, all running home. And then as if a door had opened, rushing winds brushed the ground. Tiny whirlwinds sprang up, iskoki, the Hausa called them, the same word as Holy Spirit, a mighty rush of wind. Across the way, women snapped clothes from the bushes where they were drying. All around, Isabel heard the last mangos hitting the ground. She could now hear the rain coming across the tin roofs of the town. It was one of her favorite sounds. Her heart trembled, trying to remember. Doves shot like streamlined rockets from tree to tree. Rain.

The world was turning. Isabel stood and waited, and the rain came, and she turned in it until she was drenched.

＊ ＊ ＊

Finally one June morning, Isabel opened her eyes to see first light slanting through the window, and a tiny bubble of expectation filled her chest. Nick slept. She swung her legs out of bed, dressed, and went to fetch Catherine, who was sitting upright in her bed, patting the sheet and singing softly. She saw her mother, smiled, and held out her arms. Isabel scooped her up and covered her in kisses, dressed her, set her on her own two feet, and the two of them headed for the kitchen. Isabel made coffee, and then she and Catherine stepped out into the morning. The garden plants were huge. Isabel couldn't believe she hadn't noticed. Everything looked so vibrant. The lane was quiet. Two orange lizards scooted by. Catherine pointed. "Lis, lis."

"Yes! Yes! Lizard. You bright girl. You brilliant girl."

Later Isabel would remember that morning light as a miracle. Perhaps it was Sarah, saying, "Go to Catherine. Love her for me." For the first time, Isabel thought she might live.

Kufana

•••••

August 1965

Isabel received a letter from her grandmother.

We have a good offer on the five acres, significantly more than the five hundred you need. A young man wants to purchase the land to annex to a small farm he's developing adjacent to ours. He is the nicest fellow, marrying soon. He plans to build a house on one acre, and he means to raise goats! Isn't that quaint? Think how little Catherine will love that when you return! We miss you so much and look forward to that day. As soon as the transaction is complete, we will send what you need for dear Daniel.

It was just like her grandmother not to labor over Sarah. She knew Isabel was still in mourning. But she would focus on the living child, as Daniel had. She would treat Isabel as if she were yet whole. She held the letter close to her chest and then placed it in her top dresser drawer. Everyone needed an ancestor. Nigerians knew that. Bobby knew that. Gram was her ancestor, the one who would lead her even beyond death.

♦ ♦ ♦

By August, Isabel's art classes had become so popular she had to order paints and paper through Chellarams every month. But she didn't order brushes. Instead, she and her students learned to make them from reeds, horse tail hairs, chewing sticks. They created stamps for prints, carving small blocks of wood to create an image. Often, Catherine and Oma came to the lessons. Catherine was a patient observer, only occasionally trying to steal a young girl's paintbrush or chew on a block of wood. Isabel wondered if the

Sarki might like the students to paint a mural on one of his compound walls. Ornately painted walls in Arabic patterns were a staple of Hausa architecture. She imagined a scene reflective of town life with a vehicle or two, goats and chickens, trays full of tomatoes, a mango tree. The town would be strangely unpeopled because of the Muslim injunction against human images. She couldn't help that. The students would submit ideas on paper first. She would select the best artists for the most difficult parts. Then they would create a composition to transfer onto the wall. The first step would be to whitewash it. Even Catherine could help with that.

The chief gave permission, but he wanted only the boys to work on the project. The girls could contribute images and help in the planning. They would not be part of the mural painting. "But I am an artist," Isabel said. "I'm teaching them. Why can't your own girls participate? They create all kinds of arts. They weave and sew and make baskets and pots."

"They do so to help their families and their husbands and to enrich the homestead."

"And to beautify."

"It is true. But they do so in the compound, not in the public areas."

"That's not true. I've seen women weaving baskets while selling tomatoes in the market."

"Even so, that is the women's area of the market."

"What if we let the boys do one wall and the girls do another."

One of the chief's translators offered a long explanation. "The chief cannot permit it. He has already extended too much freedom to these girls. They will marry soon. He hopes they use what you have taught them in their crafts. It may be a benefit to their husbands. The boys, on the other hand, can use what they have learned to do leather work to sell, or to make drums and decorate mosques, even their homes. They will support their families."

Isabel was stumped and angry, but at present these feelings were useful to her. They got her mind working. Walking home, she plucked two yellow flowers from a bush on the roadside. The dancing woman descended into her brain like Aurora triumphing over night, airy and swathed in white cloth, bearing fruit and flowers.

A gloriosa lily bloomed at the edge of her yard. She plucked it. She plucked two red hibiscus from the shrub at the side of the house. At her front door, she took her sandals off. In the sunroom, she unveiled the dancing woman and turned her around. She laid the flowers at her feet. She placed her hand on the figure's head. "Who made you?" she whispered. She felt a movement at her center as if a small cabinet had opened. If most of the so-called Noks were men, why had this dancing woman been created? Isabel had not found other Noks in the backyard. Was hers an exile, a woman out of her home country?

Isabel made a cup of tea. She sat with the dancing woman, tapping her toe against the table leg. Something was coming to her. "Hello?" Isabel felt a stirring. She had reasoned with the chief to include the girls in her lessons. She had forced his hand, but she must do more. That evening she tried to talk with Nick about her conundrum, but he was preoccupied with an irrigation system. With Catherine in bed, Isabel sat with the dancing woman and hand-stitched the sleeve facings in a new blouse. "What happened to break your hand?" she said to the terra-cotta. She finished the hem, made her knot, and broke the thread with her teeth.

Several days later, the chief sent word that Isabel might have the girls paint a mural on a wall facing inward to his wives' cooking area. Entrance huts made these cooking areas private so no one but women would see them and the girls wouldn't be on display as they worked. Isabel didn't like it much, but she was glad for the girls, so she agreed.

That night she woke again, clawing out of sleep, howling. Nick pulled her back down into the bed and held her.

"I feel like there's a bag over my head. Something heavy is on top of me. I'm suffocating. It seems evil, so it can't be Sarah. What is it?"

"A bad dream," he said.

◆ ◆ ◆

In the daytime, Isabel turned to her students and their projects and left the garden to Nick. She hardly ate. She spent her hours occupied with patterns for the mural, but the children kept changing her designs. They introduced abstractions. At first, she thought they were simply unsure of their capacities to render an automobile or tree or drum. After a week, she began to see that they were asserting themselves with images they knew, letters from the Arabic alphabet, symbols like those she had seen at the king's palace in Zaria, arabesques that started with a circle, then a leaf. She urged them to mix the two styles, a tree here, a symbol there. Isabel was out of doors so much that her skin matched Catherine's. She still worried that they had not obtained a passport for the girl and herself. Yet she thought little of Bobby Tunde. He was in the *before.* She was in the *after.* Sarah's passing had pushed her to the other side of doubt and into faith. Not in God. But in her claim on this child. No one would touch her. Nick would never hear the story of Bobby Tunde. Isabel refreshed the flowers at the dancing woman's feet. She didn't pray to her. She didn't pray to anyone. She sought refuge, like the mother bird in the ground nest, somehow miraculously staying alive.

She watched for signs of her husband's grief, but she could not decipher what was grief and what was the result of his accident or the pressures of his job. When he walked, his left shoulder was now a little lower than his right. He often sighed deeply. His laugh was less quick. He had been the one, when she was stupefied in her sorrow, to pack up Sarah's clothes. Isabel never asked where they went. He now planned his projects with the thought of handing off to someone else when the family went on leave in six months.

In the margins of a drawing tablet, Isabel jotted sentences. *I can hold on to myself by painting: brush to paint and paint to paper. I cannot control the paint, but the act of painting leads me forward. Color choice becomes intuitive. This is a mystery I do not understand. It is the opposite of the night terror. I feel almost whole. Every day, I wake up to paint. It is what I live by.* This is what she should have said to Beatrice. Perhaps Beatrice might then observe that Isabel had taught others to paint and thus made herself useful.

◆ ◆ ◆

Nick engaged a local photographer to come take pictures of Isabel and Catherine. The two of them sat on a bench in the side yard of the house, the concrete brick of the outer wall behind them, color-ful crotons to either side, Catherine in Isabel's lap. In late September, the family of three traveled to Lagos to get a new passport for Isabel and Catherine. They took Nigeria Airways and arrived at the Lagos airport in a little over an hour. It would have taken two arduous days by car. They stayed at the Bristol Hotel on Lagos Island, where, in the cool evenings, they could walk down to the marina and see the great freighters at sea.

On the second night of their stay, they ventured out to a new Chinese restaurant. Isabel put on lipstick for the first time in months and wore the garnet clip in her mass of hair, now grown even with her chin. The restaurant shone like a jewel itself, all lit in red. They were given a table near the front windows, where they could look out over the street and watch the cars glide back and forth. Most of the guests were well-to-do Nigerians, the women wearing abundant gold jewelry and glamorous dresses. Isabel once more felt she had really taken on the missionary look in her cotton dress and low heels. Passing by their table on his way out, a well-dressed man stopped to speak to Catherine.

"Where are your parents, little one?" he said.

The sticky remnants of a fried banana glazed Catherine's face. She bounced a bit. Finally, she pointed at the stranger and said, "Dada."

"No, honey. He's not Dada," Isabel felt herself blush. She pointed to Nick. "Dada." Her husband's forehead seemed to pulse in the red light.

"You see. She recognizes me." The man smiled largely.

"Have we met?" Nick said.

"I don't believe so. But your daughter wears a halo above these curls. She is a Nigerian cherub."

"She was born in Kaduna." Isabel placed a hand on her daughter's back.

"Truly," the man said, "the child is uncanny. She has Nigeria in her."

"My wife says she favors her," Nick said.

Catherine nodded.

"Indeed. In your time here, your wife has taken on Nigeria as well." The man touched his cap in a gesture of departure.

"Bye, bye," Catherine said.

"I suppose she doesn't look much like me," Nick said glumly.

Isabel drank her jasmine tea, trying to settle her nerves. On the ride back to the hotel, she held Catherine in her lap. "She may look like me, but she has your good nature," she said, to reinstate the narrative she had worked so hard to establish, Nick as Catherine's father. They were a trinity. Nothing bad could happen.

◆ ◆ ◆

The next morning a soft wind blew as they drove over the bridge toward the U.S. Embassy on Victoria Island. The Atlantic sparkled in the distance. Armed with Isabel's old passport and multiple photographs of Isabel and Catherine, they stepped into an office. A young American man behind the desk looked so innocent Isabel wondered if he had finished college. How old did she look after four years in Nigeria, the loss of a child, and the weight of a damning secret? She wished she had worn more makeup and a nicer dress for the morning's business. "Everything appears to be in order," the young man said. "It'll take about a month to get the new passport. You can send someone to pick it up, or you can return for it."

Nick looked at Isabel. "I'll come back for it. We had the experience of losing our passports some while back, and I'd rather not go through that again." Isabel felt the promised passport pull Catherine to her in a tighter embrace.

Back at their hotel, they changed into swimsuits and drove to Bar Beach for the afternoon. The sun was high and the sand blinding white. Here and there, a Nigerian family walked the beach fully dressed, children running into the surf to wet their legs, then calling in delight and rushing back to the safety of their parents. Nick claimed the shade of a palm tree. It rose with a graceful curve, and the light through the fronds danced across the sand. Isabel wished for her paints. She would try to remember the scene for later. The waves were high, but Nick went in to swim. Isabel watched.

Catherine quickly escaped her sandals, running in spurts away from Isabel, pausing thoughtfully, and then running back. Nick seemed too far away. Occasionally, he would disappear and then emerge again. Isabel gathered Catherine up and hurried to the surf, motioning to her husband to come in. Catherine demanded to be put down. Isabel held her tight by the hand, letting the child wade. Nick clambered in through the waves, the skin graft on his arm white as ivory, but he looked strong, glistening with salt water. Dripping wet, he embraced Isabel and Catherine, and she felt the lock click into place that would keep them safe forever.

◆ ◆ ◆

When Isabel returned from Lagos, three of her students came to call, two boys and a girl. "Please, mah, come." All of them looked radiant, as if they had seen an angel and were calling her to witness it. The girl led her into the women's compound. Isabel's other female students stood beside their mural, shy and beautiful as nymphs. They had completed the work. She ran to hug them, praising them over and over: for the stylized palm tree, the cooking fire, the clay pots, the loom. "You are brilliant," she said. The boys' mural was more abstract, though they had incorporated a stream, a mango tree, and a cow, of all things. She bowed to them, held their hands, and praised them lavishly.

"Please, mah," one of the boys said. "We don't wish to finish. We wish to paint more." Her heart overflowed. For these children, painting was the gift she had brought. She had not come to this country empty-handed.

Kaduna

♦♦♦♦♦

October–December 1965

What does one do to celebrate the second birthday of a twin whose sister is dead? One bakes a cake. One invites guests. The father makes a playhouse from old crates. Of herself and her husband, Isabel thought, *We are paper dolls in our paper stands. Our clothes hang in front. Our backs are gray. We are flat.*

But on the day of the party, the Sarki's niece appeared with two toddlers. Elise showed up with one of her colleague's young daughters. Amina arrived with her youngest son. The children made their own games, which had little to do with Pin the Tail on the Donkey or Ring Around the Rosy and everything to do with tag, squeals, somersaults, and squeezing every bit of juice out of the oranges they were given. Catherine wore the leafy crown threaded with ribbon that Isabel had made, until another child pulled it off and they had great fun destroying it. The children ate cake, and then they all fell back like exhausted warriors and each one was carried home. Catherine fell asleep in Nick's arms.

A gift arrived from Tunde the next day, a small, soft drum. Nick looked at it. "Nice. I guess he meant for the girls to share it. The guy is an enigma."

"Catherine will love it," Isabel said, closing the subject.

The dry season settled in again.

Early in November, Nick flew to Lagos to pick up the new passport for Isabel and Catherine. Since that night at the Chinese restaurant, Isabel had wondered if they should try for a second child, for him. But she hadn't spoken about it yet. She wasn't sure she was ready. On the front porch, she picked up the sounds of someone pounding yam. A man on a horse passed on the road. The African rain tree across the way threw a spray of shadows so that everyone who walked under its limbs disappeared briefly, only to reappear again a little farther along. Isabel tapped her cheek with her index finger. She should try to socialize, to create a home where friends came and went, for Catherine's sake as well as her own. She went indoors. At the kitchen counter, she made a list of friends to invite for tea and cards: Rebecca, Elise, and Beatrice. Yes, Beatrice, though she hadn't seen her since tennis and the comment about Isabel's painting "pastime."

Elise had settled into her own flat in Kachia, on the other side of town from Hugo. She was the first to arrive. She looked trimmer than Isabel had ever seen her. She wore a blue dress with a belt and fashionable sandals. Isabel hugged her. "You're looking so smart."

"The women at the dispensary approve my new look. A few have asked if I'm taking a special pill to restore my youth."

"If you are, please share your potion." All at once, the other guests arrived, and Catherine woke from her morning nap. Elise managed Catherine as Isabel served iced tea and coffee and sugar cookies. They settled into a game of whist, Catherine beside Isabel at the table, supplied with crayons and paper. Isabel wasn't very good at the game, so she was paired with Rebecca, the best player, and Elise and Beatrice made a team. She and Rebecca lost every game.

The women talked through the latest news from Kaduna, complained about the ongoing dry season and what it did to their skin, and shared expectations about what they hoped to find at the commissary for their holiday parties. Rebecca reported on a book she was reading by a woman from Rhodesia, titled *The Grass Is Singing*. "By Doris someone. With a title like that, I was expecting something lovely and melodic. Instead, a British woman falls in love with her servant, and he ends up killing her!"

Isabel saw herself sitting in the back garden, Daniel bringing tea. Would he ever bring a knife? "The situation in Rhodesia is extreme," Elise said. "Whites took all the good farm land. They displaced Blacks from their own homelands."

"I suppose so," Rebecca said. "Beatrice, you're in a better position than we are to know how Nigeria compares to Rhodesia."

"What makes you think I'm an expert on Rhodesia?" Beatrice said. "Anyway, I'd have to read the book. Why don't you loan it to me when we're back in Kaduna."

Isabel was so humored by Beatrice's retort that she nearly spit out her tea. So she hadn't been singled out for critique. Beatrice considered it her civic duty to meet bature with candor when they made flimsy assumptions or made themselves at home in her country without some aim to contribute to it. Beatrice was a friend, an honest one.

"I'll be happy to," Rebecca said, shuffling the cards, though they were through playing.

A knock at the door interrupted them. Isabel opened it. It was Amina with her daughter, Latifa. Amina took the chair Isabel offered. Latifa was dressed modestly and curtsied around before taking a seat on the sofa. She seemed suddenly tall, and she had a different air about her. Isabel chalked it up to the self-confidence she had gained at the dispensary.

Sudden as a four o'clock flower opening, Amina said, "My daughter will marry. The man has paid a handsome bride price."

"Oh no," Isabel said before she could catch herself.

"How wonderful," Elise said, glaring at Isabel. "Tell us, Latifa."

"He is a Hausa man from Zaria, a student in veterinary research." She pulled a white handkerchief from her sleeve and turned it in her hands. A large smile spread across her face.

"Congratulations," Elise said.

"How long have you known him?" Isabel said. If Amina had noticed her gaffe, she wasn't letting on.

"Since I was a tyke," Latifa said.

What a poised and knowing woman she has become. How? When?

"We must have a toast," Elise said.

Little Catherine followed Isabel into the kitchen to get more Coca-Cola and lemonade. "Mommy keeps getting surprised, honey." Her daughter watched, hands clasped behind her back, stomach pushed forward. "You never know what to expect. I only say this because you will forget. My mother didn't plan anything for me. But I'll do better by you." Catherine held her hands out. "You want Coca-Cola?

You're too young. But it's a special day." She poured the bubbly liquid into a cup for her daughter. "Now carry that back to your chair. You can do it." Catherine held the cup tightly, focused on the contents.

Regaining the living room, Isabel heard something about Latifa enrolling in classes. When she asked, the girl turned to her. "Yes, to prepare me also for veterinary medicine. My work with Mrs. Van Dijk has given me a lift. I'm quite surprised, really, I am, how it all worked out. Allah is great."

Isabel held the tray as her guests took their drinks. "It seems such a short while ago you were a young girl in my yard eating butterscotch."

"Yes," Latifa said. She seemed entirely at ease with her plans.

For Isabel, the rest of the room had fallen away. Only Latifa was in her sights. "Somehow I saw you as a basket weaver, an artist. Your hands are so nimble"

Latifa raised her hands. They were long and slender. They would be perfect for bringing calves into the world, or tiny horses, or piglets. "I once found an orphaned baby crocodile and brought it home to Mum. She let me raise it in a pen near the creek until it was time to let it go."

Would wonders never cease?

◆ ◆ ◆

Plumping the cushions after her guests had left, Isabel said aloud to herself. "I thought I needed to save Latifa, but Amina-the-warrior-woman was saving her daughter all along. Saving her daughter and crocodiles. Ha!"

"Ha!" Catherine said and wrinkled her nose.

◆ ◆ ◆

The next week, Nick, Isabel, and Catherine arrived at the administrative office in Kaduna for Catherine's birth certificate. Isabel noted how, with the exception of the Nigerian flag, everything was brown, and being brown, everything seemed relaxed. The clerks were Nigerians, the window shutters were brown, chairs and desks were brown. The man who helped them wore a brown shirt with ivory embroidery at the neck. He asked for Isabel's passport, the one that held the picture of mother and daughter and served for both of them. Nick produced it from his shirt pocket. The same man opened an ink pad, picked up a squat brown stamp, inked it, and applied it firmly to the page. "You may make her an American on paper," he said, "but it doesn't matter. She will always be Nigerian. She was born here."

Nick chuckled. "I've heard that before."

◆ ◆ ◆

How could it be Christmas again? So much time had lapsed in mourning that Isabel had hardly taken account of the passing months. Christmas was the ochre-colored season in Nigeria: papayas, carrots, oranges, and tangerines—and sometimes even her skin when coated with harmattan dust. She pulled out the silk balls her mother had sent last year, and Catherine helped decorate. She no longer called for Sarah, which sent the longing back to lodge in Isabel's heart. A Christmas without their firstborn. Every ritual emphasized Sarah's absence, from lighting candles to homemade paper chains to fixing potato soup, Sarah's favorite. "We must visit her grave," Isabel said. Catherine took a cookie with sprinkles to leave at the headstone. Nick laid a spray of bougainvillea on the grave. Isabel wished she could lie down and spend the afternoon on the sandy soil beside Sarah, that they could eat their Christmas dinner there, build an open roundhouse over Sarah's dwelling place.

On Christmas morning, Isabel placed a brand-new baby doll under the tree, soft plastic with eyes that opened and shut and a change of clothes. Catherine found her, undressed her, left her in the floor, and went back to the old doll.

In early January, Ramadan returned, the muezzin calling for prayers and people fasting morning and night.

Kufana

•••••

January 1966

Daybreak. Isabel heard Daniel in the kitchen. She found him sitting on a chair, illuminated only by the faint light that came through the window. "Have you heard the news?" he said. "Rebels have absconded with the prime minister. They are killing everyone."

"What?"

"Prime Minister Balewa. They have abducted him in Lagos."

Isabel knew who he was, of course, the country's head of state who had sent the military into Tiv land. Now he had been taken. By whom? Isabel flipped on the overhead light. "Where have you heard this? Who has been killed?"

"I have heard from the BBC. And from a woman in the next compound who just arrived from Kaduna. Also, last night rebels entered the compound of the prime minister of the North in Kaduna and shelled his house." So many prime ministers, Isabel thought, one for each region, as well as Balewa, prime minister of the country. "He is killed, and his wife," Daniel continued. "My neighbor—the one who returned this morning—she heard the blasts."

"Who has done this?"

"Army officers. They have attacked Lagos and Ibadan as well. The premier of the West is also dead."

"My Lord, Daniel. Is Balewa dead?"

"No one knows. I am fearful. When big men riot, smaller men pay."

"It sounds as if the big men are now dead."

"No. The big men are now the military. Remember what they did in Tiv land? A massacre. Who will stop them now? They are killing their own leaders."

Nick appeared in t-shirt and shorts, holding his razor, his face half covered in shaving cream. "There's been a coup. I heard it on Voice of America."

"Daniel was just telling me. What do we do?"

"Nothing. Kaduna must be a madhouse. Some general is leading the government."

"Ironsi, sir. General Ironsi. He was not part of the coup. But as military leader, he is now head of state."

"Well, I hope he's got a good head on his shoulders," Nick said.

"Did the neighbor you spoke with this morning have any more details, Daniel?"

"She said the soldiers are everywhere, truckloads of them. She got through the roadblock because she knew one of the men."

Isabel thought of the green passports, the fresh new one she had in her possession with the photograph of her and Catherine. If need be, they might drive west and cross the border into Dahomey. But that was a far distance, and there would be roadblocks there too.

Daniel remained silent all day. The world seemed brittle. Reports on the BBC suggested many Nigerians were happy to have their wealthy leaders deposed. They had not been representing the poor, working people, simply taking on the roles of the departing British. Isabel tried not to think of the handsome prime minister of the North, killed with his wife in their home. How? Shot in the head? She thought briefly of Bobby Tunde in Ibadan, where the prime minister of the West was now dead.

Nick said they would stay home for the next few days. When Daniel came back in the evening, he reported that the Sarki had been touring the town. There was no trouble in Kufana. Still, he wanted to get home before dark, so he cooked dinner and Isabel sent him on his way.

Amazingly, the next day, women passed by on the street carrying their loads of prepared foods to sell as they always did. A young Hausa man showed up on their doorstep with a sewing machine mounted onto a block of wood, which he appeared to be carrying from house to house. He wanted to know if Isabel had work for him. Not wanting to disappoint, she found some cloth and asked him to cut and hem napkins, save the larger portion as a tablecloth, and hem that too. She found another piece of fabric and asked him to make a dress for her, using one she presently owned as a pattern. She had Daniel bring a table and chair out for the tailor, and he set up shop on her front porch. Throughout the morning, the man's sewing lulled her. Still, Isabel felt it was quite possible that at any moment, soldiers would push their way into the house. An army truck would drive down the street followed by another. Daniel had told her that in Tiv land, the army men, instead of a bribe, sometimes took women. Her throat constricted.

The government had turned like a hand on a table. Now what? Plunder and death? Her body felt prickly and tight. In the coming days, nothing happened in their vicinity. Daniel left each night before dark. Kufana stayed calm. The bougainvillea on the side of the house bloomed bright red, one of the few flowers that could withstand the dry season. Elise came and brought a wooden truck for Catherine, an odd gift since Isabel and her little family were to take leave soon. Six days after the coup, they heard on the radio that the prime minister's body had been found on a roadside near Lagos.

What had the poor man endured for those six days? Or was he dead the whole time and finally dumped? It would be better to die on the spot than to be taken to some remote location in the bush. Isabel pictured Nick's body in the smashed Suburban on the side of the road. Her edginess grew. Catherine drank in her mother's feeling. One morning, Isabel found red circles on her daughter's arm. Had she gotten ringworm? In all of the hubbub, she had let her daughter become infected. She lashed out at Oma. "Let me see your arms." Oma's arms were pristine. "Has there been an animal in the yard?"

"No mah."

"How do you explain this?" She pulled Catherine forward and pointed to the circles on her forearm.

"She bites herself."

Isabel sucked in air. "That's not true."

"From last week," Oma said, standing her ground.

Isabel pulled Catherine up and carried her to the bathroom where she ran cool water over the bites. No skin was broken, but she could see now the girl's little teeth matched the marks. "My darling. No, no. No biting." Catherine cried and clung to Isabel. At her wits' end, Isabel put on Tunde's record and played the song she knew was written for this child. *Baby's skin golden like the sun.* She felt more relaxed listening to Bobby Tunde's music and dancing with her daughter.

When Elise dropped by, Isabel asked her about Catherine's behavior. "It's a sign of her grief," Elise said. "Wasn't she pulling on her hair too? It's all of one piece. Be patient with her."

"But isn't there something I can do to get her to stop?"

"Not really. Time will heal her. And the safety of your constant love. If she ever learns of Bobby—and I expect at some point she will—she will push against you. Your love must be unconditional."

♦ ♦ ♦

Over the next two weeks, Isabel played Tunde's album, both sides, over and over.

"The music is fine. It makes me feel at ease," Daniel said.

But his eyes were still overcast.

"Do you feel safe here?"

"I need to purchase a motorcycle. In case I must go."

"Everything seems to be getting back to normal in Kufana. Why would you need to go? The Tiv had nothing to do with the coup."

"People are not careful when it comes to blame. A cutlass can fall on the head of an innocent."

"How much does a motorcycle cost?"

"The one I am seeing is two hundred pounds. It is very expensive, but it will carry me."

"I see." Because of Daniel, she had gone to Kaduna for the party at the British Rest House and brought Catherine back, a flicker of possibility that became a girl. She had the money he needed in her dresser drawer.

Daniel stepped outdoors. She saw him through the screen, engaging with a woman across the hedge. She had no reason to delay. She went to her room and opened the drawer to find the envelope full of pounds supplied to her during Nick's illness. She would tell

Nick later. "Here," she said, handing Daniel an envelope. "I hope it's enough for your motorcycle."

"Thank you, madam. God is great."

"It's a selfish gift. I couldn't bear it if anything happened to you."

✦ ✦ ✦

It was the end of Ramadan. In spite of everything, families came out, all dressed up, prepared to break the fast. Children arrived at the door, asking for treats. Isabel was ready, but she tried not to look too hard, fearful she might see a mother with twins.

One day, Nick showed up for lunch, bringing a small package for Isabel from the U.S.

"Hmm," she said, picking it up. "Not Christmas. No one's birthday." The return address was her grandparents'.

"It's probably a little something for Catherine."

Nick pulled out his pocketknife and cut the twine in two places. Isabel tore at the paper. She couldn't believe her eyes. "Tampax? Gram thinks I need Tampax?"

"Lower your voice," Nick said.

"But Tampax?" Isabel whispered. She started to laugh. Her funny, darling grandmother was worried she didn't have Tampax.

"What's for lunch?" Nick said.

"I'm not sure. Daniel's in charge." Isabel was a little disappointed not to have gotten a new blouse or a pretty new bra. "I'll be right there," she said. In the personal storeroom, she pushed aside a box of Kotex. Just as she put the Tampax on the shelf, she saw that it was taped. "Because someone opened it?" she whispered. She pulled the tape back and opened the small box. It was full of folded paper. She slipped it out, and ten fifty-dollar bills fluttered to the floor. Daniel's five hundred dollars. Her brilliant grandmother had smuggled in the money. She picked up the bills and stuffed them back in the box.

Kufana

·····

February 1966

Isabel remained at the table as Nick finished breakfast. Catherine sat with them, eating orange slices. "Peter and Beatrice are returning to the East," he said. Beatrice, Isabel thought, who spoke her mind. "I've offered to follow them in the Suburban to the other side of the Benue. We'll be fine. I'll be back in three days. But I'm carrying my passport, just in case. Keep yours tight. If there's another coup, we may have to leave the country."

Catherine finished her orange. Juice dripped down her chin. "All gone," Isabel said. She wiped the girl's hands and face. "Why don't you go find your crayons?" She patted her daughter's arm. The bites were still there. Isabel turned back to her husband.

"You mean we might leave through different airports?" Catherine started drawing before she took a seat. One long swoop and she had what she called a bird.

"I'm just mentioning it," Nick said. "The Agency is getting a phone installed here at the house. We should have done it a long time ago. There's nothing to worry about."

"Have you forgotten the accident you were in not so long ago?"

"I'll be home by Sunday. Do you want Mary Linderman to come and stay with you?"

"No. I'll be fine. I may invite Elise."

Peter and Beatrice arrived in their car to spend the night. They were quiet and retired early to the guest bedroom. Isabel was ashamed of her own worries. Even though Peter was assured of a job at a university in the East, something much more profound was at stake for these two than she could fathom.

"I hope you can return, and we can play more tennis," she said to

Beatrice over coffee the next morning. Isabel meant it. She was now impervious to anyone's criticism of her painting.

"I hope so," Beatrice said, but she didn't look at all sure that they would be back.

At the door, Isabel hugged her friend. "I pray for your safety." She shook Peter's hand, kissed Nick, and the trio were off, morning light glinting off the back of the Suburban.

As it turned out, Elise was not able to come and stay with Isabel even one night. The head nurse at the dispensary had gone into labor.

◆ ◆ ◆

The next day, Bobby Tunde showed up at the front door. Isabel had the sense she had vaulted through time. She steadied herself against the doorframe. "My husband is away."

"Ah. I am sorry to miss your husband. I have only now learned of your loss."

She stared at him. It seemed as normal as day for him to be here, to be speaking. Yet she had almost convinced herself that he was only a dream.

"Your daughter, Sarah."

Isabel felt her body tilt. She thought she had put Sarah to rest. She was Catherine's mother now. She had their passport. She was giving art lessons. She was planning to go home. She was solid in the dark, not a filmy thing. Her heart tightened. "It is true." She swayed.

"I thought you may already have left."

"I suppose in some way I have." She could not let him in. She closed her eyes.

"Isabel? You are trembling. You should sit." Tunde put a hand on her wrist. She stared at his silky fingers come to claim Catherine.

He removed his hand. She stepped back. She closed the door on him. She found Catherine in her bed, sucking her thumb and holding her old baby doll. She had just wakened and still held the warmth of her nap. Isabel sat on the floor beside the girl's bed. A little later, Catherine kicked her softly in the back.

"Mama. Popsicle," she said.

Isabel picked her up, carried her to the kitchen, and sat her on the counter. She pulled out a homemade popsicle from the freezer. Catherine put it to her teeth, then her tongue. Isabel leaned against the counter with the girl's legs spread around her until the child finished. Catherine's mouth was purple now, like a hibiscus. Isabel lifted her daughter to the floor. Out the window the lemon tree glittered, deep green, wildish, its limbs poking out at odd angles, large, yellow fruit still hanging here and there. Isabel stepped out the back to pluck a fruit. When she returned, she called for Catherine. The girl had opened the front door onto Bobby, who had not moved from where Isabel had left him. "You might as well come in." Catherine scampered off.

Bobby spoke as if there had been no intermission. "I came from Ibadan to Ogbomoso to Ilorin to Bida and then here, in order to avoid Kaduna. Even so, I faced too many roadblocks. My car was searched every time."

Isabel thought of Nick on the road, being stopped, the Suburban searched. "Will you travel back to Bida tonight?" she said. "There's no hotel here."

"I have a relation in Kufana. I will lodge with him."

"In Kufana? I had no idea."

"Mrs. Hammond, there is a great deal you do not know."

"What's that supposed to mean?"

"I had a twin sister. She died of measles when we were six years old. The disease did not even touch me. I remember her hands. She had a small blemish on the tip of her right index finger where the skin was white as ivory. Her eyes were so large and lovely you felt she had come directly from God. I did everything she told me to do. We pretended that the blemish on her finger could work magic. Our favorite pastime was to sit at the piano and pluck tunes. She died while my mother was still here in Nigeria with my father, the four of us. I have always felt guilty. As if I did something to cause my sister to die and my mother to leave."

Isabel sensed Sarah nearby. "Do you still miss your sister?" she said.

"Sometimes still, I feel the wind of grief blowing through me." He paused. "Recently I had a dream in which a child was picked up by a large bird and carried across a lake. This dream came to me two nights ago. As soon as I had it, I knew the meaning. You are preparing to travel. You mean to take Catherine with you to the U.S. I cannot let her go without some agreement."

"What do you mean? She's an American citizen. We have a passport for her."

"We both know she is my daughter."

"We already have an agreement. You said you wouldn't interfere in my life. You said you would never come between a mother and her child." Isabel's voice rose. She was a fool for trusting him, for allowing him into her house for that ridiculous naming ceremony. She'd thought that if she appeased him, he would go away. But she had desired him too. She had sometimes believed she loved him, or could. "You told me you have children. Nick and I have only this one." A play on his sympathy, yes, but her panic and fury were too strong. Her voice rose. "Go ahead, then, tell my husband whatever you wish. He won't believe you. I will deny it."

From somewhere, Catherine began to wail.

"There is no need to alarm the child. Let us find her."

They found Catherine in the sunroom in her aloneness. The three of them stepped out the back door. Catherine took off for her wooden truck.

What if Isabel could go into a private garden with this man and hide there with Catherine? Would she go? Would she abandon her bulky American husband for this musician, who shared her sensibility and felt a great river running just beneath the earth's crust? She had little interest in returning to the U.S. Yes, she felt guilty that she had been gone so long. She had not thought enough about her parents and their grief over a grandchild taken before they even met her. She missed her grandparents. When Isabel thought of the face of God, she saw Gram. She must go home for them. And then come back.

"In some other life, I would have loved you," she said.

"Even in this life I have loved you," Tunde said, turning to look at Isabel.

"No. You do not love me. You said you had come to comfort me in my loss of Sarah, but you have come to threaten me."

He walked away. Isabel heard a car door open and shut. Tunde came back, holding something wrapped in white cloth. He gave it to her, and she opened it, the figure of a small person carved in wood—not at all like the dancing woman. This sculpture featured a slightly protruding stomach, foreshortened eyes and legs. It was polished to a shine.

"It is an Ibeji, to house Sarah's soul. Don't talk, please. Just listen." Tunde wiped his brow. His own struggle was showing through his calm. "Every child has a spiritual counterpart in heaven. With twins, the connection to the spiritual counterpoint is twice as strong. Sarah has met her double. You must keep this one and honor it so that Catherine feels her sister is still here and does not follow her to another realm, as twins are prone to do. Most white people cannot believe this. They cannot even open their minds a little. But you can. You have shown me. I have seen how the sculpture in your house speaks to you. You are an artist. You know that most of the world is hidden."

Isabel cupped her hands, and Bobby laid the sculpture there. It felt warm, and she brought the gift to her breast. "Thank you," she said. "But this doesn't mean you can lay claim to Catherine. We will take her with us. She is not a Nigerian."

"Yes, you will take her with you, but you are wrong. She is a Nigerian. At some point, she will learn. When she is ready, I will seek her. In your country or here."

"That won't be soon."

"You are insightful, Isabel, but you do not know God's time. I have no doubt that one day Catherine will know me as her father. First let me see her for one moment. Then I will take my leave." He called Catherine, who came running but stopped abruptly before him. He picked her up and began to sing the song from the record: *Baby's skin golden like the sun.* Catherine pulled back to stare at him, apparently dazzled that the music came out of his mouth and not the record player. She placed her finger on his lips, and he kept singing though he laughed a little. Tunde walked with Catherine, who held her head alert as the wind lifted her curls. She seemed perfectly content, and Isabel thought, *She feels at home.* At last, Bobby set Catherine down next to Isabel. "Good-bye for now, Kehinde," he said, placing his palm on her head. "Good-bye, Aduke." *Loved like a waterfall.* And then clearly and fully, in the presence of Isabel and Catherine and God, he let the tears come and flow down his cheeks.

Isabel heard his car start up and heard the tires gain the pavement, and then Bobby was gone. She felt the river splitting at its delta.

◆ ◆ ◆

That evening, after dinner, she asked Daniel to sit with her at the table.

"Yes, madam."

"I have your money for nursing school." She pushed a white envelope across the table. It contained the bills her grandmother had sent. Daniel opened it and looked inside but did not pull the money out. He set it down.

"It's yours," Isabel said. "Five hundred dollars. For nursing school. Have you applied?"

"Not yet, madam."

"You should apply now. You can start. When we get back in a year, we can see how far this has taken you."

Daniel looked out the sunroom windows. "I am grateful," he said.

"You are welcome," she said. "You deserve it. More than I do."

◆ ◆ ◆

Nick returned the next day, weary and on edge. He and the Okwus had encountered over a dozen roadblocks and many young soldiers with guns slung over their backs. "I drove right through one before I heard the soldiers yell. When I stopped and reversed, this kid—he hardly looked fifteen—shoved his rifle in the window. He backed down when he saw I was with USAID. Folks on lorries were all forced to get out. The soldiers went through their belongings and took anything that appealed to them." Nick jiggled one knee. "I just wonder what's going to happen. Peter doesn't think the North

is going to lie quietly after having their premier killed in Kaduna.
It's that family thing."

"What family thing?"

"You can criticize members of your family or your own regional
premier, but you don't want an outsider coming in and killing him.
Remember, the coup plotters were mostly Igbos. Peter says the
Hausa won't stand for it. It's why he wanted to leave. Before anything else happens."

And we have to leave too. Isabel's heart lurched as she looked
around the house—the sunroom, the dancing woman and now the
Ibeji, the cocoa pod curtains, and through the windows, the garden,
the lemon tree, the avocado tree. Even with her sorrows, sorrows so
great she believed the world would break apart, this place was home.
Bobby was here.

Kufana

•••••

March 1966

March brought no relief from the dry season. Isabel packed while Nick made last tours of his projects, wrote reports, and tied up loose ends. Except for the clothes they were carrying and a few special items, their household goods would be stored with the Fergusons in Zaria until they returned in a year. Pulling framed watercolors down to store, Isabel touched the walls and wondered at the strange truth that the world would hardly register their departure. Daniel's shiny new motorcycle rested at an angle by the back step, but it didn't seem to bring him the happiness it would under different circumstances, if the country were not sitting on a powder keg. Catherine was their single source of liveliness. She pulled pots out of kitchen cabinets to bang together and scattered old newspaper that Isabel was using to pack dishes.

Beneath every day, the thought of Bobby Tunde ran like a runaway train. Isabel felt the rumble. She yearned to tell Nick. She could explain. That February at the Kaduna rest house was so long ago. She and Nick were now inextricably bound—by his accident, Sarah's death, their thousand mistakes and celebrations. She should tell him here, now, and they could leave it behind. But it would damage him more than the accident. Her aloneness created sorrow. The other lamentation, held just below her heart, was leaving Sarah's little grave. One afternoon, wrapping dishes, Isabel began to sniffle and then cry. Catherine hugged her legs. "Mommy has a boo-boo?" she said.

"Yes, honey, Mommy has a boo-boo." Isabel leaned down, lifted the girl, and held her close. "But I'm much better now that you've hugged me." She looked at the dancing woman on the corner table in the sunroom before the window. *Don't you have a last message for me?*

Kufana

•••••

March 1966

Nick yawned, pulling on his pajamas. Isabel was already in bed, her eyes closed, ready for sleep, exhausted from a day of packing and Catherine running around full tilt and no Oma because Oma had had to attend a family funeral, which might take days.

"I almost forgot to tell you. Your friend is coming by to bid us farewell," he said.

"Elise?"

"No. The musician. Bobby Tunde. He sent a courier to my office. Maybe he wanted to surprise you."

Isabel pushed up on her elbows, her heart in her throat. "What did you tell him? We can't entertain now. The whole house is packed."

"Who cares? He'll just come and salute us. He's a little goofy, but I like the guy. You don't need much to entertain him. He entertains himself."

Nick bent to turn off the lamp.

"Turn that back on. I can't have him over tomorrow. You'll have to send him word not to come."

"I have no idea where he is."

"Well, when is he coming?"

"After lunch. I've got to get some sleep."

Deep in the night, Isabel finally slept. She dreamed of soldiers at the roadblocks, only middream things got mixed up and they were light-skinned soldiers with guns trampling the garden. They broke through the door into the sunroom. She could see them through the walls. They headed for the bedroom. They were almost here. Nick was their leader.

•••

In the morning, Isabel considered driving Catherine to Elise's dispensary for the day. But Elise would be working; she couldn't do that. Instead, she fixed her hair. She put on a belted dress made from a print of yellow roses and continued to pack. Nick was holed up in a corner of the guest room at a table doing paperwork, having given up the office next to the bicycle shop. Again, she longed to tell him of the infidelity. *I will not*, she thought. *It is my penance.*

Daniel was sitting for an entrance exam in Kaduna.

She set the table for lunch, pulled the lever on the ice trays, filled the glasses, and poured tea. She had saved one precious jar of Skippy peanut butter for sandwiches. She cut two oranges into wedges. Her husband appeared at the table, looking weary but wearing a smile. He did not seem quite so big anymore. Isabel supposed she had readjusted to his size. That, or his hard work had worn him down. His shirt hung at his shoulders. He would rebound in the U.S. But why did Americans need to go home if they didn't want to? If she could just stay here, Tunde wouldn't need to come say good-bye.

"If Tunde weren't coming, we might take a last trip to the Kaduna Falls."

"We can still do that." Nick ate his sandwich.

"I wish we didn't have to leave right now."

"You need a break."

"Actually, I don't. I'm quite happy here. Catherine needs more time to mend before facing another transition. She loves the house and the yard. So do I."

"That's natural. You've put so much into the place. But we'll be back, if not to this very house, to another, and you'll fix it up just as well."

Her mind churned, and she recalled the dream of the soldiers with their guns, breaking into the bedroom, her husband coming to search her things or arrest her.

♦ ♦ ♦

Isabel got Catherine down for her nap. Nick was back at the desk in the now otherwise empty room. She went to him. "Honey, we need to talk."

"What is it?" His back was to her. She could tell him without having to see his face.

A wash of pink obscured her vision. She was aloft, over the Kagoro Hills, flying, Catherine in her arms. Her only job was to hold on to Catherine.

"Isabel? What is it?"

Nick turned in his chair. He looked tired.

"Nothing," she said, the great burden settling in her again. "It can wait."

♦ ♦ ♦

She watched for Tunde, and as soon as she saw his car, she stepped out onto the front porch. "Please," she said to him. "Please say nothing. Let us part as friends."

"Is this how you greet a guest?" he said. "With this lack of faith? Your husband has invited me. Let us go into the house."

"Just promise me." Isabel backed up to the door. "Please. I care for you. Don't you know that? Isn't that enough? We'll return. Please."

The door opened behind her, and Isabel fell back against her husband's chest.

"What's going on out here? Come on in, Bobby."

There was nothing she could do then. It was out of her hands. Her fate lay between these men. What a fool she had been to think she could keep it all, not just the secret, but her fantasy; her second self; her infatuation with a Nigerian songwriter; her dear American husband; her daughter; her painting; her home; the garden; the lemon tree; the dancing woman; Elise, who gave and gave; Amina and her daughter, Latifa; the chief; Daniel, whom she loved though she knew he did not love her. She had lost Sarah. Wasn't that a great enough price?

"Let's have some music. I don't think we've packed up the record player," she said. "There's lemonade in the refrigerator. I'll get it. Nick, put on a record." Anything to avoid a lull, a slip, conversation that might lead to discovery. She had righted herself after almost blurting a poisonous confession.

"It'll wake the baby," Nick said.

"Let her wake. I'm sure Mr. Tunde wants to say good-bye."

In the kitchen, Isabel reached for three aluminum glasses she planned to leave behind. Outside the window, a tiny bird with a long black tail wobbled on a wire. Up and down he went, perfectly balanced in his black-and-white plumage. All she needed to do was stay so balanced. At the doorway, she could see that Nick had selected a record. He lowered it onto the turntable, lifted the arm, and placed the needle on the record's edge. After a moment of silence, Bobby's voice lifted from the black disc. Nick had chosen "Golden Like the Sun." Bobby was seated on the sofa. "Ah," he said. Isabel advanced with the lemonade.

"Our daughter loves your music," Nick said.

Catherine appeared from her room, rubbing her eyes with her fists. She moved shyly when she saw Tunde, kept an eye on him and skitted sideways, like a watchful crab, over to her mother. She clutched Isabel's skirt.

"Hello, Kehinde," Bobby said. He sat on the edge of the cushion, elbows on his knees, hands clasped in front. "So you like my music, eh?"

The child said nothing but took a step forward, her eyes locked on Tunde. Clearly, she remembered his recent visit. She recognized him as the source of the song and more than that perhaps. Isabel's heart ached with all its leanings: toward her husband, her daughter, Bobby Tunde, herself. Catherine began to sway to the beat.

"I told you," Nick said, grinning.

Isabel delivered the drinks. "I forgot the cookies," she said.

Maybe she could just let these three spend thirty minutes together. Bobby would keep his promise and leave. In the kitchen, she organized a platter of oatmeal cookies along with some English biscuits. In the doorway, she watched Bobby slide from the sofa onto his knees. He took Catherine's hands as she bobbed and danced, looking back at Nick and then at Bobby, smiling at her audience of two.

Isabel should open a bar of Toblerone. She backed into the kitchen, pulled the chocolate from the refrigerator, and broke the cold bar into triangles.

Suddenly the music stopped. Isabel heard Nick's voice. "The two of you. Just now. The two of you in profile."

Who was he talking to?

Isabel listened, not daring to show herself.

"She looks like."

She looks like what? Isabel peered from the doorway. Nick's face went slack. His shoulder dipped even further. He looked as if he had caught a glimpse of himself in the mirror and yet not seen himself but someone else, as if, perhaps he had been erased. He set the arm of the record player to the side. There was a tiny click.

"She looks like you," Nick said. He had the funniest expression on his face, as if he had been shot but hadn't realized it until at last he looked down and saw the blood oozing out of his chest.

Bobby stumbled over his words. "You mean? Yes. We share the same musical taste. Quite right."

Bobby never used phrases like that. *Quite right.*

"More zaka," Catherine said. *More music.*

If only Sarah were here, dancing with her sister, so all of the focus wasn't on Catherine.

"Just a minute, honey," Nick said to Catherine, staring at her as if she, too, had been transformed into someone else. He looked away from his daughter and then back at her. Then he turned to Tunde with the same bewilderment. "No. No. Just now, in profile. If I didn't know better."

Bobby said something Isabel didn't catch. Then he laughed.

"I saw something," Nick said. "A resemblance. Can't you see it yourself?" He reached for Catherine and turned her head sideways.

Nick's hand was as big as their daughter's head. Suddenly Isabel feared his power.

Bobby had scooted back into the sofa cushions. "Zaka!" Catherine shrieked.

"I don't know. What is this you're saying? I never saw a child . . ." Bobby broke off. He so clearly didn't want to hurt any of them.

"My daughter resembles you. She looks like you. Her coloring." Nick was on the edge of his seat.

Isabel held the platter of cookies, her hands shaking. "What happened to the music?" she said, moving into the living room.

"Look," Nick said. "Catherine's forehead, her nose, even her hairline. She looks like our friend here." Her husband appeared perplexed, and then he actually did look down at his chest as if he had just now heard the gunshot. When he brought his face up, the furrow between his brows had deepened. His face had gone still.

Finally, finally, finally. The truth.

Isabel wished she had been in the accident, that she had taken the blow.

Bobby's eyes were fixed at a midpoint on the wall where a painting had hung.

"Zaka?" Catherine tried once more.

Nick pulled himself to standing. He seemed to take in air. Now he had the look of a scientist teasing out relationships among species. This was the moment Isabel had dreaded and swerved around for months, even years. But this time she, not her husband, was going to hit the tree.

"I see I have caused a disturbance," Bobby said. "I must take my leave."

Nick had his hands on his hips, his eyes fixed like a laser on Bobby as the man pulled himself up from the sofa, stepped to the door, opened it, stepped out, and closed it behind him.

Nick turned his gaze to Isabel. "Did you sleep with that man?"

Was the bird she had seen from the kitchen still bobbing on the wire? Yes. She knew that it was. Yes was the answer. "Yes," she said. Isabel stood with the cookie tray. She might drop the whole platter.

"I need you to come here." His voice was even but full of warning.

She could feel the dangerous anger emanating from her husband. She was caught. There was no way out. She put the tray on the table.

"I need you to explain to me."

"I can't."

"My God." He kicked the base of the sofa, and it screeched forward against the tile floor because the sisal rug had already been taken up. "Is this some kind of joke? Have you lost your mind?"

Isabel stood in the middle of the room, her hands crossed over her chest. "We can't talk now, like this. With Catherine." She motioned to their daughter, who stood between them, looking back and forth, one hand on her stomach, the other on the top of her head.

"You're not going to direct this conversation. You're not going to tell me what to do now. What a box of shit this is."

Isabel trembled at her husband's crudeness. He had never spoken so in her presence. Had she created this in him?

Catherine began to cry.

◆ ◆ ◆

Fifteen minutes later, after he had thrown the lemonade with the glasses into the garden and broken Bobby's record in two, Nick drove away in the Suburban. He didn't look at Isabel, nor did he speak to her, though he picked up Catherine and kissed her once on the cheek.

◆ ◆ ◆

Daniel arrived for the evening.

"How was the exam?" she said, knowing she could not muster the appropriate energy for so important a moment.

"I met it well," he said and smiled.

She was sure he had. She had no doubt that he would excel. To his intelligence was added intuition, which is why he was not fooled by her excuse about Nick's absence. She didn't have the will to carry through with a charade. All she could do was follow Catherine around and tend her needs. Nothing good could come of what had happened. When Daniel left for the night, she bathed her daughter, put her to sleep, and then crawled into her marriage bed alone. Thunder rumbled far away. She prayed for rain, but it did not come.

Nick did not return the next day. Isabel feared he might have followed Tunde. He would kill him. Or he would go somewhere, get drunk, and kill himself in a worse accident. Daniel prepared meals and left them on the table, then sat on his chair in the backyard until she sent him home. Isabel had no transportation, but where would she go if she could? She had no strength even to imagine an escape.

All she could do was keep breathing and care for her daughter. Thus she moved through the hours like a doe shot in the flank, dragging through the forest with its fawn by its side. Without Catherine, she would not have bothered to keep going.

Finally, Nick returned on the afternoon of the third day. He looked gray and gaunt, but he was dressed, appeared to have showered and slept somewhere. He would not speak to her. He disappeared into the extra room with his papers. He would not acknowledge Catherine. Isabel made up stories about Daddy's work and how he had to finish it all so that they could play later, and she distracted her by digging with spoons in the dirt and creating a feast of mud pies. She let them both get dirty, let dirt lodge in her fingernails. Indoors, she was surprised the walls didn't flow with water, her grief was so consuming.

A letter came from Beatrice in the East. They were settled in a house on the university campus, which was surrounded by a circle of hills. She described the library, the faculty club, the dining hall, and even the zoo, though she seemed wistful about Kaduna. Isabel wished she could flee to her friend.

A week after Tunde's visit, Nick sat down at the dinner table, though it was two in the afternoon. "Can I bring you something?" Isabel said.

He ignored her question. "I've had some time to think. We have to put this behind us. Just put it behind us. I'm sorry for nothing I did. You should be sorry." He looked up at her. "I'm surprised I'm not angrier than I am. I don't want to know any more about your affair. Don't tell me if it happened more than once."

"It did not."

He looked at her as if she were a troublesome pet.

"The passport hardly mattered. I'm glad you had to worry about it, but Catherine was born in our home. I have been with her from the beginning. You say you slept with your musician friend. Let's say he is the biological father. I don't know how that works, and I don't want to know. But I am her father. Do you understand that?"

"Yes. I do." Silence hung between them. "Where did you go?"

"It doesn't matter." He got up from his chair, letting it scratch noisily against the bare floor.

◆ ◆ ◆

Isabel continued to pack. One morning she created a small fabric pouch, wrapped the silver link in cotton balls, and sewed the thing up like a sachet. She put it in the bottom of her suitcase. Oma was back and took care of Catherine during the day. Nick worked on his reports. One night after Catherine was down, he stood at the threshold of the bedroom. "Why, Isabel. That's what I keep asking myself. I thought we were so in love. Why did you do this?"

It was long ago. She was a different person then. What would she say? *Bobby and I shared a night on a porch, rain pounded around us. My throat ached with longing. He had a kind of light in him.*

"You were gone. I was lonely. You didn't pay enough attention. You didn't care about my need for a purpose. You never said I was beautiful."

"That's it? I needed to tell you you were beautiful?"

"It happened when you were gone all the time. I was here alone. I didn't have any support."

"You wanted to live here in Kufana. What do you mean by your purpose? We came here together."

"Being an artist, contributing something that's mine. I didn't know how to create a life for myself out of air. I was entirely dependent on you for everything."

"I gave you everything I had. You must have thought I was a fool. My God, we had that man in our house. I befriended him. You two knew. Every time. You've humiliated me. If you needed more from me, you should have told me. I would have tried." He turned and left.

Isabel heard a creak, like a house settling, or perhaps the beginning of a house falling down.

◆ ◆ ◆

The next morning, just before light, shots rang like firecrackers, one after another. Isabel thought they were over, then there were more,

and glass shattered. She heard someone in the house. They were being invaded. She couldn't move. She watched for the bedroom door
to fly open, and when it did, she screamed.

"It's me," Nick said. He put Catherine down on the rug, then
reached for Isabel and pulled her out of bed and onto the floor beside them.

The two of them lay facing one another, their family a stone fruit,
with Catherine the seed. It was chilly. Still they lay so, Isabel shaking, waiting to hear more shots. Catherine turned from one parent
to the other, sticking her searching fingers into their mouths, eyes,
noses. "What is Cathy doing?" she said.

"We're playing tent." Isabel pulled the sheet from the bed over
their heads.

Catherine swatted it down and pulled it over her head again. Isabel looked at Nick's face, a foot away from hers, and saw a softening. Painful certainty rising in him. *He loves us. He wants us safe. He
cannot walk away.*

At last, the three of them climbed into bed together. Nick kept his
arm over Isabel and Catherine, and they slept.

◆ ◆ ◆

In the daylight, they discovered a bullet had destroyed a windowpane at the front of the house and lodged in a far wall of the sunroom. The Sarki and his young son—the one Isabel had seen reading
to him long ago—arrived as she and Nick stood in the kitchen, trying to decide if they were safe another minute in the house. The
chief had heard of the shattered window, though how the news had
traveled Isabel could not imagine.

"One drunken man has caused the damage," he said. The chief
motioned with his hand, and the son took over telling the story.
"The man was angry and began shooting all about. His bullets
struck no one. We are grateful."

"I see," Isabel said.

"He must repair your window."

"My company can take care of it," Nick said.

The chief shook his head, and the son spoke. "My father says we will repair this damage as the town wills, not as your company prefers."

A local carpenter came and covered the broken pane with a piece of plywood, and throughout the day Isabel conjured the moment of peace on the floor even as a gunshot rang through their home. Nick's instinct was to hold them. He didn't want to want to, but he did. She suggested they go visit Sarah's grave.

"I'd like to do that," Nick said. So the three of them walked to the churchyard.

There was little to take with them. Even the bougainvillea was bare. Isabel cut a palm frond from a young tree bordering their yard and let Catherine wave it as they walked. The small headstone held only the words *Sarah Marie Hammond* and the dates of her short life. Someone had recently brushed the ground with a broom. The gesture touched Isabel. "Elise has promised she will keep it neat and tidy," she said, not looking at her husband. She didn't try to explain to Catherine that her dead sister lay below the dirt but showed her how to lay the frond across the grave. They walked home in silence, Catherine sucking her thumb.

With a rational explanation for the gunfire and the danger behind them, Nick returned to being cool and aloof, warm only with Catherine. Still, Isabel knew what she knew. He would stay. He took Catherine into the guest room where he set up a little desk for her with paper and crayons and brought in her wooden truck and her baby doll. They lived so for the next week as Isabel continued to pack, reassured but unforgiven, her heart a wound.

Late one afternoon, Daniel flew through the back door like a swooping crane. "Madam! I am accepted to nursing school." He waved a letter. Isabel took it from him and scanned it. Tears came to her eyes. "I'm so happy for you," she said. She would take this joy with her along with her sorrows.

Kufana
•••••
April 1966

Ten days before they were to depart, the windowpane was replaced. After the repair was made, Isabel cleaned the glass with lemon juice and newspaper. The pane was slightly imperfect so that looking through it the world was warped, and it seemed exactly right that it should be so. Isabel said nothing about the imperfect glass to Nick, who didn't notice. She called on the chief to say thank you and took a painting she had done the first year they were here. It was a street view that showed his compound in the distance. She wished she could have it properly framed, but she didn't have time. When she arrived, he was sitting in his inner court and waved her in. Once they were seated together and she had received her Coca-Cola, he spoke again of his boredom.

"All of this trouble we have in Nigeria." He made a circle with his hand. "I dislike it. It does not satisfy me to think of war. I yawn at war. So how are we to find satisfaction? Good food in the pot is not enough. Even a new car is not enough." His English had improved dramatically.

Isabel couldn't agree more. It was difficult to find real contentment in good times, almost impossible in trying ones. "I should have given you painting lessons," she said. "You might enjoy doing something with your hands."

"The king's arm is for governing."

"Yes, but it leaves you with longing."

"It is true."

"Even when our stomachs are full, we want more." This would always be true.

"You have spoken what my own head says. Give me one lesson. I will try your painting."

•••

With only days left before departure, Isabel stood in the Sarki's courtyard armed with two easels, paints, brushes, and paper. After breakfast, she had told Nick of her mission, and he had nodded and disappeared into his room with Catherine, having set Oma to laundering their daughter's clothes to ready for travel.

Isabel wore an old dress with quarter length sleeves and a yellow and blue scarf tied around her hair. It was one of her favorites, always bringing compliments from Nigerian women. A lovely tree sat in the middle of the courtyard. Isabel set up her supplies. A breeze flowed along the ground bringing with it the scent of earth and water. When she looked up from her preparations, she saw that a line of youngsters, some of them her students, had gathered silently on a wall at some distance. One of the older boys wore sunglasses and a cap advertising Ovaltine. Isabel forgot her sorrows. She was just pouring water into two glass jars when the chief and his attendants appeared. The chief wore one of his white gowns. She had not thought to tell him to wear something darker or old. Likely, he would not have done so. She curtsied and lowered her head.

"Welcome, Mrs. Hammond. I thought you would bring your husband."

"He has to work this morning." His comment surprised her, given how often she had visited on her own.

"And what of your daughter?"

"She is with my husband."

"That is good. She is old enough by now to wait on him."

Not yet three? Old enough to wait on her father? But Isabel had seen very small Nigerian children deliver food and drinks for their elders, lay down their mats, and wave fans for them.

"Yes. Well. Shall we start? I have a full pad of watercolor paper left, so though we have only one lesson, we can paint several pictures."

The chief clasped his hands behind his back and came over to look at her setup while his entourage drifted off to sit in the shade of the veranda. "You might want to throw your sleeves up over your shoulders so that you don't get the cloth in the paint or topple the rinse water." Isabel was still dubious. "You have several possible subjects just here in your courtyard." She pointed to a cluster of pots, the arched entrance to the compound, a single palm that rose high above the roofline. He studied her suggestions. "With watercolor you paint the background first in light washes and leave white space to fill in your primary subject." *What is my primary subject?* "So, for example, if you want to paint those pots, first put a light color wash in the top third of the page to represent a wall. You can darken it later. Leave white space for where the pots will be." *I feared the open space in my own life.* "And for the ground in front of the pots, you might try a pale yellow or gray. You see how there are shadows? You will come back for those." *And I filled the expanse too hastily.* "Would you like for me to demonstrate?" *I thought I was uncommon, set apart, immune. Nothing truly bad could happen to me. I even thought I was bold. I was impatient, like my mother. Why have I never seen that?*

"Yes," the chief said.

Isabel demonstrated, trying not to be too good at what she was doing because she didn't want her pupil to be disappointed with his own attempt. In five minutes, she had finished her watercolor sketch, throwing in a little bit of grass and even a bird, along with an extra pot off to the side that wasn't actually there.

"Ah, I see. You use your head to guide you."

"Yes, and your heart. Much of painting is observation but also intuition."

The chief raised his chin. He selected a broad brush to begin and piddled it in water. Then he chose a watered-down dark gray before bringing brush to paper. In a moment, he had achieved the suggestion of the house wall. Isabel watched. He rinsed the brush and came back with a mixed pink wash for the foreground. He left the far right of the paper blank. In a moment, he was lightly dabbing in a palm tree, though the tree in his courtyard was behind them. She felt she must intervene before he tried the fronds. But he was already plopping them in with nice deposits of color by pressing the brush on the paper and turning it sideways and back. He rinsed the brush and then stood aside to consider his next move. Isabel wondered if he was going to ignore the pots and paint an altogether different scene from the one she had. Perhaps it would be inappropriate for him, a chief, to imitate her design.

The chief looked sideways at his painting, and then he approached the paints again and selected orange and brown, which he mixed on the pallet with water until it looked like clay. His pots were much larger than Isabel's, as impressive as his large front door, as large as the great pots she had seen in pictures of Crete. He created several large pots, all in a row, like soldiers. One stood out as much larger than the others.

"Very nice." She clapped.

The Sarki didn't look at her but at the painting, considering his progress. "How do I make them look round, like your own?"

"You shade it and make shadows." She pointed. "As you can see from those pots there in your yard, where the sun hits them, they are lighter. At the edges, they are darker. And they are darker still at the ground where the light doesn't reach." *If the light shines in the darkness, does darkness also transfigure the light?*

The chief returned to his task. One of his full sleeves fell from his shoulders, but he didn't push it up. He worked until the pots took on some semblance of depth. Soon he was darkening one side of the ground in front and the wall behind. The composition was shaping up quite nicely. With one lesson, the chief had created a sense of reality in his painting along with his leaps of imagination. He seemed to wonder if he was finished and decided he was not. He reached over to dip his brush into a circle of red paint, and as he did, his sleeve fell into the orange and brown.

"Ah!" Isabel said.

The chief observed the color for a moment as if to determine its significance. Then he threw the voluminous sleeve up over his shoulder and in the same motion deposited a broad swath of red at the base of his composition. He came back several more times until he had created a kind of lop-sided rectangle.

"A rug," she said.

"You have read my mind."

"I have another guess. The pots represent your wealth."

"No. You see how round and full they are. They represent satisfaction. Everything is well." He patted the air down as if to show calm. "No war here."

Isabel's head felt full of airy waves. Was that joy? She couldn't remember. "It's good. It's very good." She wanted to hug the Sarki or at least pat his back, or shout, but she was sure she should not. "While that one is drying, would you like to try another?" She was trembling, she was so happy. When had she felt so alive?

"Yes, of course."

"Very well, you paint and I'll paint my own, and we'll compare when we're finished." The Sarki's red rug might as well be a magic carpet. Isabel felt herself taking off. She conjured the Kagoro Hills. Gray cliffs, huge mounding green of hill, blue slope of valley, white craggy rock. Above it all floated the pink tint that traveled with her, sometimes visible, sometimes not, the flag of herself. She was consumed in her work. Her strokes were strong. She lived now on an eighth continent. It was a hilly country with plains below filled with farms, and beneath the soil dwelled a country of ancient sculpture left by some genius people who had for their own reasons needed to create something so beautifully expressive that their longing would outlast them. Among the farms growing corn and groundnuts and beans was a peculiar acreage spotted with pecan trees and smelling of pine, her grandparents' land. Isabel couldn't paint all of this, but she saw it. Hardly thinking, she added a little stone, the resting place of Sarah Marie, the daughter who would never return and never leave. She added an open structure with a red roof. Using abstractions of triangle and circle, she gathered her clan: Elise, Amina, Beatrice, and even Rebecca, who had come to accuse but left confessing. And scampering among them, in and out of the structure, ran Catherine, a slash of green movement.

Isabel placed the hard end of her paintbrush against her front teeth and looked up, and there was Bobby Tunde, ten feet away, wearing a white Oxford button-down shirt and black trousers.

"Good day," he said.

She thought she must be imagining things. Bobby. Bobby. Bobby. Suddenly the day seemed far advanced, as if she had slept through years and walked through a portal to another time. She looked about to be sure of her surroundings. "What are you doing here?"

"The Sarki is my brother." He moved in her direction until he was close and she could smell him, a mix of Lux soap and citrus.

She could see the green flecks in his eyes. It seemed she was looking through glass, as if she were in a car. In her mind, she rolled down the window separating them. He smiled, and his look was so familiar and kind she knew she was in the presence of someone who knew her better than anyone else, someone who had been waiting for her all of her life, even in a life before this one. He moved sideways to get closer, and she felt he comprehended her. He was joining her. She smiled in the delight of friendship, deep intimacy, a gift given out of thin air. She was a girl again, on South Pine Street, trembling in hope.

"What? How can he be your brother? He is a Hausa man. And you've never told me." She had forgotten her pupil, who continued to work on his own painting.

"My father's mother also gave birth to the chief's mother, who came north and married a Hausa man."

"You're cousins, then, or something like that." She looked back and forth at the two men and saw no resemblance, unless it was their manner of holding themselves.

"Yes, as I said, we are brothers."

The chief looked up and scowled. "There is too much noise here." He tucked his head and focused again on his painting.

Isabel bubbled with joy. Everything that had happened to her was hers, for better and for worse. She might wake and discover this moment was a dream, but the sense of Bobby's presence would stay with her.

"You have found yourself," he said.

No. It was not a dream.

"You have found your source."

He was right. A well deep within her had begun to fill. She apprehended it, like a pregnancy, like groundwater. Isabel pried her attention from the musician and looked at the chief's work. He was trying diligently to conjure a parked motorcycle but the effort was failing. It came to Isabel in a flash that she could not take the dancing woman to the U.S. The chief would not allow it. Nor could she have Bobby Tunde. The pink sky was hers, but he and the sculpture were not. Where would she leave the terra-cotta? She had no idea how to get it to the man who had come to the house. Could she re-plant it in the garden beneath the soil? No one at USAID was work-ing on cultural preservation. There was no solution. Isabel held her breath as the chief continued his work. But he was about to make a mess of it, overworking the motorcycle and detracting from the arched compound entrance that he had lightly conjured beyond it.

"May I?"

The chief looked up.

"You're very close. Be careful not to try too hard." She moved slightly forward, and he stepped back. "Just a tilt to the front wheel of the cycle. A little shadow here." The chief watched her move-ments. "Now. See. You don't show everything. Leave something to the imagination." She pointed to her head.

When she looked up, Bobby was gone. But his scent was still there. She felt very much the need to sit down, have a cup of tea, and hold her daughter. What she felt was a deep need to be home.

"Chief," she said, "I can leave some paints and paper for you to continue your art. To fight your boredom." Had Bobby Tunde just been here? The Sarki hadn't spoken to him. He was still at work on the painting, feathering in what appeared to be an open fire with a large round pot set to cook. But if Bobby was the chief's cousin that would explain how he heard her voice, how he knew of the twins' birth, Nick's accident, Sarah's death. "I must leave for now. I don't know if I will see you again before we depart." She should say something about the sculpture. She must bring it to him, but she couldn't commit to it yet. She would do it tomorrow. He looked at her briefly.

"I think this one will satisfy me," he said, and she knew he didn't mean this one picture but painting itself.

She sorted out some paints to leave and placed them with an entire folio of watercolor paper, and then she stepped out of his courtyard without looking back, though she could have sworn that someone watched her, perhaps even prayed for her.

Departure, Kufana

•••••

April 1966

I t came to her like a vision as she walked back to her house, hers for one more day.

A woman danced. She held a bird in her hand, the bird more comely than the woman, downy feathered with a pale red breast, its eyes large and knowing. The vision shifted, and Isabel saw that the dancer was a work of art. Another woman was modeling the dancing woman out of clay, a bird in her lifted hand. She applied a glaze in one dash of movement. A fire blazed. The artist-woman drew the clay woman from the kiln. Again, the vision shifted, this time to grassland and rock. The artist-woman held the dancing woman who held the bird. She placed the dancing woman on the rock. She brought a crude instrument down upon her own creation, and the dancing woman's hand broke off, as well as the bird. The bird turned a brilliant turquoise. It took flight. The artist-woman picked up her creation and put her in a basket lined with fragrant leaves and headed home. When she arrived there, she saw that both of her children were well and the water pot was full and a mound of clay waited for her next creation.

Isabel was home. She walked up the steps where the crown of thorns yet bloomed.

••••

When it seemed yet midnight, Isabel felt Nick nudge her.

"Time to get up. I've brought you a cup of coffee."

He sat on the edge of the bed. Isabel sat up and pushed her hair out of her face. Nick handed her the coffee. He looked serious. Perhaps he meant to tell her that once they were home, he planned to divorce her. He had decided to get over loving her. She would

be left to make her own way. She would have to be a secretary or
a bank teller. The coffee cup was warm in her hand. She took a sip
and closed her eyes. Whatever happened, she could always paint.
Nick placed his hands on her sheeted knees. He was ready to speak.
Speak, then. But she kept her eyes closed and cradled the cup, taking
another sip. Though they had not slept together for a month, she
knew exactly where the skin graft began on his arm, where the long
scar started down his thigh. She could imagine her thumb pressed
at the thickening of the healed bone in his left arm where the break
had been. She knew exactly where the tube had been shot into his
chest to re-inflate his right lung, knew the white round scar.

"How are you feeling?" he said.

She opened her eyes. He had put his wedding ring back on.

"How about you?"

"I miss you," he said.

"I miss you too. Do you think you can ever forgive me?"

"I have to. But it's a selfish forgiveness. I'm doing it for me." The
same words had come from her mouth, speaking to Daniel when
she gave him money for his motorcycle.

◆ ◆ ◆

Isabel opened the front door, stepped onto the porch, and closed the
door behind her. She held the terra-cotta in her arms like the child
she was leaving behind and moved into the silence. The sun was coming up. Low on the ground, pale mist hovered like mosquito netting
and wetted the path. Above her, the barest hint of pink sky emerged
behind the tall palms. Isabel hunched into her sweater in the chill
air and breathed in the smell of morning fires. Something shook the
hedge next to her. She veered to her left, and a rooster high-stepped
out onto the path. The animal amused her, and she laughed. Her long
stride filled her with jubilation, and when she reached the road and a
bicycle came by, she observed it with the assurance of her own power.
Several fires were visible now. She crossed the road.

She never counted blocks. There weren't blocks in Nigeria. Instead, she knew the time it took to reach the baobab, and beyond
it, the chief's compound. As she knew where the children were in
the homes she passed, gathered with their mothers around the fire.

As she knew how the compound animals still huddled in their corners and she knew the eldest girls had gone to collect water, or if they had collected it yesterday, they now ladled it into a pot for morning cleansing. She did not know the heart of a girl, like Latifa, who would soon be wed. She was closer to knowing the heart of Amina, who wanted the best for her daughter and who had masterminded the most promising outcome in the churning world of modern Nigeria. She knew a gun had fired a bullet that had lodged in her house. She knew the chief feared war, as Daniel feared trouble, as Elise trembled when she learned of her husband's infidelity, as her own husband feared a permanent rift. Isabel felt no dread and wondered at the miracle of it. Was this grace?

She felt her twoness but in a different way. There was the young, inexperienced Isabel who had come to Nigeria, and now there was the older Isabel, more damaged but more capable of love, of offering herself out of her fault, because she was human and frail and yet, knowing so, she could accept her strength, which was to persevere, to give everything.

"I will not say good-bye," she had told Elise. "Pretend I am here, and I will do the same. We'll be back in a year." Elise had not seemed convinced. With Amina, she had touched her heart and said, "I will not forget you." She had not said good-bye to Daniel yet. A ray of sun shot across the road, and her body passed through it. *I am in eternity right now. I will always be here.*

She saw him as she drew near the chief's compound, in his white suit, shirtless, leaning against the corner of the housefront. Of course he was there. When she was closer, she saw that his feet were bare, and she remembered them, light brown on the bottom, darker on top, the nails of his toes smooth as river rock. Now she clasped the dancing woman against her heart with both hands. It seemed she could feel the ancient woman's beating heart, her deep sigh. Ten feet from Bobby Tunde, she stopped. "I have brought her for you to hold. Tell the Sarki I have returned her. There is a man at Ahmadu Bello University who wants to study her. He calls her a Nok. Perhaps together you two can find him."

Tunde stepped away from the house and came closer so that she could see his eyes.

"I have discerned the sculpture's message," she said.

"And what is that?"

"In life we are broken, but we can also set ourselves free. In fact, we must. It is our duty."

"How did you come to this understanding?"

"The figure here. Look where her hand is broken off. It was done on purpose by the artist. The figure was holding a bird. The woman who made her broke the hand to release the bird."

"How do you know this?"

"It came to me in a vision."

Bobby's gaze rested on the sculpture still in Isabel's possession. "I see. I will tell the Sarki." Bobby Tunde took a deep breath, and as he exhaled, he seemed close to tears. "And now what of you?"

They breathed together.

"I must leave for now. This afternoon we travel to Kaduna. We fly to Zaria and on to London tomorrow. I'll be home in two days."

"That's a funny way to put it."

"What do you mean?"

"Home."

"Yes. You are right. In some ways, this place will always be home. My children were born here. And perhaps I was reborn. And where is your home?"

He moved his arm in the shape of an arch, and she took him to mean *Here, this place, this land.*

"May God be with you," he said.

"She is."

For a moment, Bobby looked startled, and then his eyes danced.

"You are blessed," he said.

The dancing woman passed out of Isabel's hands and into his. "Farewell," she said.

"I will see you again," he said. "And our daughter." He held his hand at his heart.

To keep herself from falling into his arms, Isabel turned and stepped back through the portal, holding her own wondrous life in her hands.

Acknowledgments

My deepest thanks to all those who helped and supported me through the writing of this book.

Thank you to the visionaries who created the North Carolina Museum of Art and especially the African Art Collection where this novel began with a Nok sculpture.

I thank Robert Doty and Sena Naslund, to whom this book is dedicated, for steering me into a life of literature, which has been for me church, art form, community, ecstasy.

Thanks to so many who answered questions and acted as research assistants. Chief among those is D'Anna Shotts, librarian and researcher extraordinaire, who exchanged hundreds of emails with me over the course of several years, as she lived in Nigeria, answering every sort of question about Hausa land, Kaduna, northern Nigeria, its plants, birds, religious practices, languages, politics, architecture, history, and landscape. Her assistance made it possible for me to create verisimilitude in the writing of the novel. She recommended several books at this novel's beginnings. *Dancing Woman* would not exist without her.

Thanks also to Amanda Maples, curator of African art, North Carolina Museum of Art (NCMA); Rebecca Nagy, who obtained the Nok sculpture that resides at the NCMA and who is an expert in Nigerian arts; Yomi Durotoye, friend and correspondent who has answered every sort of question I might pose to him; and Baker Hill, who answered numerous questions about language and place.

Deep thanks to Nell Joslin, my steady writing partner, who listened to me read this book aloud over years of composition and talked with me about the art and life of literature.

Thanks to many others who listened to or read portions or all of the novel in draft: Liza Roberts, Therese Ann Fowler, Diane Chamberlain, Valerie Nieman, Katy Yocom (cheerleader extraordinaire), Peggy Payne, Yomi Durotoye, and Susan Ketchin.

Thanks to several people who shared portions of their life experience with me: Ardith Fuglie, who spent years with her husband in Nigeria as a USAID couple; David Fuglie, their son and a friend to me growing up in that country; Ric Rothney, also a child of USAID parents in Nigeria and a friend in childhood; John Kessel, who shared stories about his Catholic Sicilian mother (though I created for Isabel a Catholic Sicilian father); and Alan Reberg, who resided for a time in Tiv land and answered many questions about history, culture, and folklore. My character, Isabel, and indeed all of the characters and their personal situations in this novel are entirely fictional and bear no resemblance to anyone I know or with whom I spoke.

Thanks to friend and medical doctor David Dixon, who answered questions about brain trauma from a car accident and possible treatments and outcomes.

Thanks to childhood friend Laurie Pitman, who brainstormed with me when I was at the very beginning of this novel and planted seeds for how the plot might unfold.

Thanks to bookseller, Suzanne Berube Lucey, for an afternoon of conversation when I was stuck in the midst of this project.

Thanks to Jackie Meier, artist, who read the novel for its depictions of watercolor composition and helped me get it right.

My deepest thanks to my agent and friend Joelle Delbourgo for reading and advising me on all of my books, and especially for her persistence with this one, composed during the pandemic and its aftermath as the market for literary books became even more fraught. I am hugely grateful for her passionate intelligence.

Thanks to Lynn York and Robin Miura for loving this novel and committing so much to it and giving it the perfect home. Thanks also to Arielle Hebert and Michael Levatino, who round out the Bair team and brought such energy and care to this book.

Thanks to the Virginia Center for the Creative Arts for gracious time and space to devote wholly to writing. In my time there, Kathryn Levi, Fiona Donovan, and Sarah Dorsey were special friends in writing who remained devoted to this book's success. Thanks to the Naslund-Mann Graduate School of Writing for literary community and inspiration. I depend on the sustaining companionship of faculty and students I have met there. Thank you to North Carolina State University, which has afforded me a professional home for decades, for recognizing novel writing as research, and for financial support for research trips and writing fellowships. Thank you to concurrent Heads of English Laura Severin and Jason Swarts for encouraging my work.

Thank you to my cousin and her husband, Marilyn and Doug Hesser, for loaning me their beautiful beach home for ten days of editing.

Thank you to Beth Sheffield, advocate always and owner of a cottage getaway in her backyard.

Thank you to Diane Chamberlain for a one-week writing retreat with her at her Topsail Beach condo.

Thank you to Mallory Cash for my author photo and for the hours she spent getting it!

A special thanks to Annie Frazier Crandell for re-creating my website and making it extra special.

Thank you to Kaye Publicity and Caitlyn Hamilton-Summie, publicist, for getting this novel into the world and noticed.

Finally, thank you to my departed parents who gave me everything and still speak to me. Thank you to family who surround me and offer bouquets of love in months and years of solitude necessary to writing: Andy Orr, Joel Orr, Scarlett Orr, and Joy Edwards. And thank you to my sister, Becky Neil Albritton, there in Nigeria from the beginning.